Gateway To A New Beginning

September 1873 – January 1, 1874

Book # 21 in The Bregdan Chronicles

Sequel to Walking Toward Freedom

Ginny Dye

Gateway To A New Beginning

September 1873 - January 1, 1874

Copyright © 2024 by Ginny Dye

Published by Bregdan Publishing
Bellingham, WA 98229

www.BregdanChronicles.net

www.GinnyDye.com

www.BregdanPublishing.com

ISBN# 9798339438892

All rights reserved. No portion of this book may be reproduced in any form without the written permission of the publisher.

Printed in the United States of America

Book # 21 of The Bregdan Chronicles 3

With my deepest gratitude to

<u>AWOHALI</u>

My Cherokee Grandmother

My life to live

My wings to fly

I am you

You are me

A Note from the Author

My great hope is that *Gateway To A New Beginning* will entertain, challenge you, and give you hope and courage to accept new beginnings. I hope you will learn as much as I did during the months of research it took to write this book. Once again, I couldn't make it through an entire year, because there was just too much happening. As I move forward in the series, it seems there is so much going on in so many arenas, and I simply don't want to gloss over them. As a reader, you deserve to know all the things that created the world you live in now.

Writing this book was an adventure – and something of a miracle. I almost died three times in March of 2024. I didn't die. I lived.

I will continue to create as long as I have breath.

Always passionate, I am now more passionate than ever. Passionate to be a voice for the world. Passionate to empower every single person who reads one of my books – but especially women because too many of you don't understand your power.

As a reader, you know it's not the events of history that fascinate me so much – it's the people. That's all history is, you know. History is the story of people's lives. History reflects the consequences of their choices and actions – both good and bad. History is what has given you the world you live in today – both good and bad.

This truth is why I named this series The Bregdan Chronicles. Bregdan is a Gaelic term for

Book # 21 of The Bregdan Chronicles 5

weaving: Braiding. Every life that has been lived until today is a part of the woven braid of life. Each life reflects the **Bregdan Principle**...

**Every life that has been lived until today is a part of the woven braid of life.
It takes every person's story to create history.
Your life will help determine the course of history.
You may think you don't have much of an impact.
You do.
Every action you take will reflect in someone else's life.
Someone else's decisions.
Someone else's future.
Both good and bad.**

My great hope as you read this book, and all that will follow, is that you will acknowledge the power you have, every day, to change the world around you by your decisions and actions. Then I will know the research and writing were all worthwhile.

Oh, and I hope you enjoy every moment of it and learn to love the characters as much as I do!

I'm constantly asked how many books will be in this series. I guess that depends on how long I live! My intention is to release two books a year – continuing to weave the lives of my characters into the times they lived. I hate to end a good book as much as anyone – always feeling so sad that I must leave the characters. You shouldn't have to be sad for a long time!

You are now reading the 21st book - # 22 will be released in spring of 2025. If you like what you read, you'll want to make sure you're on my mailing list at www.BregdanChronicles.net. I'll let you know each time a new one comes out so that you can take advantage of all my fun launch events, and you can enjoy my BLOG in between books!

Many more are coming!

Sincerely,
Ginny Dye

Book # 21 of The Bregdan Chronicles 7

Chapter One
September 7, 1873

Carrie Wallington pushed back the stubborn tendrils of black curls that had escaped her braid and used a sleeve to wipe the sweat from her face. After two days of cooler weather had tempted her with the promise of fall, summer had returned with a vengeance. Hot humidity was determined to have another say beforc the season turned.

Carrie had left the medical clinic early to take No Regrets and Granite for a swim. The horses had raced into the James River, lying down to roll in the cool current before they jumped up and pawed at the water exuberantly, casting huge rainbow sprays that glistened in the sun and soaked Carrie to the bone. It was a pure delight.

As they headed home, the horses trotted easily down the sunbaked road bordered on both sides by towering tobacco plants.

No Regrets shook her head to dislodge a huge horsefly.

Granite, trotting along beside them, kept up a constant motion with his long, silky tail to keep the flies and mosquitoes from his body. In three months, he would be two years old. He was already almost sixteen hands of gleaming beauty. His steel gray body, damp from the swim, glowed darker in the sunshine. Waiting another fifteen months, when he turned three, to ride him would be agony, but Carrie was committed to giving his bones and joints time to fully form. In the meantime, she spent every moment she could with him.

Carrie leaned forward to swat more insects off her mare's neck, wincing when streaks of blood remained where they had bitten. "Sorry, girl. The swim washed off the fly repellent. We're almost back to the barn. I'll wipe more on you and your son as soon as we get back." No Regrets' ears flicked backward to indicate she was listening.

Granite snorted, swung his head back to nip at a horsefly, and shot her a reproachful look.

Carrie laughed but felt guilty. "I know, Granite. I should have put a bottle of repellent in my saddlebag. I was so focused on getting to the river, I forgot."

She and Susan had started making their own fly repellent two years earlier. The mixture of apple cider vinegar, cold tea, and herb tinctures was incredibly effective at keeping the bugs away from the horses, but in the hot Virginia summer, it was a never-ending battle to keep enough repellent on them. They were careful to never run out.

Carrie, eager to give them relief, urged No Regrets into a faster trot. As they swept around the final curve before the barn, she caught a flash of color out of the corner of her eye. She frowned when she realized it was Frances, sitting in the grass beneath a towering oak tree. What was her daughter doing outside on such a hot afternoon? Even from a distance, she could see and feel the tension in Frances' body.

Carrie waited for Frances to look up so she could wave a greeting, but the girl kept her gaze intently on the ground. Concerned, she wanted to stop right then, but it was important to get the horses back to the barn. She would return to check on her daughter.

Minutes later, she dismounted and led the horses into the barn. It was hot, but the open Dutch doors at the back of every stall, and the massive doors open at both ends of the barn, allowed a breeze that offered a bit of relief.

"Howdy, Carrie!"

Carrie grinned as Hobbs walked forward from the tack room. "Hello, Hobbs." He'd been on the plantation less than two weeks, but he had already become a welcome fixture. She could still see the eager boy who had been under Robert's command during the war, but also saw the man who had matured and gained wisdom in the hard years since. She was thrilled he had returned to work on the plantation after years in Oregon. He worked hard and had a natural connection with the horses.

Hobbs reached out for No Regrets' reins. "I'll take her."

Carrie, thinking about Frances against the tree, smiled her gratitude. "Thank you. They had a good swim, but they need to be wiped down with repellent. Can you take care of both, please?"

"Sure can," Hobbs agreed. "I sorta forgot how miserable Virginia humidity can be. I hope Miles is right that the weather will cool off soon."

"Not soon enough," Carrie retorted. It had been a long summer. She was ready for crisp days and nights, and the glorious colors that would soon adorn the trees. If nothing else, at least it would be cooler when they got to Boston.

The thought of Boston increased her worry about Frances. Something was bothering her daughter. She patted No Regrets' neck and nuzzled her face into Granite's forehead. "I'll be back with treats later, boy." Granite nickered softly as she left the barn.

The heat wrapped around Carrie once more, but she pushed aside the vision of cold lemonade that was surely waiting for her on the huge porch. It would be there when she was done talking to Frances. The tree leaves hung heavy with the weight of summer as she walked toward the field, but she could already see the faint beginnings of color change. Huge clumps of purple asters mingled with yellow and white yarrow, which provided a haven for the multitude of bees and butterflies that danced over and into their blooms. Flashes of green and red sparkled from ruby-throated hummingbirds darting through the air.

Despite the oppressive heat, Carrie began to relax. Her daughter was an avid birdwatcher. It was possible she was simply making the most of one of her last days on the plantation. Carrie's frown returned as she thought about how soon Frances would be leaving. She didn't know what Frances was feeling, but she was certain how *she* was feeling - anxious about sending her daughter into the world, and sad to have her so far away.

Frances was hunkered down beneath the tree. Her head rested against the rough bark, as she stared at the ground.

Carrie left the road and picked her way through the grasses and flowers. Frances looked up but said nothing. Carrie sat down and took her daughter's hand.

After several minutes of silence, she felt Frances relax slightly, but the troubled look didn't leave her eyes. Carrie waited. She had learned words weren't always necessary. Sometimes, merely being with someone and letting them know they weren't alone, was enough. She had learned Frances would talk about what she was feeling when she was ready. Her oldest daughter, adopted at age twelve, was a deep thinker. She would ponder long and hard about something before she was ready to put it into words.

"I'm afraid." When Frances finally spoke, her words were soft and trembling.

"I imagine you are," Carrie replied. "You're about to do a very scary thing."

Frances looked up with beseeching eyes. "Were you afraid when you left for medical school?"

"Terrified," Carrie admitted. "I had dreamed about it for such a long time." She thought back to those days. The war had delayed her going to school until she was almost twenty-four. Frances was not yet seventeen. How much more terrifying would it be at such a young age? Not for the first time, Carrie thought of encouraging Frances to wait until she was older, but life had made her daughter mature beyond her years. "Dreaming about going to medical school was one thing, but actually doing it was another."

"Exactly!" Frances gazed at her with relief, but her eyes remained clouded with trouble. "I don't know if I can do it, Mama."

Then don't! Carrie took a deep breath, biting back the words that wanted to escape her mouth. She thought of Abby, grateful for the lessons the woman had taught her when she had been Frances' age. Abby had refused to give her answers. The older woman's response to almost every question was to ask a question or invite more information. It was maddening at times, but when Carrie finally reached conclusions, she knew they were her own.

"Tell me how you're feeling, Frances."

Frances looked distressed. "Boston is terribly far away. I don't know when I'll see you and Daddy again. And Minnie. Russell. Little Bridget!" Tears filled her eyes. "I want to go to medical school and become a doctor, but I wish I didn't have to go away to do it."

From the moment Frances announced she was going to the newly developed Boston University School of Medicine, Carrie had developed an appreciation for what her father must have felt when she had made her own bold announcements.

Carrie spoke carefully. "Are you certain you're ready?"

Frances stiffened. "Are you saying I'm *not* ready?"

Carrie smiled, keeping her voice even. "I didn't say that. I merely asked if *you* are certain you're ready."

Frances sighed and lapsed into silence again.

Birdsong filled the afternoon air. Distant calls from men working the tobacco fields floated toward them. The harvest was not for another month, but it was evident the crop would be bounteous. A rabbit jumped into view, caught sight of them, and bounded quickly into a thicket of brambles.

Carrie was content to wait. Patience had never been one of her virtues, but she was learning how to be patient with her children.

"I think I am," Frances finally murmured.

Carrie waited, knowing her daughter wasn't finished speaking.

"I've always loved helping you," Frances continued after another long pause. She met Carrie's eyes. "Things changed for me during the train wreck."

It was easy for Carrie to pull up the terror she felt when she discovered Frances, Moses, and Felicia had been on a train that was wrecked and robbed by Jesse James and his gang. She could imagine how terrifying it had been for Frances to be responsible for medical care to injured passengers.

"I took care of those people myself. I wasn't helping you. I wanted you to be there to tell me what to do but you weren't. I knew what to do because you taught me. It was scary." Frances' voice grew thin. "I was scared when I understood those people had only me to help them. No one but. me. I can still hear the cries of the injured people."

Carrie squeezed her daughter's hand, caught between intense pride and horror at what Frances had experienced. Again, she understood how her father felt when she headed off to Chimborazo Hospital every day during the war.

"I realized I knew what to do," Frances continued. "I helped those people. I learned from working with you, Mama."

"It's the most amazing feeling in the world to know you can help people, Frances. You're the best student

I've ever had." Carrie's pride for her daughter roared past the horror of the train wreck.

"Am I old enough, Mama?"

Carrie paused, determined yet again to speak carefully. "Do you believe you are?"

"Not another question, Mama. Not this time. You are my mother, but you are also my teacher, and you're the best doctor I know. I need to know if you think I'm old enough."

Carrie met her eyes for a long moment before she nodded. Her daughter was right that she needed an answer. "You're old enough, Frances," she said decisively.

Frances caught her breath. "Really?" she whispered.

"I was taking care of the slaves in the Quarters when I was your age," Carrie continued. Frances had heard these stories, but she needed to hear them again. "I was nineteen when I started work at the hospital during the war."

"Weren't you scared?"

Carrie managed to smile. "Every day. Every hour. Every moment." Her smile faded. "I overcame my fear because I knew I was needed. I knew those soldiers counted on me. Dr. Wild counted on me." She thought of the doctor who had given her the opportunity to treat soldiers during the war, and then saved her life when Bridget had died at birth, almost taking her to the grave, as well.

"How did you do it?" Frances pressed. "How did you overcome your fear?"

There was the crux of the matter.

Carrie's smile was effortless this time. "*Courage rising.*"

Frances nodded slowly. "That's what you, Janie, and Elizabeth said to each other when the Bregdan Clinic in Richmond was attacked."

"Several times an hour," Carrie agreed. "Micah taught us about courage rising." She thought about the man who was once her father's slave but was now a trusted friend who helped manage her father's Richmond home. "His daddy, who lived his entire life as a slave, taught him. He said whenever something or someone scared him, he would whisper *courage rising*. It helped him do the things he was afraid of."

"So, it's alright to be afraid?"

"You wouldn't be human if you weren't afraid," Carrie assured her. "I was afraid to walk into the clinic every day after the attack. I whispered *courage rising* more times than I could count." She grasped Frances' other hand and stared deeply into her daughter's dark brown eyes. "I'm having to whisper *courage rising* many times a day again."

Frances looked confused. "Why?"

"Because I'm terrified to send you out into the world," Carrie admitted. "I'm not ready to not have you with me. I'm not ready to lose my daughter." She watched doubt begin to simmer in Frances' eyes. "You're ready, honey. You're young, but you have experiences and knowledge the older medical students won't have. They may doubt you at first, but it won't take them long to realize how much they can learn from you."

"I don't want you to be sad," Frances replied.

Carrie chuckled. "You could wait until you're thirty-five to go to medical school, Frances. I still wouldn't be ready to lose my daughter. Your grandmother tells me that is a normal part of being a mother. You can't allow my fears or sadness stop you from doing what you're meant to do. Any more than you can let your own fears stop you."

Frances took a deep breath. "I'm coming back, you know. We are going to practice medicine together, Mama." Her voice left no room for doubt.

"That's the plan," Carrie agreed, forcing her voice to stay even.

Frances narrowed her eyes. "I *am* coming back."

Carrie thought about Old Sarah as she formulated her reply. Rose's mama had talked her through many times like this. "I know you intend to return, honey. I want that, too. I've learned, however, that life seldom follows the path you believe it will." She thought about the countless times her life had taken an unexpected turn. Many things can happen to change the plans we make."

A hawk's screech split the air around them. She and Frances looked up at the red-tailed hawk circling above them, soaring on the air currents produced by the heat. Carrie watched thoughtfully, noticing how it floated, lifted, and fell without ever moving its outstretched wings. "Life is like the currents carrying that hawk, Frances. When it took to the air this morning, it didn't know where the air currents would take it. It simply decided to fly." Her voice grew firmer as the truth of her words eased her own fear. "Life is like that. You've decided to go to medical school. It's your time to fly.

Until you spread your wings and actually take flight, you can't know where life will take you. Life might bring you back here, or it might not."

Protest flared in Frances' eyes, but Carrie held a finger to her daughter's lips. "I would love that to happen. I hope it does..." She paused, wanting more than anything to give Frances the freedom she deserved. "Honey, if life takes you somewhere else, I will cheer you on and be your biggest supporter."

"But I want to practice medicine with *you*, Mama," Frances repeated.

"It means the world to me that you want to do that." The hawk soaring through the cloudless sky had shown Carrie what she truly needed to give her daughter. "What I want you to know, however, is that my greatest hope is for you to follow your dreams and live *your* life. Things in America are starting to change for women. You have opportunities that older generations never had. I want you to make the most of them, and I want your choices to be what you want, not what you think I want." She paused. "Do you understand what I'm saying?"

Frances' eyes filled with worry. "It's scary to think I'm going to go to Boston and have the freedom to make my own decisions."

The hawk screeched loudly again.

Frances tilted her head back and gazed at the soaring bird. When she looked back down, her face was wreathed in a smile. "You believe I'm ready, so I'm going to believe it too. When I'm too scared to breathe, I'm going to whisper *courage rising.*"

"I'll be doing the same thing," Carrie said, relieved to see their conversation had chased the shadows from Frances' eyes. "In the meantime, there's a lot to do to prepare you and Felicia to move to Boston. Rose and I are going to have a wonderful time with you girls."

Frances' eyes brightened even more. "It's going to be tremendous fun," she proclaimed. "Even though I'm afraid, I won't be alone. Felicia will be there with me, building her business empire while I go to school."

"That she will be," Carrie agreed. Once again, she and Rose would be worrying about their children together. She found comfort in that.

Frances threw back her head and laughed. "It's my time to fly, Mama!"

The sound of rattling wheels pulled their attention from the sky. Carrie and Frances looked toward the road as the plantation wagon rounded the curve.

"You two going to sit under that tree all day?" Abby called as she pulled the horses to a stop. Sunlight glinted off the silver strands in her soft brown hair. "Or are you coming swimming with the rest of us?"

Rose was perched on the driver's seat next to Abby. "There's enough room left for you two in the wagon, and I'm told there's enough food for everyone."

"Ain't never not been enough food for this wild bunch!" Annie yelled from where she sat in the back of the wagon, surrounded by the children.

"Come swimming with us!" The children yelled.

Minnie stood up and waved her arm, her red hair blazing like a flame. "Come on, Frances! I won't have many more chances to go swimming with my sister!"

"Me either!" Russell yelled.

Two-year-old Bridget, held tightly in her big brother's arms, was determined to be heard. "Swimming!"

Carrie exchanged a glance with Frances. "Are you interested in a swim? I was down at the river with No Regrets and Granite, but other than getting sprayed with water, I can't say I was actually swimming."

Frances responded by scrambling to her feet. "Let's go!"

John, Rose's ten-year-old son, ran up to Annie as soon as they finished unloading on the shores of the James River. "Grandma, I'm starving! Jed and Hope are real hungry too. Can we have something to eat before we swim?" he asked with a bright smile.

Annie placed her hands on her ample hips. "You can wipe that big smile right off your handsome face, John. I know you figure you can get anythin' you want with that smile. It ain't happenin' today. Ain't nothin' comin' outta that basket of food 'til I been in that water. I don't reckon none of you gonna starve in the next little while." She shook a finger in his face and turned to stride toward the glimmering blue-green water laced with small whitecaps that danced farther from shore.

Rose stood beside Carrie. "Can you believe it? It took us years to get her into the water. Now it's all she wants to do."

Carrie laughed. "We should have had the men force her into the river long ago." She pulled off her boots. "I'm going in with Annie!"

Annie was stepping into the water, her dress billowing around her, when Carrie caught up. The children splashed and played, their squeals of delight filling the air. "You know, you would be much more comfortable with breeches on," Carrie told her.

Annie stopped long enough to snort her disdain. "Ain't no one livin' ever gonna catch me in a pair of them breeches." She waved her hands around her body. "Least I can do for people is cover this big body up with a dress."

Carrie frowned. "You're beautiful exactly as you are, Annie. Breeches or a dress won't make a bit of difference."

Felicia ran up in time to hear the exchange. "You know, Grandma, back in Ancient Rome women didn't wear anything to swim."

"What you be talkin' 'bout, girl?"

Felicia grinned mischievously. "They swam in the nude!"

Annie gaped at her granddaughter. "That right?"

"You clearly spend too much time in the library, Felicia," Carrie said with a laugh. "In case you're not aware, we don't live in Ancient Rome."

"It's a pity," Felicia retorted. "I bet the water would feel magnificent without clothes."

Annie shook her head. "I don't know about you, Felicia girl. Ideas like that gonna get you in a heap of trouble someday."

Felicia grew serious. "It's not thé *idea* that's the problem, Grandma. It's knowing when it's alright to say what you're thinking. There are plenty of times I don't say the things I'm really thinking, but that doesn't mean I can't think them." She burst into laughter. "Right now, I'm thinking I want to swim with my grandma."

Annie reached for the hand Felicia held out to her. "Let's go swimming!"

Carrie joined them happily, ducking beneath the cool embrace of the water. When she emerged, her children splashed water into her face. She fought back, relishing the cries of delight and fun. A quick glance revealed Rose and Abby had joined them.

When she heard a roar behind her, she knew Annie had engaged in the battle. She hoped Moses would join them soon. There was little he enjoyed more than watching his mama have fun in the river after a brutal lifetime of slavery and endless work. Annie loved her life on the plantation, but it had taken ten years of freedom to release the bondages of slavery enough to allow herself to have fun.

When Carrie had had her fill, she waded out of the water and sank down onto one of the large logs the workers had moved to the shoreline. She was content to watch as the revelry continued.

Rose joined her a few minutes later. "What fun!" she exclaimed.

Carrie grinned. "Where are Alice and Gloria? I thought they were joining us." Everyone on the plantation had fallen in love, first with little Gloria, and quickly with her mother, Alice. Alice, beaten brutally in a Richmond alley after trying to save her little girl from an assault, had almost died from an infection. Her broken arm and leg were healing, but it would take time for them to be strong again.

"Alice is out walking with Matthew," Rose answered. "She's definitely committed to her rehabilitation. Since you took off her casts, she never misses a day to strengthen her muscles. Matthew's story of regaining his ability to walk and run after breaking both legs has given her hope. She tried to talk her into joining us, but Gloria insisted on staying with her."

Carrie smiled softly. "That little girl certainly loves her mama."

"She does," Rose agreed. "I suspect she's afraid that if she lets Alice out of her sight, something terrible might happen."

"That's not surprising," Carrie replied. "It hasn't been that long since the attack. They both need some time." She turned the conversation in a different direction. "How is Gloria's reading coming along?"

Rose smiled brightly. "Gloria is a smart little girl. She's already reading, and so is her mother."

"Alice is reading?"

"She's every bit as smart as her daughter," Rose proclaimed. "They spend their evenings reading to each other when they return to the guest house. They're determined to make up for lost time."

"That's wonderful!" Carrie exclaimed.

Annie waded from the water, her face wreathed in a smile. The sun bounced off the droplets clinging to her mostly gray hair. "Anybody out there be hungry?" she called.

Within moments, the river was empty.

With the food distributed, Annie made her way to the log where Carrie, Rose, and Abby sat. She approached Rose with determination sparkling in her eyes. "What you hear from June?"

Rose swallowed her bite of fried chicken and wiped her mouth. "We haven't heard anything in a while." Rose felt a wave of guilt. It had been ages since Simon, June, and their children had been to the plantation. How had she let that much time go by?

Carrie frowned. "I haven't heard anything from Perry and Louisa either. How long *has* it been?"

"Too long," Rose replied, determined to do something to change it.

"Yep, too long," Annie agreed. "You reckon my girl knows how to swim?"

Rose laughed. "I have no idea."

"Well," Annie declared. "That ain't be right. I want my girl to go swimmin'. She be a grown woman, but she ought to swim."

"You're right," Rose answered. "I'll send one of the men over to Blackwell Plantation tomorrow to extend an invitation. We'll get them here before the summer is over."

Annie nodded with satisfaction.

Thomas, Anthony, Moses, and Miles were on the porch when the group returned home from their swim. The last remnants of the setting sun gilded the gleaming white house with a golden hue. The sentinel oak trees whispered in the breeze that had picked up as the sun sank below the horizon.

"About time y'all got back," Moses called. "A man could starve around here."

Annie jerked her thumb toward the wagon bed, which was quickly emptying of children. "There ain't much food left in that basket, but you can have it. Ain't no grown man gonna starve unless they choose to. Any of you can walk right into that kitchen and get food if you figure on starvin' to death."

Moses turned to Miles. "When did your wife learn to talk to her son like that?"

Miles grinned. "She ain't saying nothing but the truth, Moses."

Moses looked back to his mother, his eyes dancing with fun. "So, you get to go swimming while the hardworking men around here go hungry?"

"I reckon that be the way it is, son." She shook her finger at him before she relented. "There be a whole plate of ham biscuits right there in the kitchen, boy. Right next to them extra cookies I made. I reckon if you can manage to get that big 'ole body of yours in there, you can find it."

Anthony sprang from his seat. "Thanks, Annie! I'll get them."

Carrie watched the exchange with a smile, but her amusement faded when she saw Minnie walking toward the edge of the woods, away from the other children. Even from the porch, she could tell from her shaking shoulders that her daughter was crying.

Chapter Two

Frances was leaving the barn when she noticed Minnie walking toward the woods. She could feel, more than see, her sister's distress. She hurried to catch up with her and slipped an arm around her waist. Minnie shook from the force of her tears. "What's wrong?" she asked with alarm.

Minnie leaned into her. "I wish you were still my best friend," she sobbed.

Frances held her tighter. Guilt suffused her as she thought of the time she had been spending with Felicia. "I *am* your best friend."

Minnie shook her head. She sniffled and managed to bring her tears under control. "No," she said. "You're not." She blinked her blue eyes as tears threatened to overflow again. "You're leaving me and going to medical school. You'll be living with Felicia. She's your best friend."

Frances' heart ached at the pain etched in her sister's face. She searched for the right words. The six years separating them had never been more evident. "You will always be my truest best friend, Minnie, but more importantly, you will always be my sister. Nothing will ever change that."

"You're leaving," Minnie said.

"You'll leave someday, too." Frances thought about the disastrous fire in the Philadelphia tenement house that killed Minnie's family. "You can't change fire protection laws if you stay on the plantation. You say you want more from life. You're going to have to leave to find what you want."

"Why?" Minnie demanded, her eyes sparkling with distress. "Maybe everything I want is right here. Maybe I won't have to go anywhere. Maybe I'll never leave the plantation!"

"That could be true," Frances conceded, although she knew it wasn't. "However, that isn't true for me. I can't be a doctor unless I leave. I can't come back and practice with Mama unless I go to medical school."

"That's not true," Minnie said stubbornly. "You help her right now. You helped those people on the train. You're leaving me because *you* want to become a fancy doctor!" The distress in her eyes were an accusation.

"That's true," Frances agreed. "When I was eleven, like you, I didn't know what I wanted to do, but that changed. I want to be a doctor—I want to be as good a doctor as Mama—and I need to go to school to do that." She saw protest flare in her sister's eyes again. "Perhaps I could learn everything I need to know from Mama without going to school, but a lot of people won't let me help them if I'm not a real doctor."

Minnie's eyes pierced her. "You want people to call you *Doctor* Frances Wallington," she accused. "Don't forget I'm your best friend. I know you."

Frances felt a spark of anger, but she swallowed it because her sister was speaking the truth. "You're right, Minnie. I do want to be *Doctor* Frances

Wallington. When my family died from the flu, I thought my life was over. When I was stuck in that orphanage, I never believed I could be anybody other than a poor orphan. My life changed when Mama rescued me. I started dreaming I could be someone. When I began to think I could become a doctor, I realized how much I wanted to be one." She paused. "Is that so wrong?"

Her sister's face crumbled. "No, it's not wrong, Frances." Minnie's voice wavered. "Except you haven't been home from San Francisco very long. I thought you would be here longer. I wish you could become a doctor without leaving me."

"Me too," Frances told her. "I told Mama today that leaving my family is the hardest thing about going to school." She decided to go for full honesty. "I also told her I'm terrified."

Minnie looked at her with surprise. "Terrified? Why?"

Frances relayed the conversation she'd had with Carrie earlier. "I'm going to be saying *courage rising* a lot."

"Can I say it too?" Minnie asked quietly.

Frances smiled. "Only if you promise to write me every week."

Minnie pretended to consider. "I might..." she said slowly. "If you do the same thing. You *are* the one leaving me, after all. You should probably promise to write me *twice* a week."

Frances would agree to anything at this point. She couldn't stand the aura of devastation that encompassed her sister. Regardless of their age difference, nothing would change the fact that Minnie was her best friend.

"What's going on here?" Russell appeared from the deepening dusk. He took one glance at Minnie, put his arm around her, and glared at Frances. "What did you do to her?"

"I didn't do anything!" Frances exclaimed.

"She's crying," Russell said. "Minnie doesn't cry."

Minnie looked up at Russell. "Frances didn't do anything. I'm sad because she's leaving, but she's making me feel better."

Russell's frown melted away and his eyes dropped. "I don't want you to leave either."

Frances hugged her brother. Russell hadn't been with them long, but she loved him deeply. "I'll miss you, too."

Russell turned to Minnie. "We may be losing Frances, but we have each other. Will you feel better if I promise to irritate you more? It shouldn't be hard." He grinned mischievously.

Minnie managed to smile. It didn't reach her eyes, but she was trying. "I suppose that will help."

"We'll do lots of things together," Russell proclaimed.

Frances was thrilled they would have each other. Being the same age, the two were close from the moment Russell arrived on the plantation. "I'll be home for Christmas. It won't be that long."

Both looked at her doubtfully.

Frances was eager to release the tension. "I heard Annie say there was a tray of cookies in the kitchen."

"I'm stuffed from the picnic at the river," Minnie replied.

"You can never have too many cookies," Russell stated. He grabbed his sisters firmly by their hands and pulled them toward the house.

Carrie, sequestered behind a bush, watched her children walk toward the house.

"They are quite special."

Carrie swallowed her scream when Rose's voice sounded behind her. "Where did you come from?"

"I saw you walking over to talk to Minnie before Frances joined her." Rose grinned. "I wanted to hear. I figured if you could eavesdrop, I could too."

Carrie ran the conversation through her mind again. She had hidden behind the bush, not to eavesdrop, but to give her daughters their privacy. Hearing the conversation had been a bonus that warmed her heart. She had been intent on listening and hadn't heard Rose join her. "They are indeed special."

"You must have said wise things to Frances earlier," Rose commented.

"Thanks to your mama and Abby," Carrie responded. "I like to think I'm passing their wisdom down through the generations."

"Mama would have been impressed." Rose's eyes sparkled with tears for a moment before she dashed them away. "I will never quit missing her." She took a deep breath and changed the topic. "I can hardly believe our girls will be gone in ten days. We missed them when they were in San Francisco, but we knew they were coming back."

"Actually, you didn't know that," Carrie reminded her. "Felicia might have stayed in San Francisco with Mrs. Walker."

"That's true," Rose conceded. "I'm lucky she's at least back on the East Coast."

"At least the girls will be together," Carrie knew her words were more for herself than Rose. They'd had this discussion dozens of times since the girls decided to move to Boston.

Right on cue, Rose added, "We'll have an excuse to go to Boston anytime we want. We'll see the girls, as well as Peter and Elizabeth."

Carrie nodded. There were times those words made her feel better about the girls leaving. Other times, like now, they meant nothing. Rose had experienced Felicia being gone for long stretches of time at Oberlin College, but Frances had spent much of the last five years working alongside Carrie at the clinic. She could feel the dark void waiting for her when she left her daughter in Boston.

Rose reached out and shook her shoulder. "Stop being maudlin," she scolded. "They're not gone. Besides, we're going to Boston to get them settled. If we really don't think we can live without them, we won't leave Boston. Perhaps we'll move in with them."

"Our other children would love that," Carrie said wryly. "Not to mention the fact the girls would throw us out." The sheer ridiculousness of the suggestion made her smile.

"Let's go get one of those cookies before none are left."

Carrie chuckled. "I doubt the men even let the children near them. Besides, I can't eat another thing."

"Neither can I, but everyone is starting to wonder why we're hiding in the bushes."

Startled, Carrie looked toward the house. Anthony, Moses, and her father were standing on the edge of the porch, staring in their direction. She cast about in her mind for a reasonable explanation to be crouched behind a bush, but quickly realized there wasn't one. She had been eavesdropping on her children, plain and simple.

"Ready for that cookie?" Rose asked with a smile.

Carrie laughed and moved away from the bush. "Let's go have a cookie."

They were at the base of the stairs when Russell ran from the house and grabbed Anthony's arm. "Daddy, it's time!"

Carrie, realizing her son had granted her a reprieve from being questioned, climbed the stairs and joined them. "Time? Time for what?"

"We can't say," Russell responded, his eyes wide with anticipation. He tugged Anthony's arm again. "It's time." His voice had gone from excited to firm and unyielding.

Anthony nodded. "We have to hitch the wagon back up."

"No, we don't," Russell replied. "I told Miles we would be needing it."

"Yep," Miles drawled. "Your boy done told me how things were gonna be tonight."

Anthony grinned. "You were that certain I would say yes?"

"It's *time*," Russell repeated.

"I suppose you're right." Anthony ruffled Russell's hair.

Carrie listened to the interchange with complete confusion. "What are you two talking about? What do you need the wagon for?" As soon as she asked the question, she thought about the long nights in the workshop. Was she finally going to discover what they had been doing?

"You'll see," Russell said, the little-boy excitement back in his voice. He danced to the edge of the porch. "Don't anyone go to bed until we're back!" With those words, he and Anthony ran down the stairs and disappeared into the darkness.

"Where in the world are they going?" Frances asked as she appeared at Carrie's side.

Carrie had her suspicions but didn't know anything for certain. She shrugged nonchalantly. "I have no idea, but we'll find out soon enough."

"It's dark," Frances protested. "How can they drive the wagon?"

"They gonna have plenty of light," Miles answered. "That big moon 'bout to pop up over the trees."

In response to his words, the full moon that had been lurking below the horizon rose over the dark band of forest in the distance. A glow spread over the pasture and illuminated the road, spotlighting the wagon as it disappeared around the curve. By the time they arrived home it would be high in the sky.

Bridget, held securely in Abby's arms, clapped her hands. "Ooohh...pretty moon."

Carrie swept her daughter into her arms. "You are absolutely right, my beautiful girl. Do you think you can stay awake to wait for Daddy and Russell?"

Bridget nodded solemnly.

Abby smiled. "I'll give her ten minutes. She's exhausted from the fun down by the river."

Carrie sank down into an available rocking chair, cuddled Bridget close, and hummed quietly. Her daughter laid her thick black curls against Carrie's chest and closed her eyes. Nothing gave Carrie more joy than rocking her little girl to sleep. At two and a half, Bridget remained a little small for her age, but she was growing quickly. Now that she was loved, safe, and well-fed, her body was healing from her rough beginning living under a bridge.

As predicted, Bridget fell fast asleep, her breathing even and regular. Carrie gazed down at the long, black lashes resting on plump cheeks tanned by the sun. Her heart swelled with such deep love, she suddenly found it difficult to breathe.

"How long is it going to take Russell and Anthony to do whatever they're doing?" John asked.

Moses shrugged his massive shoulders. "I have no idea." He and Anthony were very close, but he was as much in the dark as everyone else. "Anthony hasn't told me their secret, just like Russell hasn't told you. I would say it's quite important, though."

"I don't think it will take long," Carrie added. "Whatever they went to get must be finished or they wouldn't be bringing it back."

John looked doubtful.

Moses knew how hard it was for his energetic son to stay still, even after an afternoon at the river. "Why don't y'all go play a game of tag?"

"It's dark," Hope said, coming to lean against her father's leg.

Hope wasn't comfortable in the dark, but Moses didn't want her to be afraid. He encouraged the children to be cautious, but the adults were right there to watch them. He didn't want her fear to stop her from having fun. "That's true, honey. It's also true that you're seven years old. When you're seven, you're old enough to play in the dark."

Hope regarded him suspiciously, her soft brown eyes a complete tiny replica of Rose. "I am?"

"Cross my heart," Moses assured her. "When you're seven, your eyes can see better in the dark. It makes you much better at playing tag." He bit back his smile when he saw Rose's eyes widen.

John decided to play along. "Daddy's right, Hope. I could see better in the dark when I was seven. That's why I'm not afraid anymore."

Hope turned to her big brother. "You're not afraid of the dark, even a little?"

"Nope," John said firmly. "Playing tag in the dark is more fun."

"What if I hide and none of you can find me?" Hope stepped closer to her father, her own suggestion frightening her.

John looked thoughtful and then reached out his hand. "How about if we play together tonight? You can hide with me." He paused. "As long as you're real quiet."

Hope leapt forward to take his hand. "I'll be *real* quiet," she promised. "Let's go hide."

Moses watched as the children raced down the stairs and out into the yard. He was proud of his son for choosing to be a good big brother.

"When you're seven, your eyes can see better in the dark?" Rose settled into the rocker next to him. Chuckles sounded around the porch.

Moses shrugged, his lips twitching. "It could be true."

Rose laughed. "It's nonsense, but it got Hope playing with the other children. Well done."

Carrie returned from putting Bridget to bed and sat down in her rocking chair. "I rode through the tobacco fields today. It seems even taller than two days ago."

Moses felt a surge of satisfaction. "It is. The heat is miserable to live with, but it's great for the tobacco. This year is going to be a bumper crop."

"The workers must be quite excited," Abby said. "Their percentage of the profits will make such a huge difference."

"They're making big plans," Moses responded with pride. "It still amazes me that every plantation doesn't work this way."

"Ignorance and greed are powerful forces," Thomas said. He smiled slightly. "So is stupidity. I had one of our esteemed neighbors stop me on the road yesterday and light into me about how we treat our workers. When he was done, I told him the dollar amount of our crop last year and asked him how his plantation had fared. I could tell our profit shocked him, but he told me it didn't matter." His smile disappeared. "He said what we're doing is wrong because we're letting our workers believe they're as good as we are."

Moses was done feeling angry about others' attitudes. Instead, he laughed. "You can't argue with stupid, Thomas."

Laughter rippled around the porch.

Moses took Rose's hand, enjoying the warm breeze. It was too dark to see the children, but he reveled in their yells and laughter. Even Felicia and Frances had joined the children playing tag. The sound of the two girls filled him with a sudden sadness. "I'm going to miss those two," he said quietly.

Rose squeezed his hand but didn't speak.

Moses knew she was remaining silent because she doubted her ability to control the emotion she was feeling. He thought about the three months he had spent with Felicia and Frances, traveling across the country and experiencing San Francisco. He knew he would treasure every moment of it for the rest of his life. "I'm glad you're going to Boston with her."

Rose squeezed his hand again.

"I reckon we all gonna miss them," Annie said. "It's hard to believe them young'uns be old 'nuff to move off to Boston and live on their own."

A heaviness settled on the porch as they listened to the voices drifting toward them from the darkness. The moon was bright enough to outline figures darting from tree to tree. An occasional firefly lit the night with its golden glow. Tree frogs sang their chorus, while a nearby owl added to the symphony.

"Enough," Abby said. "They're not gone today. Besides, it's the natural order of things. Those two girls are ready to go out and make their mark on the world, and we have a wonderful trip to New York and Boston with them."

"Speak for yourself," Thomas grumbled.

"Are you jealous?" Abby teased.

"I am," Thomas admitted.

"Too bad, my dear. This is a female outing." Abby's voice softened. "I will miss you though, my dear husband."

Thomas leaned forward in his rocker. The lantern light glistened off his silver hair and made his blue eyes sparkle. "Will you miss me enough to consider letting me join you? If I promise I won't interfere with any of your female togetherness?"

"What would you do in New York City?" Carrie asked.

"I've been corresponding with Wally," Thomas revealed. "If I can convince y'all to let me join you, he will take me to the Stock Exchange. I would be quite happy to sit in the seat of American finance while you women gallivant around the city. It's something we've talked about. I have no interest in playing the stock market, but it would be fascinating to witness firsthand."

Abby looked at him in amusement "You've been planning this?"

"I prefer to use the word *hoping*," Thomas replied. "With me there, it will be easier to keep Wally out of the way. I can help take care of Bridget, which will give you more time with Nancy when the girls leave for Boston. I'm sure Wally and I will have plenty to talk about every night in his study. You'll have even more female time," he said persuasively.

Moses listened to the exchange, curious to see how it would turn out. Thomas had told him the day before that he hoped he could talk the women into letting him join them. He had lamented that Moses couldn't join them because of the harvest, but Moses had assured him he had no desire to go. The noise, crowdedness, and pollution of the city didn't appeal to him. As far as he was concerned, there wasn't another place in the world as special as Cromwell Plantation.

"You're serious about this aren't you, Father?" Carrie asked.

Thomas hesitated. "Only if it won't interfere with your time with the girls. I know how special this is going to be. I can travel up another time. My feelings won't be hurt if you prefer for me to stay here."

Moses doubted that was true.

Rose was the first to speak. "I don't have a problem with it."

"It will be the best of both worlds for me," Abby said. "I'll have you girls to myself during the day but sleep with my husband at night."

"Will you tell us about the Stock Exchange?" Carrie asked. "I admit it's a mystery to me."

"I promise to tell you everything I can. That is, when Wally and I are allowed in your presence," Thomas replied with a wink.

"The Stock Exchange?" Felicia appeared, her face gleaming with sweat as she leaned over to catch her breath. "What's this about the Stock Exchange?"

Abby answered. "Thomas has talked his way into joining our women-only trip. He and Wally are going to spend time at the Stock Exchange."

Felicia whirled toward Thomas. "Really? I want to come with you!"

"Felicia!" Rose protested.

Felicia took her mother's hand. "For one day, Mama. Mrs. Pleasant and I have talked about the Stock Exchange. I want to see it for myself. I've dreamed of the day I'll be able to invest my profits. Since I'm going to Boston to begin my financial empire, I believe it's only right that I should experience the Stock Exchange."

Moses knew that Rose couldn't argue the soundness of Felicia's reasoning. She would have to release her expectation of spending every moment of the trip with her daughter.

"I understand," Rose replied. "I'm thrilled you'll have the opportunity."

Felicia turned back to Thomas. "You'll take me?"

"Of course," Thomas agreed. "I would love to."

Felicia clapped her hands. "I'm sorry the harvest will keep you from going, Daddy."

"Don't be," Moses replied. "Even if the harvest was over, I'm not going anywhere. I'm happy to be back on the plantation. I have no desire to go to New York City. I have no desire to go *anywhere*."

Frances stepped out of the shadows. "I think we should leave earlier and spend more time in the city," she announced.

Carrie gazed at her daughter in the lantern light, admiring her flushed cheeks and sparkling eyes. "You do? Why?"

"Because there's so much to do. We need more than two days, especially with Felicia wanting to go to the Stock Exchange. Besides," Frances added, "it will be fun to spend more time with you."

Carrie laughed. "You know I can't say no to that."

Frances grinned. "I do make a compelling argument."

"I agree with her," Felicia said. "I'm excited to get to Boston, but I want to experience more of New York City. Who knows when we'll have the freedom to return?"

Carrie exchanged a look with Rose and Abby that confirmed their agreement. "We'll leave three days early, on the fifteenth, and stay in New York City until the twenty-first., instead of leaving on the eighteenth." She thought about the changes she would have to make with the clinic schedule, but she was sure Janie and Polly would be alright with it. "I'll let the Gilberts know about the change."

"That sounds like a wonderful plan," Abby replied. She turned to Thomas. "I have a change of my own to propose. Since you'll be with me, there's no reason to hurry back. How about if we spend another week in the city before we come home?"

Thomas smiled. "That sounds perfect. I'll let Wally know we're coming. By the time we get home, things should have cooled off here."

The sound of wagon wheels in the distance stopped the conversation. Within moments, the children rushed onto the porch, crowding the edge as they peered down the road.

"Daddy and Russell are back!" Minnie exclaimed. "Will you tell us *now*, Mama?"

Carrie laughed. "I honestly don't know what's in that wagon. Your daddy and Russell have kept it a secret from me as well." Truth be told, she was as eager as everyone else to discover what it was.

Russell bounced up and down on the seat as Anthony pulled the wagon to a stop.

A peek at the back of the wagon revealed nothing but a mound of blankets.

Anthony beckoned to Moses as he stepped down. "Would you help me with this?"

Russell held up his hand. "No, Daddy, I can do it. We did this together. I want to help you carry it up!"

Anthony smiled. "Together it is, son."

Carrie's heart swelled as she watched her husband and son. They had always been close, but whatever they had been doing in the workshop had obviously made them closer.

Russell joined his father at the back of the wagon. They released the back panel and pulled the blankets forward slowly. With the surprise covered, they carried it up the stairs, taking each step carefully.

"What is it?" Minnie exclaimed. "You have to show us right this minute!"

Russell looked at his oldest sister. "Frances, will you please uncover the surprise?"

"Why me?" Frances asked as she stepped forward.

Anthony draped an arm across her shoulders. "Because it's for you," he said. "Russell and I have been working on this for the last month."

Frances wore a look of astonishment as she gingerly pulled at the blankets. Her mouth dropped open when it was revealed. "A cedar chest!" She held a hand to her mouth as she leaned closer to examine it. "It's beautiful!"

Carrie understood her daughter's reaction. The chest was exquisite. In the lantern light, the rich wood, varnished to a high shine, reflected their admiring faces.

Frances knelt and ran her hands over its surface.

Russell dropped down next to her. "We engraved your name in the lid," he proclaimed.

Frances gently traced the letters of her name, her face filled with awe.

"Look inside!" Russell opened the latch and lifted the lid. The smell of cedar filled the warm evening air. "Feel how smooth it is."

Frances ran her hands over the inside, closed the lid, and ran her fingers over the ornate engraving on the top and sides again, lingering on her name.

Carrie saw her trembling lips and knew what an emotional moment this was for her daughter.

Finally, Frances sat back and looked at her father and Russell. "You did this for me?"

"Of course," Anthony replied tenderly. He laid a hand on Russell's shoulder. "It was your brother's idea. He brought in the cedar logs from the woods. Even when I couldn't help, he was cutting the boards and planing them. He spent hours sanding them smooth."

Frances threw her arms around Russell. "Thank you! I love it!"

She ran to her father and hugged him tightly. "I'm sorry," she mumbled against his chest.

Anthony shook his head, confused. "Sorry for what, honey?"

"I was upset you spent so much time at the workshop with Russell. I wanted to spend time with you. I wouldn't have felt that way if I'd known what you were doing, but I'm glad you kept it a surprise. I'm sorry for being jealous." Frances kept her head pressed against his chest.

Anthony frowned. "I should have thought about that. We wanted it to be ready before you left." He tilted her face up. "Will you spend time with me before you go, honey?"

"Of course," Frances said, her eyes filling with tears. She stepped back and looked around the porch. "How am I ever going to leave y'all? No matter how wonderful medical school is, I'm going to miss the plantation and the times we've had on this porch." Her voice trembled with emotion.

"You have to leave," Russell replied. "We didn't build this chest so you could stay home!" His tone was playful, but his expression was sad.

Minnie stepped up and put an arm around her sister. "Courage rising."

Frances laughed. "Courage rising," she agreed.

Carrie's heart swelled with happiness. She felt the same surge of pride she'd felt earlier as she hid in the bushes listening to them talk. She had yearned for a sibling when she was growing up alone on the plantation. Rose had been the closest thing to a sister, but the reality of her best friend being a slave made things complicated.

Her children would always have each other.

"One week," Frances said in wonder. "We leave in one week."

"One week," Felicia echoed.

Chapter Three

Carrie tightened the cinch on No Regrets' saddle and led her to the mounting block. Granite stood to the side, snorting in the early morning air. The heat wave had finally broken. While it wasn't quite cool, the oppressive, muggy air had disappeared in the wake of a vicious storm two nights earlier. The sun lingered below the tree line, but the early dawn revealed it would be a beautiful morning. A half-moon hung slightly above the western horizon.

Carrie absorbed the beauty. She was happy to be going to New York and Boston with the girls, but she hated leaving the plantation. No matter where she went, nothing was as beautiful as her own home. She would miss it every second she was gone.

Granite snorted again and stomped his hoof impatiently.

Carrie laughed and stepped onto the mounting block. "Alright, your highness. We're going!"

"Mama, wait a minute!"

Carrie looked up with surprise when Frances appeared. "What are you doing out here?" Her daughter was not known for being an early riser.

"It's my last morning," Frances replied.

Carrie could tell Frances was trying to control her emotions. "Would you like to go for a morning ride?"

"Can I?"

Carrie grinned with delight and dismounted. "Of course. Nothing would make me happier. Let's get Peaches tacked up."

Within a few minutes, the beautiful palomino mare was saddled and bridled.

Frances looked sad when she mounted Peaches. "I'm going to miss her. I missed her while I was in San Francisco, but this time is different. It could be years before I'm really back on the plantation."

Carrie didn't try to tell her that wasn't true. She fought to keep her voice even as she thought about how long it could be before Frances returned—*if* she returned for more than occasional visits. "I missed Granite every single time I had to go away. It was the hardest thing about leaving. It still is."

"Will Peaches be alright?"

"Absolutely," Carrie said. "She will miss you, but we'll take good care of her. Minnie has promised to ride her and give her carrots every day." She smiled. "Since your little sister is happier in the kitchen than she is in the barn, that should tell you how much she loves you."

"It does," Frances replied. She looked toward the horizon as the sun broke free of the trees and cast its first golden beams on the day. "It's beautiful!"

"There is no more beautiful place in the world," Carrie declared, basking in the glory of a new day. Her eyes roamed over the fenced pastures full of horses. The house glowed white in the sunshine. She pushed aside the thought of her daughter leaving tomorrow. She wouldn't be saying goodbye until she and Rose left Boston to return home. Until then, she could pretend it wasn't going to happen.

"Mama, if I ask you a question, do you promise to say yes?"

"What kind of question is that?" Carrie demanded. "I have the distinct impression I'm being set up."

"That's because you are," Frances replied. Her playful tone didn't cover the seriousness of her expression.

Carrie gave herself a little time by signaling No Regrets into an even trot. Peaches fell into stride beside her. Granite cavorted around them with his usual energy. When they were several hundred yards from the barn, Carrie slowed to a walk. "What's your question?"

Frances shook her head. "You haven't promised to say yes."

Carrie regarded her daughter, admiring how the sun caught the summer highlights in her hair. She knew she had no reason to hesitate. Whatever she wanted to ask, she had already thought it through carefully. Carrie couldn't imagine anything she would refuse, but if Frances needed to turn this into a game, she might as well play along. "This is obviously important to you."

"It is," Frances said. "I promise you it's nothing bad. In fact, I think you'll be happy you said yes."

Carrie considered her daughter's words. She could continue the verbal sparring for a while, but she already knew she would say yes. "I promise."

Frances spoke quickly. "I want Minnie to come with us to New York and Boston."

Carrie's eyes widened. Whatever she had been expecting, it wasn't this. "You do?"

"Minnie is sad, but she is going to be sadder when I leave. She's already afraid she's not my best friend anymore. She thinks she's been replaced by Felicia. It will be easier for her if she comes on the trip with us. That way, she won't be left out."

"She'll miss school," Carrie muttered, more to herself than to Frances.

"Rose said it won't matter," Frances replied. "I already asked her. Minnie is really smart. Missing school won't hurt her. Besides," she added persuasively, "a trip to Boston will be quite educational."

Carrie laughed. Minnie had already been to both New York City and Boston, but every new trip would certainly provide new experiences. More importantly, Carrie agreed it would make Frances leaving the plantation a little easier. Nothing would erase the ache of missing her sister, but perhaps the memories of their trip together would provide some comfort. "Yes, honey, I would love to have Minnie join us."

Frances whooped with joy and urged Peaches into a canter.

Carrie caught up to her quickly. A good morning had turned into a spectacular morning.

"Mama, that's not fair!"

Rose sighed as she looked at Hope's defiant expression.

"If Minnie is going on the trip, I should be able to go too!"

Her and Carrie's carefully planned trip to New York and Boston had spun wildly out of control. She wasn't upset that Thomas and Minnie were joining them, but she wouldn't deny it would make things more complicated. Adding a seven-year-old into the mix would mean less time with Felicia. However, she understood Hope's feelings, and was certain she would feel the same. Frances' sister was joining them. Since Hope was Felicia's sister, she should be able to come too.

"Hope is right, Mama."

Rose hadn't heard Felicia come up behind them. She turned and raised a brow in question.

"I want Hope to come," Felicia said.

Rose doubted that was completely true, but she appreciated Felicia's desire to include her little sister on such an important trip. Her oldest daughter had become a caring, compassionate adult. Rose could put aside her own expectations and be as mature as Felicia.

Hope peered up at her. "So, I can come, Mama?"

Rose smiled. "Yes, honey. I would love for you to join us."

Hope clapped her hands excitedly. "I need to pack!"

Minnie was already upstairs doing that very thing. Rose could hear Minnie's excited chatter through the open window. The little girl had almost burst with excitement when Frances announced she wanted her best friend to come. The sadness that had engulfed Minnie like a cloud for the last week disappeared in that one golden moment.

Hope wrapped Rose in an exuberant hug. "Thank you, Mama."

Rose looked into her daughter's excited face. Hope was glowing with pride that she had been included. Rose was suddenly certain the trip was going to be extraordinary. It didn't matter that her careful plans had gone awry.

They were going to have a glorious time. It would be a trip all of them would treasure.

Shortly past noon a wagon rolled down the long driveway. Their company had arrived. Everyone had hoped for a longer visit, and having it happen the day before their trip wasn't ideal, but the fact it was happening at all was wonderful.

Annie walked to the edge of the porch, her face split by a wide smile. "My June be here!" she announced. "It's been way too long since I seen my baby girl!"

Moses grinned. "June isn't exactly a baby girl anymore, Mama. She's twenty-nine years old. She has two children." He winked. "Or have you forgotten?"

"I ain't forgotten nothing. June will always be my baby girl," Annie retorted, her eyes flashing with fire. "It don't matter none that you be big as a tree, Moses. You gonna always be my baby boy, and I' gonna always be your mama." She wagged a finger at Moses. "Don't you never forget that, boy!"

Moses laughed, though truth be told, his mama was an intimidating figure when she was angry, even when she was fake angry. "I won't forget," he promised.

Annie shaded her eyes and watched the wagon as it rolled closer. "It's been way too long since I seen them grandchillun of mine. I can't believe little Simon is eleven and little Ella be five."

"I'm going to play with Ella," Hope announced.

"We all will," Felicia said.

Hope tossed her head. "Yes, but you're old. You're not as much fun to play with."

Laughter exploded from everyone on the porch.

"I'm not old!" Felicia protested.

Something akin to sympathy crossed Hope's face. "Maybe. But you're not as much fun as I am."

Felicia scowled. "Don't make me sorry I told Mama you should come on the trip with us."

Hope smirked. "You won't be sorry. I'll make sure everyone has *fun*!"

Laughter rang out again. Before Felicia had a chance to respond, the wagon stopped in front of the porch.

"Mama!"

Annie hurried down the stairs and wrapped her daughter in her arms. "June girl! You be a sight for sore eyes." When she released June, she held out her arms to her grandchildren. "Simon! Ella! Come here and let me see you. I can't believe you be the same chillun I saw last time."

"Grandma!"

Moses hugged his sister and shook hands with his brother-in-law. "Simon, I'm glad you're here."

Before Simon could respond, Perry Appleton and Louisa stepped down from the wagon. Their eight-year-old son, Nathan, had already run off to play with the children.

A flurry of greetings didn't distract Moses from the trouble he'd seen lurking in Simon's eyes. The two had been friends for a long time. Their years serving during the war had cemented their friendship. The long gap since they'd last seen each other hadn't changed how well he knew him.

Carrie leaned back against the log and watched the children play in the river. Abby and Louisa laughed and splashed along with them. Despite Annie's pleas and admonitions, June refused to get into the water. She had planted herself on a log and refused to move.

"I hope she enjoys being dry," Rose said. "The men will be here soon."

Carrie chuckled. Annie had made Moses promise to step in if she couldn't convince June to swim.

"I heard that."

Carrie hadn't realized June had walked up behind them.

"I don't know what you're talking about," Rose said innocently. "I was simply telling Carrie the men will be here soon. Everyone is hungry, but Annie won't let us eat until everyone arrives."

June glared at Rose. She wasn't as tall as her brother, but she was a formidable woman. "*I hope she enjoys being dry?*" Her eyes flashed. "My brother might be a giant of a man, but it will take more than him to get me into the water."

Carrie thought it wise not to reveal that Annie had enlisted more than Moses to accomplish her goal. "The river really is wonderful," she offered. "I believe you would love it."

June sank down next to Carrie with a troubled expression. "Do you want to know *why* I won't go in that river?" When Carrie nodded, she continued. "When I was young, I was pulling worms off the tobacco plants with my best friend, Delilah. It was fierce hot that day. When the overseer had gone to another part of the fields, Delilah ran down to the river. Our plantation was much farther north, but it was this same James River. She wanted to splash water on her face because it was fierce hot." Her voice faltered.

Carrie tightened, dreading what was coming.

Rose took June's hand, offering her courage to continue.

June took a deep breath. "Delilah was standing right at the edge of the river when the overseer came back. He pulled out his whip and told her he would teach her a lesson she would never forget." Her voice faltered again. "He hit her... with the lash... over...and over." Tears rolled down her face. "Delilah was so scared. She turned and ran - right into that river. She didn't know how to swim..." She wiped at her face as she fought to catch her breath. "She never came back up."

Carrie allowed her tears to flow. "I'm sorry," she whispered. She thought about the time she had saved Rose from being whipped by their old overseer, Ike Adams. She couldn't imagine what she would feel if she couldn't have saved her best friend.

"I'm sorry," Rose echoed. "That's horrible."

June sighed heavily. "Then you know why I won't get in the river."

Rose shook her head. "I know why you haven't gotten into the river *yet*, June." She squeezed her sister-in-law's hand tighter. "You are a strong, brave woman. You have overcome an incredible amount to be who you are. You've fought through a lot of fears. The river is simply one more."

June jerked her hand away. "I'm not afraid," she snapped.

Annie joined them. "Of course you be afraid. So was I."

June gazed up at her mother, her eyes full of tears.

"I be there that day too, June girl. I watched that ole river swallow Delilah, and I held her mama for lots of nights while she cried for her baby." She glanced at the water. "I thought that ole river ain't be nothin' but pure evil."

June's expression said she agreed.

"But that ole river ain't evil," Annie continued. "That overseer be the evil one. He drove little Delilah to her death with that whip of his." Her eyes settled on the river again. "I decided I weren't never gettin' in that water. I got alright with the rest goin' in, but eber time I thought about gettin' in, I couldn't see nothin' but Delilah disappearin'."

"Mama..."

Annie held up her hand. "I ain't done. I spent my whole life makin' decisions 'cause of the fear I lived with every day. I lost your daddy." Her voice trembled with emotion. "Sam be a good man!" she said fiercely. "They done killed him anyway. My little Carmen got beat to death right in front of me. They crippled my little Sadie. I had to watch that too." She reached out and laid her hand on June's shoulder. "They sold you away from me when you ain't but fifteen. They sold Moses away. I didn't think I would ever see y'all again."

Carrie's heart felt like it would explode. Annie wasn't saying anything she didn't already know, but hearing it laid out was almost more than she could bear.

Annie continued. "Ever'body I cared 'bout got ripped away. There weren't nothin' left but pain and fear. When Moses came and found me, and brung me here, I knew I was safe, but the fear was real deep in me. Ain't easy to let go of that fear, June girl." Her voice grew more firm. "Rose be right 'bout you being a strong, brave woman, but you got the fear deep in you too."

June looked at her defiantly. "Getting in that river won't get rid of my fears, Mama."

"Not all of them," Annie agreed, "but you got the chance to get rid of one of them, June girl. There ain't nothin' evil 'bout that river. That water feel better than you can even imagine. I reckon God done made rivers for lots of reasons, but I know for sure one reason be because they fun to get in."

"What made you finally get in the river, Mama?" June asked. The anger in her voice had been replaced by a fearful longing.

"It weren't my idea, sho 'nuff." Annie smiled. "I put up a pretty good fight, but I knew I weren't gonna win, so I went ahead and walked in."

"What did it feel like?"

Annie's smile widened. "Like nothin' you can imagine. Bathin' in a washtub ain't nothin' like havin' that water wrap right 'round you. It be cool on a hot day. It be real soft too. I'm gonna be real sad when that water be too cold to get in."

The deep sparkling blue of the James River reflected the cloudless sky. Close to shore, nothing marred the mirror image of the towering trees on the bank. Further out, the current ran fast while white caps danced.

"I've done learned some thin's since I been here," Annie continued. "It ain't no lie that life is full of fear, but I done learned that I can choose hope over fear. When I step into the big ole James River, I be choosing hope every single time," she said triumphantly.

June didn't look away from the water.

Carrie could feel the battle raging inside June. She knew how hard it was to overcome fears, but she couldn't truly understand the deep fear June lived with after watching her friend drown.

June drew in a deep, shaky breath. "Will y'all go in with me?"

Annie nodded. "Of course, baby girl."

Carrie and Rose stood, each reaching out a hand to June.

"You'll stay with me?"

"Every second," Rose promised.

"I'll be right there with you, June girl," Annie assured her.

"You'll never be alone," Carrie added.

June took their hands and faced the water. "Let's go swimming," she said weakly.

Annie whooped with joy and surged forward, leading the way as she parted the waters.

Carrie and Rose linked their arms with June's and walked slowly into the river.

The children cheered and clapped when the water lapped at June's waist.

June stood stiffly for several minutes, shallow breaths a testament to her fear.

Annie faced her with a comforting smile. "Feel the water, June girl. Close your eyes. Lift your face to the sun and feel the water."

June obeyed her mother's instructions. A breeze ruffled her hair, and the sun warmed her dark skin.

The children, sensing the sacred moment, fell silent and watched.

Birdsong filled the air, punctuated with the cry of a hawk wheeling overhead.

Gradually, peace softened June's face. She lowered her hands and swirled them through the water. A soft smile transformed her face.

"Ain't it wonderful?" Annie asked tenderly.

"It's wonderful," June agreed. She opened her eyes and took in the vast expanse of the river. "I think I understand why you love it, Mama."

Behind them, the men rode up and dismounted.

Simon's mouth dropped open when he caught sight of his wife in the water. "I never thought I would see the day." He looked at Moses. "I was certain we would be carrying her in kicking and screaming."

Carrie heard his words. "No kicking or screaming, Simon. Your brave and beautiful wife walked in on her own."

Simon knelt to remove his shoes and waded into the water to be with June. "What made you get in? I been trying to get you in the river for a lot of years."

"I know," June agreed, a smile suffusing her face. "They helped me see I could choose fear or hope. I've had so much stolen from me. I decided it was time to take my life back. I chose hope."

Annie raised her arms in a gesture of triumph. "My baby girl done chose hope!" She stepped forward and wrapped June in an embrace. "I'm real proud of you, honey."

"Thank you, Mama," June whispered. "Without you, I never would have done this." She looked at Carrie and Rose. "Thank you."

Simon laughed loudly, swooped June into his arms, and spun in circles. Water swirled around them, catching the light in diamond droplets.

It was a moment no one there would ever forget.

"I was terrible to Carrie when we were growing up," Louisa told the children at dinner that night.

Carrie watched her friend. Louisa's blond hair framed blue eyes. She was older but remained a delicate beauty. Louisa had been her nemesis when they were younger, but that was behind them. Why was she bringing it up?

Perry looked equally puzzled.

The rest of the adults at the table fell silent as they waited to see where the conversation would go.

"Why?" Minnie demanded.

"Did Mama do something mean to you?" Russell asked.

"Of course she didn't," Frances protested.

Carrie opened her mouth to assure her children she hadn't been perfect, but Louisa beat her to it.

"Your mama tried to be kind to me," Louisa replied. "I was horrid."

Minnie looked at Carrie. "Is that true, Mama?"

Carrie searched for the right words but came up empty.

Louisa laughed. "Your mama would probably never tell you how horrid I was. Even tonight, she can't find the words to speak the truth."

Memories assailed Carrie. Louisa had indeed been horrid when they were growing up. She had looked for every opportunity to insult and demean Carrie. To top it off, she had tried to turn Robert against her and take him for herself. It hadn't worked, but not for her lack of trying. The war had caused her to grow up. Louisa had transformed into a woman who was a true friend, but memories never truly left once you experienced them.

"Why were you horrid?" Minnie persisted. "I don't understand."

"I was horrid because I was unhappy," Louisa said, speaking directly to Minnie. "I didn't like myself very much, so I took it out on Carrie every chance I got."

Minnie looked confused. "Did it make you feel better to treat Mama badly?"

"I thought it did. The truth was that I was jealous of your mama."

Louisa's words left Carrie dumbstruck. They had never talked about their growing up years. They had simply left it in the past as their friendship had evolved.

"Why?" Russell asked.

"She had the life I wanted," Louisa admitted.

"What?" Carrie couldn't hold back her exclamation. She glanced at her father. Thomas looked as shocked as she felt.

Louisa smiled at Carrie. "It's true. My mama wanted me to be the perfect plantation daughter, so I was. Your mama wanted the same thing, but you chose to be your own person." She glanced at Thomas, who listened intently. "My father refused to step in and support what I wanted. *Your* father bought you a horse. He let you ride. He let you *compete* in the tournament." She looked back at Carrie. "I was **so** jealous I could hardly stand it."

Louisa spoke to the children again. "Even though I was terrible to Carrie, she was the one who made sure Perry lived after being wounded in the war. She made certain I could spend time with him and nurse him back to health. She should have turned me away at the hospital door, but she chose compassion."

Minnie looked at Carrie. "That must have been really hard, Mama."

Carrie didn't bother to deny it. She was still trying to absorb the confession. "Louisa is my friend now. That is what's important."

When Minnie looked doubtful, Carrie wondered if Louisa's conversation wasn't random. Most of her words had been directed toward Minnie. What did

Louisa know about her daughter that she didn't? She thought back over the afternoon.

Though Blackwell Plantation was on the river, too, Louisa had admitted that afternoon that she'd never been swimming in it. That must have been another thing her mother hadn't allowed to happen. Once she'd stepped into the water, she refused to come out. She had spent far more time in the river with the children than she had. Had she overheard something?

When she caught Louisa's eyes, her friend gave her a nearly imperceptible nod of acknowledgement.

Frances and Felicia were on the porch when Carrie went upstairs to their bedroom. She needed private time with Minnie.

Minnie, sitting cross-legged on her bed, looked up with a bright smile. "Hi, Mama! I can't believe we're leaving in the morning. I'm excited!"

Carrie settled down next to her. Since she didn't have a lot of time, she decided to get straight to the point. "Are you excited because you're going on the trip? Or because you're leaving something hard behind, honey?"

Minnie's smile faded. "Did Frances tell you?" Her expression reflected the betrayal she felt.

"No," Carrie assured her. "It was Louisa's conversation at dinner tonight. She seemed to be speaking directly to you. I'm assuming she overheard something at the river today. Is someone treating you badly, Minnie?"

"No, Mama!"

Carrie remained silent, watching the expressions race over her daughter's face. She was content to wait. Muted voices rose from the porch below. A soft breeze ruffled the curtains, carrying in the earthy smells of the countryside. The aroma of freshly cut hay filled her senses with delight.

After several minutes, Minnie sighed heavily. "Missy isn't very nice to me, Mama."

There was a lot unspoken in those simple words. "What has happened?"

Minnie hesitated. "Frances is the only person I've told. She asked me about it today. Mrs. Appleton must have heard her." She looked distressed. "Missy says if I tell anyone, she'll make things worse for me."

Carrie's anger flared, but she forced her voice to remain even. "I'll make sure that doesn't happen, honey. You can tell me." When Minnie continued to hesitate, she added, "Mean people want you to be afraid of them, but you should never let fear stop you from trusting the people you love. You never have to be afraid of anyone. You have me and Daddy. You have Russell. Frances. Your grandparents. Everyone on the plantation loves you and believes in you. We will always take care of you."

"You can't always be there, Mama," Minnie stated sadly.

Carrie, as much as she wanted to deny it, knew that was true. Louisa had been the most horrid when no one was around to witness it. "Tell me what's going on."

Minnie's face turned red as she fought for control. She remained silent for a long moment before she spoke. "Missy tells me I'm ugly and stupid. She pinches me when no one is looking." Her voice was slow and halting. "She makes fun of what I wear. She told me I wasn't good enough to live on Cromwell Plantation." Minnie stopped, her lips quivering. "One day she tripped me and made me fall. She stood there and laughed at me."

Carrie's anger roared in full fury. She hated that her beautiful daughter had been treated so terribly. She wrapped Minnie in her arms and held her close. "Absolutely none of that is true, Minnie. I'm sorry you had to hear it." Her thoughts were spinning. "Who is Missy?"

"I don't know her last name," Minnie told her. "Russell says she didn't use to be horrible."

"Russell?" Carrie was confused. Minnie had been at the school far longer than Russell. "How does he know?"

"He lived with her under the bridge."

Carrie's anger dissipated as quickly as it had flared. She was upset Minnie had been treated badly, but she had an instant image of a small, skinny girl with haunted eyes crawling out of the wagon when the children had been brought to the plantation to meet their adoptive parents. She remembered that Missy had been adopted by Graham and Melissa Highland. She didn't know much about them. They had never been to the clinic, and until now had not had a child in school.

Minnie huddled closer into Carrie's embrace. "Why does she hate me **so** much, Mama?"

"She doesn't hate you," Carrie said, thinking about Louisa's words. Later, she would thank her friend for alerting her to the situation. "She's jealous of you, Minnie."

"Why?" Confusion twisted Minnie's face.

"Because you have the life she wishes she had, honey." Carrie wiped a stray tear from her daughter's face. "I think the important thing is to figure out a way to change things."

"I don't think we can," Minnie said in a defeated voice.

"Oh, we can," Carrie replied, certain she would find a way to stop the bullying. "For the next few weeks, though, you have nothing to worry about. Since we're leaving in the morning, you won't be here for Missy to torment. You'll be having the time of your life in New York City and Boston!"

Minnie's sadness melted away. "That's right!"

Missy would be even more jealous when Minnie returned, but Carrie would think of a solution.

She had to. Minnie's devastation had broken her heart.

Chapter Four

The predawn hours had been a flurry of excitement and tearful farewells. The girls were eager to begin their adventure, but their presence on the plantation would be sorely missed.

Anthony and Moses watched as Carrie, Rose, and the others drove off in the wagon laden with trunks and the food Annie had insisted on sending, even after stuffing them with cinnamon rolls for breakfast.

"So, it's just the men," Anthony said.

"I been called a lot of things in my life, but I ain't never been called a man." Annie appeared behind him holding a tray with cups of hot coffee. Her eyes snapped with indignation. "I ain't sure either of you be needin' this coffee after all. I'll just be takin' it right back inside."

"We need it, Mama," Moses said hastily. "Thank you for bringing it out."

Annie eyed Anthony. "You want to say somethin' different, Mr. Anthony?"

Moses hid his smile as Anthony squirmed beneath his mama's baleful expression.

"What I *meant* to say was that it would be only the men around, with *you* running things, Annie. We know nothing could work around here if you weren't taking care of us."

Annie assessed him for a long moment. Finally, she nodded and handed over the tray of coffee. "Now you talkin' like you got some sense in your head. Just you don't forget it."

Perry walked out onto the porch, his big hand covering a yawn. "I heard everyone leaving, but I couldn't force myself out of bed." He yawned again and chose a chair in the morning sun. "Louisa will be down soon. It's been a wonderful visit, but we have to get back to Blackwell. Simon and I need to make sure the tobacco crop is successful."

Moses had no trouble understanding their need to leave. "Do you expect a big crop?"

Perry shrugged. "It will be alright, but not as big as yours."

"Why not? You've got the same number of acres planted." Moses wondered if this had to do with Simon's troubled expression.

"Yes..." Perry's voice trailed off into silence.

Moses' level of concern increased. "What is it?"

"We've had to make a few changes," Perry said evasively.

Moses could feel the tension vibrating in Perry's body. He exchanged an alarmed look with Anthony. What was going on?

Before he could say more, Simon joined them on the porch. "Good morning!"

Perry visibly relaxed. "Morning, Simon. We need to be leaving soon."

"Yep," Simon answered. "June and Louisa are getting the children dressed."

"Cinnamon rolls be waitin' for you in the kitchen," Annie said. "I appreciate y'all comin' for a visit, Simon. I been missin' y'all somethin' fierce."

"Seeing June in the river made the trip worth it. That, and your cinnamon rolls, will keep us coming back."

Moses watched his friend closely. Concerned he wouldn't have the opportunity to get him alone, he decided to tackle the issue head on. "Is something wrong, Simon?"

Simon tensed. "What are you talking about, Moses?"

"I can tell you're hiding something. I have Perry dancing around a simple question. So, I ask again. What's going on? What kind of changes have y'all had to make?"

Simon and Perry exchanged a long look.

Moses interpreted the vow of silence they had evidently made.

Perry was the one to finally answer. "Like I said, we've had to make a few changes. It's not a big deal."

"You mentioned the few changes already," Moses replied. "I still don't know what kind of changes." It was obvious Perry didn't want to answer. That served to make him more determined. "I don't know you very well, Perry, but for June's sake I need to know if something is wrong. Your reluctance to answer is alarming."

"We've had some trouble," Perry said slowly, once again locking eyes with Simon.

Moses walked over to stand in front of Simon. "What happened? I'm tired of trying to pull it out of you two."

He was counting on their friendship to make Simon talk.

"Perry, we might as well tell them. They know something is wrong. It won't help us none to hide it." He met Moses' eyes squarely. "The neighbors aren't thrilled with how Perry has been running things," Simon began.

"The Klan," Moses said flatly. Anger began to bubble.

Simon shrugged. "Whether they are actual Klan members or not hardly seems to matter. There doesn't seem to be a white man in the area who isn't upset about the way things were being run."

Moses focused on one word. "*Were*?"

"The Klan got Perry when he was on his way home one night. They beat him up pretty good and told him if he didn't change things, they would kill him the next time."

"And go after Louisa and Nathan," Perry growled, his eyes full of anger and desperation. "I can't let that happen."

Moses' heart sank.

"Blast that Klan," Annie seethed. "I don't know why they hate us so much. Who cares if them men get paid what they earn?"

"What did you do?" Moses asked.

Perry clenched his fists. "We continue to pay them well, but we don't pay a percentage of the crops anymore. The men know to keep their wages a secret. They all understand the harsh truth of danger."

Simon scowled. "As overseer, I hated being the one to tell them they were losing the percentage. We told them the truth though—why we were doing it. They said they understood."

Moses immediately realized why the Blackwell crop was less than Cromwell's. Perry and Simon had taken away the motivation for the men to work as hard as possible. He wanted to insist that the workers could keep their profit percentage a secret, like they were doing with their income, but he was certain it would come out eventually. A change in lifestyle, or someone overhearing a boast, could put Perry and his family in grave danger.

"That's why we haven't come to visit," Perry admitted. "We didn't want to tell you about the change, but mostly, we don't want to bring trouble to Cromwell. If the Klan sees us coming to visit, it might make things worse for y'all."

Annie's eyes snapped with fury. "You mean it's the Klan that kept me from seein' my baby girl and my grandchillun?"

Simon looked ashamed. "I'm sorry, Annie."

Perry continued. "Things on Blackwell aren't like here on Cromwell. Our men are loyal, and they're good workers, but they aren't going to stand guard like your men do here."

"Because they don't consider the plantation their home," Moses remarked. "It's a place to work."

"I know that's part of it, but it's more than that, Moses. The men who first came to Cromwell to work fought with you in the war. Most of the ones who have joined you in the years since can say the same thing. They have a different type of loyalty. My men respect me, but they see a white man who fought to keep them as slaves. Even though I've changed, that's not something they're likely to ignore. It creates a different environment."

Moses couldn't deny the truth. He thought about the large number of men he hadn't been able to add to his work force. "Simon, what happened to the men I sent to Blackwell for a job? They served with us."

"They came, but they were disappointed when they found out things weren't going to work the same as they do here." His eyes burned with frustration. "Most of them headed north where they might have the opportunity of being treated equally. I can't say I blame them."

Moses wondered if Simon still received a percentage of the profits, as he and Perry had initially agreed. That was a conversation they would have privately.

Perry had made the only decision he thought he could make. "I'm sorry you were attacked, Perry." Without the Cromwell men to provide constant protection, Moses might well have made the same decision to protect Rose and the children. "Are you alright?"

"I healed," Perry said quietly, but he wouldn't meet his eyes.

Moses knew it must have been bad. Perry's body may have healed, but fear still haunted him.

"Are June and the children safe?" Annie demanded.

"I believe so," Simon said. "I run things, but I don't make the decisions. The Klan doesn't have a problem with me."

Moses disagreed, but he wasn't going to point that out with his mama there.

She took care of it for him.

"I ain't no fool, Simon," Annie said. "The Klan got a problem with anyone that got black skin. Especially a black man that works for a white man they got a problem with. Your skin be real black. Them men workin' for you gonna protect you if the Klan comes?"

Simon opened his mouth to answer, but she didn't give him a chance to respond.

"Them men workin' there gonna take care of my June and them chillun?" Annie's voice grew harder with each word.

Simon's silence was his answer.

Moses ground his teeth. He wanted to tell Simon to leave Blackwell immediately and bring the family to Cromwell. Simon's next words dashed any hope of his brother-in-law accepting the offer.

"We're not going to leave. Perry and Louisa have been good to us. We work well together, and Blackwell Plantation has become our home. I'm not going to run because of the Klan." Simon took a deep breath. "If I do, I'll spend the rest of my life running."

June stepped onto the porch. Clearly, she had been listening to the conversation. "Simon is right, Mama. We work for Perry and Louisa, but they are our friends, and our children love each other. I might struggle with a lot of fears, but we're not going to give the Klan the power to make us leave. We hope that someday things will change."

Moses looked sharply at Perry.

"I told them they should leave," Perry said, his blue eyes sad beneath his thatch of blond hair. "I appreciate the fact they've decided to stay, but I worry about them every day. They moved into the house with us. We figure we're safest if we're all together."

Moses felt helpless to do anything. They didn't live close enough for him to send men to provide protection. They were on their own.

"Are you doing anything to protect yourselves?" Anthony asked. His green eyes were dark with concern.

Perry grimaced. "I have guns with me everywhere I go. I've taught Louisa how to shoot, and Simon taught June. And..." he paused.

"Go ahead and tell them," Simon said. "They may need to know it's there one day."

Moses tightened at the expression on his friend's face. It was obvious Simon was anticipating something bad.

"We've dug a big cellar under the house," Perry revealed. We built a door in the floor that's covered with a thick rug. It's not foolproof, but we can put the children down there if we're attacked." He paused. "Only the four of us know it's there. Until now."

Moses thought about the tunnel. Perry and Louisa didn't know the Cromwell secret. Simon and June did, but he knew they would never reveal it.

"Is the cellar large enough for all of you to hide there?" Anthony asked. "Four of you with guns might not stand much of a chance against a large group of the Klan, and leaving the children down there alone could be disastrous."

"Hide down there while they destroy my home?" Perry demanded.

"A destroyed home is better than a dead family," Moses said bluntly. He understood Perry's desire to protect their home, but the house would mean nothing if his family was killed, or if the children were left down there to fend for themselves. He suddenly understood why Simon had said they might need to know about the cellar someday.

Perry's defiance melted away like a candle before a flame.

Moses thought about the space Perry and Simon had already dug. Perhaps there was a way he could help after all. He locked eyes with Anthony.

"Perry, there's something we would like to show you." Anthony said. He started toward the front door. "Simon and June already know about it," he added.

Moses watched Simon's eyes widen. "Come inside with us, Simon." He turned to his sister. "Will you wait here for Louisa and the children?"

"Of course," June replied.

Annie smiled. "You doin' the right thing, Mr. Anthony."

Moses followed the other men into Anthony and Carrie's bedroom.

Perry looked around, obviously confused. "What are we doing here?"

Instead of answering, Anthony strode forward and pulled the hidden handle on the large mirror attached to the wall.

Perry gaped at the hidden entrance that appeared when the entire mirror opened away from the wall smoothly. He stepped closer. "Is that a...?"

"Tunnel?" Anthony finished. He lit four candles on the small table inside the doorway and handed them around. "Join me."

Perry, his eyes wide with astonishment, stepped into the tunnel and peered into the darkness. "Where does it go?"

"All the way to the James River," Anthony informed him. "It was built by Carrie's ancestors to provide protection from Indian attacks. It was unused for a long time, but it's been used quite a lot since the war began. Even after the war, it has provided protection from the KKK. The children and Annie have been kept safe here."

Moses understood the shock on Perry's face. He remembered every detail of the day, alerted by a statement he wasn't meant to hear, when he had found the door hidden by underbrush on the banks of the river, and then followed the tunnel to Carrie's room. Not even Carrie had known that a tunnel existed behind the mirror she had peered into for the first eighteen years of her life.

Moses had saved her moments before Union soldiers broke into her bedroom.

"You knew this was here?" Perry asked Simon.

"It's a Cromwell secret," Simon responded. "I would never reveal it to anyone. It did, however, give me the idea for the cellar room."

Perry continued to look around at the sturdy brick walls with amazement. "Why are you showing this to me?"

Moses stepped forward. "Because we would like to help you and Simon dig one at Blackwell."

Simon's mouth dropped open. "What?"

Perry opened his mouth, but no words came out.

"If our plantations were closer, I could have my men offer protection," Moses told them. "That's not possible, so we're going to do the next best thing. I think we know it's only a matter of time before the Klan comes to pay a visit. The two of you, and two women who have recently learned to shoot, might not be able to hold them off. Your hole under the floor is a beginning, but we can take that hole and create something that will truly protect you."

Perry looked skeptical. "We can't possibly build something like this. Where will we get bricks? How will we make it tall enough? The four of us can't pull this off."

"Not something equal to this," Moses agreed. "Have you ever talked to Matthew about how he escaped from Libby Prison during the war?"

The astonishment on Perry's face deepened. "Matthew escaped *Libby Prison?*"

Moses smiled. "Get him to tell you sometime. It's quite a story." His plan solidified in his mind. He was certain Matthew and Harold would be eager to help with the tunnel, but he brought his thoughts back to the present. "The point of the story is that he and a few other men were responsible for digging a fifty-five-foot-long tunnel beneath the prison grounds. Ultimately, more than a hundred men used that tunnel to escape. About half of them made it to freedom without being recaptured. Matthew was one of them."

"The tunnel was nothing fancy," Anthony added. "It was wide enough for the men to crawl through. That's what we'll dig at Blackwell. It can be improved over time, but we can quickly provide the protection you and your family need. It will afford you a way to escape the Klan."

Moses could tell Perry was considering the possibilities.

"About sixty feet from the house, there's a thicket of dense bushes. If the tunnel came out past the bushes, it would only take a few minutes to run to the river. No one in the house would see us." Perry spoke slowly as he envisioned what could be created.

"We could have a boat hidden at the river," Simon added. "One big enough to hold everyone. The odds are that the Klan will attack at night."

"I agree. Cowards prefer to do their dirty work at night," Moses growled.

"We'll have the cover of darkness to float down the river," Simon added. "If we're quiet, they won't even know we're not in the house until we're out of danger."

"What about the plantation?" Perry protested.

Moses understood Perry's concern. He would feel the same way. "What's more important? Your family or the plantation?"

"My family, of course," Perry snapped. "But I have to be able to provide for them. Not to mention they need a home. What if the Klan decides to burn down the house when they can't find us?"

Moses wouldn't insult him by denying that was a possibility. "Then you'll rebuild."

"Or we decide to go somewhere else," Simon said.

Moses clenched his jaw. He was aware each of them might someday be forced to make a different decision about where they would live and raise their families. He couldn't imagine leaving Cromwell Plantation, but he could see signs the Democrats were taking back control of the South. What would happen if the Klan was given free rein? He forced his thoughts away from that possibility.

"None of us have the answers," Anthony said. "We certainly don't have control. The one thing we can do is protect our families and deal with whatever happens." He paused. "Do you want us to help you build the tunnel, Perry?"

Louisa stepped through the door. "Yes."

Perry jerked around. "Honey…"

"I heard most of your conversation," Louisa said. Her voice was tight with emotion. "I lost my entire family to that blasted war. I will *not* lose my husband and child to protect the plantation." Her delicate features twisted with agony. "We've had tough times before, Perry. I can handle tough times. What I can't handle is living life without the people I love." She smiled at Simon. "That includes you, June, and your children. You are my family."

Louisa took time to look at the portion of the tunnel she could see. "It's extraordinary!"

"Honey…"

Louisa held up her hand to stop his words. "We are building that tunnel, Perry."

Perry chuckled and took her hand. "I've been trying to tell you that I agree with you."

Louisa managed a small smile. "Good. It's time to go home in order to get started." She walked toward the bedroom door and then swung back around. "When can you come to help us?"

"We'll be there tomorrow," Moses replied. "I'm hoping to have Matthew and Harold with us." Leaving the plantation to build a tunnel would complicate his schedule, but he couldn't live with himself if something were to happen to any of them—but especially to June. He had to do what he could to help.

"It will go faster if our men help," Simon observed. "We could pull them out of the fields for a couple hours."

"True," Moses agreed, "but the tunnel will only be safe if it's a secret. You know your men are hard workers, but do you trust them with your lives?"

Simon sighed heavily. "No. Louisa is right. It's time to go home. We have a tunnel to build."

Perry was stepping into his wagon when Hobbs emerged from the barn. He watched as Hobbs approached. "Who is that?"

"Warren Hobbs," Anthony answered. "He is a longtime friend of the family. He moved back to the South last month after a long stretch in the Pacific Northwest. He works in the stables with Carrie and Susan." Anthony saw no reason to mention Hobbs' previous involvement with the KKK.

Hobbs reached the wagon. "Hello, Anthony. Susan wanted me to tell you she and Harold won't be here for dinner tonight."

Anthony frowned. "Is she alright?" Susan had given birth two weeks earlier to a beautiful daughter, Susan Jessica Justin.

"You know how she is, Anthony. Amber told her to stay home for another couple weeks—that she, Clint, and I could take care of things—but Susan made Harold bring her over this morning."

"Is she alright?" Anthony repeated. Janie and Polly were handling things at the clinic while Carrie was gone. He knew Janie would come immediately if Susan needed her.

"She says she is, but she looks tired. Harold is going to take her home."

"And baby Jessica?"

"Cute as a button," Hobbs said with a wide smile. "She looks like a doll with that curly red hair."

Anthony grinned, determined to shake off the anxiety that had settled on him like a dark cloud after the revelations of the morning. "Exactly like her daddy and his twin brother."

"Yep," Hobbs agreed.

"Hobbs, I want you to meet Perry & Louisa Appleton. This is their son, Nathan. You already know Simon and his family."

"Pleasure to meet y'all," Hobbs said.

"You too," Perry replied. He nodded at Hobbs' wooden peg leg. "If you don't mind me asking, how did you lose your leg?"

"Same way about fifty thousand other men did during the war. I caught a bullet during one of the battles. The doctor who treated me when I first got wounded was able to save my foot and most of my leg, but it ended up shorter. I had to wear a platform shoe, but at least I had my leg. They even put me back fighting. I thought I was one of the lucky ones." His face twisted. "Until I got out to Oregon. Somehow, I got an infection where the initial wound had been. It got bad real quick. The doctor said he couldn't save it, so my leg came off above the knee."

Anthony was certain that if Carrie could have treated him, he would still have his leg, but few doctors had her level of passion for her patients.

"I'm sorry," Perry said. He reached down and pulled up his own pant leg. "I lost mine at Gettysburg."

Hobbs leaned down to peer at Perry's leg more closely. "What kind of a fake leg is that? I've never seen anything like it."

Moses leaned down, as well. "I've heard about these new legs, but I've never seen one. That looks to be an engineering marvel."

Perry grinned. "Getting this prosthetic changed my life. I used to have the same wooden peg you do, until I met James Hanger."

Hobbs kept examining the leg. "Who?"

"James Hanger," Perry repeated. "As far as anyone knows, he was the first soldier to have his leg amputated during the war. He had just joined the army when the Battle of Philippi happened in West Virginia. He was eighteen and never had the chance to formally enlist. His leg was mangled by a cannonball when he was in a barn trying to calm the horses. It was a Union doctor that saved his life by amputating his leg."

Hobbs stood up straight with a look of disbelief. "A Union doctor saved a Confederate soldier? Why?"

"He was a good man. Of course, Hanger was a prisoner of war for six months before being released in a prisoner exchange, but he came home alive. He went home with a wooden peg leg like the rest of us. The thing is, he was an engineering student at Washington

College, here in Virginia, before he left to join the army. He hated that peg leg. When he got home, he decided to create a better prosthesis. He wanted something better for himself, but he also knew there were going to be a lot of men who would need them after the war."

Hobbs leaned down again to examine the leg. "Are those hinges?"

"The leg is crafted from whittled barrel staves, rubber, and wood, with hinges at the ankle and knee," Perry confirmed. "The hinges make it work almost like a real leg. You can't tell I have a fake leg when I walk."

"Can you ride a horse like a regular person?" Hobbs asked keenly.

Anthony knew Hobbs felt very self-conscious about riding with his leg. He very seldom rode, and only when no one else was around.

"Pretty much," Perry assured him. "We both know nothing can truly replace a leg, but my life is much easier since I got this prosthetic."

"Where did you get it?"

"Hanger has a business in Richmond. The government has a program to pay for a new leg for veterans."

"The government pays for it?" Hobbs demanded.

Perry nodded. "It takes some time to jump through all their hoops, but mine didn't cost me a penny."

"Richmond?" Anthony was astonished. He'd never heard of the man, and Carrie had never mentioned him. He was certain the veterans she treated would want an opportunity for a better prosthetic.

Anthony could well imagine how much easier Hobbs' life would be if he could get rid of his wooden peg leg.

Just as he was about to offer to bring Hobbs to see Dr. Hanger in Richmond, he hesitated. Was it safe to take Hobbs into town? What if someone from the KKK recognized him? Any attempt would take careful planning and consideration. A quick look at Moses' face told him he was thinking the same thing.

"What time will y'all arrive tomorrow?" Perry asked.

Anthony was more than willing to change the subject. "We'll be there by ten o'clock." He briefly explained the need for a tunnel at Blackwell Plantation to Hobbs.

Hobbs scowled. "The KKK has got to be stopped!"

Anthony again considered telling Perry about Hobbs' earlier involvement with the Klan, but he decided not to reveal it. It was Hobbs' story to tell. They should get to know him before they passed judgment on his past mistakes.

Hobbs looked thoughtful. "I think Amber and Clint can do without me tomorrow. Would you like more help?"

"The more the merrier," Anthony responded. "You know how to keep a secret. The sooner we can get it dug, the better."

"Thank you!" Perry said fervently.

"We appreciate all the help we can get," Simon added.

"It will be my pleasure," Hobbs replied, his eyes shining with sincerity.

Anthony understood Hobbs was still trying to make amends for his involvement with the Klan.

"We'll see you tomorrow," Perry said. He lifted the reins and urged his horse forward.

Anthony and Moses stood with Hobbs as the wagon rolled down the drive.

"That leg is something," Hobbs muttered.

Anthony knew it wouldn't be fair to let fear of the KKK keep Hobbs from regaining as much mobility as possible. "We'll go find Hanger when Carrie and the rest come home."

"You reckon it's safe to go to Richmond?" Hobbs asked hesitantly.

"We'll be careful," Anthony assured him. "We'll arrive after dark and go to the clinic early in the morning. You'll be safe at Thomas' house."

"Anthony is right," Moses added. "it's been my experience that KKK vermin don't like early hours. They prefer to terrorize their victims late at night in order to hide their identity under their ridiculous hoods."

Hobbs looked down at his peg leg. "I'd sure like to find out if I qualify for that government program."

"We'll make it happen," Anthony promised.

Hobbs watched the dust plume in the distance. He waited until it disappeared around the final curve. "You figure we have time to get the tunnel dug before the Klan does something bad?"

Anthony wasn't certain of anything, but he forced himself to nod. The alternative wasn't something he was willing to contemplate.

Moses provided the words he couldn't find. "We'll get it done in time." His voice grew forceful. "We have to."

Chapter Five

The sun was still resting below the horizon when Moses moved the wagon forward. He was astonished how much food his mother had managed to put together in one day. There were baskets bulging with enough biscuits and fried chicken to keep an army working.

Hobbs held his hand to his stomach. "I[SK1]'ve only been here two weeks. I still can't believe y'all eat like this every day," he groaned. "I'm stuffed."

"Mama wanted to make sure you had enough breakfast to fuel you for the morning. You're going to need every bit of it," Moses warned him.

"Believe him," Matthew said. "It's much easier digging a tunnel when you have real food to eat. I was about half my size by the time I was thrown in Rat Dungeon at Libby Prison. The tunnel didn't have to be as big, but it was harder to dig it when I was close to starving."

"Anthony told me you and a bunch of prisoners escaped through a tunnel." Hobbs voice was thick with amazement.

"He was a hero," Harold said. "He helped save a lot of lives."

"It wasn't just me," Matthew protested. "A small group of other prisoners helped." His eyes darkened with the memory. "In the end, more than a hundred men escaped through that tunnel. Not everyone made it, but over half ended up free." He scowled. "The rest were recaptured." The reality of what must have happened to the men who were recaptured would always haunt him.

"Where did you go when you escaped?" Hobbs asked.

"Right here. Even though Robert was a Confederate soldier, he was my best friend. We were college roommates before the war. When I showed up at Thomas' house looking like a ghost, he didn't turn me in. He and Carrie hid me in a wagon, brought me out here, fattened me up for a few days, and put me in a boat to float down the river to freedom." He frowned. "There were close calls, but when we got to Fort Monroe, we knew we had made it."

"We?" Hobbs asked.

"Another one of the prisoners was about to be caught. He dove into the river to escape, and I floated by at the right time to pull him out. We finished the trip together."

"That war seems an awful long time ago," Hobbs said. "And there are times it feels like it never ended."

Moses knew exactly what Hobbs meant. He often wondered if the North winning the war meant anything. With what was going on in the country, it seemed like the South had actually won—or were at least convinced they had.

"What's going on down in Louisiana?" Hobbs asked. "I overheard Susan say something to you, Harold. I've been wanting to ask."

Moses saw both Anthony and Matthew stiffen. The five months that had passed since the Colfax Massacre had diminished their pain and memories, but he knew from Carrie that nightmares continued to haunt Anthony on a regular basis. He suspected the same was true for Matthew. Things you could forget during the light of day could too easily consume you in the dark.

"Louisiana is a blight upon our nation," Anthony said bitterly.

"No one is paying for what happened down there at Colfax?" Hobbs demanded. "I read your articles when I was in Oregon, Matthew. Are they actually going to get away with it like nothing happened?"

"Oh, there is an attempt being made to hold the men accountable for what happened down there." Matthew's lips twisted with disdain. "If Louisiana follows its pattern though, a trial won't happen until next year, and no one will be convicted. They'll be released to live their lives," he said angrily. "After murdering hundreds of men and destroying entire families."

"What about the Fourteenth and Fifteenth Amendments, and Grant's Enforcement Acts against the Klan?" Hobbs protested. "Those were supposed to change things."

"You can pass all the amendments and acts you want," Moses responded. "If there aren't people willing to enforce them, they don't mean a thing." He thought about the train porter he had met on the way to San Francisco. He had learned more about Angola Prison from Matthew since his return. "Louisiana has developed very powerful ways to control and terrorize the freed slaves. So far, no one has been able to stop them. It merely gets worse."

"Is he right?" Hobbs asked the others. His expression revealed his distress.

"I'm afraid he is," Matthew said. "I hope there's accountability for the Colfax Massacre, but I don't believe it will happen. When the story first came out in the newspapers, public opinion against Louisiana was strong, but by the time any possible trial rolls around, most people will have forgotten."

"What do we do?" Hobbs asked.

Moses understood the fear glittering in his eyes. Hobbs would not be treated well if he was recognized by someone who remembered his betrayal at the KKK convention six years earlier. Hobbs' question was one Moses dealt with almost daily. *What do we do?*

"We build tunnels," Moses said flatly.

Anthony attacked the wall of dirt in front of him with focused anger. Hobbs' questions earlier brought back the fear and anger he had spent the last months attempting to repress. Nightmares of the Colfax massacre plagued him, but his determined focus on Carrie, the children, the plantation, and River City Carriages, had helped him greatly. He was grateful for a full life.

He gritted his teeth and slammed his pickaxe with as much force as he could muster in the confined space. When the earth in front of him crumbled beneath the onslaught, he grabbed his shovel and pushed the dirt behind him.

The others would put it in buckets and send it down the line to the cellar that had already been dug. Louisa and June were carrying the buckets of dirt outside.

Simon was almost as big as Moses. With seven of them taking turns digging, they could make the tunnel tall enough for everyone but him to walk through easily. It would make their escape faster if they didn't have to crawl. It was tall enough for Simon to run hunched over. With more time, they could make it taller.

Sweat poured from Anthony's face and his breath became ragged as he worked. His efforts worked to peel away the layers of dirt and rock, but it was impossible to erase the faces of the massacred freedmen at Colfax. Lantern light flickered in the tunnel. It was enough to illuminate his work but not enough to free him from the regular nightmare that invaded his days. The cramped tunnel trapped him in his memories. He registered the laughter and cheerful talk of the others behind him, but nothing penetrated his desperation.

Anthony jolted when a large hand clamped on his shoulder.

"I'll take the pick for a while," Moses said, his deep voice reverberating in the confines of the tunnel.

Anthony shook his head. "I've got it," he muttered. He raised his arms to attack the dirt again.

Moses reached forward and grasped the pickaxe. "Stop," he ordered. "You need to get out of here for a while. Go up and help move the dirt out of the house."

Anthony gripped the handle tighter. "I'm fine," he snapped. All he could think about was smashing into more dirt and rock. He needed it to erase the images swarming his mind.

"It's not going to stop the memories," Moses said, keeping his voice low. "I know what Hobbs' questions did to you this morning. A time will come when the faces of those men won't make you stop breathing, but that time is not today. I wasn't even there, but I can't stop envisioning the massacre either. If Felicia hadn't chosen to go to San Francisco, I would be one of those bloated corpses. There's not a day that goes by that I don't think about how close I came to dying."

Anthony released his grip on the pickaxe. He hadn't realized until that moment how much Moses struggled with what had happened. He'd been too lost in his own memories. "I'm glad you weren't there," he said hoarsely.

"Me too," Moses said. He pried the axe from his friend's hands. "Go move dirt," he commanded.

Anthony was suddenly eager to be out of the tunnel where he could breathe fresh air. He squeezed past everyone and scrambled up the sturdy wooden ladder Perry and Simon had put in place in the cellar. Louisa and June were busy carrying buckets of dirt out into the bushes where it could be spread. It was imperative they did not leave evidence of what they were doing. Perry had directed the workers to the fields on the far side of the plantation for the day. There were no prying eyes to discover their actions.

Anthony left the house and took deep breaths. Gradually, his heart stopped racing, and his head quit pounding.

June appeared at his side. "You alright, Anthony?"

Anthony managed a smile. "I decided I would come help you and Louisa with the buckets of dirt for a while. That alright with you?"

June's answer was to hand him a full bucket of dirt.

Darkness had fallen before they tunneled out into the clearing behind a hedge of bushes sixty feet from the house. It wasn't far enough away to be truly safe, but if everyone remained silent, the odds were good they could creep through the woods to the river and escape on the boat hidden along the banks.

As they emerged sweaty and exhausted from the tunnel, they slapped each other on the back, hugged, and shook hands.

Little Ella, who had long ago succumbed to fatigue, was asleep in her bed.

Nathan and Junior., working side-by-side with the adults during the day, stared at the tunnel they had helped build.

"Are we really going to need this, Daddy?" Nathan asked. The darkness didn't conceal the fear in his voice.

Perry had not revealed what happened to him, but his son was intelligent enough to put the pieces together when his father had arrived home bruised and bleeding.

Perry laid an arm across his son's shoulders. He hated that his eight-year-old had to live in fear. "I hope not, Nathan. I hope we never have to see this tunnel again, but if we need it, we'll be grateful it's here."

Gateway To A New Beginning   92

"Because the men who beat you up are going to come after us?"

"Us too," Junior. said, standing close to his best friend. "You really believe the tunnel will save us if the Klan comes, Daddy?"

Simon walked to his son. "I do," he said firmly.

Perry hated the necessity of this conversation. He hated that he wasn't certain the tunnel would save them if they were attacked. It would give them a chance to get away, but moving through the woods at night would be risky. He tried to erase the vision of their home burning as they ran for their lives.

Perry looked at the tired faces surrounding them. "We couldn't have done this without your help. Thank you. I don't know how we can repay you."

"I reckon we can start by going back to the house and pulling out the baskets my mama sent," Moses replied. "I'm so hungry I'm about to start gnawing on the branches."

His words broke the tension.

Nathan and Junior. took off running for the house.

"Y'all better hurry if you want any food!" Nathan yelled over his shoulder.

Anthony snorted. "They have no idea how much food Annie packed in those baskets. There's not a chance we can eat it all."

Anthony regarded the crumbs scattered on the table with a look of astonishment. "I can't believe we ate everything."

Matthew chuckled. "Never underestimate the hunger of men and boys after digging sixty feet of tunnel in a day. It's amazing to me that we got it done." He stretched his arms high above his head. "My body is going to feel this for a few days."

"I would imagine digging is easier when you haven't been starving in a prison," Hobbs commented.

"I won't disagree with that," Matthew replied.

June sat back and rubbed her stomach. "And never underestimate the hunger of women who hauled thousands of buckets of dirt into the woods. Personally, I think we had the harder job."

"I agree with you," Anthony replied. "I was actually happy to get back into the tunnel and grab the pickaxe." Moses' words had helped him make it through the day. "At least those of us in the tunnel were taking turns. You and Louisa carried buckets all day long."

"I still can't believe y'all came to do this," Perry said. "We would have worked on this for weeks and not had it finished."

Moses knew how true that was. There was a lot that could be done to improve the tunnel, but it was a huge step in providing protection. He cared deeply about Perry, Louisa, and Nathan, but it was his fear for June and her family that drove him. Since he couldn't convince them to come to Cromwell, at least he had done what he could to improve their odds of survival if the worst happened.

"You're staying tonight, of course," Louisa said through a yawn.

"We are," Moses agreed. It would be pure folly to navigate the roads at night. The five of them would be sitting ducks for the Klan. "We'll leave at first light. We need to get back."

Anthony met his eyes evenly over the table.

Moses knew Anthony felt the same concern he'd been feeling. Now that the tunnel was done, his worry moved to his mama, John, Jed, Russell, and Miles. He wouldn't relax until he was back at home.

Hobbs stood next to the window. "Is there anyone keeping an eye on Blackwell tonight?"

Perry nodded. "There are five men stationed around the house and barns. There aren't enough to stop an attack, but they'll alert us to danger."

Moses thought about how easily tired men, exhausted from a full day in the fields, could be sneaked up on, but there was no sense in piling more worry on what he already felt. Every person in the house was exhausted and needed rest. He hoped his fatigue would allow him to sleep.

If the Klan attacked, at least the tunnel was waiting for them.

———⚜———

Moses sagged with relief when the wagon pulled away from the Blackwell house the next morning. Louisa and June wanted to fix them breakfast, but he had insisted they needed to return to Cromwell. No one would starve before they got home. Besides, he knew his mama would have a meal waiting for them.

"We're going to get wet." Hobbs pointed his finger at the thick clouds dipping lower as they moved east.

"Looks like it," Moses agreed. The air was thick with humidity but at least it wasn't hot at this time of day. They had slickers handy in case the skies opened. The road appeared empty, but he scanned the woods as they rode, watching for any movement or flashes of color. He hated the uneasiness he felt, but the air spoke of danger. Each of them had checked their guns before they set off, making sure they were loaded and easily accessible.

"Do you believe it will ever be different?"

Moses looked at Matthew, who sat on the bench seat next to him. "Do I believe blacks will ever stop watching for trouble?" He fought to swallow his anger. "At this point, it's hard to believe my children will ever have that luxury. It's going to be a long time before white Americans see blacks as anything but a problem and a threat to their perceived superiority." He hated how certain he was of his belief.

"Do you truly feel alright about Felicia living in Boston?" Matthew asked.

"She's far safer there than anywhere else I could have picked. You know as well as I do that bigotry exists everywhere. All we can do is increase our odds the best we can." Moses tensed at a movement in the woods, relaxing when a buck stepped out to graze. "If I could keep all my children on the plantation forever, I would. Since that isn't possible, I'm grateful Felicia didn't choose somewhere in the South or out in San Francisco."

"Trouble is coming!" Hobbs called sharply.

"From behind us!" Anthony snapped.

Moses twisted around to see a group of horsemen galloping toward them. There was no evident reason to expect they meant trouble, but Moses was certain they did.

"Pull to the side," Harold ordered. He had risen and stepped up to the wagon seat. "When they see they haven't caught us by surprise, they may think twice about causing trouble."

Moses stopped the wagon, reached for his gun, and swung around on the seat to face backwards. He was grateful he was the sole black man. The Klan would think a little harder about attacking a wagon full of white men.

Anthony pulled off his hat. "Hobbs, put this on," he urged. "No one needs to see your red hair."

Moses quickly realized what the real danger was. If Hobbs was identified, it was going to turn bad quickly. He untied the bandana from around his neck. "Use this to cover your face," he said quickly, his mind racing. "Lie down and cover yourself with that blanket. If anyone asks, we'll tell them you're sick."

Hobbs obeyed; his eyes wide with anxiety.

Moses forced himself to breathe evenly as the horsemen drew closer.

The group of six men pulled their horses to a stop when they reached the wagon. Their eyes blazed from lined, stern faces. The first rider, a portly man who appeared to be in his fifties, swept the wagon with his penetrating gaze, noting no doubt that Moses and the others were armed but had not drawn their weapons.

After several long moments, the man spoke. "Where you boys headed?"

Anthony answered authoritatively. "I don't see that our destination is any of your business. Who is asking?"

"Theodore Poulton," the man snapped, his face red with anger. "I reckon me and my men have a right to know where you're going."

"And where you came from!" A tall, thin man with a tattered blue hat pulled down over his limp hair added the question. His dark eyes glittered with barely contained meanness.

Anthony remained calm. "What exactly gives you that right? Far as I know, Virginia roads are open to the public."

Theodore scowled and looked away from Anthony, his eyes boring into Moses. "You're an awful big nigger," he spat.

Moses eyed him silently.

"You the nigger who owns part of Cromwell Plantation?" Poulton asked.

"Would it matter?" Moses responded, allowing his voice to take on a hard edge. He wouldn't start anything, but he wouldn't be intimidated.

Matthew stood. "There is no reason for you men to have any business with us. We'd appreciate it if you move along." He pulled his pistol from his waistband smoothly, his voice tight with anger.

Moses chose to keep his own gun hidden as his friends pulled their weapons. He could grab it easily if needed, but the sight of an armed black man could make things worse.

"Y'all been over at the Blackwell Plantation?" Poulton demanded.

No one answered. The only sound was the incongruent birdsong lifting from the trees. The beauty clashed with the fraught tension filling the air.

Moses fought the impulse to kill the man on the spot.

Anthony rose to stand beside Matthew. "I believe you've been asked to move along. I don't know about my friends, but my patience is wearing thin." His voice was commanding and stern.

At that moment, a man at the back of the group moved his horse forward.

Moses instantly knew this was the true leader of the group. His body language was relaxed, but animosity radiated from him. He held himself with an air of authority.

"We're sorry you're feeling inconvenienced, gentlemen." The man's eyes bored holes into them as he slowly appraised their group. He smiled casually. "We've had a bit of trouble here recently. We're doing our part to keep the roads safe."

"What kind of trouble?" Anthony asked.

The man assessed Anthony thoroughly before he answered. "Oh, some people who don't seem to know how things work in this part of Virginia," he said pleasantly.

Moses gritted his teeth, certain this was the group who had beaten Perry.

Anthony's return smile was as fake as the leader's. "I'm certain you've done your best to clear up any misunderstandings."

"We have," the man agreed. "We'd hate to have to clear up any more *misunderstandings*." His meaning was unmistakable.

"We'd hate that too," Anthony responded, "especially since the consequences would be grave for you gentlemen." He pulled out his second pistol. "We're done being polite. We might catch a few bullets in a fight, but I can promise not a single one of you will walk away from this encounter. We don't want trouble, but we're not afraid of it." He raised his pistol and pointed it toward the leader.

Their adversaries had lost the element of surprise. Before they could even draw, they would be shot. Moses's stomach roiled at the thought of more senseless violence. He felt sick that these men might take out their rage on Blackwell Plantation. Bullies didn't like to be bettered at their game; they would discover a way to vent their rage.

The leader spat into the dirt, cursed, and reined his horse away. "Let's go, men," he called. "I don't believe our friends are going to cause any trouble today."

They remained silent as they watched the group ride out of sight.

Moses again fought the urge to return to Blackwell and force Simon and June to come home with him. He knew they would refuse.

"Pleasant gentlemen," Matthew said sardonically.

"Can we please go home?" Hobbs asked as he sat up and shed the blanket.

Moses was sure Hobbs had been the most frightened. If those men—most certainly Klan members—had recognized Hobbs, they wouldn't have hesitated to shoot him on sight, regardless of whatever consequences came with killing a traitor.

"That sounds like an excellent plan," Anthony responded. "Of course, I think it best if I empty my bladder before we continue." He leapt from the wagon and stepped to the side of the road.

They chuckled as Anthony broke the tension.

The skies chose that moment to open. What started as a light rain quickly became a pounding downpour. Moses pulled on his slicker and tossed one to Anthony.

"Let it rain," Harold called loudly enough to be heard over the deluge. "The vermin will be less likely to come out."

Moments later, they again rolled at a rapid pace down the road. None of them would breathe easily until they were back at Cromwell.

Chapter Six

Annie listened closely as Moses told her about the new tunnel. Driving onto the plantation and finding the house standing, with no evidence of trouble, had released the tight bands of worry around his chest. He stretched out his long legs and leaned back in the rocker, devouring the ham biscuits she had greeted them with. He talked in between bites. The food they had eaten the night before had long worn off.

"You reckon that tunnel gonna keep them safe?" Annie asked sharply.

Moses thought of the cruel, hard eyes of the men who had accosted them that morning. He wanted to alleviate his mama's concerns, but she would see right through an attempted lie. "I think it will give them their best chance of escape."

Annie twisted her lips and eyed him. "There gonna be trouble out there, ain't there?"

"Probably," Moses conceded.

"What you ain't telling me, Moses?" Annie wagged her finger at him. "You oughta know by now that I gonna get the truth out of you."

"We had a little trouble this morning," Moses admitted. He told her a shortened version of the encounter with the men who had come after them.

Annie's face tightened as she quickly connected the dots. "You reckon it be them men who beat up Mr. Perry?"

Moses sucked in a surprised breath. "You know about that?"

Annie snorted. "You think my June girl ain't gonna tell me something important like that?" She smirked. "Oh, she didn't want to, but I could tell she be hidin' somethin' from me. I made her tell me."

Moses chose the truth. "We did all we could to keep them safe, Mama. They won't be able to fight off an attack but they've got a good chance of escaping through the tunnel and reaching the river. They'll be able to float down to Cromwell, and Simon knows where the hidden door is on the riverbank."

"How come you didn't talk my June Girl and that Simon into leaving Blackwell with my grandbabies?" Annie demanded. "You be her brother."

Moses managed a chuckle. "You're her mama. How'd you do when you tried that?"

Annie sighed heavily. "I ain't raised nothin' but hardheaded chillun."

Moses' smile was genuine this time. "That's because we have a hardheaded mama."

Annie smiled, but the stark pain in her eyes did not diminish.

Miles walked up onto the porch in time to hear the last part of the conversation. He laid a leathery hand on his wife's shoulder. "They may be hardheaded, but June and Simon be real smart, Annie. They know trouble could be comin'. They gonna keep an eye out."

Moses nodded. "Everyone is sleeping downstairs, close to the room with the tunnel entrance."

"That tunnel door opens in the floor?" Annie asked.

"It does," Moses said. He knew what she would say next.

"How they gonna cover up that door once they get inside the tunnel?"

"They won't be able to, Mama," Moses admitted. If the marauders came inside, they would realize where the family had gone. It wasn't like the Cromwell tunnel, where closing the door completely concealed its existence. "They'll get through the tunnel as fast as they can. Once they're out, it won't be easy to follow them." He decided not to mention that it would be impossible to conceal the sound of seven people running through the woods. They would at least have a head start.

"All they have to do is reach the boat," Anthony added. "Once they're on the river, no one will be able to follow them."

Moses' earlier feeling of peace completely evaporated as he was reminded of the probable scenarios. They had given their family and friends on Blackwell Plantation the best opportunity for escape, but it remained fraught with danger.

"Daddy!"

Jed dashed from the barn and ran up the porch steps.

Unaware of any impending doom, Jed's face was wreathed in a brilliant smile. He skidded to a stop and reached for a ham biscuit. "Do you want to come riding, Daddy? We got the horses saddled. We figured you would want to go ride the fields now that you're home.

I'm pretty sure the tobacco grew more when you were gone!"

There was nothing Moses wanted more than to be out in the tobacco fields with the boys, but he didn't want to leave his mama with her worry.

"You go on," Annie said, reading his mind as easily as she had since he was a boy. "I got work to do on dinner. That blackberry cobbler ain't gonna make itself."

Alice appeared at the door in time to catch Annie's words. "It ain't gonna make itself, but that doesn't mean Gloria and I didn't go right ahead and make it."

"You done made the cobbler?"

"Three of them," Alice replied.

Moses watched the conversation with a smile. Alice continued to make remarkable progress. When she wasn't exercising her leg, she could be found in the kitchen. She and Annie had become close friends, bonding over cooking and stories of slavery.

A little girl, a tiny replica of her mama but for the light eyes and caramel skin that revealed her white father, appeared at Alice's side. "I helped too!" she announced.

Annie grinned down at her. "You did?"

Eight-year-old Gloria bobbed her head, causing curls to dance around her face. "I helped the boys pick the blackberries this morning. That was before I helped mama put the cobblers together. I reckon they gonna be the best blackberry cobblers anyone ever ate!"

Gloria still woke up crying from nightmares caused by her rape in the alley, but the security of the plantation was the refuge she needed to heal.

Annie took the girl's hand. "I reckon we best go find out if that be true."

Moses was relieved to see the trouble fade from Annie's eyes.

Alice and Gloria had become family. There had been no talk of when they might return to Richmond. No one wanted them to leave. Hope would be heartbroken if her best friend in the world returned to Richmond.

Even though his mama would never admit it, cooking for everyone on the plantation had become too much for her. Moses planned on talking to Alice soon about hiring her to help in the kitchen. She and Gloria lived in a room at the guest house. Different plans could be made for the future, but there was no hurry. They felt safe in the guest house and they loved being so close to everyone.

"Let's go, Daddy," Jed said. "I know you've only been gone for a day, but I swear the tobacco is even taller than when you left!"

Moses smiled. John loved the plantation, but he didn't have Jed's passion for farming. Moses was certain who would take over his work when he was gone. His smile faded as Jed clambered down the steps. Would any of them be on the plantation when that day came? What price would they have to pay to remain in the home they loved?

John and Russell led the horses from the barn, their faces full of excitement.

Moses pushed aside his thoughts, determined to focus on the boys. He couldn't predict the future. The past years had taught him he had nothing beyond today. A day riding with the boys was guaranteed to be a good day.

He reached the barn and mounted his towering bay gelding, Champ.

John was already astride Cafi, his chestnut gelding.

Russell sat tall on Bridger, the gelding's black coat glistening in the sun. His white blaze was even more beautiful in the light.

Jed ran to Tucker and mounted his buckskin gelding. "Let's ride!" he called.

Moses laughed as the foursome took off at a trot. The boys were confident, skilled riders. The condition of their horses attested to their commitment to giving them excellent care. He and Miles had trained them well.

It was sometimes difficult to comprehend how vastly different his sons' lives were than his had been at their age. He'd done nothing but work in the fields, often feeling the lash if he wasn't fast enough. Because he was big and tall, little consideration had been given to his age. He was expected to do the work of a man from the time he was John's age.

John looked back at him and pointed at the leather bag tied to his saddle. "Grandma made us food!"

Moses had eaten half a dozen ham biscuits on the porch, but he could always eat more. Pushing aside the remnants of his heavy thoughts, he grinned and released Champ into a canter.

The boys whooped and surged ahead to join him. The four rode abreast down the wide, raised road between the tobacco fields. They scared up a flock of bobwhites that scattered before them, while hordes of butterflies danced across the tops of the tobacco.

Moses felt a surge of pride. Jed was right; the tobacco was taller than when he had left the morning before. The sun and rain had done their magic. With fair weather and a stable economy, they should have their best harvest yet. Abby's prediction of financial hardship ahead for the country had lodged in his mind, but he wasn't truly concerned. Trouble might come, but he didn't believe it would come soon.

Tall, green tobacco plants stretched toward the sun as far as he could see. Pink and white blossoms swayed in the breeze, making the fields look like a huge, lush flower garden. Once the tobacco was cut, they would pull it into the drying barns to hang in huge sheaves. It usually took four to six weeks to dry it out enough to transport it to Richmond.

Moses eyed the crop carefully and reached a decision. It would be two weeks earlier than he had anticipated, but they would harvest next week. The tobacco was ready.

"Daddy?"

Jed had ridden up close beside him. Moses brought Champ down to a walk. "Yes, son?"

"I heard Uncle Thomas talking about the tobacco tax before he left for New York. Is it going to create a problem for the plantation?" Jed's voice and eyes were serious.

Moses considered how to answer the question. "What did you hear about it?" He needed time to formulate a reply.

Jed's expression was thoughtful. "Uncle Thomas said the government is trying to make back the money they spent on the war by taxing our tobacco. He thought it would ease up after a few years, but that hasn't happened." Jed frowned. "He said they are closing a lot of the factories in Richmond because there isn't as much tobacco coming in. What will we do if we don't have a place to take our crop?"

"That won't happen," Moses assured him. "It's true there are many small farmers who can't keep growing tobacco because the high taxes make it impossible for them to make money, but that isn't true for us."

Jed didn't look convinced. "Uncle Thomas said if things don't change, there won't be a tobacco farmer in the area that will be able to make it."

Moses regretted that Jed had overhead Thomas' conversation. The boy was too young to separate fear from caution. He'd had too much fear in his short life. "How exactly did you hear this, Jed?"

Jed looked back at him earnestly. "I wasn't trying to hear it," he said. "Felicia asked me to get a book for her out of the library before she left for Boston. I was about to walk in when I heard Uncle Thomas and Aunt Abby talking about tobacco." He looked slightly ashamed. "I know I shouldn't have listened, but it was about *tobacco,* Daddy."

Moses chuckled. "I understand." He hoped questioning Jed about *how* he got the information would make him hesitant to continue the conversation, but Jed's words dashed that hope.

"So, are we in trouble?"

Moses realized John and Russell were listening to their conversation closely.

"Small farmers are in trouble," he admitted. "A lot of tobacco farms are going under. It makes no sense for them to grow a crop they can't make money from. That's the reason factories are closing. There isn't enough tobacco coming in to keep them operating. Our harvest is different, because it's large enough to make it profitable." He decided not to mention that even though they were soon going to have their best harvest, the tobacco tax would take a larger amount of their profit than normal. Though they would have a bigger harvest, he didn't know that the profit margin would be larger. The best he could hope for was that the increased profit would cover the tax.

"Won't we make less money?" Jed observed shrewdly.

Moses couldn't decide whether to laugh or cry. Jed's whole focus was on the tobacco. Rose had said their son excelled at math, and he could well imagine the boy poring over numbers in the library. Truth be told, Jed might have a better understanding of the income issue than he did. Moses preferred to focus on farming and let Thomas handle the business aspects. He knew he and Rose had a bounteous amount of money in the bank. Jed's questions, though, made him realize he needed to pay more attention.

"I tell you what, Jed." Moses respected his son's business acumen and his desire to be closely involved with every aspect of farming. "When we harvest the crop and start sending it to Richmond, you can work with

Thomas and me on the books. You'll be able to see exactly how the finances work."

Jed nodded seriously. "That would be good, Daddy."

"Now that y'all have that worked out, can we please go have fun?" John asked.

Moses signaled Champ into a canter, and then released him into a ground-eating gallop. He was done talking. He wanted to ride through the vast fields, enjoying the results of everyone's hard labor.

An hour later, they lounged on the beach after washing off the dust and sweat from their ride. The horses had plunged into the water to cool off and drink. Satisfied, they were grazing contentedly in the field. The James River, placid when they arrived, was starting to churn with whitecaps, an early warning of a storm that approached from the west. Dark cumulus clouds had begun to thicken, creating a stark contrast with the clear blue sky overhead.

Moses was keeping an eye on the storm, but they had plenty of time before they needed to head home. "Are you going to open that saddlebag, John?"

John shrugged nonchalantly. "I'm not that hungry, Daddy. Perhaps we should wait until we get home for dinner."

"John is right," Jed piped in, his eyes wide with innocence. "We don't want to spoil our dinner, Daddy."

Moses choked back a laugh. "That's probably wise." He reached quickly between the boys and snatched the saddlebag. "Russell and I will help you by eating it all ourselves. I'll tell your grandma how wise you were."

"Hey!" John yelled. He leapt up and grabbed for the saddlebag.

His son was growing like a weed, but Moses easily held it above his head out of reach.

Within moments, the four of them were wrestling on the shore, laughing loudly. The boys didn't have a chance of overcoming Moses, but it wasn't for lack of trying.

Moses gained new awareness of how strong John had become. His ten-year-old son was quickly gaining the strength of a man.

Finally, more interested in eating than in playing, Moses shook the boys off easily and held the saddlebag high in the air. "I'm assuming y'all have decided you're going to eat?"

"Give me that fried chicken," John yelled. Leaping high, he could almost reach the food Moses held out of reach.

"Please," Moses reminded him.

John rolled his eyes. "Give me that fried chicken, *please*."

Moses grinned and settled down on a log. "Let's see what we have here." Dinner would be waiting when they got home, but he'd never known the boys to not be hungry. He pulled out mounds of fried chicken wrapped in cloth, biscuits slathered with sweet butter, and a mountain of oatmeal cookies. "Now we're talking!"

Silence fell as the four of them consumed the feast. When they finished, they slipped down from the log to sit on the bank. They gazed out over the river, watching as fish jumped and swallows dipped down to snatch bugs from the surface of the water. No one spoke.

Moses felt the peace of the river relax him, pushing other thoughts out of his mind.

"This is kind of great," John said. "I've never been down to the river when it was just us guys. I love the girls," he said hastily, "but this is kind of great, too."

"Yeah," Jed agreed. "We ride the fields together, but we never come down to swim and eat without everyone else."

"Maybe next time my dad can come too," Russell said. "The girls are going to be gone for a while. Maybe we could do it again."

Moses was startled to realize how correct they were. They rode the fields together and loved it, but they had never taken the time to simply have fun. "I promise we'll come back and play soon, boys." He would talk Anthony into joining them the next day. Their wives and the girls would be gone for several weeks, but it wouldn't be that long before fall cooled the river. He wanted to take advantage of the time they had by creating memories for the boys.

"I'm glad we couldn't go to Boston," John said thoughtfully. "At first I felt left out because I wasn't a girl, but the plantation is better than a city any day!"

Moses couldn't have agreed more. He stuffed the cloths back into the bag and stood. "I don't know about y'all, but I sure could use my share of that blackberry cobbler waiting at home."

"Yes!" Russell yelled. "I'm still hungry."

"And there are no girls around to tell us we *shouldn't* still be hungry," Jed stated. "You know what else I realized? Most of the Bregdan Women are gone on the trip. That means the plantation is being run by Bregdan *Men* now!"

"That's right," John agreed. "Our first official job as Bregdan Men is to tell Alice and Annie that we need blackberry cobbler every day!"

Jed shook his head firmly. "That can be your job, John. I'm not going to be the one to tell Grandma that! We'll probably end up without any cobbler at all."

John looked thoughtful. "You could be right. I'll think of something else for our first official job."

Moses watched the boys as they caught and tacked their horses. *Bregdan Men.* They had a point. He was determined to make the most of the time they would have together.

As he swung onto Champ, he had a vivid image of the men who had confronted them on the road. Gritting his teeth, he pushed the image aside. He hated feeling out of control. He couldn't stop what might happen at Blackwell, but he could be here for the boys.

Chapter Seven
September 17, 1873

"You seem restless." Abby settled down on the porch swing next to Carrie.

Carrie had been pretending to read a book, but she had no idea what was on the page in front of her. "New York City feels different." The city was different every time she visited, but this time it seemed more extreme.

"It's a city on the move," Abby agreed.

"It's more than that," Carrie murmured. Wally and Nancy's home was many blocks from the frenetic pace of downtown, but the time they had spent in the chaos during the last twenty-four hours had seeped into her soul. She set her book aside and reached for a newspaper she had read earlier. "Are you familiar with Mark Twain?"

Abby nodded. "Vaguely. He was a correspondent for a San Francisco newspaper when he came to New York City six years ago. If I remember correctly, he wasn't fond of our town."

"He's actually quite famous now. He's in high demand as a writer and speaker. I found this in the library. It was written by Mark Twain in 1867." She lifted the newspaper and began to read. *"I have at last, after several months' experience, made up my mind that New York is a splendid desert – a domed and steepled solitude, where the stranger is lonely in the midst of a million of his race. Every man seems to feel that he has got the duties of two lifetimes to accomplish in one, and so he rushes, rushes, rushes, and never has time to be companionable – never has any time at his disposal to fool away on matters which do not involve dollars and duty and business."*

"Money fever," Abby replied. "He described the city quite astutely." The sounds of industry floated up to them. "New York has always been a place where money exchanged hands. It is the nation's business capital."

Carrie lifted the book she had been pretending to read. "This is *The Gilded Age: A Tale of Today*. Twain wrote it, along with Charles Dudley Warner. I haven't read much of it, but it seems fascinating."

Nancy joined them on the porch, her lovely eyes shining below her carefully coiffed blond hair. "I've read it. It's basically a satire of the greed and political corruption since the war ended. Because of that book, this period of time in the country has been dubbed *The Gilded Age*."

"Where did the name come from?" Abby asked.

"They got the name from Shakespeare's *King John*," Nancy answered. *"To gild refined gold, to paint the lily...is wasteful and ridiculous excess."* She smiled. "Gilding gold, which would be to put gold on top of gold, is excessive and wasteful. It's a rather apt description."

"I agree," Carrie replied. "That describes New York City perfectly. It feels like the entire city worships wealth." She frowned. "With the exception of millions of immigrants who are being used to create wealth for a few.," she added sarcastically.

Wally and Thomas joined them on the porch at that moment.

Carrie could hear Rose and the children laughing and talking in the parlor. She yearned to be inside with them, but it would be rude to walk away in the middle of a conversation.

Wally had obviously heard what she'd been saying. "It's the way business works, Carrie."

"That doesn't make it right," Carrie protested. She looked at her father. "You and Moses don't use the plantation workers. You pay them well, and they earn a percentage of the profits."

Wally spoke before her father could respond. "That would never work in New York. There is too much at stake."

Carrie watched the play of emotions on Abby's face.

"For whom?" Abby asked. "Millions of immigrants came here looking for a new life. Instead, they live in poverty while they make others rich."

Wally flushed. "They're finding jobs."

Carrie started to add that the jobs seemed to provide little more than slave wages. Wages that could not provide any quality of life in the exploding city. She remained silent, caught by the almost desperate look in Wally's eyes.

"New York City is the repository of the banking reserves of the country," Wally continued, not giving anyone a chance to respond. "New national banks provide the capital for America's railroad infrastructure, telegraph networks, and mining projects."

Carrie thought about the diamond hoax that had stolen much of Wally's money a year earlier. She saw her father and Abby exchange a concerned look. She turned to Nancy in time to see a deeply troubled expression spring to life in her eyes.

"The value of real estate and personal property has doubled in the last ten years," Wally gushed, almost as if he were convincing himself more than them. "New York's value is over one billion dollars. The value of goods produced in the city has doubled to about three hundred thirty-three million."

Carrie felt a bit frightened by the feverish shine in his eyes. She decided to change the subject. "I understand my father and Felicia are going with you to the Stock Exchange."

"They are. The Stock Exchange is a fascinating place. It's trading more than three billion dollars in securities each year. The growth has been incredible. We've got quite a bit invested in the stock market," Wally confided. "In the next few months, we will have recovered everything we lost to the diamond hoax."

Carrie noticed Abby watching Nancy closely. Nancy's body was rigid, her hands tightly clasped in her lap. Her eyes were fixed on the porch floor. This was unusual behavior for the usually warm, outgoing woman. She could feel the fear emanating from their hostess.

Abby met Carrie's eyes. Carrie couldn't read everything there, but it was impossible to miss the deep concern. What was going on?

Loud laughter floating out to them enforced her decision to go inside. "Excuse me," she stated. "I'm going in for girl time." That was exactly why she was here. No one could fault her for leaving a conversation she had grown increasingly uncomfortable with to be with the children.

"Mama!"

Carrie laughed when Bridget hollered for her. "Coming!" she called through the window. She was happy to leave the tension behind as she slipped through the front door of the sprawling, blue clapboard house.

Bridget clapped her hands happily when Carrie appeared in the dining room. "Mama!"

Carrie scooped her daughter up into her arms. She would miss Bridget greatly when they left for Boston. She wanted to make the most of their time together here. She rubbed her nose on Bridget's velvety cheek until her daughter giggled with delight and looked around the room. "What's everyone doing?"

"Making plans for tomorrow," Rose announced.

Frances looked up from a map she was examining. "I want to go back to Central Park. I'm sure it's changed since we were last here."

Minnie nodded. "We're going to ride the *El* to get there. Can you believe the train is on tracks that are *three stories* above the street? We'll be able to see over the entire city from that high!" Her eyes shone with excitement and anticipation.

Carrie chose not to point out that the *El* made life miserable for the unfortunate residents whose windows were close enough to the tracks for riders to peer into their parlors and bedrooms day and night. In places where the streets were narrow, the railway was built right over the sidewalks, close up against the walls of houses. She could easily imagine the unending noise for their occupants. For the first time, she was eager to leave New York City. The whole experience had her on edge. She wished they could leave for Boston but she was determined not to spoil the fun for the girls.

Hope jumped up and whirled around in a circle. "I can't wait to go on the *El* with my big sister!"

Felicia's voice was gentle when she answered. "I won't be with you tomorrow, Hope, remember? I'm going to the Stock Exchange with Thomas and Mr. Stratford."

Hope looked downcast for a moment, and then tossed her head. "Too bad for you, Felicia. The *El* sounds much more fun than the old Stock Market."

Carrie and Rose chuckled at the same time.

Minnie changed the topic. "Russell is going to be sorry he didn't come. He hung on every word Moses told him about the cable car in San Francisco. I bet the new bridge they're building here in the city is bigger and better than anything in California!"

Thomas walked through the door in time to hear what she said. "The New York and Brooklyn Bridge," he said. "The bridge is going to connect Manhattan and Brooklyn. Instead of everyone having to use a ferry to cross the East River, they'll be able to use the bridge. The New York State Senate passed a bill six years ago that allows for the construction of the bridge. It's taken quite a bit of preparation and planning, but work has begun."

Carrie thought for a moment. "The East River is quite wide. How long will this bridge be?"

Thomas shook his head. "I'm afraid I'm not an engineer. I don't know."

"I do," Minnie announced. "It's right here in the newspaper. The bridge is going to be almost six thousand feet long, and it will be eighty-five feet wide." She cleared her throat and continued. "To make sure ships can go underneath it, it's going to be two hundred and seventy-two feet tall, with a clearance of one hundred and twenty-seven feet above the water." She stopped reading and looked at Thomas. "Is that really big?"

"That is over a mile long, Minnie. It will be the longest bridge in the country when it's completed."

Minnie nodded, but then hesitated. "How long is a mile, Grandpa?"

"That's a good question," Thomas responded. "A mile is the distance from our house to the end of the driveway out on the road."

"That's really long!" Minnie exclaimed. She continued to read. "The bridge will have roadways and elevated rail tracks." She looked up. "Like the El we're riding tomorrow?" When Carrie nodded, she found her place in the article again. "There is even going to be a raised promenade that will serve as a leisurely pathway." She stopped reading again. "What is a promenade?"

"It's a walkway," Carrie told her. "This one is going to be raised above the road and the tracks for the *El*. People will be able to walk there without worrying about traffic."

"They are going to make it beautiful," Thomas added. "They'll add plants, oil lanterns, and benches to sit on. It will be a wonderful addition to the city."

"Minnie is right that Russell would be fascinated by the bridge," Frances said. "Mama, do you believe Russell will be an engineer?"

"He'd be a great one," Carrie replied. "On the other hand, he may decide he wants to do something completely different." Having to watch Frances go off to medical school was hard enough. She wasn't ready to think of what Russell would do in the future. She was grateful there were many years before she had to consider it.

Minnie showed them the newspaper so they could see the elaborate drawing. "Is a bridge like this hard to build? How long will it take?"

Wally was passing through the parlor when she asked her questions. He paused. "Thomas and I are headed to my study in order to not interrupt girl time, but I can answer that question. Do I have permission?"

Minnie pretended to consider before she nodded. "You have permission," she announced.

Laughter rolled through the room.

Wally sank down into an empty wingback chair. "Many men have died building the bridge."

The laughter stopped abruptly.

"Really?" Minnie demanded. "Why?"

"There has been trouble from the very beginning. Talk of this bridge started in 1800 but no one could figure out how to do it until John Augustus Roebling proposed a suspension bridge. He had designed and built other ones. Six years ago, he erected a bridge over the Ohio River between Cincinnati, Ohio and Covington, Kentucky." He frowned. "He was given the job to build our bridge, but he never got to see it started. Four years ago, while they were conducting final surveys, Roebling was pinned against a piling by a ferry. His foot was so badly crushed, they had to amputate his toes."

Carrie winced. An injury like that was incredibly painful and prone to infection. She was about to ask how Roebling was doing, but Wally answered the question before she could ask it.

"Unfortunately, he developed an infection that killed him a month later."

Somber silence fell on the room.

"Who took over building the bridge?" Frances asked.

"His son, Washington Roebling, was hired to fill his father's role. Another interesting twist to this story is that Boss Tweed became involved in the bridge's construction. It was Tweed's political machine, Tammany Hall, that approved Roebling's plans and designated him as chief engineer. It's been discovered that Tweed required a sixty-thousand-dollar bribe to give his approval, and then he demanded that he and two others from Tammany receive over half the private stock of the bridge company." Wally's lips twisted. "Even though Brooklyn and Manhattan put up most of the money, they essentially have no control over the project."

"Even with all that has happened?" Carrie asked.

"Boss Tweed escaped conviction eight months ago when

the jury couldn't deliver a verdict, but he's scheduled for a retrial soon. Surely, he will be held accountable."

Wally shrugged. "We hope so, but a large part of the New York legal system appears to be in his pocket. I suppose time will tell. I have heard, regardless of how the November trial goes, that the State of New York intends to file a civil lawsuit against Tweed. They're going to try to recover six million dollars in embezzled funds."

"What about the people you said have died working on the bridge?" Minnie demanded. "That seems far more important than the Boss Tweed man."

Carrie knew Minnie wasn't old enough to understand the ramifications of a justice system that could be bought by a powerful man, but she would be growing up in a country that reflected those decisions for many decades. As she matured, they would talk more about Boss Tweed.

Wally gave his attention back to Minnie. "Building the bridge is very dangerous." He hesitated. "The details are rather daunting."

"I'm quite intelligent, Mr. Stratford," Minnie said calmly. "I think I'm capable of understanding."

Carrie choked back a laugh. Evidently, she had succeeded in raising confident daughters.

Wally chuckled. "You're right, my dear. I'm not doubting your intelligence as much as I'm doubting my ability to explain the situation."

"I want to know why so many men have died," Minnie replied. "It's important."

Carrie understood her daughter's intensity. Minnie was serious about improving fire safety when she grew up because of the loss she had experienced. Men dying in the building of the bridge would be equally important to her.

"I'll do the best I can." Wally pointed to the newspaper illustration. "This bridge can only be built once the foundation is in place. They started by creating a caisson for the Brooklyn side. They started there because the water isn't as deep as the Manhattan side."

"A caisson?" Frances asked.

Wally nodded. "A caisson is used for underwater construction. It is a huge prefabricated hollow box almost as big as this house."

Hope gasped and looked around with wide eyes. "A box as big as this house? That's really *big*!"

Wally smiled. "You're right. It's really big. They built it in Brooklyn and floated it over to where the bridge foundation is going. It was easy to sink, but then they ran into trouble, because the river has a lot of sediment and rocks. It took many men to dig down deep enough to set it in place. They pumped compressed air into the caisson so that workers could be inside to dig the sediment."

"Was the air so that they could breathe?" Minnie asked.

"Partly," Wally answered. "I spoke with one of the young men who worked inside the chamber. There were six of them working in eighty-degree temperatures. Within five minutes they were sweating profusely, even though they were standing in icy water. The compressed air pressure had to be extremely high in order to keep the water from rising. He said they had blinding headaches every time they went down."

Thomas grimaced. "That must have been challenging."

"I agree," Wally said. "It's certainly not a job I have any interest in. Once the caissons reached the right depth, they were filled with vertical brick piers and concrete. It took a long time for them to reach the right depth because of the boulders, but they finally accomplished it."

Felicia frowned. "What a horrible job."

Carrie shook her head. "That sounds terrible. There must have been many men who suffered from decompression sickness when they came back up."

"Decompression sickness?" Frances asked. "What's that?"

"Something you never want to experience," Carrie answered. She thought about how to explain it simply. "When men breathe inside the caisson while in deep water, the air pressure is higher than on land. The deeper they go, the higher the pressure has to be. Pressurized gasses dissolve in the blood. When the men come back up to the surface too quickly, the gasses can expand rapidly in the blood. When that happens, it forms bubbles. Those bubbles lodge themselves in joints and the nervous system." She paused, thinking about what she had learned. Decompression sickness had only been understood for a couple of decades. "The men in the caisson have to come up slowly to allow the pressure to equalize and redissolve the gas in their blood. Too many people don't understand that—especially employers who want things to happen quickly. If the workers come up too fast, however, they will experience excruciating pain in their joints. People can become paralyzed. Some die."

Minnie was listening intently. "Is that how so many men have died?"

Wally frowned. "Yes. Your mother's explanation helps me understand why." He looked around the room. "Hundreds of men have indeed suffered from decompression sickness. Some have died. Others, like Washington Roebling, became paralyzed."

Minnie looked startled. "The son who took over for his father?"

"The same," Wally answered. "He was paralyzed from decompression sickness shortly after the first caisson was lowered into the river. He can no longer supervise the construction in person, so he designs everything from his apartment. He directs the completion of the bridge by using a telescope from his bedroom."

Abby looked impressed. "That is quite a feat."

Nancy, who had been uncharacteristically quiet, came to life. "You have no idea of the real story. You girls are going to love this," she said with a smile. "Washington Roebling is not the only engineer in his family. His wife, Emily Roebling, is an engineer, as well. She doesn't have a degree, but her education is as vast as her husband's. Not many people are aware of it..." She paused for dramatic effect. "What I'm about to tell you isn't well known. One of Emily's closest friends happens to be a Bregdan Woman here in New York. She's told me that Emily has pretty much taken over the project. She and Washington confer closely, but she has developed an extensive knowledge of building design and materials. She relays information to the assistant engineers, handles day-to-day supervision, and oversees project management."

Wally regarded his wife with astonishment. "Is that true? I had no idea!"

Nancy nodded. "Emily is afraid if people know, they will fire Washington. It is his knowledge and passion driving things forward, but nothing would happen without Emily."

"I'm not surprised," Felicia stated. "Women are capable of doing anything. One day,

men will realize that."

Carrie exchanged a proud look with Rose. Their daughters had grown into extraordinary young women whose generation would have a profound impact on women's rights.

"I'm going to change safety in America," Minnie said. "Especially for workers. It's wrong that workers are put into situations where they can get hurt." Her eyes blazed. "Those men shouldn't have been hurt building the bridge. Ignorance is no excuse for them getting decompression sickness!"

"I know you're going to change things," Frances responded, putting an arm around her sister's shoulders. "We both are."

Carrie watched the exchange, once more feeling gratitude that her daughters were together on

this trip. It was different from what she and Rose had envisioned, but it was better.

Wally stood up and beckoned Thomas. "It's time for us to disappear, my friend. Let's go into my office and leave the girls alone."

"There are drinks and snacks waiting for you, my dear," Nancy said. "I'll knock on the door when you and Thomas have permission to come out." Her tone was light, but her eyes remained a pool of trouble.

Bridget toddled over and lifted her pudgy arms, her eyes heavy with sleep. Carrie swept her up into an embrace. "I'm going to put this little one to bed. I'll be back down soon."

"That's what I'm here for," Abby protested. "I'll be happy to take Bridget up."

"I know," Carrie replied. "I want time with my little girl, though. It won't take her long to settle. This is one exhausted child." A quick glance revealed her green eyes were already shuttered by her thick black lashes.

Carrie knew Abby watched her speculatively as she exited the dining room, but she wasn't ready to talk about the uneasiness she felt. There was no real reason for it that she could identify, but that didn't change the reality of how intense the feeling had become in the last hour.

Chapter Eight
September 18, 1873

Thomas smiled at Felicia as their carriage rolled toward Wall Street. The usually self-contained young woman bounced with excitement on the seat. He knew how much going to the Stock Exchange meant to her. The two of them had spent hours in his office at the plantation studying stock prices. He and Abby weren't invested in anything, but it hadn't diminished his own desire to understand the market.

Felicia's head swiveled as she took in everything around her. New York was changing everywhere, but nowhere as much as in the financial district.

"How tall is that building?" Felicia asked as they rolled down Broadway. She tilted her back back to look.

"The Equitable Building is the tallest in the city," Wally answered. "They used to cap buildings at five or six stories, but they are getting taller. The Equitable is ten stories tall. It's the first office building to have a passenger elevator." His eyes brightened. "I understand taller ones are in the works."

Felicia looked suitably impressed.

Thomas knew her business mind was rapidly calculating cost and profitability.

The carriage made its way down the busy road slowly. The sidewalks were as crowded as the roadway. He couldn't help but notice how women's clothing had become increasingly complex, colorful, and restrictive, while the men's attire could only be called industrious sobriety. He didn't imagine any of them were comfortable. New York women made quite an impressive spectacle, but he imagined the Cromwell women chafed at having to dress opulently while they were in the city.

He leaned closer to Felicia. "What do you think of the clothing?"

Felicia grimaced. "I think I'm going to be happy every time I come home to breeches." She shook her head. "I know to be successful I'm required to dress fashionably, but I don't have to like it."

Thomas smiled. "Every time I see how women dress, I'm more grateful to be a man. I can't imagine how long it takes a society lady to get ready in the morning." Abby traveled with city clothing, but she set limits on what she was willing to do. She had become increasingly used to the comfort of breeches on the plantation. She loathed having to dress up now. Since she was beautiful, no matter what she wore, he didn't care.

Felicia scowled. "It's such a waste of time. I believe the day is coming when women won't have to wear such voluminous and constricting clothes. I much prefer to breathe." She grinned. "And swim!"

Thomas chuckled. "I'm quite sure you and Frances will help lead the way to freedom in clothing."

"It's hard for me, but it will be worse for Frances. She's accustomed to the freedom we have on the plantation. I had to dress up during my years at Oberlin." Felicia scanned the sidewalk. "It really is ridiculous how women have allowed societal expectations to dictate their lives and choices. Look at the ruffles, ribbons, lace, and braids. It's as if the more you have on your clothing, the more sophisticated and wealthier you appear."

"What would you wear if you had no constraints?" Thomas asked, curious what her answer would be.

Felicia pursed her lips thoughtfully. "Breeches will always be my first choice, but I don't mind dresses when I'm in public. Corsets, however, should be thrown into the river or burned." Her dark eyes blazed. "I have refused to wear one since the time it was expected for me to. Mama never told me I should, but it was required at Oberlin. My teachers finally accepted my decision. Women are finally coming to their senses and revolting."

Thomas freely admitted this was a subject he knew little about. "What do you mean revolting?"

"I've been reading about it," Felicia replied. "There is a dress reform movement that's been going on for the last fifteen years or so. They oppose corsets and advocate against their use, particularly the high-fashion trend of tightlacing to achieve ever-smaller waistlines." She scowled. "Most women have been convinced that a corset's ability to maintain an upright, shapely figure is necessary for a moral and well-ordered society." Her scowl deepened. "Besides the fact that they're terribly uncomfortable, I happen to believe corsets are physically detrimental. They are the result of a male conspiracy to make women subservient by cultivating slave psychology in them."

Thomas raised his brow. "That's a strong opinion."

Felicia didn't back down. "I believe it's true. The clothing reformers feel that a change in fashion could alter the position of women. It would allow for more social mobility, independence from men and marriage, and the ability to work for wages. Not to mention, we would have better physical movement and comfort."

Wally had been listening closely. "You feel quite strongly about this."

"I do," Felicia said. "It's not merely dress reformers who agree with me. Doctors have begun criticizing corsets, as well. Your daughter happens to be one of them."

"That doesn't surprise me." What surprised Thomas was how ignorant he was on the subject. "Will you enlighten me please?"

Felicia grinned. "My pleasure. Corsets have long presented a variety of health risks, but they are especially connected to the difficult births experienced by many women. Far too many babies have been lost and pregnancies ended because of the corset."

Thomas noticed Wally's discomfort. His friend was not used to the frank medical talk that was commonplace on the plantation.

Felicia wasn't finished. "Whites claim to be the superior race, but corsets damage a woman's uterus and ovaries, as well as damaging the babies that are born. White women are thought to be weaker and more prone to birth complications. I don't believe they're inherently weaker, but they are impacted by corsets. Compare them to the black race that whites believe are primitive and inferior. Most of us don't wear corsets. Our births are easier, and our babies are healthier. Not to mention the fact that we're far more comfortable." She shook her head. "It makes you wonder who the primitive ones are!"

Thomas didn't question Felicia's outspoken passion, but he was aware of the position she planned to take in society. "Will you wear a corset in the future?"

"Absolutely not," Felicia stated firmly. "I consider myself far too intelligent to be sucked into societal expectations. I intend to make enough money that no one will dare question what I choose to wear—or not wear."

Thomas was quite sure she would do exactly that. He'd already seen America change for women; he could hardly imagine how much it might change in the future. The day was coming when women would have the right to vote, and that right would increase their power to make changes.

Felicia's expression brightened when the carriage turned onto Fifth Avenue. "It's the Fifth Avenue Hotel!"

From Wally's expression, Thomas knew his friend would welcome a change of topic. "What can you tell us about it, Wally?"

Wally shot his friend a grateful look. "The Fifth Avenue Hotel is New York's grandest and most glamorous hotel. Have you been inside, Felicia?"

"No." Felicia admired the plain, Italianate design. "A few of the hotels in San Francisco were fancier on the outside, but I understand this one is incredibly luxurious inside."

Wally nodded. "The interior is quite opulent. I've not seen anything that compares to it. It has the first passenger elevator ever installed in an American hotel, and every room has a private bathroom."

Felicia's eyes widened.

Wally wasn't finished. "It is the gathering place for Wall Street brokers in the evening. They come for the fine dining and the chance to discuss the happenings of the day on the Stock Exchange."

Thomas could tell Wally longed to be part of that coveted group. He thought again about the conversation they'd had the night before. Wally had lost quite a bit of money the year before from his investment in what was discovered to be a diamond hoax. Desperate to recoup his losses and regain his financial stature, Wally had invested heavily in the stock market. He was quite optimistic about the returns he would soon experience. Thomas hoped Wally was right, but he couldn't ignore Abby's certainty that the country would soon experience a financial crisis. He had attempted to broach the subject of an upcoming crisis with Wally, but his friend had refused to discuss it. If it was indeed coming, Thomas hoped it wouldn't happen until after Wally had cashed in on his investments.

Abby waved goodbye to Carrie, Rose, and the girls as they rolled away in a carriage. When they were out of sight, she sat next to Nancy on the porch swing. When Nancy had announced she would stay home today, Abby was happy to join her. The allure of the city had already worn off, and there would be time with the girls that evening to hear about their adventures.

"It's a beautiful day," Nancy observed.

Abby couldn't bring herself to agree. She appreciated the clear blue sky—what she could see of it—but a thick haze lay over the city, spewed forth by the smokestacks of industry. Clanging bells and train whistles created endless noise. She fought the longing she felt for the plantation.

Perhaps she could talk Thomas into going home early. She had always loved New York, and she loved Nancy dearly, but her heart wanted the beauty of the plantation in early fall. The longer she lived on the plantation, the less she wanted to leave it.

Abby pushed aside her thoughts. "Are you going to tell me what is bothering you, Nancy?" Silence met her question. She knew her friend wouldn't talk until she was ready. She leaned back, content to wait.

As the morning had worn on, more and more carriages and wagons rolled down the road. The clattering on the cobblestones, once a pleasant sound, grated on Abby's nerves. While she waited, she envisioned the horses cavorting in the pastures, the children playing under the trees, and the never-ending symphony of birdsong.

"I'm worried about Wally," Nancy confessed.

"Why?" Abby asked gently. She knew the simple words concealed a well of bubbling emotions.

Another long silence ensued.

"He's changed," Nancy said quietly. "Wally has been a very successful businessman for decades. He did quite well in real estate and was cautious and reasonable." She paused. "Michael once told me he learned more about business from his father than he did from any college course." She stopped again, her expression growing increasingly troubled.

When nothing more seemed to be forthcoming, Abby decided to probe a little. "How has he changed?" She believed she knew the answer already. She'd seen the feverish shine in Wally's eyes and heard the hint of desperation in his voice.

Nancy finally looked at her. "He won't tell me exactly how much he has invested, but I sense it's quite a bit. Wally is convinced the stock market is the way to wealth."

Abby was grateful Thomas would never think of hiding something like that. "Why? Wally has made a lot of money in real estate. From what I can tell, real estate values are continuing to rise."

"They are," Nancy agreed, "but not fast enough for my husband. He's given the real estate company to Michael and put his entire focus on the stock market. He is at the Stock Exchange most days, and spends his evenings devouring stock reports. He is fixated on gaining vast wealth. He wants to be like Jay Gould, Jim Fisk, and Daniel Drew."

Abby absorbed this information. She had read about the three men extensively. She considered them rogue financiers determined to make a fortune by controlling prices without any concern for the economic stability of the country. Many people worshipped them as captains of industry, others despised them as criminals. She personally had no respect for them. They were a huge part of the problem pushing America to the brink.

"Why are you worried?" Abby asked. She knew Nancy was justified in her worry, yet now was a time to support and listen.

"Wally is obsessed with emulating these men to create wealth. I loved the life we had before, but it's not good enough for him anymore. I'm afraid we're going to lose everything, Abby. Since he won't tell me how much he's invested, I suspect it's everything." Nancy's voice faltered and her eyes shone with fear. "You've been telling me something bad is going to happen with the economy. I'm not the financial genius you are, but I've been watching the signs. What if you're right?"

Abby remained silent, unsure how to respond. She didn't want to feed Nancy's fear, but neither could she refute it. If she were in the same position, she would be terrified.

"The Vienna Stock Exchange crashed in May of this year," Nancy said. "Since Wally won't tell me anything, I've become determined to learn things on my own. Vienna's economy was unable to sustain the bubble of false expansion, insolvencies, and dishonest manipulations. I've read that their trouble could be replicated here."

Nancy's awareness of the European troubles impressed her. Until now, Nancy had been content to let Wally handle their business matters, insisting she had more important things to think about.

"That's merely part of it," Nancy continued. "Inflation is high. There have been far too many speculative investments, especially in railroads. The demonetization of silver in Germany and the United States has created an additional problem."

Abby's admiration grew. "What kind of problem?" She wanted to know how much Nancy had learned.

Nancy's answer was prompt. "The Coinage Act that passed this year changed the country's silver policy and depressed its price, but the real issue is that many investors believe it shows instability in our monetary policy. Investors are shying away from long-term obligations." She paused to collect her thoughts. "There have been other things that have cracked the foundation of the economy. Property losses in the Chicago and Boston fires, consequences from the Franco-Prussian war." She looked out over the city. "There is tremendous strain on our bank reserves. I don't know how long it can continue."

Abby thought carefully before answering. There had been other times she had questioned Nancy's blind adherence to Wally's wishes and decisions. Those conversations had not gone well. "You have a solid understanding," she said. "What does Wally think?"

Nancy stalked to the edge of the porch. "He refuses to acknowledge any of it," she said angrily. "He tells me I'm being paranoid and should let him continue to handle our finances."

Abby realized Nancy's fear had brought her to the end of her rope. She understood the anger, because she knew she would feel the exact same way.

"He is blindly following the brokers he has become friends with. He refuses to believe there could be trouble." Nancy's rigid back and shoulders revealed the depth of her distress.

Most of the country felt the same way, precisely as they had every other time the economy had crashed.

The allure of riches could blind even the most reasonable of men. Once again, Abby felt a surge of appreciation for Thomas. He respected her enough to heed her warnings about the economy, and they had made wise choices in the previous two years, preparing for a time when things wouldn't be going as well.

Nancy returned to her seat on the swing. "How much do you know about Jay Gould?"

Abby tensed. "Why are you asking?" She strived to keep her voice even but failed.

Nancy eyed her sharply. "How about answering my question?" As soon as the words shot from her mouth, she grimaced.. "I'm sorry. I shouldn't be taking my fear out on you."

Abby reached for both her hands. "How deeply is Wally involved with Jay Gould?"

"Too deeply, Abby. Wally hangs on his every word and does whatever he suggests."

Abby took a deep breath. She wanted to allay Nancy's fears, but lying would do nothing to help her. "Jay Gould is quite unscrupulous. You mentioned James Fisk and Daniel Drew, as well. The first I heard of Jay Gould was when he collaborated with those two men to gain control of the Erie Railroad five years ago."

Nancy thought for a moment. "I thought that stock was owned primarily by Cornelius Vanderbilt?" She laughed at Abby's look of surprise. "I've done a lot of reading since we lost money in the diamond hoax."

Abby smiled before turning serious. "Wally's friend, Gould, joined with the other two men to issue fraudulent stock that diluted Vanderbilt's shares and gave them control of the entire Erie Railroad. They made a fortune. To protect themselves from criminal charges, they put Boss Tweed on the board of directors."

"That man is everywhere!"

"Unfortunately," Abby agreed. "Their next scheme, three years ago, caused far more damage to the country."

"The Gold Ring?" Nancy asked. "I've heard of it but don't know much about it."

"Yes, the Gold Ring. That's what they started calling it when it was discovered. Gould and Fisk's plan was to buy as much gold as they could in order to inflate its price, hoard it, and eventually sell it for a huge profit. Their problem was that President Grant, as part of his effort to reduce the huge national debt from the war, planned to put U.S. gold on the market."

"Which would have lowered its value," Nancy observed.

Abby chuckled. "I feel like I'm talking to a new woman. Who are you? We've never had these types of discussions before."

Nancy shook her head regretfully. "I was content to live in ignorance. I can't afford to do that anymore. It's important that I stay informed on current events. What happened with their gold scheme?"

"Part of their plan involved bribing Daniel Butterfield."

Nancy raised a brow. "Grant's assistant secretary of the Treasury?"

Abby nodded. "They bribed him to tip them off when the gold was about to go on the market. That way, they could sell first and reap big profits. They used their influence to talk Grant's brother-in-law into pressuring the president to stay out of the gold market. That connection produced conversations with the president himself, in which they fed him false financial information that influenced his actions with the gold."

Nancy's eyes widened. "That was a bold move."

"It worked for a while," Abby replied. "Grant delayed putting the gold on the market. He

thought he was doing the best thing for America. While he delayed, Gould and Fisk gobbled up gold through September of 1870. The price rose higher than it had ever been. The time came, however, when Wall Street speculators began to suspect someone was manipulating the market. The problem was that they didn't know who.

Grant was furious when he discovered the scheme. He ordered the sale of government gold on September twenty-fourth. The consequences of the entire scheme were terrible. The price of gold plummeted and the stock market tanked. Gould and Fisk got out in time, exactly as they had planned, but other investors went broke. The newspapers called it Black Friday." She swallowed her anger. "The country went through months of economic turmoil but thankfully, a national depression was averted."

Abby had thought the crash would happen then, but the country had somehow skirted disaster. With everything else that had happened since, she didn't think they would be as lucky the next time, whenever that may be.

Nancy's eyes narrowed with disgust. "What happened to Gould and Fisk?"

"What you would expect in a city run by corruption. Persuasive lawyers, combined with corrupt Tammany Hall judges, helped them escape prison. There were no consequences. They never even went to trial." She thought about Matthew's stories of the atrocities in the South that would never receive justice. Injustice seemed to be rampant throughout the country. "Gould rebounded. He makes a fortune off Western Union and the elevated railways."

"And Fisk?"

"He had a rougher end," Abby replied, feeling a sense of satisfaction. "It was evidently quite the dramatic scene. I'm surprised you don't know about this."

"Don't be," Nancy replied. "If it didn't happen in the last several months, I would be clueless. I was quite content with keeping house and doing my charity work. Reading newspapers seemed a waste of time."

Abby knew that was true. "Did you never hear of Jubilee Jim?"

"Jubilee Jim?" Nancy looked bewildered.

Abby smiled. "That's what the city called James Fisk. Jubilee Jim loved to broadcast his wealth. He strutted around Manhattan in elaborate clothing with perfumed hair, a waxed mustache, and fingers adorned with diamonds. He was quite the celebrity in the New York social scene. He was married, but he had a showgirl mistress that his best friend and business partner, Ned Stokes, was trying to take from him."

"Quite the love triangle," Nancy replied.

"Quite," Abby agreed. "Anyway, last year things reached a head. Stokes and the showgirl mistress tried to blackmail Fisk. Fisk was livid and planned to charge both of them in criminal court. When Stokes found out, he went to the Grand Central Hotel and murdered him."

Nancy gasped. "What? How?"

"He shot him with a Colt revolver," Abby answered. "Fisk lived long enough to identify Stokes as his assassin. It took three trials, but Stokes was ultimately found guilty and sentenced last fall. He is serving time in Sing Sing Prison."

"Because of money," Nancy said bitterly. "People are crazed for it, but I don't see it make people happy." She waved her hand toward the bustling city. "It seems to do nothing but make people crazy."

"I couldn't agree more," Abby replied. She knew emotions were roiling in her friend. Hearing of Fisk's demise had obviously intensified Nancy's angst.

Nancy stared out over the city for several minutes before she whirled around. "Abby, we could lose everything." Her voice was high with desperation. "What will happen then?"

Abby didn't have an answer.

Thomas was astonished by his first sight of the New York Stock Exchange. The cavernous hall was illuminated by light pouring in through towering arched windows. The space below was left mostly empty, allowing for throngs of men who hollered and waved their arms in wild gestures. The presiding officer was elevated above the traders on a stage. Stocks were sold from a list printed on a huge blackboard. The noise was deafening.

Felicia's expression mirrored his. "I've never seen anything like this!" she yelled.

Thomas could barely hear her over the cacophony of the traders below. He thought he had arrived with a basic understanding of the Exchange, but he was completely mystified. As the presiding officer pointed at a stock, the hall would erupt with a babel of unearthly yells. Wally had explained that meant the crowd was bidding.

"What are they saying?" Felicia was intent on the floor below.

Thomas shook his head, not bothering to try to speak above the ruckus. He had no idea how

to answer anyway. He was as confused as she was. When the officer pointed at a stock, the bids came fast and furious. The air was full of hands, arms, hats, and canes all waving frantically as traders sought to get the officer's attention. The shouts and cries were louder than anything Thomas had ever heard.

As the morning wore on, the action became even more intense. The men below were stamping, yelling, and shaking their fists violently. He wondered at times if someone would be trampled to death.

Felicia's expression had morphed from astonishment to something closer to horrified fascination.

Thomas understood. He knew a few of the men below. In their private lives, he knew them to have quiet repose and dignity. He could hardly believe he was watching the same people. They were more like maniacs than sensible beings. Was this truly how American commerce was managed? No wonder the nation was caught in a cycle of economic crises.

He thought about what he and Abby had learned during their late nights in the parlor throughout the long winter. There was little to no federal oversight regulating big banks or Wall Street. The scene below was evidence that the policy was a complete debacle. He wondered how long it would take before unsuspecting investors caught up in money-fever realized the bull market was rigged against them.

Mania for stock gambling had swept the country, pulling vast masses of people into its web. The telegraph stayed busy twenty-four hours a day, with stock orders pouring in from the entire country to New York brokers. Evidently, anyone who could raise funds wanted to try their hand at the stock market. People from every walk of life came to the Stock Exchange to tempt fortune. A few won. Unfortunately, most of them lost.

Looking at the wild throng, Thomas realized he was watching a lesson in human nature. America had become a country crazy for wealth. He recognized that greed controlled people all across the world – igniting conflicts and war in every nation – but there was something about what he was watching that was especially unsettling.

Somewhere along the way, America had become a country where money was everything.

Thomas thought about the millions of immigrants pouring into the country, searching desperately for a different life. They were being swept into the vast corporate machinery running America. As far as

Thomas was concerned, they were being used as mere pawns to achieve vast wealth for the select few who owned and ran the corporations. The people who had money were desperate for more, while the masses who had nothing were desperate to get at least a little of the wealth they saw flaunted on the streets. It was a recipe for disaster and hardship for the country.

Thomas suddenly noticed a lull in the activity. The crazed shouting fell to a deafening silence

as everyone looked toward the front of the room. Wally leaned against the balcony, learning far enough over the ledge that Thomas feared he might topple over.

The presiding officer stepped up to the podium and banged his gavel. "The firm of Jay Cooke and Company has suspended!"

Wally's face went slack. His usually robust color faded into shocked whiteness.

Felicia leaned into Thomas. "What does that mean?" She didn't have to yell.

"They've filed for bankruptcy," Thomas muttered with disbelief. The announcement was grim. The Jay Cooke and Company Bank had financed most of the Union side of the war and was considered untouchable by financial trouble. However, they had invested heavily in the railroads since the end of the conflict. Abby had told Thomas it was very possible that the bank would become overextended in building the Northern Pacific Railway. Obviously, her prediction had come true.

Thomas thought of Hobbs and the others who had been laid off weeks earlier in Oregon. The country had refused to acknowledge the trouble those layoffs had foretold.

It could no longer be denied.

The question that remained was how massively the bankruptcy would impact the country. Was it a sole occurrence, or the beginning of a tidal wave that would encompass American finance?

Thomas' heart quickened when he looked at Wally. He didn't know how the bankruptcy would impact the country, but he was certain his friend was terrified about how it would impact him.

Wally's face was pale and sweaty. His eyes were wide with fright and full of an uncertainty Thomas had never before seen in the confident businessman. Not even the news of his losses in the Diamond Hoax had created such a severe reaction.

Chapter Nine

Thomas watched the scene below, wondering what was happening on the streets of the city. Any bank going under would be grim news, but the fact that it was Jay Cooke and Company transformed grim into truly disastrous. Though traders remained on the floor, the crowd had substantially diminished. Thomas felt certain a run on the banks was happening at that very moment.

Felicia leaned close enough to speak into his ear. "Is this what Abby has been predicting? Is the country's economy crashing?"

Thomas suspected it was, but the economy had rebounded two years ago after the gold debacle that resulted in Black Friday. Perhaps it could come back from this as well. "We're going to have to wait and see."

Felicia looked toward Wally. "Mr. Stratford looks terrified."

Thomas didn't bother to refute the obvious. Wally's entire concentration remained on the floor below. Wally was listening as if his life depended on it.

More trouble began at one o'clock.

Though Thomas continued to struggle to decipher exactly what was going on below, he could tell by people's expressions that stocks were weakening. Wally maintained his rigid concentration, but when the board showed Western Union had declined by ten percent since opening, his shoulders slumped.

Thomas could feel despair emanating from his friend in waves. He wanted to go to him, but Wally was a proud man. He could only wonder how much his pride had cost him.

The calling out on the floor continued.

He saw Felicia watching Wally with concern. On the one hand, he hated that Felicia was experiencing the stock market on what was quickly becoming a very black day. On the other hand, he was glad she was getting an invaluable lesson about the unstable reality of the market

and the economy.

As Felicia raised her eyes to his, the official tapped the podium lightly with his gavel, before smashing it down with a massive force that spoke of building frustration.

Thomas whirled around to watch the action closely.

"ROBINSON AND SYNDHAM, THIRTEEN BROAD STREET, HAVE SUSPENDED!"

Chaos ensued below. Shouts, wild gestures, and jostling transformed the knot of men into a caricature of confusion.

Thomas was watching the collapse of the American economy, but he was too fascinated to look away. Another smash of the gavel pulled his attention back to the front.

"RICHARD SCHELL IS UNABLE TO MEET HIS ENGAGEMENTS!"

The chaos grew louder and more extreme than what had previously surrounded them. Even the ladies in the gallery, most of them there for a day of entertainment, waved their handkerchiefs and yelled. From the expressions on their faces, it was clear they didn't comprehend they were witnessing the demise of people's hopes and dreams.

Into the midst of the bedlam came the gong rolling out a warning that the market would soon close for the day.

Thomas had experienced enough. He took Felicia's arm and edged over to Wally. "Let's go back to the house."

Wally released his death grip on the railing slowly. His cheeks were pale and hollow. His eyes burned as if they had been staring into the fiery abyss. There was no comparison to the confident man who strode into the market earlier, eager to watch his stocks rise in order to secure his future.

Once again, Thomas wondered how badly the Stratfords would be affected by what had happened. More importantly, he wondered how the economy would fare, and how deeply the trouble would impact the entire nation. He was certain that what they had seen was merely the tip of what was certain to be a very large iceberg.

New York City replicated the bedlam of the Stock Exchange when they emerged onto the street. Knots of men littered the road. Conversations rose in the air like a cloud of angry mosquitoes. Men leaned against buildings, their faces full of terror. Others looked confused. There were angry expressions, as well as faces filled with dismay.

Their driver eyed them closely when they arrived at the carriage. Wally's regular driver had the day off, so their service had sent over a replacement. The man's thick, corded neck bulged above broad shoulders. His whiskered cheeks were topped by hooded eyes. He nodded cordially, waited for them to step into the carriage, and lifted his reins to urge the horses forward.

Thomas was sure the driver had heard enough talk, gossip, and wild speculation to know the day on the Stock Exchange hadn't gone well, but he suspected the man would not have much compassion. While thousands had fallen under the spell of the stock market, the number was merely a tiny percentage of New Yorkers. The rest struggled to simply survive each day. They probably rejoiced when the wealthy few who used them and looked down on them had to suffer. He couldn't blame them.

When Abby walked outside early the next morning, clouds covering the city promised rain, their menacing darkness contributing to the pall over the city. She could feel the distress permeating the air. Or perhaps she had simply carried some of the stress pulsing inside the house with her.

Thomas sat on the swing, a cup of steaming coffee in his hand. He motioned toward a tray that held another cup. "Have you seen Nancy this morning?"

Abby shook her head and reached gratefully for the cup of coffee. "I heard voices upstairs but neither of them has come down."

Thomas looked up toward the bedroom in the far wing of the house. "I'm worried about Wally."

"So am I. I'm worried about both of them." She had not had a chance to talk with Thomas in depth since he arrived home yesterday from the Stock Exchange. One look had told her the day had been disastrous. At almost the same moment they'd returned, Carrie and the rest descended upon the house with stories of their fun and adventures in Central Park.

She had seen Wally and Nancy go upstairs. They hadn't come down for the rest of the evening. Thomas had filled her in briefly before exhaustion claimed him. Abby had lain awake most of the night.

"What do you think is happening at the Exchange?" Thomas asked.

Abby watched a carriage rattle along the cobblestone road toward them. She walked to the edge of the porch as it drew to a stop in front of the house. "We're about to find out."

There had been barely enough time to send a message to a friend in the city last night, but she was thrilled he had come on such short notice. Abby hurried down the sidewalk as a tall, elegantly dressed man stepped down onto the road. Thick gray hair covered by a top hat served to make him look even more distinguished.

"Hello, Jonathan!" She clasped the hand he held out to her and beckoned toward Thomas. "I'd like you to meet my husband, Thomas Cromwell. Thomas, this is

Jonathan MacMillan. You haven't met in person, but you should remember the name. Jonathan's information that he sent me on the Gold Ring two years ago is the reason we stepped back from investments."

"Of course I remember," Thomas replied. "I'm glad to have the chance to thank you."

The men shook hands warmly.

Abby climbed the porch steps and pointed toward the three chairs that sat waiting for them. She hoped they would have time for a lengthy conversation before the others awakened. "Thank you for coming **so** early, Jonathan."

When the men were seated, Abby answered the question in Thomas' eyes. "Jonathan and I are friends from Philadelphia, though he has been in New York for many years. He was invaluable to me in learning the mysteries of finance. When Charles, my first husband, died, he helped me navigate very difficult times. I will be eternally grateful."

Thomas smiled. "Thank you for being there for her. I assume you're not here for a social visit, however?"

Abby chuckled. "My husband is direct, Jonathan."

"A trait I admire, and one that will be needed in the days ahead," Jonathan responded.

Abby's chuckle died away as a feeling of dread clogged her throat. "It's as bad as I suspect?" She glanced at Thomas. "I sent a message to Jonathan yesterday after you returned from the Stock Exchange. He has been deeply involved for many years. I hope he will be able to give us current information."

Jonathan's expression was grim when he answered. "I drove through the financial district on my way here.

There are already hordes of men on the streets looking for answers, hoping for news that might allay their fear after yesterday."

"They're not going to hear anything like that, are they?" Thomas asked.

Jonathan shook his head heavily. "I'm afraid not. The market has taken a serious hit. You know it started with the collapse of Cooke. It has been generally known that their bank's money hasn't been worth its face value for some time."

Abby thought of Wally and Nancy with a sudden surge of anger. "It hasn't been known by everyone," she said sharply. "I'm assuming that knowledge belonged to a select few?"

"That's true," Jonathan agreed. "I wish I could say things work differently, but it would be a
lie. Rumors of difficulty have been heard for a while by well-informed financiers."

Abby knew Jonathan fit into that category. She hadn't seen him for many years, but his clothing revealed the wealth he had created. She thought of the Stock Exchange scenes Thomas had described. Limited knowledge was the only way to explain the shock that had spilled out into the streets like a menacing cloud. "I'm assuming those fortunate few managed to withdraw their investments before it collapsed?" She tried to constrain her anger, but the look in Jonathan's eyes revealed she had failed.

"Yes," Jonathan said reluctantly.

Abby's stomach tightened. It was clear he was one of the fortunate few. The Jonathan she knew wasn't a greedy man; he'd simply had the knowledge necessary to make the best decision. She and Thomas had known enough to mostly stay out of the market, but there were many she'd not been able to convince to do the same. Nancy's face rose in her mind to taunt her. "What do you believe is going to happen?"

Jonathan regarded her gravely. "Are you and Thomas in trouble, Abby?"

Abby was happy to shake her head. "We are not," she assured him. "I stepped back from investments more than two years ago, shortly before the Black Friday crash caused by the Gold Ring." She smiled. "I will always be grateful for the information, Jonathan. We have been very cautious, and have prepared for a dark time."

"I'm glad." Jonathan's relief was swallowed almost immediately by a frown. "I don't believe this is a crisis the country will emerge from unscathed. The economy is in a much more tenuous condition than it was two years ago. I believe many more businesses will go under in the next few days. Investors have been spooked. They'll continue to sell, and stocks will continue to decline. No one will be in the mood to buy for a lengthy period."

"Do you believe Western Union stocks will be hit harder?" Thomas asked.

Abby knew he was thinking about Wally. Whatever money he had put into the stock market, its value was already much lower. If Wally had bought the stocks recently, which she suspected he had, he would have bought when the value was highest. Any drop would be disastrous. With the market continuing to plummet, the values would go even lower. He might have a chance to recoup a portion of his investment if he moved quickly. Her hopes were shattered with Jonathan's next words.

"I'm sorry to say I believe it will," Jonathan replied. "I doubt there are any stocks that won't

be impacted negatively. For people who can afford to stay in the market long term, the time will come when values rise. If they were hoping for fast wealth, however, and need the money they invested, they'll be in serious trouble. At this point, anyone willing to buy will pay pennies on the dollar.

The last several years have been quite challenging for America. Speculative investments, primarily in railroads, along with massive property losses in Chicago and Boston, have put a huge strain on bank reserves. The bank reserves plummeted by more than thirty million dollars this month. Combine that with the reality of massive greed and corruption from Boss Tweed's Ring here in New York..." Jonathan's voice trailed off.

As if on cue, the dark clouds threatening the city dropped closer to the ground.

The heavy air matched the heaviness on the porch. Silence extended for several moments before he continued. "I believe there will be a run on the rest of the banks."

"Which will create more panic that will cause more businesses to go under," Abby said, the words catching in her throat. "Unemployment is going to soar." She was concerned about Wally and Nancy, but her concerns were also for Felicia. To say this wasn't a good time to strike out and establish businesses would be putting it mildly.

The skies opened. Rain poured down, quickly forming puddles in the road. Abby thought of the scores of men desperately searching for answers and likely forming long lines at area banks to take out whatever money they could. The rain would make their day even more miserable.

Abby wanted to understand the current crisis as much as possible. "What do you believe is the most important contributing factor? Does this come back to the railroads?"

Jonathan regarded her steadily. "I suppose the railroads laid the foundation for the collapse. Thirty-three thousand miles of new track has been laid across the country in the last five years. Much of the craze in railroad investment was driven by government land grants and subsidies. The railroad industry has been the largest employer in America, outside of agriculture."

Abby knew scores of those men would soon be unemployed. Their situation would create a ripple effect of collapsing businesses and increased unemployment.

"The railroads have involved large amounts of money and risk," Thomas observed.

"Very true," Jonathan said. "A large infusion of cash from speculators caused immense growth in the industry, as well as the construction of docks and factories. The problem is that the

capital is invested in projects that offer no immediate, or even early, returns." He paused. "The economy might have survived if we hadn't had continued financial setbacks. The Black Friday Panic, the Chicago Fire, the Equine Influenza." His voice grew sterner as he continued to recite the list. "The Boston Fire last year, the demonetization of silver this year. We simply didn't have the reserves to weather the challenges."

"We?" Abby asked, realizing she didn't know exactly what Jonathan was currently involved with.

When Jonathan looked at her, his eyes were dark with trouble. "I'm a partner at Jay Cooke and Company," he revealed. "I should be at the bank this morning. I'm here out of respect for you, Abby, but I can't stay much longer."

Abby felt a surge of compassion for him and a deep appreciation for his presence. "What happened, Jonathan?" she asked sincerely. "Please help me understand before you leave." She trusted him to be honest.

Jonathan met her eyes. "Cooke, along with other financiers, planned to build the second transcontinental railroad."

"The Northern Pacific Railway," Thomas said.

Jonathan inclined his head in agreement. "Cooke provided the financing—one and a half million dollars. Ground was broken in Minnesota on February 15, 1870. In order to recoup the investment, Cooke created several million dollars in Northern Pacific Railway bonds for the public to purchase, but everything that's happened these last few years has made it impossible to sell enough of them."

Abby's mind whirled with what she already knew. The Northern Pacific had been chartered by Congress in 1864. The goal was to connect the Great Lakes with the Puget Sound in the Washington Territory in order to open new lands for farming, ranching, lumbering, and mining. It was intended to link Washington and Oregon with the rest of the country. It had taken six years to find financing through Cooke.

"The railway has been unable to pay back the loan," Abby observed.

"Yes, there have been serious challenges and delays." Jonathan grimaced. "The staggering costs of building a railroad through a vast wilderness was drastically underestimated. We believed we could market the bonds in Europe but had little success because of Europe's own financial crises. Because we couldn't sell the bonds, the bank ended up owning seventy-five percent of the railroad. Cooke overextended in meeting overdrafts of the mounting construction costs." He sighed. "Investors sensed mounting trouble and began withdrawing money from the bank. Cooke believed we were about to swing a three-hundred-million-dollar government loan this month, but with rumors swirling that our credit had become nearly worthless, the loan never came through. You already know the bank filed for bankruptcy yesterday." His expression revealed he was still stunned by the collapse of the bank.

Abby's gut tightened as she thought of Wally and Nancy, but her immediate concern was for Jonathan. He had indicated his privileged information had protected him, but she wanted to be certain. He had protected her from financial destruction in the past. "And you? What is this going to do to you, Jonathan?"

Jonathan hesitated for a long moment but met her eyes evenly. "I'll be fine. Quite honestly, I anticipated the failure. Several months ago I divested from my assets that would crumble if Cooke failed."

Abby smiled. "I'm glad for you, Jonathan." Her thoughts returned to the Stratfords. "How bad do you believe it's going to be?"

"Bad," Jonathan said bluntly as he pulled out his pocket watch. "I imagine there is a run on the bank happening at this moment. Cooke won't be able to meet its obligations, so operations will be suspended. That failure will cause a chain reaction of bank runs and other failures. People losing their money is merely the first step in what's to come. Factories will lay off workers, unemployment will explode, and businesses will close."

"We're moving into a full depression," Thomas said hoarsely.

"I don't see any way the country can avoid it," Jonathan answered. He cleared his throat and

stood. "I'm sorry, but I must be on my way. I won't be able to stop what is happening at Cooke, but my presence is required."

"Of course," Abby said as she and Thomas rose to stand with him. "I hate the reason for it, but I'm happy to see you again, my friend. Thank you for making time to come talk with us."

Jonathan said his farewell and returned to his carriage. Moments later, he was a speck in the distance before fully disappearing around a corner.

Abby watched until she could no longer see him. She needed a few minutes to absorb everything she had heard. It wasn't as if she hadn't anticipated this day for years, but she was horrified by how it would impact

Nancy and Wally. Other friends and associates came to mind, but her immediate concern was for their hosts.

The squeak of the screen-door hinges revealed their privacy had ended. Abby was grateful for the time they'd had.

Nancy stepped onto the porch, her face set and drawn. Her normally sparkling eyes were lifeless saucers held in place by deep lines.

Abby enveloped Nancy in an embrace. There were no words to address the agony she saw.

Nancy finally stepped back. "I heard what he said," she whispered.

Abby hadn't known she was listening, but she believed Nancy should be equipped with the truth.

Nancy walked to the edge of the porch, her unblinking eyes focused on the roses resplendent with late-season blooms

Abby exchanged a look with Thomas, silently communicating that the women needed time alone. He nodded, stood, and walked into the house.

Abby moved next to Nancy, offering her silent support.

"We're ruined," Nancy said in a trembling voice. She raised bewildered eyes. "We've lost everything, Abby."

Abby felt the shock resonate through her body. When Nancy had said those words yesterday, she hadn't thought it possible that Wally would actually endanger their entire financial status. "How?" she asked. She knew, even as she was asking, that the how didn't really matter at that point, but it was all she could think of to say.

Nancy shook her head, unable to speak.

When Nancy could finally form words, her voice quaked with emotion. "He was desperate to regain the money we lost last year. He admitted last night that he invested everything, believing there would be a huge return very quickly…" She swallowed hard. "He paid top dollar for the stocks because he believed their value would continue to rise. Jay Gould convinced him it was completely safe. Every stock he invested in crashed yesterday." She raised her eyes. "The little we have left is in the Cooke Bank."

Abby's heart sank. Nancy had heard Jonathan reveal that the bank could not meet its obligations. Still, there might be time before that happened. "Wally should go to the bank immediately," she urged. "Cooke will try to meet its obligations for as long as it can."

Nancy shook her head again. "I told Wally the same thing. He's too ashamed to show his face. I doubt he'll leave the bedroom until you and Thomas are gone."

Abby felt an equal surge of compassion and anger. Wally was in a terrible situation, but it was one of his own making. He owed it to Nancy to try to save what he could of their money. Her mind continued to spin. She grabbed Nancy's arm. "You can go and get the money."

Nancy's eyes were bleak with hopelessness. "I'm not on the bank account, Abby. Even if I was, they wouldn't give it to me without Wally there." Tears welled in her eyes. "It's not much, anyway. Wally planned on cashing out of the market this week, so he invested almost everything."

"You have your home," Abby reminded her. "It won't be easy, but…"

Nancy dashed away a tear, her hand shaking with emotion. "Wally used the house...to get as much money...as he could to put into the market. The house will be gone soon."

Abby ground her teeth, wishing she had the perfect words. How could Wally have done this?

"What about Michael?" she asked. "Does he know?" Abby was very close to their son, Michael, and his wife, Julie. She knew real estate would be negatively impacted by the financial crash, but there would hopefully be enough business to keep everyone afloat until the economy improved. Michael would do anything to help his parents.

"Wally insists I not tell him."

"Nancy!" Abby protested. "Michael is your son."

"I know," Nancy whispered. "I don't know what to do, Abby. I've never seen Wally like this. He's completely lost."

There were people throughout the city feeling the same way. By now, the effects were beginning to be felt across the nation. The shock emanating from New York City would impact every financial market. Jonathan believed it was going to get worse. Abby knew that was true.

Nancy gripped Abby's hand. "What are we going to do?"

Abby wished she had an answer.

Chapter Ten[SK2]
September 24, 1873

"I'm worried about Mr. and Mrs. Stratford, Mama."

Rose looked away from the countryside that rolled past them on the train. "I am too, Felicia."

"Are they going to be alright?"

Rose had no idea how to answer that question. She, Carrie, and the girls had stayed in New York for a couple of extra days, waiting to see if the stock market would take an unexpected turn for the better, but the news had gotten progressively worse.

It became obvious their presence was putting additional strain on the household. Abby hadn't told her and Carrie the truth about the Stratfords' financial situation—at Nancy's request—until the morning they left. They hadn't told the girls yet.

"They've never closed the Stock Exchange before," Felicia said. "They closed it on the twentieth. How long will it stay closed?"

Felicia had talked with Thomas and Abby at length regarding the economic situation in the last few days. The country was indeed in a tailspin. The Stock Exchange had closed in an attempt to stave off more disaster. More banks had failed, leaving people destitute. Hundreds of businesses had failed in less than a week. Scores of people had already been laid off in New York City. The ripple effect had reached other parts of the country, with no relief in sight. It would take a long time for the economy to recover.

"Mama?" Felicia's voice was troubled.

Rose suddenly understood what Felicia was actually asking. "I don't know, honey," she said. She grasped her daughter's hand, grateful Hope was deep in conversation with Minnie and Frances several rows ahead. "I imagine this has made you nervous about your plans."

Felicia nodded slowly. "Thomas and Abby believe the country is heading into a severe depression."

Rose didn't pretend to be an expert on business, but she had learned to respect Abby deeply. "What do you believe?"

Felicia sighed. "That they're right."

Since she had no helpful advice, Rose decided to ask questions. "What does that mean to you?"

Felicia looked up. "You're doing that thing," she accused. "You're asking questions instead of giving me answers."

Rose smiled, not bothering to refute the obvious. "Honey, I can't help you with business advice. What I can do is help you remember what you already know."

"What do I know?" Felicia asked.

"You tell me. You've learned from Mrs. Pleasant in San Francisco, from Thomas and Abby, and from school. What does that tell you about the country's economic situation?"

Felicia grew thoughtful.

Rose settled back and waited for Felicia to speak.

Several minutes passed. The rhythmic noise of the train on the tracks was peaceful. The trees they passed were already clothing themselves in their autumn garb. It would be a few weeks before peak foliage, but it was beautiful. She was glad to be out of New York, away from the belching smokestacks that deposited a layer of grime over the city.

"Abby and Thomas reminded me that the economy will rebound eventually. We don't know when that will be, but it will happen. It's more challenging to start a business during a

tough economic time, but it's not impossible," Felicia began. "You and Daddy are going to finance my first business. Mrs. Pleasant has offered to invest in my new endeavors, as well."

Rose listened. Truthfully, she didn't know how the depression would impact her and Moses, nor Mrs. Pleasant, but they would do whatever they could to help Felicia. She and Moses would talk when she got home. There was no reason to plant doubt.

"My success will depend on the type of business I start," Felicia continued." People need an affordable place to live." Her eyes brightened. "If things are getting really tough, I should be able to buy boarding homes below the current market value. I could help people and still make a profit."

"That's true," Rose replied. In fact, she didn't know if it was true or not, but it sounded feasible.

Felicia wasn't finished. "There will be less competition to buy real estate during a depression. I'll be able to provide more affordable housing options than people currently have. Even when the economy eventually gets better, they'll likely be loyal to me, meaning I'd have longer-term tenants."

Rose listened closely, impressed with Felicia's business acumen. She began to feel her daughter's growing enthusiasm.

"I bet things will be much cheaper too," Felicia continued. "Not just the real estate, but

everything else I need. I need to be smart."

"Which you already are," Rose observed.

Felicia's face grew earnest. "Do you believe I'll be alright, Mama? Am I making a mistake?" She drew in a deep breath. "Should I go back to the plantation and wait until the economy improves?"

Rose fought every impulse to tell Felicia that was exactly what she should do, but she refused to let her own fears dictate her daughter's future. Before she could open her mouth to respond, Felicia asked another question.

"Should I go back to San Francisco and work with Mrs. Pleasant?"

Rose didn't hesitate to answer that one. "No, dear." Boston might be risky, but at least Felicia would be within travel distance. The idea of her across the country was more than Rose could bear. "I believe you can succeed in Boston."

"Really?" Felicia said breathlessly.

Rose seldom saw her confident daughter vulnerable, but neither had the economy been in such a challenging position since the end of the war. Her heart told her that wasn't the root source, however. "Talking about doing something, and actually doing it, can be daunting," she said. "I remember when Moses and I decided to leave the plantation and head north to

Philadelphia. We had no idea whether we could actually make it, and we didn't know what awaited us."

"I've never heard this story," Felicia said. "Please tell me what happened."

Rose was happy to tell the story. As the words poured out, she could feel the terror again when she told Felicia about their conductor from the Underground Railroad being murdered. His death had left them on their own. She talked about crossing the Potomac River in the dead of night in a small rowboat during a massive storm. About the weeks of travel when they were completely on their own, navigating their way to Pennsylvania, and watching over their shoulders for slave hunters. About finally reaching Abby's house, and the joy of her taking them in.

Felicia soaked in every detail. Suddenly, she threw back her head and laughed. "Why am I worried about what's going to happen? I'm going to Boston on a train. I have money to find a place to stay. I have Peter and Elizabeth waiting. I have my best friend in the world to live with me." She shook her head. "What is wrong with me? What I am facing is nothing compared to what you and Daddy faced for freedom."

Rose recognized with a start how correct Felicia was. Fear was fear, and was to be acknowledged, but her daughter was already leaps and bounds ahead of where she and Moses had started. It's what they had worked hard for, to ensure their children would never have to deal with the hardships they'd had to. The economy might be in a crisis, but she and Moses had started with nothing. They could not have dreamed where life would take them. Her confidence soared. "Honey, you have nothing to worry about. You're going to do wonderfully in Boston. There will be challenges, with or without a depression, but you will find a way to overcome them and succeed." Her voice was firm and steadfast.

"You're right," Felicia said, equally as firm. Her eyes were filled with confidence again.

Frances slid into the empty seat next to them. "Yes, you are right, Rose." Her face was filled with awe. "I couldn't help but overhear. Did you and Moses really go through such a terrible time?"

Rose smiled. "We did." There were things she chose not to tell them, but they didn't

need to know everything. Stories of Ike Adams coming after them and almost raping her on the streets of Philadelphia would merely fuel fears. She had told Felicia what she needed to know to

face this stage of her life with confidence.

Rose left Felicia and Frances as they talked excitedly, and moved up two rows to slide in next to Carrie.

"This is happening," she said quietly. Telling her and Moses' story had done much to build her

own courage.

Carrie twisted her lips and nodded. "It's happening. We're going to leave our girls in Boston." She paused for a moment. "I heard you telling Felicia about your and Moses' trip to Philadelphia. It's been a long time since I heard that story. It will never cease to amaze me what you went through. We thought we had planned it carefully, but it went terribly wrong."

"It did," Rose agreed. "The important thing, however, is that we made it to Philadelphia. We found Abby, and we had a home. We found our purpose, and then I found you again."

Carrie chuckled. "You make it sound so simple." She sobered. "It wasn't, though."

"It definitely wasn't," Rose agreed.

They were surprised when Frances appeared next to them. "Felicia and I want to hear the stories, Mama—yours and Rose's. Minnie and Hope should hear them too. Will you tell us?"

"When?" Carrie asked. "We're going to be rather busy."

"When we're in Boston," Frances answered. "We'll find the time. Felicia told me how much better she feels after hearing what Rose and Moses endured." She looked at Rose. "I want to hear about Old Sarah, too. We've heard a few of the stories, but I have a feeling we can learn a lot from her."

"It might take more than the trip to Boston," Rose said. "The last fourteen years have been rather eventful. Not to mention our growing up together on the plantation." She was thrilled the girls wanted to know the stories. She wished she had asked her mama to tell her more about her life in Africa.

"We'll do the best we can," Carrie promised. "If there is more to tell, you'll have to wait until you come home for Christmas."

Frances eyed her playfully. "Have you ever heard of a letter?"

Carrie chuckled. "I have, but I'd much rather lure you home with the promise of more stories."

Peter and Elizabeth were waiting for them when they emerged from the train station in Boston.

"Carrie!" Elizabeth called. "You're here!"

Carrie fell into her friend's arms, laughing with delight. "It's so good to see you again!"

A flurry of greetings ensued.

Peter eyed the mountain of luggage. "It's a good thing you recommended I bring a wagon instead of a carriage."

Carrie inclined her head toward Frances and Felicia. "Most of it belongs to those two."

"Every bit of it is necessary," Frances protested. "We *are* moving here, you know."

Felicia nodded. "It requires a lot to begin a new life."

"Your mother might not agree," Carrie said. It would be good to remind Felicia of how her parents had started.

Felicia slapped a hand to her mouth. "Oh my...you're right." She stared at the pile of bags and chests with guilty dismay. "Mama, you and Daddy started with just what you were wearing."

Rose stepped forward and wrapped an arm around her daughter's waist, sending Carrie a scolding look. "Which I would never want for you, my dear. I helped you pack this, remember? You're going to use it, and you will appreciate having it."

Soon, the wagon was rolling down the road under a brilliant blue sky. Carrie was thrilled to be out of New

York City. "How is the rebuilding of the financial district coming?" she asked Peter.

Peter smiled enthusiastically. "I see it every day, but I can hardly believe how fast it's being rebuilt. Most businesses were overinsured for fire. They received their money quickly, so the rebuilding began almost immediately. More importantly, they are taking the time to do it correctly. After the fire, citizens formed a committee and urged the city to restructure the layout of roadways in that area. Many of the downtown streets were reestablished to be wider and straighter before they allowed construction to begin."

"What did they do with the rubble from the fire?" Frances asked. "I read there was a great deal."

"There certainly was," Peter agreed. "When you have that many buildings destroyed, there will be tons of rubble and refuse." He grinned broadly. "They turned it into Atlantic Avenue!"

Minnie, who had been eagerly taking in every inch of their new surroundings, pivoted to Peter. "They did *what* with it?"

Peter chuckled. "They took the rubble and moved it into the harbor to expand Atlantic Avenue. It's a wonderful addition to the city." He shook his head. "There's much more work to be done, but I can't believe how quickly it's coming back to life. We seem to be on target to finish in another year."

"That's astonishing!" Rose exclaimed. "Chicago isn't rebuilding that fast."

"Chicago's fire was much larger," Peter replied. "In addition, many of the buildings weren't insured, or their insurance papers burned in the fire. In addition, laws have been passed requiring new buildings to be constructed with fireproof materials. They have to use brick, stone, marble, or limestone. All of it has to be held together by mortar." He frowned. "Unfortunately, the Chicago fire burned far more residential homes than Boston's did. Without insurance, and with the law stating they have to rebuild with fireproof materials, thousands of people and small businesses are being crowded out of Chicago."

Minnie looked outraged. "That's not fair!"

"I agree," Peter said. "Fair or not, though, that's what is happening."

Carrie's mind was on the financial panic. "How much will the economic crisis impact things?"

"I believe it may create a serious problem in Chicago," Peter said. "In Boston, not

so much. Insurance companies have already paid out the money. It's simply a time factor now."

"Are they rebuilding things the right way?" Minnie asked, her blue eyes bright with intensity.

"They are," Peter assured her. "Every building erected is being upgraded and updated. They're being rebuilt to suit the commercial nature of the district. With the roads being widened, many of the land parcels are being reassembled into larger plots."

"Won't that make land values go up? Along with the prices?" Felicia asked keenly.

"It is definitely doing that," Peter acknowledged.

Felicia frowned. "Is that true for everywhere in the city?"

"It's not," Peter assured her. "I know you're here to

look for real estate. I believe there are deals to be found, especially with the Wall Street crash."

"That's good to know," Felicia responded. "Do you have a suggestion for where we might look for a place to live?"

Elizabeth spoke for the first time. "We believe we might have the perfect solution, girls."

"What do you mean?" Carrie asked. She recognized the gleam in her friend's eyes. Elizabeth was hiding something.

Elizabeth grinned. "I'm not telling you a thing until I give you your surprise."

Carrie's curiosity grew. "My surprise?"

Elizabeth's grin widened. "I'm glad you're finally here. I don't know how much longer I could keep it a secret. There were several times I came close to sending you a telegram. Only the threat of bodily harm kept me from doing it."

"What in the world are you talking about?"

Elizabeth shook her head, her black curls dancing around her glimmering brown eyes. "I'm not telling you a thing. Since we're only a few blocks from the house, you don't have long to wait."

Hope leaned into her. "You can whisper it in my ear," she invited. "I'm real good at keeping secrets."

Elizabeth laughed and gave Hope a hug, but she shook her head. "I gave my word. I've held the secret this long. It's a matter of personal integrity to keep it a little while longer."

To keep from bursting with curiosity, Carrie went back to the conversation with Peter. She knew Minnie had questions she hadn't had the chance to ask. "Tell us about the upgrades to the buildings in the financial district, Peter."

Minnie leaned forward so she wouldn't miss a word of his reply.

Peter spoke directly to Minnie. Everyone knew her passion for fire safety, as well as the reason for it. "The city leaders understand that choices made in the past led to last year's disastrous fire. They're determined to rebuild the city in a completely different way."

"They're going to use fireproof building materials?" Minnie demanded.

"They are," Peter answered. "We're building with brick, stone, limestone and Marble. Unlike Chicago, where too many people can't afford to rebuild in the best way, Boston can do it correctly. We're also limiting the height of buildings."

"So firefighters can reach the top floors with ground ladders," Minnie stated. Her eyes glimmered with tears. "If they could have reached my family, they might not be dead."

Carrie felt her own eyes fill with tears. She would never forget Anthony's recounting of how he watched the Philadelphia fire engulf Minnie's entire family. He had left Minnie blocks away from the fire in a carriage, but she had forced her way back through the crowds and witnessed the fire consume her brother, Jack. Carrie and Anthony had brought the traumatized little girl home and adopted her.

Carrie knew her daughter would never lose her passion to make buildings and families safer from fires. Minnie spent many hours in the library reading about fire safety and the disastrous fires that swept away towns and communities far too often. Thomas and Abby made it a priority to order everything they could find on the subject.

"That's right," Peter said gravely. "Boston realizes we have to do everything possible to keep that from happening here. Fire escapes have become mandatory, and we are improving our water supply for the entire city - not merely the financial district. It will take time to complete the work, but we won't stop until we do."

"Are they putting more space between the buildings?" Minnie asked. "That's quite important in order to keep burning buildings from igniting new fires."

Carrie had to remind herself sometimes that her little girl was only eleven years old. Minnie's painful experiences had given her extraordinary passion.

"You're right," Peter agreed. "They are doing that, as well. They're building wider corridors and creating open stairways so people can get out of burning buildings. They're installing more fire alarms, too."

"In every building?" Minnie probed.

Peter shook his head and met her eyes directly. "That is the goal, Minnie, but it will take much longer to accomplish that. Rebuilding businesses that are no longer in existence is much easier than attempting to retrofit existing buildings and homes." He leaned forward to take Minnie's hand. "This is where your passion will be so important in the years to come. Every city in this country must become more aware of fire safety. We have to train city managers, but it's equally important to educate the people who work and live in the buildings. They should demand the buildings be safe."

Minnie nodded thoughtfully. "You're right." She shifted her attention to Carrie. "Mama, do you think I could meet Mr. John Damrell while I'm here?"

Carrie rolled the name over in her mind but came up blank. She looked to Peter for help.

"John Damrell is Boston's chief engineer," Peter said.

"Of course he is." Carrie shouldn't be surprised Minnie knew about him.

"Minnie, how do you know about Mr. Damrell?" Peter asked.

Minnie shrugged casually. "Felicia and Frances taught me that if you want to know something, the information is out there. I've read everything written about the Boston fire.

Grandma and Grandpa ordered the Boston Globe for me. Mr. Damrell has been a firefighter here since 1858. He's been the chief engineer since the war ended. He's been trying to convince Boston to replace and repair water mains since before the fire. They should have paid attention to him."

Peter looked impressed. "You're absolutely right, Minnie. It's too late for the buildings that burned, but the city is definitely paying attention to Mr. Damrell now."

"That's good," Minnie said. She returned to her earlier question. "So, may I meet him, Mama? I expect I could learn a great deal from him."

Carrie searched for a way to reply. She couldn't imagine such a busy man would take the time to meet with a child. She had no idea how to make it happen.

Peter saved her. "Chief Damrell happens to be a friend of mine, Minnie. I'll see what I can do."

Minnie beamed with delight. "Thank you, Peter. I don't believe he will regret it."

Carrie choked back a laugh, nearly losing control when she caught Rose's laughing eyes and saw Elizabeth's lips twitching. Truth be told, there was nothing to laugh about. Minnie's passion was real. Carrie believed her daughter would make a difference in the world of fire safety as she grew older. Probably, Minnie and John Damrell would both benefit from their meeting.

When she felt the carriage begin to slow, Carrie's attention returned to what Elizabeth had said earlier. "Am I about to discover my surprise?"

Elizabeth said nothing.

Carrie laughed aloud. "If you're trying to drive me to distraction, you're succeeding."

"That is possibly true, my friend. It's not very often that I have something to hold over you. I'm going to savor this for as long as I can."

"That's cruel," Carrie cried.

Frances grinned and clapped her hands. "Well done, Elizabeth! Mama does the same thing to us. It's about time she gets a taste of her own medicine."

Carrie scowled playfully. "What happened to loyalty, Frances?"

Frances shrugged. "This isn't a matter of loyalty, Mama. I'm telling the truth. You've told me I should embrace honesty and integrity."

The entire wagon erupted into laughter.

Carrie knew when she was beaten. She raised her head high, controlled her twitching lips, and stepped from the wagon. "I'm going to greet your parents," she said primly. "Perhaps I will discover more mature conversation inside."

"You might not," Elizabeth said mysteriously.

At that same moment, the door to the Gilbert Medical Center, attached to the northern wing of the Gilbert's sprawling home, swung open.

A slender blond woman stepped out on to the porch.

Chapter Eleven

Carrie's breath caught when her eyes landed on the figure in the doorway. She stared with disbelief and then dashed up the walkway to enfolded her friend into her arms. "Alice Humphries!"

"Alice! Is it really you?" Joy exploded in her heart as she took in her friend's dancing blue eyes, framed by blond hair. Alice was as petite as ever, but there were fine lines etched into a face that had known too much pain. "What are you doing here?"

"I happen to work here." Mischief sparkled in Alice's eyes.

"You work here? At the medical clinic?" Carrie tried to make sense of what she was hearing. How could she not have known this?

Elizabeth stepped up beside them. "Alice moved to Boston a few weeks ago. We knew you were coming, so we decided to keep her presence a surprise."

"Can we get out of the wagon now?"

Hope's plaintive voice broke into the reunion. Everyone was still in the wagon. Carrie beckoned them to get out and join them before she smiled at her friend. "You know you're going to have to answer a million questions for me."

Alice grinned. "As long as you answer the million and one questions I have for you."

Frances and Minnie, their faces openly quizzical, approached Carrie's side.

"Alice, I want you to meet two of my children. My oldest is Frances."

"Hello, Frances," Alice said warmly. "I understand you are moving to Boston to begin medical school."

"I am," Frances replied eagerly. "You're one of the women Mama went to medical school with in Philadelphia, aren't you? I've heard about you."

"There are many stories to be told," Alice answered with a smile before she took Minnie's hand. "You're Minnie. It's a pleasure to meet you. You have a passion for fire safety and love to cook."

Minnie looked surprised. "How do you know that?"

Elizabeth provided the answer. "While I was keeping the surprise, Alice demanded to know everything possible before your arrival."

Alice turned next to Rose and pulled her into a hug. "I would know you anywhere, Rose

Samuels. Carrie talked about you from the first day we met. You went to school at Oberlin, and you have a fabulous school on the plantation. You are married to Moses and have four children."

Rose laughed and stepped back. "I know about you, as well, with the exception of what you're doing in Boston working at the medical clinic. The last I heard, you were working with Elizabeth Packard to reform insane asylums."

Alice waved her hand through the air dismissively.

"We'll get to that. First, I want to meet your beautiful daughters."

Felicia stepped forward. "I'm Felicia. I'm moving to Boston as well."

Alice appraised her. "You're here to start your financial empire and show everyone what a powerful woman can do." She gripped Felicia's hand tightly. "I believe you'll do that, my dear. It won't be easy, but doing it in Massachusetts will be easier than in other states."

"Why?" Felicia asked.

"Details to come. First, I want to meet your little sister." Alice leaned down to peer into Hope's eyes. "You have to be Hope. You look exactly like your mother."

Hope nodded. "My mama is a very beautiful woman."

"Hope!" Rose protested with a helpless laugh.

"It's true, Mama," Hope replied. "Daddy tells me all the time. He says I'm going to be beautiful, just like you."

"Which you will be," Alice said firmly.

Carrie watched the exchange with amazement. She'd not seen Alice since shortly after rescuing her from the insane asylum, where she had been imprisoned by her husband, whom she had since divorced. Alice had been thin, frightened, and in shock from the trauma and abuse she had endured. Carrie had heard from Elizabeth that Alice returned to medical school for her degree before joining Elizabeth Packard in the fight to improve how asylums treated women.

Instead of writing letters, they had fallen out of touch.

This strong, confident woman was an older version of the young medical student Carrie had first met. Obviously, she had overcome her trauma and the injustice done to her.

Alice leaned down closer to Hope. "Do you know what is far more important than being beautiful, Hope?"

"What?" Hope asked.

"Being a powerful woman, like your mother. Your mama changes lives every day by being a teacher."

Hope squinted in confusion. "So I should be a teacher?"

"Maybe." Alice smiled. "Maybe not. It doesn't matter what you decide to do, only that you should do it with as much passion as your mama has for teaching."

Carrie gazed at her old friend. Clearly, Alice's years on the road with Elizabeth Packard had taught her how to empower women and give them confidence. She found herself wishing that Frances and Felicia could spend more time with her. Having both Elizabeth and Alice in Boston was going to be wonderful for the girls. She was feeling better about leaving them alone in the city.

"Dr. Carrie Wallington!"

Carrie spun around when a booming voice rang through the air. "Dr. Gilbert!" she called, climbing the porch stairs to give Elizabeth's father a hug. "It's wonderful to see you."

"It's wonderful to see you, my dear. What do you think of Elizabeth's surprise?"

"I'm thrilled to see Alice, but I'm shocked your

daughter kept the secret," Carrie said playfully. "The Elizabeth I know has never been good at keeping secrets."

"One of the benefits of being married to a reporter," Peter said. "It's taken me a while to train her, but she's coming along nicely."

Carrie and the rest laughed when Elizabeth stuck her tongue out.

Peter shook his head. "See what I have to deal with?" he said, laughter dancing in his eyes. "There is so little respect."

Gertrude, the Gilbert family cook for more than thirty years, stepped onto the porch. Her rich Irish brogue rang through the air. "Are the group of you going to stand out here yammering all day, or are you coming in to eat the meal I've slaved over?" She smiled when she spotted Minnie. "You must be the wee Irish lass I've heard so much about."

Minnie's eyes widened with delight. "I am. You're Irish too! I happen to be a wee Irish lass that loves to cook, like my mama did. Will you share some of your recipes with me?"

Gertrude pretended to think about the question. "Are you planning on taking my Boston recipes back down to the plantation?"

"Of course!" Minnie answered. "Wouldn't it be a special thing for you to know your secret recipes were being enjoyed in the South by people you love?"

Carrie was impressed with her daughter's negotiating skills. She also recognized Abby's influence.

Gertrude frowned. "What would be making you

think I love any of the lot standing here?"

"Because my mama says you do," Minnie replied earnestly. "We've been eating sandwiches ever since she was last here. She says you taught her about them."

Gertrude smiled with delight. "That right?"

Minnie nodded. "Do you have anything new to teach me? Or perhaps you need me to teach you."

Carrie practically choked at her daughter's audacity. "Minnie!"

Gertrude held up a hand to stop her protest. "You figure you have something to be teaching me, wee lass?"

Minnie glanced at Carrie with uncertainty, seeming to sense she might have stepped over an invisible line, but she answered honestly. "I might. Annie has taught me a lot of recipes, and I've learned a lot more from the books I read."

Gertrude looked at her with a puzzled expression. "You be getting recipes from books, lass? Doesn't Annie have enough recipes to keep you busy?"

Minnie met her eyes. "I believe that if I want to be a great cook, I shouldn't only stick with what I already know. I should keep learning. I have a lot of great cookbooks!"

Carrie wondered, not for the first time, if she had raised her daughters to be a little too confident, or perhaps too outspoken.

Gertrude looked surprised. After a long moment, she held out a hand to Minnie. "You come with me, little Irish lass," she said. "I suppose we'll be teaching things to each other. For right now, you can help me serve this meal."

Carrie exhaled with relief as Minnie trotted into the

house beside Gertrude.

"Mama, can I go with Minnie?"

Rose looked down at Hope with surprise. "Don't you want to stay out here with us?"

Hope shook her head. "I already know the adults are going to start talking about things I don't care about. I don't care a lot about cooking either, but there might be fresh cookies in the kitchen."

Laughter rang around the porch again.

"Go on," Rose replied. "Follow your nose. You'll find the kitchen."

Matilda Gilbert, Elizabeth's mother, chose that moment to join them. There was another flurry of greetings, until finally, she waved toward the house. "Everybody, come inside. Hot tea and cookies are waiting. I'll show Hope how to find the kitchen and come join you. Lunch will be ready soon."

———⚜———

Carrie's sides ached with laughter during the long lunch. She never tired of the easy banter that was the hallmark of a Gilbert Italian meal. The food never stopped coming, and the drink never stopped flowing.

When there was a lull in the conversation, Carrie leaned close to Minnie. "Did you learn anything from Gertrude?"

Minnie's eyes widened. "I don't know anything about Italian cooking, Mama! I'm going to learn *so* much." She grinned broadly. "Gertrude told me that when she first came here to cook, she couldn't cook Italian. Mrs. Gilbert taught her. She says there are days she feels more Italian than Irish."

Carrie laughed. "She still *sounds* Irish."

Minnie nodded, but her eyes looked troubled. "I get told at school that I still have my Irish accent." She frowned. "Sounding Irish is not always a good thing in America."

Carrie had never heard Minnie say this. She loved her daughter's lilting Irish brogue. It had diminished in the last few years, but she hoped it would never disappear entirely. It bothered her to know Minnie viewed it negatively. What had she read to give her this belief? "Never be ashamed of being Irish, Minnie. Even if you manage to disguise your accent, your red hair and blue eyes make you stand out. Being Irish is something to be proud of."

"Not everyone feels that way, Mama," Minnie replied. "Irish people aren't always treated well."

"Not everyone thinks it's good to be Italian either," Elizabeth said, reaching over to lay her olive-skinned hand on Minnie's milky-white arm. "Immigrants are not always welcome in America. Differences are too often not embraced."

"Why not?" Minnie asked. "Doesn't everyone start as an immigrant?"

Dr. Gilbert was the one to answer her question. "You're correct, Minnie. Unless you're Indian, you're an immigrant. The issue is that more and more immigrants are pouring into America. While Americans want cheap labor, they need someone to look down on. It's one of the frailties of human nature. The Irish have long had problems being accepted as equals. So have Italians, and it's only gotten worse. Unfortunately, the press has begun to circulate pseudo-scientific theories that Mediterranean types, meaning Italians, are inherently inferior to people of northern European heritage." His voice dripped with sarcasm.

"I've read things that say the same about the Irish," Minnie said. "Even though we're from northern Europe too."

"They certainly say it about black people," Felicia added. "Americans used it as an excuse to enslave millions of us."

Carrie thought about the truths she had discovered about her Cromwell ancestors. "Unfortunately, the English enslaved the Irish. They called them indentured servants, but they were nothing but slaves."

"I know," Dr. Gilbert said sympathetically. "The important thing to remember is that they are *all* wrong. The color of your skin, or where you are from, has absolutely nothing to do with who you are as a person. The true question is what you are willing to do to prove your value. It was very difficult for me to get into medical school, but I did it, and I succeeded." He looked at Elizabeth proudly. "Elizabeth did, as well."

Minnie nodded thoughtfully. "Mama told me it was hard for Elizabeth in the South, though. Even though she was a doctor."

Elizabeth grunted. "Being in the South is hard for a lot of people." Her eyes darkened. "I hated it while I was there. I feel sorry for the mindset that believes different people are inferior. Personally, I believe Italians are superior to everyone else!"

Minnie's eyes narrowed. "Well, I happen to believe the *Irish* are superior to everyone else."

Carrie stepped in. "How about if we agree that every human being is equally wonderful?"

Elizabeth rolled her eyes. "Fine." She grinned at Minnie. "Your mama was always the reasonable one." She lowered her voice to a whisper. "How about if we agree on equality for all, but hold onto the belief that perhaps we're a *little* better?"

Minnie giggled and nodded enthusiastically.

Dr. Gilbert grew serious. "I'm afraid things are going to be more difficult in the years ahead."

Carrie didn't have to ask what he was referring to. "Because of the economic crisis."

Dr. Gilbert's silver hair flashed in the late afternoon sun that streamed through the dining room window. "This crisis has been coming for a long time, but most people didn't want to see it. Abby saw it, of course. We talked about it at length when she was last here. I've been exchanging letters with her and Thomas throughout the winter."

Carrie eyed him with surprise. "I didn't know that. I realize they both spend hours in the library communicating with people across the country, but I didn't know you were one of them."

"Your parents are quite thoughtful and clear-thinking. I'm glad I listened to your mother. Because of her, I stepped back from the stock market last year. I shudder to think what could have happened if I had ignored the signs like most others."

Carrie's thoughts flew to Wally and Nancy.

Dr. Gilbert continued. "It's been less than a week. The Stock Exchange remains closed, but its closure has done nothing to diminish the panic sweeping across the country. People are already losing their jobs. Unemployment will increase as the depression deepens."

"Which means immigrants are going to be blamed for taking American jobs," Alice said, shaking her head in disgust. "Things never change."

"This is going to be worse," Dr. Gilbert predicted. "The American economy has gotten much more complicated since the end of the war. The country is heavily industrialized. The majority of workers are employed by the railroads. There's no telling how many of the railroad companies will declare bankruptcy, but I'm certain growth will grind to a halt. Men will be looking elsewhere for work, but there aren't enough jobs. They'll want someone to take their frustration out on." He scowled. "It will be immigrants."

Carrie knew he was right. She thought of everything Abby had been saying for the last few years. Her worry for Wally and Nancy was growing. She forced her thoughts back to the present, but the present was equally worrisome. What would it be like for Frances and Felicia in Boston?

"Stop worrying," Rose commanded quietly.

Carrie looked at her best friend seated to her right. It was no surprise Rose knew what she was thinking. "It's hard." She kept her voice low, hoping the conversation would cover her words.

"Worry doesn't help. You know that," Rose reminded her.

Carrie heard the words, but she saw the truth in Rose's eyes. "You're as worried as I am," she whispered.

A lull in the conversation caused her words to be heard.

Alice smiled. "I think this might be a good time to mention what I wanted to talk with Frances and Felicia about."

Carrie was grateful for a reprieve from her thoughts. "What do you mean?"

Alice looked at the older girls. "I understand the two of you are looking for a place to live while you're here."

"That's right," Frances said.

"I might have a solution for you," Alice replied. "I've only been in Boston a few weeks. I stayed here with the Gilberts until a few days ago. I've been saving money over my years of travel with Elizabeth Packard. I was able to buy a home recently."

Carrie listened intently, praying this was going where she thought it might. She could tell Rose was hoping for the same thing.

"The house is bigger than I need, but I bought it on purpose, thinking it could provide housing for young women coming to Boston."

Frances' eyes widened. "Are you saying we could live with you?"

"If it's something that appeals to you. You're starting a new life. This is a new America, where women have more rights—at least in Massachusetts. You have the freedom to make the choices that are right for you."

Carrie wanted to know more about what Alice meant

regarding Massachusetts, but that could wait. She fought to keep a neutral expression on her face. It wasn't her place to influence the girls' decision.

Frances exchanged a questioning look with Felicia and obviously saw what she was hoping to see. Her eyes sparkled with excitement. "We would love to live with you!"

Alice looked delighted. "You're certain?"

Frances laughed. "I get to start medical school while I'm living with a practicing doctor that went to school with my mama? I can't imagine anything more perfect."

Felicia looked more thoughtful. "I agree that it's perfect, but only if we can afford it. I'm afraid we won't be able to pay a lot in the beginning."

"I thought about that," Alice said. "I don't need your money. I was able to pay cash for my home."

"We won't stay there for no—" Felicia began.

Alice held up a hand to silence her. "I don't need your money, but I could certainly use help around the house." She turned to Frances. "Are you a cook like your sister?"

Minnie snorted with laughter. "Only if you're interested in a starvation diet."

Frances glared at Minnie, but she joined the laughter around the table. "I'm afraid my culinary skills are limited to eating what someone else has cooked." She grinned. "I'm quite good at that."

Carrie stepped in to help her daughter. "Don't feel bad, honey. If I remember correctly, Alice's cooking is limited to biscuits." She didn't suspect Alice's years married to Sherman Archer had changed that.

They'd had plenty of household help.

"That might possibly be true," Alice admitted. "Felicia?" she asked hopefully.

Felicia shook her head. "Mama told me I was going to regret not learning how to cook, but when you have a grandma like mine doing the cooking, I never saw a reason to spend my time working over a hot stove."

"We could never get her out of the library," Rose added with a smile.

Alice eyed them. "Well, girls, it looks like we're going to learn a new skill. Either that or go hungry."

Carrie and Rose looked at each other with delight.

Rose was the first to speak. "Being a brilliant businesswoman is a great thing, Felicia, but you do have to eat." She made no effort to hide the amusement in her voice.

"At least until I make enough money to hire a cook," Felicia retorted.

"I hope that happens soon," Frances said fervently.

"Probably not soon enough," Carrie teased.

"You're not a great cook either, Mama," Frances reminded her.

Carrie chuckled. "I won't argue that point, but I have Annie. Part of living on your own is

figuring out how to do things for yourself."

"Besides," Elizabeth added, "we never starved when we were in medical school. Our meals may not have been fancy, but we didn't go hungry."

Gertrude entered the dining room with a tray full of desserts in time to hear the comment. "I tried to teach this girl how to cook when she was growing up, but she told me she had more *important* things to do."

"I did," Elizabeth protested. "I was helping Daddy in the clinic. Besides, you were such a wonderful cook. You told me you were happy to make sure no one was hungry, as long as we were taking care of sick people."

"Really?" Frances looked at Gertrude speculatively. "Gertrude..."

Gertrude threw up her hands. "You can take that thought right out of your head, Frances Wallington. I'll not be cooking for three able-bodied women just because you're lazy!"

Felicia laughed. "It was worth a try, Frances. Perhaps, though, we can get her to teach us a few things."

Frances' eyes were dancing. "Maybe in the future. We'll keep everyone here as long as we can." She smiled at Minnie. "My little sister will keep us from going hungry. I knew she would come in handy!"

Minnie tossed her head. "Only if you cook next to me. It's time you learned how to cook. I won't always be around to keep you from going hungry."

"You could leave her here with us, Mama," said Frances.

"I will not be losing two of my daughters at the same time. You're on your own, darling. I know the three of you well enough to know you won't starve. You'll figure it out. It's one of the joys of growing up," Carrie teased.

"She's right," Rose agreed. "Besides, it will be great motivation to succeed even faster, Felicia. You'll be determined to succeed in order to hire a cook. This might actually be the best strategy to make sure our investment is returned."

Felicia appealed to Dr. Gilbert for support. "Do you see what we have to deal with?"

Dr. Gilbert added his laughter to the rest. "When we sent Elizabeth down to Philadelphia to medical school, she asked if we would send Gertrude to cook for her."

Carrie whirled on her friend. "You did what?"

Elizabeth laughed helplessly. "Obviously, the answer was no. He threw me to the wolves and told me I would have to figure it out."

"No one starved," Dr. Gilbert reminded her. He looked toward his wife. "Matilda, what happened to the days when young women were raised to become cooks and housekeepers?"

"Oh, that happens in most households, but we are in a room full of young women who desire to be anything but normal." Matilda smiled. "I seem to remember you insisting Elizabeth didn't need to learn mundane household chores, my dear."

Dr. Gilbert looked suitably abashed. "I suppose that could be true."

"*Could* be?" Matilda teased. "Face it, dear. We are surrounded by doctors and a budding businesswoman. Their focus is on something quite different."

"But..." Dr. Gilbert focused his attention on Carrie. "I thought Southern plantation daughters were raised to be proper wives."

Carrie smirked. "I'm afraid my mother was doomed to be disappointed. She tried her best, but I resisted."

"Is this what America is coming to?" Dr. Gilbert groaned. "Houses full of women who have no interest in being homemakers?" His eyes twinkled.

"Yes!" Even Hope added to the chorus from every female at the table.

"Don't worry," Felicia added. "There will always be women looking for jobs. We'll hire them and treat them with value as our equals. It will be for the best."

Dr. Gilbert pushed back from the table as everyone laughed. "And on that note, I'm going into the clinic to treat patients. They're much easier to control!"

―――※―――

Carrie inhaled the early fall air. The street in front of the Gilberts' home was empty, but she could hear an occasional carriage rolling by a few streets over. Street lanterns cast a flickering glow on the cobblestones as the wind rustled the thick canopy of leaves that stretched overhead. A few lingering rose blooms perfumed the air with their sweet scent. She could hear laughter through the closed windows as she relaxed against the cushions of the porch swing.

"May I join you?"

Carrie smiled with delight when Alice stepped outside. "I would be thrilled."

Alice settled down onto the swing and pulled a sweater closer around her shoulders. "I do believe summer is over."

"In Boston," Carrie agreed. "We'll have more hot weather on the plantation before fall truly arrives."

"I hope to someday visit the plantation," Alice replied wistfully. "I've heard many wonderful things about it."

"I'd love to have you come for Christmas," Carrie said. She'd been thinking of extending the invitation ever since the decision had been made a few hours earlier for Frances and Felicia to live with Alice. "It's a very special time."

"Invitation accepted!" A pensive look settled on Alice's face. "The last few years have been so busy that I've seldom taken a break. Coming to the plantation would be a dream come true. Thank you."

Carrie was filled with admiration. "Consider it my way of thanking you. You and Elizabeth Packard have achieved wonderful things. I'd like to hear more about it, but first I want to know how you are. I haven't seen you since…"

Alice finished for her. "Since you rescued me from the asylum. I know I've said thank you many times, but the longer I'm free and the more I've learned about asylums, the more I appreciate the risk you took to get me out of there."

"You would have done the same for me," Carrie answered.

Alice shook her head. "I'm not certain of that, Carrie. My experiences in the last few years have given me confidence in what I can do, but the woman in that asylum was someone who lived in constant fear."

"A woman who constantly lived in fear would never have had the courage to go to medical school, Alice," Carrie protested.

"Perhaps," Alice answered, "but I let Sherman take control of my life. I lived in fear of displeasing or disappointing him. I became someone I barely recognized."

"He did that to you," Carrie said, her anger resurfacing. Sherman had been fired from his job after his boss learned what he'd done. She hoped he was suffering somewhere, and not causing another wife immeasurable pain.

Alice shifted on the swing to look more directly at Carrie. "I *let* him do that to me. Yes, Sherman is a terrible person, but my fear let him take control of me. During those years, I thought often about Janie leaving her husband when he was abusive. I wanted to walk out like she did, catch a train, and go somewhere safe. I had that choice." She cleared her throat. "I didn't make it."

Alice continued. "The most powerful aspect about the last few years on the road with

Elizabeth Packard is that I was able to face my part in what happened. As she and I have fought to pass legislation and improve conditions in asylums, the thing I have loved most is talking to women in similar situations. My greatest joy has come when my words give other women the courage to walk away. There are times when marriages can be saved, but there are times a woman has to choose her own value and make the decision to leave."

Carrie squeezed Alice's hand. "I'm proud of you," she said. "I love knowing the girls will have you in their lives while they are here."

Alice smiled. "Frances and Felicia are very special. Your daughter reminds me of you. It's difficult to believe she's adopted. She has the exact same fire and passion you did when I first met you in

Philadelphia seven years ago."

Carrie blinked. "Only seven years ago? It seems as if I've lived an entire lifetime in those years."

"Both of us have," Alice said. "You've created such a beautiful life for yourself, Carrie. I'm proud of you, too." She clasped Carrie's hands in both of hers. "I'm deeply sorry about Robert and Bridget. I can only imagine the pain you suffered when you lost them. We've both endured terrible things."

"We didn't merely endure them," Carrie wiped away the tears that sprang up when Alice mentioned Robert and Bridget. "We lived through them and became better women. I don't know anyone who doesn't go through hardships. It's not what you go through that matters, it's what you choose to do with it."

Alice regarded her thoughtfully. "You've become wise."

Carrie laughed. "Wise enough to listen to my mother. I don't know where I would be without Abby. She's been a gift to my father, but she's been an equal gift to me. Combined with everything Rose's mother, Old Sarah, taught me, I have a powerful foundation. I will forever be grateful."

"I'm looking forward to getting to know Abby over Christmas."

Carrie changed the subject. "Will you tell me more about the legislation passed by Elizabeth Packard, and why you think the girls are safer in Massachusetts?"

"You already know I chose to finish medical school when I was released from the asylum and divorced Sherman. After graduating, I decided to delay practicing medicine and instead joined Elizabeth in her fight for women's rights. After what I'd been through in the asylum, I felt it was what I had to do.

Traveling with her was both challenging and eye-opening. She has been tireless in fighting for the rights of mental hospital patients, as well as bolstering the rights of married women. There are many remaining battles to be fought, but laws have been changed in Illinois, Iowa, Maine, and Massachusetts. Husbands no longer have the right to commit their wives to an asylum without due legal process. There must be evidence of mental health issues, and there must be a hearing or trial."

"It should be that way everywhere!" Carrie said. "I can only imagine how many women are suffering right this minute."

"It's terrible," Alice agreed. "Every woman I talked to made me relive my own experience." She paused when her voice wobbled.

Carrie understood the trauma of imprisonment in the asylum would likely affect Alice for the rest of her life, just as Robert's murder and Bridget's death would never leave her.

"There are regular visiting teams that monitor conditions in asylums in those four states. She's gotten laws passed that make it illegal for asylum officials to intercept patients' mail." Alice smiled. "That particular piece of legislation is named 'Packard's Law.'"

"Wonderful!" Carrie exclaimed.

"It is," Alice said. "But we've only begun. There is a tremendous amount left to do. Elizabeth has published many books, and she gives countless speeches in order to garner publicity for her campaigns, but she faces opposition from the increasingly organized and powerful psychiatric profession."

"Why?" Carrie demanded. "They should support what she's doing more than anyone. Surely they care about their patients?"

Alice rolled her eyes. "Men don't like to give up control, especially in regard to women. We can pass legislation, but it's up to each asylum to ensure it's adhered to." Her face tensed. "Women will fight an uphill battle for rights in this country for a long time. Women's property rights are what I was referring to when I said Massachusetts is safer for women. I know Frances plans to return to Virginia, but if Felicia stays in Boston, her income will be more secure."

"As a single woman or a married woman?" Carrie asked.

"Legally, either," Alice answered.

"What do you mean *legally*?"

Felicia stepped out onto the porch. "Yes, what do you mean?" She had the grace to look embarrassed. "I haven't been eavesdropping for long, but when I heard my name, I had to know what you were talking about."

Alice smiled. "I would have done the same thing, my dear." She pointed toward an empty chair on the porch. "Have a seat." Once Felicia had settled in, she asked her a question. "Are you familiar with coverture?"

Felicia's eyes narrowed with distaste. "Unfortunately, yes. Coverture is the English common law system. Married women cannot own property, control their wages, enter into contracts, or do anything autonomous to their husband's authority. They have no control over where their children live and..." Her eyes narrowed into slits. "They have to submit sexually to their husbands at all times."

Alice looked shocked. "How do you know all that?"

"Our Felicia is a walking book," Carrie replied. "There isn't much she doesn't have a solid understanding of."

Felicia shrugged. "I like knowledge, so I spend my time attaining it. That knowledge has convinced me I'm not interested in marrying any time soon. I have no intention in giving up control of my life."

"I completely understand how you feel," Alice replied. "I've been studying and reading endlessly since I divorced my husband. Ignorance is no excuse for bad choices. I never intend to make myself vulnerable again. I might, perhaps, marry again in the future, but I will protect myself."

"Back to the legal issue," Felicia prompted. "I'm not married, but isn't it true that many states, including all of the northern states, have passed *Married Women's Property Acts* to provide protection?"

"There have been steps taken in many states, but it isn't enough," Alice answered. "*Married Women's Property Acts* have made it possible for women to control real and personal property, enter into contracts and lawsuits, inherit independent of their husbands, work for a salary, and write wills."

"Aren't those good things?" Carrie asked.

"Theoretically," Alice told her. "Most of those changes were made because of concerns for family integrity and to ensure a household was protected from economic crisis." Her voice tightened. "I'm afraid the laws have very little to do, however, with a liberal conception of the role of women."

"What do you mean?" Felicia asked keenly.

"I'll give you an example. Six years ago, in 1867, the Illinois Supreme Court heard the case of a wife conveying real estate without the consent of her husband. It was quite a complicated case, so it went all the way to the state Supreme Court. When it was over, the court sided with the husband." Alice shook her head. "Their position was so ridiculous, I actually memorized it so I could share it with other women." She dropped her voice several octaves. *"It is simply impossible that a married woman should be able to control and enjoy her property as if she were sole, without practically leaving her at liberty to annul the marriage."*

"That's absurd," Carrie snapped.

"It is," Alice agreed. "Felicia, if you decide to marry in the future, you'll be more protected here, but how closely the law is followed is often solely based on the man who hears the case. You already know that not all men support women's rights."

"I'm lucky," Carrie said fervently. She trusted Anthony, but before they were married, she and Susan, advised by Abby, had taken steps to protect their business partnership in Cromwell Stables. She and Janie had taken the same steps with the medical clinic.

Alice faced her. "Are you? I wouldn't be so certain."

Carrie furrowed her brow. "What do you mean? Susan and I are sole owners of Cromwell Stables. I trust

Anthony explicitly, but we are protected."

Alice hesitated a moment but opted for direct honesty. "Carrie, you should know that Virginia has not passed legislation to protect women's rights. When it was brought to the legislature in the 1840s, they debated and rejected it. You may have papers saying you and Susan own Cromwell Stables, but there is nothing in those papers that would stand up in a court of law. In the state of Virginia, your husband is in control of your business."

Carrie was speechless. How could she not have known this? She pushed aside the spark of fear that ignited. Anthony would never attempt to take control of her financially. Neither would Susan's husband, Harold. Still, the lack of control was unsettling. Another question demanded to be answered. How could Abby not know this?"

Alice eyed her with compassion, but her tone was firm when she continued. "I know you trust Anthony, but you need to be involved in changing the laws in Virginia. Every other married woman you know is at grave risk. Even men we trust can change, Carrie. I've heard the stories over and over. Everything women own, or think they own, can be taken away from them. They have no legal recourse to get it back."

Carrie couldn't find words to respond. She struggled to process what she was hearing.

Alice wasn't done. "At least Virginia isn't as bad as Tennessee. When it was brought up to the Tennessee legislature, they stated that married women lack independent souls and thus should not be allowed to own property."

The audacity of the statement freed Carrie's tongue. "That is complete nonsense!"

"Of course it is," Alice replied, "but if you are a married woman in Tennessee, it doesn't

change the fact that you have no rights." She paused. "The same as in Virginia."

Felicia stood abruptly and began to pace the porch. "Carrie, the Bregdan Women have to fight this. You're teaching women to be independent, but the laws won't protect them!"

Carrie took a deep breath. Felicia was right.

The question was—what could be done?

Chapter Twelve

Abby hugged Thomas tightly, inexplicably anxious as he prepared to leave without her. She knew she'd made the right decision to stay in New York with Nancy, but the knowledge didn't make it easier.

"It feels wrong to leave," Thomas said.. "I wish I could do something to help Wally. Perhaps if I stay..." His voice trailed off.

Abby shook her head. "I don't want Nancy to be right, but maybe when you're gone, Wally will finally leave the bedroom. She is adamant that he is too ashamed for you to see him." She laid her hand gently on his shoulder when Thomas looked ready to continue his protest. "We've talked about this. It doesn't matter if it makes sense or not—it's how Wally feels. Nancy has never seen him like this. If your leaving will make it easier for Wally to face what has happened, we must support it."

Thomas sighed in defeat. "You'll be home in a week? Annie might never forgive you if you don't make it back in time for the picnic for the children who were adopted from the black orphanage. She's been planning this since the day they arrived from Richmond."

"I'll be home," Abby promised. "I can't leave

Nancy. Even though I feel helpless, it's important that she not be alone. Thank you for understanding."

Thomas embraced her one more time, stepped into the wagon, and motioned the driver
forward.

Abby watched until the carriage disappeared around the corner before she climbed the stairs to the house. The beautiful home that usually sang with laughter was oddly silent. Heaviness hung in the air like a threatening thundercloud.

Wally had not left his bedroom since the day the market had crashed ten days earlier. The Stock Exchange remained closed. The news had grown progressively worse as the crisis spread throughout the country. Tens of thousands of jobs had already been lost. Scores of banks had failed. More railroads had gone bankrupt.

Abby looked up hopefully when Michael walked out the front door. Had Thomas' departure already worked the magic Nancy believed it would?

Michael shook his head, shattering her hope that Wally had finally agreed to see his son. "He won't talk to me. I'm tempted to bust the door down, but Mother has kept me from doing it so far."

Abby ached for Michael. The brown curls she loved were limp and disheveled from him raking his fingers through them. Brown eyes mirrored his confusion and distress.

The economic crisis was being felt in his real estate firm, but he insisted he and Julie would be fine. His wife, having come from a life of poverty, had insisted they remain frugal, even when money started flowing in. Their simple lifestyle would allow them to weather the storm.

"How long will he stay locked in his room?" Michael asked. "He won't even allow Mother in. I've never seen her this upset and afraid." His eyes flashed with anger. "Doesn't he know what he's doing to her? He's not the only person who lost everything! People across the country are facing consequences from the crash. Most importantly to me, my mother has lost everything. Doesn't he care?"

Abby didn't have an answer. She stepped forward and wrapped her arms around him, thinking of the small boy she used to comfort when life delivered hard blows. He was a grown man, but Michael was facing things he had never been forced to confront.

"Will it get better?" Michael asked.

Abby was glad to have an answer to at least one question. "The economy will get better," she said firmly. "This is not the first financial crisis the country has faced. You weren't born when everything came crashing down in 1837. I was only twenty, but I remember it well. My father lost his business, and he lost his money when the bank closed. The situation was so bad, the banks here in New York ran out of gold and silver. More than forty percent of the banks in the country failed. Businesses closed, causing mass unemployment."

"And just thirty-six years later, we're repeating the same thing?" Michael looked toward his father's bedroom window. "How did your father handle it?"

Abby almost wished she could tell him her father had collapsed from the same despair Wally was feeling. In truth, she didn't understand why Wally had closed everyone out. At the time when he needed his family the most, he was blocking them from his life. At the time they desperately needed him, he had hidden away. "It was hard, Michael. We moved from our big house into a much smaller one. We did without a lot of things. This was before Charles and I married and started our factories. Father suffered, but he assured me there were positive forces at work that, in time, would invigorate the economy. He was right. Railroads began to expand, and the country became more industrialized. New jobs were created. Things were hard for seven years, but as my father predicted, the economy improved."

"The very railroads that proved to be part of the solution back then are the core reason of our demise now," Michael said bitterly.

"The country hasn't learned its lessons," Abby said.

"Will it ever?"

Abby took a deep breath. "I honestly don't know. Individuals can learn lessons, but the economy is often impacted by mass greed and corruption beyond our control."

Michael looked thoughtful. "Julie and I have you to thank, Abby."

"What do you mean?"

"You talked with Julie last year about your fears for the economy and your concerns about what corporations are doing to the country. I didn't want you to be correct because business was going well, but Julie believed you. She insisted we remain frugal and not join in my father's investments." He closed his eyes for a moment. "If I didn't love my wife so much, I would be in the same situation as my father. He urged me to invest in the same companies he did this last year. He was angry when I refused..." Michael's eyes darkened with pain.

Abby's heartache increased. "You and Julie did the right thing, Michael. Your parents will get through this."

"Will they?" Michael demanded. "Mother tells me they've lost everything. I checked with my friend at Cooke, and he confirmed my father put up the house as collateral for a loan so he could invest more heavily in the market. He also confirmed they've lost the little money they had left when the bank closed." He clenched his fists in frustration. "Julie and I have been frugal, but I lost money when the banks closed, as well."

This was news to Abby. "How much?"

"Not everything," Michael assured her. "Julie insisted we keep most of our money at home when she saw signs of what you had predicted. I was too busy working to pay attention to the indicators that were there." He shook his head again. "We have some money, but not enough to save this house."

Abby felt what had become a familiar flash of anger toward Wally. His greed and fear had created an untenable situation for his family. Hiding in his bedroom wouldn't solve it, but she supposed she could understand his reluctance to face the consequences of his decisions. Still, Nancy needed her husband. Michael needed his father. He had looked up to him since childhood, and relied on his advice.

"You'll take it one day at a time," Abby said, forcing herself to remain calm. She knew it was a weak answer, but it was the only one she had to give. "When everything around you is dark, focus on taking the next step. In time, there will be light to illuminate that step." She took Michael's hand. "Nothing is going to change quickly, but it will change."

Abby wanted to assure him that his father would emerge from the bedroom and offer a plan to recover from this massive setback, but she couldn't bring herself to make a promise there was no evidence to support. Her only choice was to hold onto hope.

Two days later, Abby found Nancy huddled over a cup of hot tea at the kitchen table. A stiff breeze off the Atlantic had brought in cooler air during the night. Her friend would normally be exhilarated by the promise of fall; laughing and singing with joy. Today, her hunched shoulders revealed nothing but fear and confusion.

Abby didn't have to ask if Wally had left the bedroom. Nancy hadn't seen her husband for six days. He had refused to eat anything during that time and demanded the newspaper be placed outside his door. News of the Stock Exchange's continued closure dominated the headlines.

"He didn't even take the paper this morning."

Abby wanted to cry when her friend peered at her through red, swollen eyes. She wrapped an arm around

Nancy's shoulders. "I'm sorry," she whispered. She longed for something more to say, but she knew nothing would hold meaning. She could do nothing except be there.

"I'm scared," Nancy said, her voice barely audible. "I don't know the man in that bedroom. I don't know what to do for him." She paused. "It's only money, Abby. I know we've lost everything, but we didn't have much when we started our marriage. We can make more money." She shook her head. "I'm confused. Michael is confused. Why won't he come out of the bedroom? Nothing will change until he does."

Abby had no answer. She could only hope her presence made her friend feel less alone.

Michael appeared at the kitchen door. "Father?"

Nancy smiled at him sadly. "No, dear."

BOOM!

Abby jerked from the power of the explosion.

Nancy screamed with fear and covered her ears as she looked wildly around the kitchen.

Michael ran to the backdoor, peering out into the yard. "What was that?"

Abby knew instantly but couldn't bring herself to say the words. She fought to breathe through the horror

When Michael didn't see anything outside, he whirled around and stared up at the ceiling with stunned disbelief.

Abby watched as realization set in. She forced herself to stand. "We need to go check on your father." She tried to keep her voice steady but failed. Her whole body was trembling.

Nancy jerked her hands away from her ears. "Why?"

Abby couldn't find the words to communicate her fear. "I'll go upstairs," was all she could manage.

"Why?" Nancy's forced whisper ended on a shrill note.

Abby said nothing as she left the kitchen and made her way toward the staircase. She felt as if she were walking through deep mud as she started up the steps.

Michael rushed past her, racing up the stairs two at a time.

Abby wished she could stop him, but nothing would soften the impact of what they were about to discover. The moment she'd heard the explosion, she'd known it was a gunshot. The idea that Wally could be lying in the bedroom, alive and needing help, was the only thing that gave her the courage to finish climbing the stairs.

Michael stood outside the bedroom, frozen in place, with his hand on the doorknob.

Abby gently removed his hand and pushed open the door.

Michael collapsed to his knees the moment it swung open. "No," he groaned. "No..."

Bile rose in Abby's throat as tears streamed down her face.

Wally, a revolver by his side, lay slumped against the bedroom wall. Blood splatter created a gruesome halo behind him.

His sightless eyes stared through them.

"No! No! No!" Nancy's scream filled the air. She ran to her husband and dropped to her knees. "Wally! Wally! No!"

Abby started forward.

Nancy whipped her head around. "Help him! Michael, you must go for help!"

Abby laid a gentle hand on her shoulder.

Nancy jerked away, her expression manic. "Abby, he needs help. You must get help!"

Abby met Michael's eyes across the room. Devastated pain radiated from his entire being.

Wally was dead.

Abby knelt down beside her friend. "I'm sorry, Nancy," she whispered, wishing she didn't have to speak the next words. "Wally is dead."

"He is *not* dead!" Nancy screamed. "Why aren't you getting help?" Her voice grew harsh and panicked. "Michael, go get help for your father. Why are you not moving?" Her eyes blazed with desperation.

It was Michael who pulled his mother to her feet and wrapped her in his strong embrace. "We can't help him, Mother. He's dead." His voice trembled, but his words were resolute.

Nancy tried to break free, but he held her firmly.

"I'm sorry, Mother. Father is gone."

This time, the words broke through Nancy's fog of denial. She whimpered and began to shake uncontrollably, sobs wracking her entire body. "Why?" she whispered. She buried her face in Michael's chest. "Why?"

Abby did the only thing she knew how to do; she took control of the situation. "Michael, take your mother downstairs to the kitchen and make a pot of tea. I'll go contact the authorities."

As she spoke, a cry sounded from the bedroom down the hall. Bridget was awake.

Michael shook his head. "Mother needs *you*, Abby. Bridget needs you. I'll take her downstairs and wait until you get Bridget, but then I'm going to the authorities. I'll send for Julie, as well."

Abby nodded. Michael knew what to do, and where to go, because of his years on the police force.

Michael led Nancy toward the door. When her knees crumbled beneath her, he lifted her gently into his arms, cradled her against his broad chest as she continued to sob, and left the room.

Abby's heart swelled with both grief and tenderness as she watched him care for his mother. Nancy was going to endure unimaginable pain, but at least she wasn't alone. Michael and Julie would take exceptional care of her.

Michael paused at the top of the stairs. "What are you going to do?" he asked quietly.

Abby was already writing the telegram in her head that would explain why she wouldn't be at the picnic for the adopted orphans. "I'm staying with your mother," she said. "For as long as she needs me." Though Charles hadn't died from suicide, she knew what it was like to lose a spouse.

She knew how easy it was to lose hope.

Chapter Thirteen

Carrie pulled her sweater tighter to her body. The front that had blown in the night before had dropped the temperature down to close to forty. Though the sun was bright, the weather warranted a sweater. It was her favorite kind of day.

She, Rose, and the girls were returning from a day of shopping. The carriage bulged with bags of necessities, or at least what Frances and Felicia deemed necessities. Carrie was loath to dampen their enthusiasm by pointing out that they would probably never use much of what they'd bought. The girls were starting a brand-new life, and she wanted it to be full of joy and possibility.

Minnie and Hope had done their fair share of finding things they were convinced they couldn't live without. In all fairness, she and Rose had found items not to be discovered in Richmond. The sweater hugging her was one of them. Anthony would laugh when he saw their luggage. The entire day had been so much fun that neither she nor Rose had found it in their hearts to refuse any of the girls' purchases.

Peter and Elizabeth had joined them for lunch. It galled Carrie that they couldn't have entered the restaurant without a man to escort them, but she had to believe that would change in time. The day would be a memory she would always treasure.

When the carriage pulled up in front of the Gilberts' home, a telegram delivery boy was leaving the porch. He jumped into his carriage with a tip of his hat, and urged his horse forward at a rapid clip.

Dr. Gilbert waved an envelope in their direction. "Does one of you happen to be Dr. Carrie Wallington?" he called.

Carrie leapt from the carriage and hurried up the walkway. In her experience, telegrams were a vehicle for either joy or tragedy. Which would this be?

"Who is it from, Mama?" Minnie asked.

"It's from Abby!" Carrie eagerly tore open the envelope, hoping for good news. What she read wiped the smile from her face and ripped the air from her lungs. She stared at the single sheet of paper in shock.

"Carrie?"

Rose's voice broke through. Carrie read the brief message one more time, hoping the few seconds would have somehow changed its contents. They had not. She handed the telegram to her best friend.

Rose grabbed the railing to steady herself as she read. "No," she whispered.

"Mama?" Frances' voice was small and frightened. "Is it Grandpa? Daddy? Is something wrong?"

"No," Carrie assured her. She reached for the telegram, closed it, and slid it into her pocket. "Your father and Grandpa are both fine. Let's go inside where we can talk." She managed to keep her voice steady. Dr. Gilbert watched her with deep concern but remained silent. She gave him a tremulous smile as she walked into the house.

When they were seated in the parlor, Carrie pulled out the telegram again. The girls were old enough to know the truth, even Hope. Hiding it would serve no purpose. She cleared her throat and forced herself to read the unimaginable words.

Wally is dead. Suicide. Staying on with Nancy indefinitely. Meet you at Grand Central Station with Bridget on your way home. No need to stay in New York. Advise arrival. All my love. Abby.

When Carrie finished, no one made a sound. Even the birds fell silent as specks of dust floated through the beams of sunlight shining through the window.

Felicia spoke first. "Mr. Stratford killed himself?"

Felicia had spent the most time with Wally. "Yes," Carrie said. "I'm so sorry."

"Why?" Frances blurted out.

"Because he lost everything when the market crashed," Felicia answered. "I saw the look on his face that day at the Stock Exchange. He looked the same as my first father had when the policemen in Memphis beat on our door during the riot. My father knew he was going to die. I was very young, but I knew he didn't have any hope left. I saw that same look on Mr. Stratford's face."

Carrie knew it was possible. No one else in the parlor had seen Wally since the morning they'd gone to the Stock Exchange. He had sequestered himself in his bedroom for the rest of their visit.

"Poor Nancy," Rose said quietly. "She was already distraught. They lost everything, and now this." Pain radiated from her eyes.

"What will Mrs. Stratford do?" Minnie asked.

"I don't know," Carrie answered. "I do know she has your grandmother. Grandma is staying in New York **so** that Nancy won't be alone."

"She has Michael and Julie, too," Rose reminded the children. "She isn't alone."

"She's losing her home," Felicia said.

Carrie was surprised at the lack of emotion in her voice.

Rose heard it too. She reached over and took her daughter's hand. "Felicia?"

Felicia met her mother's eyes squarely. "Mr. Stratford lost everything, and now he's left his wife alone to deal with it." The lack of emotion in her voice was replaced with anger as her eyes sparkled with tears. "How could he do that?"

Rose looked toward Carrie with a helpless appeal.

Carrie wanted to respond with a wise answer, but the truth was that she was asking the same question. She wondered if Abby would know what to say.

Dr. Gilbert cleared his throat. "May I?"

"Please do," Rose implored.

Dr. Gilbert turned to Felicia. "Honey, there are people who believe money is the answer to everything. They believe their worth depends on how much money they're able to accumulate. When their money, or their ability to make money, is taken from them, they see no reason to keep living."

Felicia listened closely but her expression lost none of its anger. "Mr. Stratford has a wife and a son. That should have been his reason."

"I agree with you," Dr. Gilbert said steadily. He looked pensive. "Hope can be an elusive thing."

"Hope?" Felicia demanded. "What does that have to do with this?"

"Everything," Dr. Gilbert replied. "I heard you speak the summer you traveled with Sojourner Truth. Do you remember how you felt in Memphis when you watched your parents be murdered by the policemen?"

Rose took a deep breath but didn't interrupt the conversation.

Understanding began to dawn in Felicia's eyes. "I wanted to die with them," she said. "I didn't see a reason to keep living." She paused. "I was going to throw myself on their bodies so the police would shoot me too." Her voice shook with the memory. "Moses saved me."

Carrie thought of the devastated, frightened little girl who had arrived on the plantation seven years earlier.

"If Moses hadn't saved you, what would you have done?" Dr. Gilbert pressed.

"I would have died," Felicia admitted.

"Because in that moment, you had no hope," Dr. Gilbert said gently. "You couldn't see the future because your pain was too great. You wanted the pain to end, so you were going to die with your parents."

Felicia gazed at him. "I understand," she whispered. "Mr. Stratford lost his hope."

"Well, it's still a sin!"

Carrie whipped her head toward Minnie when she spoke. Had she heard her daughter correctly? "What?"

"Suicide is a sin," Minnie repeated, her expression a mixture of defiance and fear. "My first mama told me that. So did my first daddy. Catholics believe suicide is a sin." Her voice trembled. "Mama, is Mr. Stratford in Hell now?"

Carrie struggled with how to answer such a huge question. She opened her mouth, but nothing came out.

"Of course he's not in Hell," Felicia said firmly. "I may not completely understand why he left his family, but I know it's not some kind of unforgiveable sin."

"How do you know that?" Minnie demanded. "Are you saying my parents lied to me?"

Carrie wanted to step in, but since she had no idea what to say, she decided to let the conversation play out. Suicide had never been a topic of conversation. She'd known some soldiers who had committed suicide, and there had been moments she'd contemplated it herself after Robert's and Bridget's deaths, but she had never discussed it with anyone, not even Rose.

Carrie hated that Wally's death had become about *how* he died, but she couldn't change that reality. Perhaps Felicia had something helpful to contribute. The expression on Rose's face said she agreed, so Carrie settled back to listen.

"I had a friend at Oberlin who committed suicide," Felicia began. "We weren't extremely close, but it upset me. It upset me enough that one of my professors pointed me toward literature about suicide. I was sad she was gone, but I was mostly upset because I heard other students talking about her going to Hell. I didn't want to believe that was true."

"Just because you don't want to believe something doesn't mean it's not true," Minnie argued.

"You're right," Felicia replied. "I didn't change my mind until I did a lot of research. It helped me, Minnie." Her expression was full of compassion.

Minnie relaxed a little when she realized she wasn't being attacked for her belief. "What did you learn?"

"First, I started from the premise that the God I know wouldn't punish someone who was in so much pain that they would kill themselves," Felicia said. "My friend, Marion, was a lovely person. Then, something very bad happened to her..." Her voice trailed off."

Carrie knew Felicia was wondering what was appropriate to discuss with Hope in the room. Since they were discussing suicide, however, she thought Hope was old enough to hear about rape. Gloria had probably talked to her best friend about her rape in the alley, but it wasn't Carrie's decision to make.

Rose solved her dilemma. "You're saying Marion was raped."

Felicia looked at her with surprise. "Yes," she said slowly.

"That's what happened to Gloria," Hope said angrily. "Men did a very bad thing to her."

"You're right, Hope," Felicia answered. "Rape is a very bad thing." She returned to the story. "Marion kept getting sadder and more depressed. She went from being outgoing, to becoming completely isolated." She frowned. "I was so focused on my studies, I didn't truly see what was happening until it was too late. She left a letter saying she simply didn't want to live her life anymore because she had no hope it would ever get better." Felicia shook her head. "I know what Christians believe about suicide, but I couldn't accept that God would punish someone who went through something terrible by sending her to Hell."

"She should have trusted God to give her hope," Minnie said stubbornly. "Not kill herself."

Carrie looked at her daughter with surprise. She realized they had never discussed religion. Carrie believed in God, but she didn't consider herself an overly religious person. Evidently, Minnie had been deeply influenced by her Catholic parents before they died.

"Perhaps," Felicia agreed. "I believe Dr. Gilbert is right. When my parents were murdered, I was ready to commit a form of suicide. I wanted the policemen to kill me. If Daddy hadn't saved me, I would be dead. Would God have sent me to Hell because I couldn't live with my parents' murder?"

Minnie opened her mouth to argue again but remained silent.

Carrie knew Felicia's question had turned a religious belief into something quite personal. She watched conflicting emotions race across Minnie's face.

When Minnie spoke again, it was to ask a question. "You said you did research?"

Felicia nodded, relieved to leave her own history and return to the knowledge she had gained. "Suicide has always existed. Even in ancient times, there were people who chose to kill themselves. The Romans and the Greeks had a pretty relaxed view of suicide. There was a Greek thinker named Pythagoras who was against it, but his stance was based more on mathematical than moral grounds. He believed there was a finite number of souls for use in the world, and that the sudden and unexpected departure of one would upset a delicate balance. Aristotle condemned suicide, but only because he believed it robbed the community as a whole of the services of one of its members."

Carrie listened closely. She'd never considered the history of suicide.

"In Rome, suicide was never a criminal act, but it was specifically forbidden in three cases," Felicia continued. "You couldn't commit suicide if you were accused of capital crimes, if you were a soldier, or if you were a slave."

Frances looked shocked. "What sense does that make?"

Felicia rolled her eyes. "The reason behind the three cases was the same. It was *uneconomic* for those people to die."

"*Uneconomic?*" Rose exclaimed.

"The State lost the right to seize property if a person accused of a crime killed themselves before their trial and conviction," Felicia explained. "Of course, they closed that little loophole when it was decreed that those who died prior to trial had no legal heirs, which meant the State got everything."

"Convenient," Carrie muttered.

"Quite," Felicia replied. "If a soldier committed suicide, it was treated as if he deserted. The military didn't want to lose an asset. In the third case, if a slave killed himself within six months of purchase, the master could claim a full refund from the former owner." She let her words sink in. "On the other hand, the Romans fully approved of suicides committed as an alternative to dishonor. They considered them something like a *patriotic* suicide." She paused. "The truth is no one made a big deal of suicide until the Christian Church."

Matilda and Elizabeth had walked in during the discussion. They hadn't heard the news about Wally, but they had heard most of the conversation.

"The Catholic Church is very opposed to suicide," Matilda said.

Minnie looked at their hostess. "Are you Catholic?" When Matilda nodded, she looked relieved to not be alone with her beliefs. "My first family was Catholic. My mother told me she was very devout."

"As most Irish are," Matilda answered. "As well as Italians."

Carrie's knowledge of Catholicism was limited, but she wanted to understand her daughter's beliefs better. "What do Catholics say about suicide?"

Before Matilda could reply, Dr. Gilbert interrupted her.

"You should know, dear, that Wally Stratford committed suicide yesterday. Everyone has found out."

"That's terrible!" Matilda and Elizabeth said in unison.

Matilda had never met Wally, but Elizabeth had stayed with the Stratfords on one of her visits with Carrie. She had become quite close to the couple.

"Nancy must be devastated," Elizabeth cried. "And Michael. How awful for them."

"Abby is with her," Carrie told them. "She's going to stay as long as she feels it is necessary."

"What a blessing for Nancy," Matilda murmured.

"Is Mr. Stratford going to Hell, Mrs. Gilbert? No one will tell me. Felicia doesn't believe he will, but my first mama would say he'll go to Hell because he killed himself."

Matilda hesitated, her expression deeply troubled.

"Please tell me the truth," Minnie pleaded. "I'm old enough to know the truth."

Carrie agreed Minnie was old enough, but she had misgivings over whether any religion held the entire truth. She had fought this same battle when she was forced to decide her personal beliefs regarding slavery. "Honey, you're old enough for the truth, but truth can sometimes be complicated. People can look at the same situation and see things very differently."

"I understand, Mama, but I still think I should know what my parents believed."

Carrie couldn't disagree with that. She gave Matilda a small nod.

Matilda looked conflicted as she answered. "Catholics believe death by suicide is a very serious matter. We believe one's life is the property of God. To destroy that life is to say that you, instead of God, are in control of that life. We don't believe that's true." She took a deep breath. "Catholics believe suicide is an unforgiveable sin."

Minnie looked distressed. "So, Mr. Stratford *is* in Hell?"

Matilda looked trapped.

Carrie was sure Matilda had never had her beliefs questioned by a child, nor in a situation so close to home. She supposed it was easier to believe suicide was an unforgiveable sin, until it affected someone you cared about.

Minnie furrowed her brow as the silence stretched out. "Mama, you have always told me that *I'm* in control of my life."

"I have," Carrie agreed. She didn't feel the need to say more at that moment. Questioning was good, though Carrie was glad to have been eighteen before asking questions about slavery. Her daughter was grappling with very serious issues at a young age.

"You should know what the Catholic Church does to people who commit suicide," Felicia added in a tight voice.

"What do they do?" Minnie asked.

"Jesus had been dead for six hundred years before Christians decided suicide was a sin that had to be punished," Felicia told her. "Catholics won't conduct funeral services for people who kill themselves, and they can't be buried in a Catholic cemetery. Their family members are made to live in shame because they committed the unforgiveable sin."

Minnie looked horrified when she turned to Matilda. "Is that true? Is that what the Catholic Church does?"

Matilda looked as if she wanted to flee the room, but she met Minnie's eyes and answered honestly. "Yes."

"Do you believe that's right?" Minnie asked with a trembling voice.

Matilda's olive skin turned a paler shade. "I've never known anyone who committed suicide, Minnie," she confessed. "I suppose it's been easy to believe those teachings. I didn't know Wally Stratford, but I know many of the people who loved him. Most of whom are in this room." She took a deep breath, obviously facing her own struggle. "I'm not sure what I believe now," she admitted as she took Minnie's hand. "We're both going to have to think about what we believe."

"Wally wasn't Catholic," Carrie told Minnie "He will receive a proper service and be buried in the family plot." Abby hadn't said that, but she was confident that was what would happen. Nancy would allow nothing less.

"Mr. Stratford was a kind man. He told me all about the Brooklyn Bridge. Do Catholics really believe he doesn't deserve a proper funeral?" Minnie insisted.

"Minnie, it's not only Catholics that believe suicide is wrong," Felicia said. "In America, it's illegal to commit suicide. If Mr. Stratford had failed in his attempt, he could be in jail now."

"Jail? How would that make him have hope?" Frances asked angrily. "You're saying it's better he actually killed himself!"

Minnie looked thoughtful. "How do you punish someone who is dead?"

Carrie, despite the seriousness of the conversation, had to choke back a laugh. Leave it to her daughter to cut through to the crux of the matter.

"You can't," Felicia said bluntly. "The crime is used to punish the family and cause them to live in shame -

instead of helping the family who lost the person they loved."

Minnie shook her head. "So, it's not just the Catholic Church?" Her confused look intensified. "Does every church believe suicide is a sin? Does every church believe Mr. Stratford is in Hell?"

It was time for Carrie to do more than listen. "Honey, there are a lot of different religious beliefs about many issues. When I was growing up, my church taught me that blacks were inferior to whites, and that the only way they could survive was to live as slaves."

"But that's completely wrong!" Minnie exclaimed.

"I know that now," Carrie replied. "When I was growing up, though, I believed what everyone around me believed. I didn't have a reason to think about it differently."

Minnie eyed her. "What made you change your mind?"

"Rose," Carrie said simply, glancing at her best friend. "You know she used to be Grandpa's slave, but she was my best friend for as long as I can remember. We did everything together." She smiled. "My father told me blacks were inferior, and not as smart as I was, but I knew Rose learned how to read before I did, just by listening in on my lessons." She shook her head. "As I got older, it seemed wrong that she couldn't have the same life I did."

Minnie sighed heavily. "You're right, Mama. That was wrong. Moses and Miles were his slaves, too." Her expression grew more troubled. "It's hard to understand how Grandpa did that."

"Grandpa would say the same thing, because he believes so completely differently now. It's hard for him to accept how he used to be." Carrie paused. "When I turned eighteen, I began to realize how wrong slavery was, but I had to wrestle with beliefs I'd been taught my entire life. If I changed my mind about slavery, it meant I would be going against my family and my neighbors. I would be going against the church." She thought about Robert. "I had to decide if my beliefs were more important than love."

"Love?" Minnie asked. "What do you mean?"

"By the time I began to question, I had met my first husband, Robert. He owned slaves and believed everything my father did. I loved Robert very much, but I knew that if I decided slavery was wrong, it would mean the end of our relationship."

Minnie absorbed what Carrie said. "That must have been hard. What made you finally change your mind?"

Carrie smiled warmly. "I realized the God I knew would never want someone to live in slavery. I had never gone to church very much because there wasn't one close to us. My church was being outside. I saw God in the flowers, in the animals, in the growing tobacco, in the trees..." She relived in her head the moments on the plantation that had introduced her to God. "After what seemed like endless months of struggle, the answer was actually quite simple." She thought back to the experience in her clearing that had blown away the cobwebs of confusion. "I had listened to so many voices—loud voices—that proclaimed the reasons black people were supposed to be slaves. I had listened to equally loud voices that said it was a horrible sin for anyone to be in slavery. They condemned all slave holders, including my father. The voices were shouting in my head, demanding I believe them."

Minnie hung onto every word as Carrie spoke.

Carrie realized she did have the answer for her daughter. She'd had it the entire time. "I finally realized I needed to know God's heart. I was alone in my clearing for a long time one afternoon, desperate for an answer. It was as if God took me into a little bubble and showed me the world from his view. I saw him cry when families were ripped apart at slave auctions. I saw him weep when some abolitionists lashed out with hate. They wanted slaves freed, but they weren't doing it in the right way." She brightened. "I saw him smile when slaves reached freedom in Canada."

"Like Miles," Frances said.

"Like Miles," Carrie agreed. She looked around the room. "It's really so simple. The Bible says it in one sentence. *Thou shalt love thy neighbor as thyself.*" She smiled. "I only need to love people. That's all any of us need to do. Love other people like we want to be loved." She paused, feeling once again the sense of freedom that had poured through her that day. "From that moment on, I knew slavery was wrong and that I had to take action against it."

Minnie stared at her in wonder.

Carrie could practically see the wheels revolving in Minnie's brain.

"Believing someone is going to Hell because they did something you don't agree with isn't very loving," Minnie finally said.

"That's true." Carrie said no more. Her daughter needed to think this through for herself.

"To condemn someone to Hell because they lost hope isn't very loving," Minnie continued. She stood up and walked to the window to look out over the back yard.

"I agree with you, honey."

Minnie fell silent as she gazed out the window. Her red hair caught the light of the setting sun, seeming to catch fire. Her stiff figure revealed her emotional turmoil.

The room fell silent with her, seeming to sense a pivotal moment.

She eventually looked at Carrie. "Do you love God, Mama?"

"I do," Carrie replied.

"But you don't believe everything the church teaches?"

"There are a lot of churches, honey. They teach different things. I believe I have to listen to God and make the decisions that feel right to me. I believe my decisions should revolve around loving people."

The cloud lifted from Minnie's face as she smiled. "Then, I suppose it's okay to be Catholic, like my first family. It's the only thing I have left of them. That doesn't mean I have to believe everything they do." Her voice grew firmer. "I don't believe Mr. Stratford is in Hell, Mama. He was a good man who lost hope because of what happened. I don't believe God would punish him for losing hope."

Carrie thought her heart would burst with pride. "I believe you're right," she said tenderly.

Rose spoke for the first time. "How about we grieve for a wonderful man whom we loved? Regardless of how he died, the world lost someone special. Nancy lost the husband she loved with all her heart. Michael lost his father. We lost our friend."

Stark silence fell over the parlor as the sun slipped below the horizon, leaving the room in shadows.

Carrie wondered how many other families and friends were dealing with a similar grief. She was certain Wally was not the only person who had committed suicide after the market crash. He wasn't the first, and he wouldn't be the last. The consequences of the corruption and greed that had caused the crash would be felt for a very long time.

"How long will Grandma be in New York?" Minnie asked after several minutes.

"I don't know," Carrie replied. "She won't leave Nancy until she's certain she'll be alright."

"That could be a long time," Minnie said sadly. "Losing someone you love is very hard." She looked away. "I'm glad Grandma is staying, but I'm sure going to miss her."

Carrie walked over and pulled her daughter into a tight embrace. Minnie knew more about loss than she should at her young age. She admired her daughter's courage and maturity to face difficult questions and issues. "I love being your mama," she whispered into Minnie's ear.

Minnie pressed her head against Carrie's chest. "And I love being your little girl," she whispered back.

Chapter Fourteen

The plantation bustled with activity when Carrie and the others arrived home.

Annie appeared on the porch, a wide grin on her face. "Well, ain't y'all a sight for sore eyes! Welcome home!" She shaded her eyes and looked off into the distance. "Thomas gonna be back with the boys in a bit. Y'all got here earlier than we figured you would. They took off on a ride, but they be real excited for you to be home."

Hope leapt off the wagon and dashed up the porch stairs to throw her arms around Annie's waist. "I missed you, Grandma! I had an absolutely splendid time in Boston, but I'm happy to be home."

Annie gave Hope a tight squeeze but looked over her head toward Rose with an amused expression. "*Absolutely splendid?*"

Rose laughed. "Felicia taught her new vocabulary words. Those seem to be her favorite. There are many things that are *absolutely splendid.*"

Hope tossed her head. "It *was* absolutely splendid, Grandma!" She looked toward the house. "Are there any cookies inside? Gertrude is a good cook, but she couldn't make cookies like yours."

Annie beamed with pleasure. "What do you reckon?"

"Cookies!" Bridget's shriek of delight added to the chaos.

Hope ran back to the wagon to swing Bridget down, grabbed her hand, and ran with her into the house. "Cookies!"

Minnie moved more slowly, her eyes lingering on her bedroom window upstairs.

Carrie knew now that she was home, she was fully realizing Frances would no longer share a room with her. Minnie had experienced living in the room alone when her sister was in San Francisco, but this was different; Frances would only return on holidays. She slipped an arm around her daughter's waist. "I know," she said softly.

Minnie's eyes glimmered with tears. "I miss her, Mama."

"I do too," Carrie replied. Waving goodbye to Frances and Felicia when she boarded the train to return to Richmond had been one of the hardest things she'd ever done. Rose was used to saying goodbye to Felicia when she went to Oberlin. Other than the trip to San Francisco, which had seemed endless to Carrie, she'd not been separated from Frances since she'd adopted her. How was it possible that she had flown the nest?

Carrie forced a smile. "Eighty-one!" she said cheerfully.

"What?" Minnie asked. "What does eighty-one mean?"

Carrie smiled brightly, hoping it didn't look as forced as it felt. "It's only eighty-one days before Frances and Felicia come home for Christmas! With Alice! The days will fly by faster than you can imagine." From the moment she left Boston, she had been attempting to convince herself of the same thing.

Minnie looked doubtful. "Eighty-one days seems like an awful long time."

Rose walked over and slipped her arm around Minnie as well. "You'll be surprised. School will help the days pass quickly."

Carrie watched as a shadow filled Minnie's eyes. She was reminded of the conversation they'd had before leaving for Boston. The nonstop activity of the trip had pushed it from Carrie's mind, but the dread on Minnie's face brought it roaring back. She had promised to find a solution to her daughter's problem. She leaned down to whisper in her ear. "It's going to be alright, sweetie. I promise."

Carrie had to find a way to fulfill that promise. She would start by talking to Rose. She was confident they would create a solution.

Anthony waved a hand when Moses appeared. "Our wives and girls brought most of Boston home with them. Since half of this belongs to your family, I think you should come help me unload it."

Moses' deep laugh filled the air. "If you don't mind, I think I'll kiss my wife and daughter first."

Rose flew into his arms laughing. "I missed you!"

After he had picked Rose up, kissed her, and swung her around, he looked toward the wagon. "Where is my little girl?"

"Your daughter went inside for cookies," Rose told him. "She knew there would be an absolutely splendid choice because of preparation for the picnic tomorrow."

Moses eyed her. "Absolutely splendid?"

Rose laughed. "It won't take you long to catch on. Hope was quite eager to see what goodies she would have to choose from."

Moses narrowed his eyes. "My daughter chose cookies over seeing her father?"

Hope appeared at the door clutching a handful of cookies. "I chose cookies *first*, Daddy." She squealed and jumped into his arms, her fists still grasping the cookies. She squealed louder when Moses lowered his head and snatched a cookie out of her hand with his mouth. "Daddy!"

"That will teach you to put food before your father," he grumbled through his mouthful of molasses cookie. When he swallowed, he lowered his head to snatch another one.

"No, Daddy!" Hope squealed again. She wiggled wildly and managed to slide through his embrace. As soon as her feet hit the porch floor, she darted down the stairs. She waved the cookies in the air triumphantly. "Catch me if you can, Daddy!"

Moses laughed as she ran into the backyard. "You said something about a lot of luggage, Anthony?'

Anthony inclined his head toward the mountain in the back of the wagon. "I picked them up at the station in a carriage. I figured that leaving Frances' and Felicia's luggage in Boston would greatly reduce what they had. When I saw what they unloaded from the train, I went back to the stables and switched to a wagon."

Exactly as Carrie had predicted, Anthony laughed when the pile of their belongings kept growing at the train station. He teased them mercilessly on the way home, but she knew he would be quite pleased when she gave him the new boots and winter coat she had bought.

The boys would be pleased with their gifts, as well.

Rose had gone in and out of many stores before she was able to find clothes large enough for Moses, but her perseverance had paid off. The salesclerk raised his eyebrows in shock when she described her husband's size, but he managed to pull a good selection of clothes from the racks that would fit Moses.

Annie clapped her hands. "I know y'all been traveling, but there be a lot to do 'round here before tomorrow. Rain or shine, there gonna be a whole heap of people showin' up. We got work to do!"

Rose laughed. "I happen to know you already have more food prepared than a *whole heap of people* could possibly eat in a day."

"Girl, you don't know nothing about what it takes to feed a whole heap of people. If it were left up to you, ever'body comin' tomorrow would starve."

Rose laughed again. "That is very likely true, but since it's you doing the cooking, I'm not the least bit worried."

Minnie gave a fleeting glance toward her bedroom window before she ran up the porch steps. "I'm home, Annie. Tell me what you need."

Annie's eyes shone with approval. "That's more like it." She pulled Minnie to her in a tight hug. "I missed you, girl. Don't you be leaving me again for a while."

Minnie grinned. "I won't, Annie. I promise."

"When that sister of yours comin' back home?"

"Eighty-one days," Minnie said in an effort to match Carrie's brightness. "Just eighty-one days."

A distant call caught their attention. Moments later, Thomas, Russell, John, and Jed came trotting up, broad grins spread across their faces.

"You're home early!" Thomas swung off his horse.

"We were eager to get back," Carrie replied as she moved into his embrace. "We left Richmond before dawn."

"It's about time you got home, Minnie!" Russell said. He gave his sister a hug before he looked around. "You really left Frances in Boston?"

"We did," Minnie confirmed. "She and Felicia are going to be very happy there."

Carrie was glad to see the light return to her face. Minnie would continue to miss Frances, but having Russell would make it easier.

John and Jed welcomed Hope home, before they each snatched a cookie from her hands.

"Stop!" Hope commanded. "These are *my* cookies!"

"Plenty more where these came from," John mumbled around a full mouth. "We're hungry."

Jed took pity on Hope and pulled her toward the house. "Come on, Hope. We'll get more."

Hope stuck out her tongue at John.

Carrie grinned happily. They were indeed home.

With the wagon unpacked and Bridget settled into bed for a nap, Carrie was free to run upstairs, slip out of her dress, and don her riding breeches and boots. She had heard Granite's whinny as soon as she'd stepped from the wagon. She'd been a good mother and daughter for the last hour, but her heart yearned to be with her horse.

She ran down the stairway and paused at the door to call over her shoulder, "I'm going for a ride!" She deliberately let the screen door slam loudly enough to cover anyone's reply. She had missed Granite the entire time she'd been gone.

She was headed toward the barn when Miles stepped out, leading two horses. No Regrets was already saddled and bridled, her coat gleaming in the sun. Miles held Granite by a lead rope. Her colt stared in her direction, his ears pricked forward, and his eyes focused on her. He let out a shrill whistle as soon as she drew near.

Carrie laughed when Granite buried his head against her chest. She stroked his face, taking as much joy in the reunion as he did.

"This boy been antsy all morning," Miles told her. "I swear he done knew you were coming home today."

"Of course he knew." She patted No Regrets on the neck. "Thank you for getting them ready."

"You figure I woulda done anything diff'rent?" Miles demanded.

"No," Carrie assured him. "You've always known exactly what I needed." Memories filled her mind. Miles had taught her most of what she knew about horses. He had brought Granite home to her. It was because of him that her father had been willing to grant her freedom when she was young. She owed her friend more than she could ever repay.

"How was life in the big city?" he asked.

Carrie wrinkled her nose. "Big. Crowded. Noisy. Smelly. Boston is better than New York, but I was happy to get on the train to come back to the plantation."

Miles eyed her closely. "You sure 'bout that?"

He knew her well. "I would have been happier if Frances and Felicia had changed their minds and returned with us, but I'm truly happy for them." A vision of her daughter waving goodbye brought a mist of tears to her eyes. She forced the image from her head. "Felicia is already making big plans. Your granddaughter created a map of the city in preparation for her real estate search." She had already sent home a letter telling everyone about Alice offering them a place to live. "Both of them love Alice's house. They'll be safe and happy there."

"Felicia gonna do big things," Miles replied. There was a serious glint in his eyes. "But more than anything, I want her to be happy. Ain't nothing means more than that." He shook his head. "I hate that Mr. Stratford let that market crash steal his hope. Killing himself done hurt a heap of people. I'm hoping Felicia figured out money can't mean everythin'."

"I couldn't agree more." Carrie reached for No Regrets' reins. She needed to escape talk of suicide and stolen hope. "I'm going for a ride."

"Best thing for ya." Miles stepped back and disappeared into the barn.

Carrie mounted No Regrets, unhooked the lead rope from Granite's halter, and took off at an easy trot. They were having an unusually warm Indian Summer Day, but a stretch of cool nights had already painted the trees glorious shades of red, yellow, and orange.

Carrie rode along the well-worn roads, letting the peace and beauty of the plantation envelop her and wash away the remnants of New York and Boston. It was hard to believe she had ever longed to leave the plantation. Her home was the only place where she was truly happy.

The verdant green of the tobacco was gone, leaving endless brown fields with short stumps that would soon wither away. Anthony had told her the crop was as bountiful as they'd hoped, but he had evaded the question when she asked when it would be transported to Richmond. She didn't press the issue. She would get the full story tonight after everyone went to bed. The time in Boston had given them a reprieve from the reality of the economic crash, but she suspected that wouldn't last for long.

The fields were fallow, but the woods rang with the sound of axes biting into trees, and the loud calls and laughter of the plantation's workers. With the harvest complete, and the sheaths of tobacco drying in the barns, the men had begun cutting firewood for winter. The trees had been felled and bucked into sections earlier that spring to give them time to season. They were being split into firewood that would be stacked close to the house in the covered wood shed, with an especially large supply going outside the kitchen door, beneath the overhang.

Once Carrie was confident No Regrets was warmed up, she urged her into a canter. When the mare asked for her head, Carrie gave it to her. No Regrets settled into a smooth gallop. Carrie whooped with joy. Her ebony hair whipped behind her, while loose, curly tendrils snapped around her face. Carrie leaned low on the mare's neck, and let the wind blow her concerns away.

She was home.

With Minnie, Russell, and Bridget tucked into their beds, the allure of the porch on a fall evening overruled Carrie's exhaustion. She took Anthony's hand and pulled him outside, thankful for the blankets across the back of the rocking chairs.

After a warm day, a cool northern wind had started to blow. Annie would be happy the weather wouldn't be too hot for the picnic tomorrow. Miles had eyed the sky, tested the wind with his finger, and assured her it would be a perfect fall day.

Thomas sat with a cup of steaming hot tea. "I thought you would go straight to bed."

"I planned to," Carrie replied, "but it's so beautiful outside tonight, I couldn't resist coming to the porch. I longed for it the entire time I was gone. You are an added bonus." She had seen Moses and Rose disappear into their room earlier. The hallway had been shadowed, but she could have sworn she saw tension in Rose's shoulders. With the children asleep and the windows closed to hide conversation, she decided to ask the questions that needed answers.

"What have you heard from Abby? When I stopped off in New York to get Bridget, there was no time to talk at the train station, but she looked terribly sad and distressed. I've worried about her ever since."

"Nancy is a mess," Thomas said bluntly. "They had the funeral service, but very few people came. It wasn't public knowledge that he committed suicide, but since he hadn't been ill and with the news of the crash, the assumption was made. Of course, the assumption was correct. I think people don't know what to say or how to react."

"Wally was a friend to many in the city. Most importantly, a woman lost her husband," Carrie said indignantly. "That should have been the only reason needed to be there for her."

"I suppose."

Carrie was surprised by his tone. Shadows hid his face. "Father?"

Thomas sat silently for several moments before he replied. "My heart breaks for Nancy, but I'm angry at Wally. I can't believe he left her in the middle of such a mess. His mistakes cost them everything, but instead of fighting to make things right, he decided to end it."

Carrie understood how he felt. She couldn't comprehend how Wally could have left Nancy behind to deal with everything alone. She knew Wally had lost hope, but it had become Abby's job to convince Nancy there was still reason to have hope for herself. Her father missed his wife terribly. Even before Wally's death, Carrie knew Abby had been ready to leave the city and return home to the plantation. "What is Nancy going to do?"

"She doesn't know," Thomas answered. "Wally truly lost everything when the market crashed. She'll be able to stay in the house for another month before the bank repossesses it."

Carrie felt sick. Nancy and Wally had lived in their home for more than thirty years. Michael was raised there. It had been completely paid for, until Wally had mortgaged it to put money in the market. She'd heard Nancy talk about growing old together with Wally in that house, sitting on the porch while they watched their anticipated grandchildren play in the back yard.

She gripped Anthony's hand tightly. "You better never do that to me," she said.

"Never," Anthony promised. "Whatever happens in life, we'll go through it together."

Carrie believed him, but Wally had probably proclaimed the same thing, until the realities of life had knocked hope from him. Her thoughts flashed to Moses and Rose. "Father, how is the crash going to impact the tobacco crop?"

Thomas was silent for a long moment. "We don't know," he admitted. "The crop was bountiful, and it's drying beautifully, but we won't know the true scope of the economic impact until it's taken to market. We were already dealing with higher taxes. We don't know how badly the crash will impact it." He paused. "The prices will be lower, but we don't know how low."

"How bad has it gotten?" Carrie no longer had the distraction of getting the girls settled in Boston. As the impact of the crash spread through the country, the ramifications would be more strongly felt.

"More than a dozen railroad companies have declared bankruptcy," Anthony told her. "Since they employ the majority of Americans, tens of thousands of men are out of work. Factories are closing at a frightening pace. There is nowhere for them to find jobs. It's only going to get worse. More railroads will declare bankruptcy, and more men will be unemployed. Families will suffer. Unemployment will force other businesses into closing their doors because people won't have money to spend."

"New York has been hit the hardest," Thomas told her. "It will continue to spread quickly to the rest of the country. When Cooke Bank, the most influential bank in the country, failed, it eroded public trust in the banking system."

"They are in business enough to take the Stratford's home," Carrie said angrily. "Cooke Bank closed with the remainder of their money, but they're taking the house. That is terribly wrong."

"You're right," Thomas replied. He stood and walked to the edge of the porch.

Carrie could feel the tension radiating from him. His hands were clenched on the porch railing. She knew that even his beloved plantation would not ease her father's heart and mind. It had been only eight and a half years since the end of the war. He had been forced to start over after the Confederate defeat. The South was fighting to regain economic prosperity. The crash would be felt harder here than anywhere, because they had started from such a weak position.

"Abby was right the entire time. We are headed into a severe and prolonged economic depression," Thomas said in a flat voice.

Carrie wondered how it would impact the plantation, but especially the stables. They had heeded Abby's warnings and had been careful, but would it be enough? What would happen to the plantation workers who were counting on their share of the profits if there were no profits? Questions pinged through her mind.

Anthony read her mind. "Everyone here will be alright. We'll probably have to tighten our belts, but we'll be alright."

Carrie knew there was more than the plantation at stake. "What about River City Carriages?"

"We've seen a reduction in business," Anthony admitted. "With less business travel, there will be fewer people needing transportation." He took a steadying breath. "It will get worse."

"Your drivers?" Carrie asked.

"I imagine Marcus and I will have to start letting men go fairly soon. There simply won't be enough business." He frowned. "I hate the hardship it will put on them."

"What about the horses?" Carrie asked, already making plans in her mind.

Once again, Anthony had already considered options. "We'll bring most of them out to the plantation if we need to. We don't know what will happen to the cost of feed, or if we'll even be able to get it when the depression deepens. Moses and I have talked about it. It's too late to plant anything this year, but we'll clear more land to use for pasture and hayfields in the spring."

Carrie knew it was necessary to plan for the long-term. "We'll make it work. The hay crops have been as productive as the tobacco yield. We'll build more lean-tos in the field to provide shelter." She smiled. "Your horses will probably enjoy their vacation."

Anthony grinned. "You're probably right. Susan told me the same thing, but she said the two of you would talk about it when you got home. If necessary, I'll sell some of the horses."

Carrie shook her head. "That will be a last resort. You know you'll probably get pennies on the dollar for them." She was grateful the foals had been purchased and paid for in the spring. Their new owners would arrive within two weeks. She and Susan would hold onto every penny. They had discussed buying more mares, but that would be put on hold. "We'll hunker down and wait for things to improve." She had no idea how long that would be, but they would take it one day at a time. They had no other choice.

"How will the crisis impact the factories?"

Thomas moved away from the porch railing. "Again, we don't know. We're in a better position than most because we have no debt. Abby and I have been smart the last few years. We made no improvements we couldn't pay for without a bank loan. We have substantial funds available, but the amount of business will dictate how many of the workers we can keep on." His voice was troubled. "We know every family that works at the factories. It breaks my heart to think of putting any of them into hardship. We'll do the best we can to keep people working, even if we have to reduce their pay."

"They'll appreciate it and work even harder," Carrie predicted. With winter coming, people would be even more anxious. "The economy may suffer, but people will continue to need clothes and uniforms. Your factories will be operating when others go bankrupt and close their doors because they overextended in the last couple years."

"We're counting on that," Thomas replied.

Carrie knew that her father, exactly as he had before the war, had converted most of the cash he held in the banks into gold bars more than a year earlier. He'd done the same in early 1860, secreting the bars away deep in the tunnel. His wisdom, even when he'd been confident the Confederacy would win, had enabled him to bring the plantation back to life when the war was over. It gave her comfort to know they had prepared the same reserves for the current crisis.

Carrie and Anthony had followed her parents' example. They weren't wealthy, but they would make it through. She suddenly regretted the spending spree they had enjoyed in Boston. What had she been thinking? She would apologize to Anthony that night.

Carrie had more questions. "What about Moses and Rose?" Carrie asked. It was the most pressing question in her mind. "Where do they have their money?"

Rose never discussed with Carrie where she and Moses kept their money, but surely Moses had discussed it with his business partner. Rose knew what Thomas had done before the war, but Carrie had no idea what decisions she and Moses had made.

Carrie grew more nervous as the silence lengthened. "Father?"

"I'm not sure," Thomas finally answered. "Though he has a stash of money here, I know Moses had most of his money at the Freedman's Bank in Richmond. He and Rose are committed to supporting the bank."

Carrie's heart began to pound. She hated the idea of her friends in financial trouble after everything they had endured and accomplished. "Is the Freedman's Bank still operating?"

"It is," Thomas assured her, but his voice was halting. "I don't know for how long, though." He answered Carrie's next question before she could ask it. "I don't know if they'll take it out or not. I know they're worried their actions will cause a run on the bank, because they're one of its largest depositors. If others see them withdrawing money, they'll most likely follow suit. The bank will fail."

Carrie felt sick. "You mean they're simply going to wait to see what happens?" She shook her head. "Couldn't they take out smaller amounts? Perhaps that would keep a run from happening. It could be perceived as normal business withdrawals."

"Perhaps," Thomas agreed. "Moses and I have talked about it. He knows we won't make what we're used to making with this year's harvest, but he's going to keep whatever earnings there are here at the plantation. He's hoping it will be enough to see them through." His voice grew more confident. "We've saved money, Carrie. We'll be alright for a long while. We have plenty to plant next year's crop—and the year after if we need to. We won't make money like we have been, but we'll make enough. There will always be a demand for tobacco – especially in Europe."

Carrie's mind worked through scenarios. "What about Felicia? Is the money they promised to invest in her business in the bank?"

"I haven't asked," Thomas said. "I'm concerned, but I don't want to pry."

Carrie knew he was right. Another thought sprang to her mind. "What about the plantation workers?"

"The original workers who own land here will tighten their belts and delay plans, exactly as we will, but I don't believe anyone will go hungry. They'll continue working toward their future."

"And the rest?"

"That's another question we don't know the answer to. I can promise we'll do the best we can to keep people employed, even if everyone takes a big pay cut. Each man will have to make his own decision about whether to stay or go."

Carrie knew tough decisions would have to be made. Every plantation worker's wife was part of the Bregdan Women organization. They helped support their families by making quilts that were shipped north for Nancy to sell to her friends. Was all that over? The consequences of the crash seemed endless. She wondered if the men whose greed and corruption had caused the crash had any idea of the suffering they had caused. Or if they cared.

Carrie had come outside looking for peace. All she wanted now was to crawl into bed with Anthony and feel the strength of his embrace. She reached for his hand and stood. "I think this day has been enough for me. I need it to end. Thanks for talking to me, Father. I love you and I'll see you in the morning."

Carrie snuggled closer to Anthony, grateful for the thick quilt that insulated them from the cool breeze blowing in through the window. It would soon be cold enough to warrant closing it, but she loved fresh air while she slept.

"We're going to be alright," Anthony reminded her.

"I know," Carrie answered. "It's the people I love that I'm worried about."

"Worrying won't change anything," he said gently.

Carrie smiled and raised her head to kiss him. "Such wisdom."

Anthony chuckled. "Do you think I haven't been listening all these years? How many times have you told me that same thing?"

"I knew there was a reason it seemed familiar," Carrie teased.

"I've been waiting for the right moment to share that particular tidbit of wisdom with you."

Carrie sobered. "I know you're right, but there are endless questions demanding answers."

"Nothing that can be answered tonight," Anthony said. "The questions will be waiting for you tomorrow morning, *after* you've had a good night's sleep."

"But—"

Anthony's lips silenced hers.

Chapter Fifteen

Dewdrops glistened in the early morning sun when the men started pounding nails into boards to create long tables to hold the food for the party.

Rose joined Annie in the kitchen. Her mother-in-law had sweat dripping from her face, but she beamed with joy. Rose felt a rush of love for the woman who had made this moment happen. "The day is finally here."

Annie looked up from the counter where she had laid out a dozen blackberry pies and cobblers. "Those chillun are gonna know how glad we be to have them around here!" she declared.

"I think they already know," Rose said with a smile. "They're doing well in school. They seem happy in their new homes, and I've talked to the parents. They are thrilled that their families have grown."

"I done gone 'round to check on each of them," Annie responded. "I be the one to set it up for them chillun to come out here to the country. It be my job to make sure they be happy." She pushed her hair away from her face and squinted her eyes toward the back of the house. The screen door let in the noise of the pounding. "Them men done with the tables?"

"Almost," Rose assured her. "The wagons should start pulling up soon. The children are setting up games outside. Everything will go smoothly," she promised.

Minnie pushed open the door and stuck her head inside. "Do you need me, Annie?"

"No, ma'am. You ain't working in the kitchen today, young lady. I want you outside with them other chillun. You done plenty already." When Minnie looked doubtful, she waved her hand. "Git!"

Minnie grinned broadly. "Yes, ma'am!" She disappeared as quickly as she had appeared.

"Where are Alice and Gloria?" Rose asked. "I thought they would be here."

"They be here real soon," Annie replied. "These here pies and cobblers be the last thing that needed cookin'. We was up real late last night. That little Gloria couldn't hardly keep her eyes open when I shooed them out, but she weren't gonna leave until her mama came with her." She wiped at her gleaming face again. "They's gonna meet us outside when ever'body gets here."

"They're here!"

Rose looked up as the faint call floated in through the screen door. "Looks like the fun is about to begin."

Annie pulled off her apron and patted her hair.

Rose smiled and decided not to tell Annie she had added white flour streaks to the gray strands that already covered her head. No one would notice.

"Let's get out there!" Annie declared.

Annie didn't believe she'd ever felt such a deep sense of satisfaction.

Loud laughter and endless conversation filled the air. The entire day had been a resounding success. Despite Rose's belief that too much food had been prepared, the long wooden tables were empty of everything but crumbs.

The children were playing together. Adoptees, their new siblings, and the plantation children were running around in a wild game of chase. The bright smile on every face brought a deep surge of joy.

"Thank you, Annie."

Annie turned to see Ruby Babcock. The woman's paisley dress somehow managed to look crisp and fresh, even after a full day. Dark eyes flashed from her wrinkled face. "Howdy, Ruby."

"I can't begin to tell you how much joy little Sonya brings us. We didn't figure we would ever have children again. There were folks that said we were too old to start over again, but Sonya don't seem to mind none."

"Of course she don't," Annie replied. Luke and Ruby had lost both their sons during the war, shortly after emancipation had allowed them to join the Union Army. They were seventeen and eighteen when they were killed in the same battle. When the couple offered to take one of the children from the orphanage, she knew whoever they got would be extremely lucky. "Sonya knows how much you love her." She waved her hand toward the grove of trees where the children were dashing around. "Just look at the smile on that face. That be a happy little girl."

"Not as happy as we are," Ruby answered. She gestured over her shoulder toward a knot of men standing to the side. "Luke talks about that girl nonstop. Wouldn't nobody ever know he ain't her real daddy."

"Luke be raisin' that little girl," Annie replied. "He be her real daddy, sure 'nuff."

Ruby grew thoughtful. "We found out more 'bout her first family. Her daddy was killed during the war, right after she been born, so she never knew him. Her mama brought her to Richmond two years after the war ended. She figured they would have a better life. They did. It wasn't anything fancy, but her mama cleaned houses, and they had a big room to live in. Until her mama up and died two years ago. There weren't no other family to take her in, so Sonya ended up at the orphanage."

Annie frowned. "Too many stories like that out in this world. I be real glad Sonya got a happy endin'."

"Because of you," Ruby said. "I don't know if anyone else woulda given us the chance to have another child. They woulda figured we were too old. Thank you."

"Love don't know age," Annie said. "Besides, I reckon there be lots of grandparents with young'uns to raise. That war took a lot. The years *after* the war done been real hard too. That's why there be so many younguns in that orphanage."

"Are you going to bring more out here?" Ruby asked.

Annie raised her brows, pretending she hadn't been thinking about that very thing. "More?"

Ruby smiled, seeing right through her pretense. "I'm just saying that if you bring more, it would be real nice for Sonya to have a little sister or brother."

Annie might have been thinking about it, but she hadn't made plans of any sort. Ruby's words changed that. "You don't care if it be a boy or a girl?"

Ruby shook her head. "Not a bit. Me and Luke decided we got enough love and energy for more than one."

Annie grinned. "I'll keep that in mind."

"You're a good woman, Annie," Ruby said. "We're all real lucky because of you."

Annie's felt tears pricking the back of her eyes. "Thank you, Ruby. I appreciate that sho 'nuff."

Annie swiped at her face. The sweat dripping down her forehead kept getting in her eyes.

Rose looked up from where she was putting away pots and pans. After the day Annie had experienced, Rose wasn't going to let her do everything. Usually her mother-in-law would have shooed her out of the kitchen, but this time Annie had merely nodded her acceptance. That fact alone put Rose on alert. She narrowed her eyes. "It's not that hot in here, Annie. Why are you sweating that much?"

Annie glared at her. "It's plenty hot when you be putting biscuits in a hot oven. I gots to get everythin' ready for the mornin'. Breakfast don't cook itself 'round here."

That was true, but there was something about the look in Annie's eyes that set off alarms.

"Rose! I missed you!"

Rose knelt to wrap her arms around Gloria. She'd seen the little girl during the day, but they'd had no time together. "Hi honey. I'm sorry I didn't get to spend time with you earlier. The picnic never seemed to slow down. I hear you worked very hard to get the food made. Every bite was delicious!"

Gloria smiled broadly and bobbed her head. "I did! I reckon this be the best picnic ever."

"*Was* the best picnic ever," Rose corrected.

Gloria rolled her eyes. "Jed told me I should get used to this."

Rose bit back her smile. "Used to what?"

"Used to being made to talk right," Gloria replied. She shook her head, but her eyes glittered with fun.

"*Correctly* would be a better word than *right*," Rose said. Gloria was a smart little girl. She had come incredibly far in the brief time she'd been here, but it was Rose's job to help her continue to improve.

Alice joined Annie at the counter. "You keep telling her how to do things *correctly*," she said. "If I ain't learned anything else here, I've learned it's important to speak correctly. It changes how people look at you."

Rose opened her mouth but stopped when Alice held up a hand.

"If I *haven't* learned anything else." Alice's eyes gleamed with humor. "I wanted to see if you would correct me too."

Annie shook her head. "Oh, she's gonna do that. She done gave up on me, but I don't never go nowhere, and I don't care none what other people think. Here on the plantation, my cooking do all the talking I need to worry about." She faced Rose, waiting for a challenge.

Rose laughed heartily. "Not to mention the fact that you're my mother-in-law. I'm not your teacher."

Gloria smiled at her. "I'm very glad you're *my* teacher, Miss Rose!"

"I am too," Rose replied, giving her another hug. She swung her attention back to Alice. "How is your leg doing? I watched you earlier. I could barely detect a limp."

"Getting stronger every day," Alice said happily. "I've been walking everywhere on this plantation with Matthew. When I get tired, he tells me Rome wasn't conquered in a day, and makes me keep going."

Rose chuckled. "That sounds like Matthew."

"I didn't know what he was talking about at first, so I asked Mr. Cromwell. He sent me into the library to learn about it." Her face brightened. "That library is really something. I've never imagined seeing that many books in one place. Me and Gloria..."

"Gloria and I," Rose corrected.

"Right. *Gloria and I* have been going into the library every day when we're done helping in the kitchen. It's become our favorite place. We could learn about anything in that library, but there are a lot of books we can't read," Alice admitted.

"*Yet*," Rose said gently. "You can't read them yet, but that will change. I used to sneak into the library at night when I was a little girl here. I would carry the books back to my room and read them with little candle stubs. If I'd gotten caught, I would have been in serious trouble, but nobody ever found out." Her thoughts flew to the past. The plantation butler, Sam, had known. He'd saved candle stubs for her, and she knew he provided needed distraction a few times when she was hiding under the table, praying she wouldn't be caught. Hope's full name was Samantha Hope, a tribute to the man who had loved Rose like a father. He died the same night Hope was born. "You were a little girl here?" Gloria stared up at her with wide eyes.

Rose could see her mind attempting to make sense of the timeline. "Yes, Gloria. I was a slave here until I was nineteen."

Alice gasped and clapped a hand to her mouth. "I didn't know." She cocked her head. "You were really a slave here?" She glanced at Annie. "You didn't tell me."

"Ain't my story to be tellin'," Anne replied.

"You're part of the family now. The stories will come out in time," Rose said. Alice and Gloria hadn't been on the plantation long, but they truly had become family. "Moses and I were both slaves here, though he was only here for about a year before we escaped and went to Philadelphia."

Alice looked confused. "Isn't Moses part owner of the plantation?"

"When did you come back?" Gloria asked.

Rose saw Annie's eyes narrow with impatience. The storytelling could wait until after the kitchen was clean and ready for the morning. She put a finger to Gloria's lips. "No more answers right now. I'll answer all your questions soon."

"Promise?" Gloria demanded.

"I promise." When Rose looked up again, she noticed Alice staring at Annie with concern.

"Are you alright, Annie?" Alice asked.

"Right as rain," Annie barked. "You and Rose both be worryin' 'bout nothing. Can't an old woman get a little hot? In case y'all forgot, we had a real busy day. I ain't nothing but a little tired."

Alice's concerned look didn't fade." What can we do?"

Rose left the kitchen in search of Carrie. She found her leaning over Bridget's small bed, laughing with the little girl as she giggled. Rose watched for a moment, delighting in the love they shared, and cleared her throat.

Carrie looked up with a broad smile that faded quickly. She straightened, pulling her daughter into her arms as she did. "What's wrong?"

"Perhaps nothing," Rose replied. "I'm worried about Annie."

"Why?"

"She's sweating more than usual in the kitchen."

Carrie raised a brow. "She's *sweating more than usual*? Is she cooking?"

"Don't ask me ridiculous questions. You know me better than that, Carrie Wallington. There is something not quite right. Alice noticed it too." She huffed impatiently. "It's going to be hard having two Alice's in our life. When Alice in Boston comes to visit, it's going to get complicated."

"Yes," Carrie agreed. "It was quite rude of the Alices not to consider us."

Rose chuckled. "You're right. I sound ridiculous."

"Only about the Alice's," Carrie agreed. "I know you well enough, however, to believe you about Annie." She placed Bridget back on her bed and straightened. The little girl opened her mouth to protest, but then gave a mighty yawn and laid her head on her pillow. "Tell me exactly why you're concerned."

"She is sweating more than usual, but it was her eyes..." Rose's voice trailed off. "I realize that's weak evidence."

Anthony entered the room and kissed Bridget's head. "How's my sleepy little girl?"

"Ready for bed," Carrie replied. "Will you read to her and put her down for the night?"

"Of course," Anthony eyed her her more closely. "Is everything alright?"

"I'm about to find out," Carrie told him. She tucked her hand around Rose's arm. "Let's go see Annie."

Rose led the way, her concern growing, though there was no obvious reason for it to. She increased her speed.

"Did you say anything to her?" Carrie asked.

"Yes, but you know Annie. She told me I was imagining things and reminded us there was a picnic today!" Rose rolled her eyes. "She said she had a right to be tired."

Carrie smiled. "The picnic was incredibly important to her. I don't think I saw her sit down all day. She certainly deserves to be tired." When they reached the kitchen, she put a finger to her lips. "Don't say anything. I want to see her for myself."

Rose was more than happy to remain silent. She was trusting Carrie to know what to do.

Carrie strode into the kitchen, all smiles. "I know I shouldn't be hungry after today, but is there anything for a woman who happens to be starving right this second?"

Annie, bent over the counter as she filled fluffy biscuits with ham, nodded. "There be a tray of biscuits on that table right there. How 'bout you take it on out to the porch? Moses done been in here snatching some. You'd think they ain't spent the whole day stuffin' their faces."

"No one can resist your biscuits." As Carrie spoke, she was examining the older woman. Annie hadn't looked up yet, but her shoulders seemed slightly slumped and there was a tired tilt to her head. Neither was to be unexpected after her long day.

Annie finally lifted her eyes. "You be right 'bout that, Carrie. Ain't nobody can make biscuits like me and Alice."

"And me!" Gloria announced. "I helped too."

"That you did," Annie agreed.

Carrie's eyes narrowed. She saw exactly what Rose had been talking about. Annie's eyes were flushed with fever. "Annie?"

"Yep?" Annie didn't look back up from the mountain of biscuits.

"How are you feeling?"

Annie jerked her head up and scowled at Rose. "Girl, I done told you I be fine. What you be goin' and getting *Dr. Wallington* for?" Her scowl switched to a glare. "I'll tell you the same thin' I told her, Miss Carrie. I be fine. That be the truth."

"That's a lie," Carrie retorted.

Annie's eyes flashed with fire. "You be callin' me a liar? You might be a fancy doctor, but I'm old 'nuff to be your mama. I be the one who keeps things runnin' 'round here. You shouldn't oughta be forgettin' that!"

Carrie smiled. "You are correct, Annie. They are the very reasons we're not going to let anything happen to you. We love you and count on you." Her voice gentled. "Please tell me what is truly going on. I can't help you if I don't know. I realize you're used to powering your way through any challenge that comes your way. I'm asking you not to do that right now." She walked forward and put a hand on Annie's arm, shocked by the heat radiating from her.

Carrie whipped around. "Rose, get a bucket of ice," she ordered. "Bring it to the guest room."

Rose ran for the icehouse.

"What be the matter with you, girl?" Annie snapped.

"You have a high fever," Carrie told her calmly, thankful she had learned how to control the emotion in her voice. She didn't want to scare Annie, but it was time to make her pay attention.

Carrie put an arm around Annie's waist and pushed the kitchen door open. "Can you handle things here in the kitchen, Alice?"

"I can," Alice said steadily. "She gonna be alright?"

"Of course," Carrie replied, grateful Rose had come for her. "Annie needs to lie down, so we can reduce her fever."

"Fever?" Annie shook her head. "That's pure nonsense. I ain't nothin' but too hot from cookin' biscuits."

"I wish that were true," Carrie replied, as she walked Annie into the hallway. "I know how important your cooking is," she said softly. "You don't want anyone else to get sick if you have the flu, do you?"

Annie, who had opened her mouth to retort, snapped it closed. "I have the flu again?" Her eyes clouded with anxiety.

Carrie didn't want to scare her, but she did want her to understand how serious her fever could be. They'd come close to losing Annie in the past from the flu. She wasn't going to take any chances, especially with Annie being older.

"I could make someone sick?" Annie's face twisted with distress.

Carrie wondered if she already had but wasn't going to say it. Annie would be horrified, especially after being with so many people for the picnic. "I don't have answers yet," she said soothingly as they walked slowly down the hall. "We're going to the guest room, where I can take your temperature. Let's figure out what we're dealing with."

Annie tried to jerk away, but the effort made her stumble. When she looked at Carrie, there was a mist in her eyes. "I reckon maybe I ain't feelin' so good," she admitted.

Carrie was glad they were almost to the guest room. "You're going to be alright," she said soothingly.

She prayed she was right.

Rose filled the bucket with ice and hurried back toward the kitchen.

"Hello, wife!" Moses called as he waved from the front porch.

Rose put the bucket down and hurried over to him. "Your mama is sick."

Moses' smile disappeared. "What's wrong?"

"We don't know yet," Rose answered. "Carrie ordered me to get ice, so I know Annie has a fever." She tried to hide her worry, but the expression on Mose's face revealed she had failed.

Moses jumped down from the porch and took her hand. "Let's go find out."

They entered the kitchen together.

"They're in the guest room," Alice told them. Her eyes were dark with concern.

Moses dipped water into the bucket, while Rose gathered up the needed cloths. Carrie should have whatever remedies were needed in her medical bag, or they would be on the shelves in the basement. The house was as well stocked as the medical clinic, unless surgery was needed.

When they got to the guestroom, Carrie hurried toward the door. She nodded with relief when she saw the ice water. "Just what I need." She reached for it eagerly, but Moses shook his head.

"I'll take it in. I want to see my mama."

Carrie stepped aside, but Moses didn't move.

"What's wrong with her?" Moses whispered.

"She has a high fever."

"How high?" Moses asked.

"One hundred and four."

Rose gasped. "Annie was in the kitchen cooking with a temperature of one hundred and four? How?"

Carrie shrugged. "We know how stubborn and strong-willed she is. She doesn't want to admit it when something is wrong."

"What's causing the fever?" Moses asked.

Carrie frowned. "I don't know yet. I suspected the flu, but she's not exhibiting any other flu symptoms. My best guess is that she has some kind of infection, but I have to examine her further." She moved back to the bedside. "The most important thing at the moment is to bring her temperature down. Put the ice bucket beside the bed and leave," she ordered. "Rose and I will take care of her."

Rose knew what that tone of voice meant. Dr. Wallington was worried.

Moses carried the ice water to the bedside. He leaned down to kiss Annie's forehead. "I love you, Mama. You're going to be alright."

Annie tried to speak, but whatever she was going to say came out as a groan.

Moses kissed her again and hurried from the room.

Minutes later, they were stripping Annie's clothing off her.

Annie was slumped against the pillows, sweat beading her face and body. She moaned in gratitude when they began to bathe her with cold cloths.

After several minutes, Carrie looked up. "You should get Miles," she said softly.

Rose felt a rush of alarm.

Carrie took her hand and gripped it firmly. "There's no reason to be frightened, but I don't know what I'm dealing with yet. I've learned to not take chances. Miles needs to know."

Rose looked at Annie slumped against the pillows with her eyes closed. "Alright." She placed a tender kiss on her hot forehead. "I love you," she whispered.

Annie didn't respond.

Rose blinked back tears and hurried from the room.

Moses was waiting for her.

Rose tried to smile reassuringly but knew she had failed when his eyes narrowed with concern. "Carrie doesn't have a diagnosis, but your mama is resting." She wasn't going to tell him that she suspected Annie was unconscious.

Chapter Sixteen

Carrie continued to bathe Annie with cold water. It was imperative she get the fever down. While she bathed her, she pressed gently on Annie's body, searching for the source of the suspected infection. As much as she hated the fever, it helped her rule out many other possibilities.

While she was pressing her abdomen, Annie moaned loudly and opened her eyes in protest.

"Hello," Carrie said gently, relieved to see she was conscious. "Can you tell me what hurts, Annie?"

Annie turned fever-glazed eyes toward her. "Stomach," she mumbled. "So hot…" Her eyes fluttered closed again.

Carrie continued to press, praying her fears weren't true, but confident she was correct. Her mind raced as she considered the ramifications.

Miles rushed into the room, his face tight with panic. "What's wrong with my Annie?" He stepped close and took his wife's hand, but she didn't respond.

"I'm not absolutely certain," Carrie said truthfully, realizing Annie had lapsed into unconsciousness again. "She's running a high fever, but I'm working to bring it down."

Rose entered the room behind him. "Janie will be here soon," she announced.

Carrie felt a surge of relief. "How?" She had been wishing her partner was with her. With Frances in Boston, it was just Carrie and Janie again. Besides the ache of missing her daughter, she also missed working side-by-side with her.

"Thomas and Matthew talked on the porch for a while after the picnic. He and Janie left for home shortly after you went upstairs to put Bridget to bed. I knew they couldn't have gotten too far in their wagon, so I sent Moses after them." She looked at Annie with worried eyes. "He took an extra horse so Janie could ride back with him."

"Thank you," Carrie said gratefully. Her mind continued to absorb the ramifications of what she suspected. When she looked up, Miles was watching her shrewdly.

"You know what's wrong with her," he said bluntly. "You got to tell me the truth, Carrie Girl."

Carrie wanted to deny it, but if the roles were reversed, she would insist on the truth. She beckoned Miles into the hallway. "Please keep working to bring her temperature down, Rose. I'll be right back."

"Of course," Rose answered, her eyes bright with concerned curiosity.

Carrie wouldn't share her suspicions in the room. If Annie happened to regain consciousness, she didn't want to add fear to her pain. She pulled the door closed and turned to Miles.

"Tell me."

Carrie took a deep breath. "I suspect Annie has appendicitis."

Miles looked confused. "What's that?"

"There is an organ in the body called the appendix," Carrie explained. "Quite honestly, though we know it exists, it's rather something of a mystery. It looks remarkably like a worm attached to the colon. We're not certain of its purpose, but we do know it can become inflamed and cause serious disease."

Miles listened intently. "How you gonna fix it, Carrie Girl?"

"I'm not sure it *can* be fixed," Carrie said carefully.

Miles shook his head impatiently. "Stop playin' games with me," he scolded. "We be way past that kinda nonsense. Just tell me straight up."

Carrie knew Miles was right, but it didn't make the conversation any easier. "The belief now is that the only cure for appendicitis is to remove the appendix. The first successful surgery was in 1735. While the surgery is done, it's not common."

As she talked, she played over in her head what she had learned about the appendix from reading books after medical school.

"You ever done one?" Miles asked. When Carrie shook her head, his expression grew more intense. "You reckon you can?"

Carrie took another deep breath. She had been asking herself the same question since the moment she'd made her diagnosis. "I don't know," she said honestly. "I've read about the surgery, but I don't have any experience. I'll do whatever it takes to try to save her, Miles. Janie will be here to help me, but she's never done the procedure either." She paused. "I've studied it and read about it, but that isn't actual experience. You should also know that infection could still take over. There's just not a lot known about this." She hated that she couldn't be more positive, but she owed it to him to be honest.

"You got some magic herbs to take care of that infection?"

Carrie thought of Jed's father. She had fought hard to save Morris when infection had set in after his wounds from the Klan attack in South Carolina. Despite their best efforts, he had died. She tried to keep her voice steady. "I promise to do everything I can. It's up to you to decide, Miles. I don't know if Annie will regain consciousness without the surgery."

Miles swallowed hard, his eyes moist with unspoken emotion. He took both her hands in his own leathery ones. "You do what you got to do, Carrie Girl. You bein' honest with me. That's all I can ask for. If it don't go well and I lose my Annie, at least we gonna know we did what we could. Ain't nobody can do more than that."

Carrie nodded her head slowly. Her heart pounded with trepidation, but she would do what Miles asked. Even if the operation was successful, that didn't mean infection couldn't still kill Annie. Taking the ruptured appendix out was just the first step.

"You gonna do the operation here?" Miles asked.

Carrie wanted to say no, but she was afraid to move Annie. With a fever this high, the appendix had clearly ruptured. As much as she yearned for the clinic, moving her could be deadly. She doubted Annie would survive it. "No," she said firmly. "We'll do it here."

"What you need?" Miles asked.

"I need you to wait outside for Janie," Carrie ordered, glad to have a clear direction to give her old friend. He needed to *do* something. She pulled a pad of paper and a pencil from her pocket and began to write furiously. The house was well-stocked for most emergencies, but not for surgery. When she was finished, she handed the paper to Miles. "Tell Janie to go to the clinic and get these supplies. The rest of what I need is in the basement supply room. I'll send Rose down."

Miles nodded, spun on his heel, and strode out of the room.

Carrie prayed Janie would arrive soon. Her partner was the only one she could trust to have the knowledge to bring the necessary supplies.

Rose looked up when Carrie entered the room. "Surgery?" she whispered.

Carrie almost smiled when she realized Rose must have had her ear pressed to the door during her conversation with Miles. The smile faded when she fully realized what she and Janie were about to do. She merely nodded, pulled out the paper and pencil again, and started to write. "I need you to go to the basement storage room and get these supplies."

Rose nodded and took her hands just as Miles had a few minutes earlier. "You're going to do your best, Carrie. That's all you can do. The rest is up to God."

Carrie blinked her eyes rapidly, refusing to let tears form. There would be a time for crying; for now, she had to focus. Merely doing her best wasn't acceptable when it came to Annie. She couldn't imagine the plantation without the domineering woman who hid a heart of gold behind her bluster and stubbornness. "Please have Anthony boil at least five large pots of water. We have to sterilize everything possible and I'm going to need a lot of water during the operation to keep the instruments clean."

"Of course." Rose paused and looked at her closely. "You've had an extremely long day with the picnic, Carrie. Both you and Janie. Do you have it in you to perform such a challenging surgery?"

Carrie managed to smile this time. "We'll be fine," she said firmly. "Part of being a doctor is pushing through fatigue. Medical emergencies rarely come at a convenient time." A sudden thought struck her. "Rose, tell Minnie she doesn't have to go to school tomorrow."

"What?" Rose asked in a perplexed tone. "Where did that come from? Minnie doesn't have to go to school? Why ever not?"

"We'll talk about it later," Carrie replied. "I have a surgery to prepare for."

"But..."

Carrie understood Rose's confusion, but it wasn't something she could do anything about at the moment. Glad she had remembered Minnie's dilemma; she would worry about how to resolve it later. She merely didn't want to make things worse on her daughter's first day back at school after their trip. "I promise I'll explain later. For now, please go get what I need," she said urgently. "I'll keep bathing Annie until Janie arrives. If her fever goes higher, we'll have more problems than a ruptured appendix." She couldn't bring herself to give voice to her fear that Annie could have a stroke.

Rose hurried from the room.

Carrie turned back to Annie, troubled by the woman's shallow breathing. Thank goodness Rose had come for her. Annie's odds for survival weren't very high right now, but if she had stayed on her feet in the kitchen much longer, she likely would have collapsed and died there. She began to hum softly as she continued to lay ice cold cloths on Annie's face and body. If Annie could hear her, it would help soothe her fears.

Carrie wanted to cry with relief when Janie finally pushed through the door. Rose had already delivered the needed supplies from the basement. She was taking care of Bridget, while Thomas kept the boys occupied. Anthony was waiting on orders from her.

Moses was right behind Janie, his arms laden with supplies from the clinic. His eyes flashed across the room. "My mama?"

Carrie didn't have an answer for him. "We're going to do the best we can, Moses," she said gently.

Moses met her eyes steadily before he spoke. "I believe in you, Dr. Wallington. And you, Dr. Justin. If anyone can save my mama, it will be you two."

Carrie wanted to scream at him not to say the words coming from his mouth. For the last hour she had sat alone and watched Annie's breathing become increasingly shallow. Used to running *toward* people who needed help, this time she wanted to flee the room – not be the one responsible for saving the woman they all loved and counted on.

"You can leave now," Janie said firmly. "We've got this."

When Moses had left the room, Janie stepped close to Carrie. "Stop thinking like that right this moment. I'm here. We have everything we need. We've worked medical miracles before. I think tonight is a wonderful time for another one."

Carrie blinked back tears. "I'm glad you're here," she whispered.

Janie reached forward and tilted her face up until their eyes met. "Remember when you had to do an emergency C-section on me when Robert was born? You had never done one before and you were afraid you couldn't do it. Do you remember?"

Memories of that terrifying night came flooding back. "I remember."

"Tonight is no different," Janie stated. "Except that we're smarter and more experienced. You're not alone. We're going to do this together." She placed her hands on Carrie's cheeks and looked deeply into her eyes. "We've got to hold on to hope, Dr. Wallington. We never have more than that when we go into surgery. This time is absolutely no different." Her voice softened. "Hold on to hope, my friend."

Carrie felt Janie's words penetrate the fear in her heart and mind. Once penetrated, the paralyzing fear faded away like the fog before a blazing sun. "You're right," she said forcefully. "We've got this."

As soon as she spoke, the door opened again. Anthony slipped in with buckets of hot water and a collection of containers.

Moses followed him, carrying more.

"We already have more water boiling," Anthony told her. He walked over and leaned down to kiss her gently. "I love you, Dr. Wallington."

Carrie smiled at him and then gestured toward the door. "Thank you. Please leave our operation area. Do not come back in until we tell you to. We don't want any more contamination in the surgical suite. You can leave the hot water outside the door," she said authoritatively.

Janie chuckled. "There is my partner. She has returned."

Carrie smiled at her and then began to describe the surgery they were about to perform. She had spent the waiting time deeply immersed in medical books that described the operation. She was as ready as she could be.

"Where's Grandma?" Hope asked. "She's not in the kitchen. Grandma is always in the kitchen. We asked Alice, but she told us to ask you."

John and Jed crowded close to Moses to hear the answer.

Moses met Rose's eyes above their heads. The love he saw there gave him the courage to answer. "Your Grandma is sick," he said gently. "Carrie and Janie are taking care of her."

"Is she going to be alright?" John demanded.

"How can she be sick?" Jed asked. "She didn't seem sick at the picnic."

Moses had asked himself the same questions. Miles had come outside and explained about the appendicitis, but he knew he couldn't give the children an adequate explanation. He looked across the porch. "Thomas?"

While Moses had ridden to bring Janie back, Thomas had delved into the library.

"Your Grandma has something wrong with her appendix," Thomas said. "It's a little organ that can cause very big problems if something goes wrong." He paused. "Something went wrong."

"Why?" John asked.

Thomas shook his head. "Nobody seems to have an answer for that. Carrie and Janie are going to fix the problem."

"They can fix it?" John demanded.

Moses knew his oldest son wanted the truth, but he had Jed and Hope to consider, as well. He wasn't going to make uncertain promises. "Do you know any better doctors than Carrie and Janie?" he asked.

"No!" Hope said loudly. "Carrie and Janie are the best doctors in the world."

"You're right. The best doctors in the world are working on your grandma." Moses could tell from John's expression that his son knew what he was doing, and that he understood.

"How long is it going to take?" Jed asked, his face tight with fear. "When can we see Grandma?"

Moses understood Jed's fear. The best doctors in the world couldn't save his father. What if they couldn't save his grandma either? "I don't know," he said honestly. "It's going to be a while, though. I think y'all should go to bed. Grandma would want you to get rest after the long day you've had with the picnic."

John was shaking his head before Moses finished talking. "I'm not going to bed while Grandma is having surgery," he said decisively.

Moses looked to Rose for help. He knew the children were exhausted, but he also understood their desire to stay up. He was doing the same.

Rose came to his rescue. "Let's make a deal," she said brightly. "You don't have to go to sleep, but I do want you to go up to your rooms and lie in your beds. You're tired. We'll come get you as soon as we know how your grandma is. How does that sound?"

Hope looked doubtful, but she was the first to nod. "I suppose that sounds alright." A big yawn slipped out of her mouth.

"I guess," Jed replied reluctantly. His gaze was locked on the front door, as if he hoped Carrie or Janie would walk through it at that instant.

Moses knew the surgery was going to take a long time. He looked at John. "Son?"

"Fine," John muttered. "I don't like it, though. I'm not going to sleep. You promise to come up and tell us as soon as you know something?"

"I promise," Moses said solemnly. He remembered his determination to be with his father the night Sam was hanged for his escape attempt. He'd had to sneak away into the darkness. He knew his mother had been terrified when she discovered him gone, but he'd simply had to be there. It was a night he would never forget. It continued to haunt his dreams, but given the chance, he would make the same decision. Even though his father never knew of his presence, Moses had the comfort of knowing he hadn't died alone.

Moses pulled his three children into his arms. "Grandma loves you so much. She's going to fight to keep being here for you. You can count on that."

Rose stood, blinking away tears, and shepherded the children toward the door. When they were inside, Moses looked around the porch. "Where is Miles?"

"In the barn," Anthony replied.

"He said it was the only place he could stand to be while Annie is in surgery," Thomas added.

Moses understood. The barn was where Miles found peace.

Thomas cleared his throat. "Moses, have you talked to Alice?"

Moses blinked, fighting to make the rapid shift in his mind. "Alice?"

"Yes. It's going to be a long time before Annie will feel like being in the kitchen again, no matter how much she'll want to," Thomas said. "She seems to trust Alice. You had talked about asking Alice to stay on long-term in order to help your mama, even before she got sick."

The door opened as he finished speaking.

Alice walked out, lines of weariness etched on her face. "Gloria is staying with Hope tonight," she told them. "Rose thought it would help keep Hope's mind off her grandma." She looked around the porch. "Is there any word?"

Moses shook his head. "There won't be for a while," he said solemnly.

Alice glanced at a rocker. "Can I join you in waiting? Your mama has become like a mama to me, too. We're friends, but I always dreamed of having a mama like her. I can't go to sleep until I know she's alright."

Moses nodded and handed her a blanket to ward off the chill fall air. "You can wait inside if it gets too cold."

"I'll be fine," Alice replied as she pulled the blanket around her shoulders. "Fresh air makes hard things easier. When I was a slave, I sat outside every night. It made facing a new day a mite better."

Moses smiled. Her words made his decision crystal clear. This was a woman made for country living. "Alice, would you consider staying here on the plantation?"

Alice's eyes widened. "What do you mean?"

"You and Gloria have become family," Moses answered. "To all of us, but especially to my mama. We've known for a long time that there would be a day when running the kitchen by herself would be too much. We were counting on the right person coming along to help her. It didn't take me long to know you are the right person."

"I see."

Moses felt a moment of unease. Alice wasn't jumping at the opportunity. What if she didn't want to stay. Suddenly, he realized what the issue was. "With a salary, of course."

Alice's eyes got wider. "You gonna pay me to cook with Annie?" Her disbelief brought back the language she was working to shed.

"Everyone who works on the plantation gets paid," Moses replied. He suddenly thought about the reality of the market crash. What could they truly afford to pay her?

Thomas seemed to read his mind. "You and Annie are crucial to making the plantation run smoothly. We can't work if we can't eat." He smiled. "Most of us would starve if we were left to our own devices."

Alice nodded. "That's what Annie tells me."

Moses chuckled. Once again, he knew they were making the right choice. Alice knew how to speak her mind. After surviving the vicious attack in Richmond, he supposed not much would frighten her.

Thomas named a salary.

Alice's eyes grew so wide, Moses was afraid they might pop from her head. "That much?"

"You'll earn it," Moses told her. "You've seen how hard Annie works. It will fall on you until she's well enough to cook again." Even as he spoke the words, he realized that might never happen. The look in Alice's eyes said she knew the same thing.

"I ain't afraid of hard work," Alice replied. Then she hesitated. "Where are me and Gloria gonna live?"

"I'm hoping you're comfortable in your room in the guest house," Moses answered. "It will be easier for you and Gloria if you're close to the house. We can talk about a change in the future when you want to."

"The guest house is just fine," Alice assured him. "Probably for a long time." Joy radiated from her face. "Gloria is going to be mighty happy. She told me the other day that she didn't want to never leave the plantation. Or Hope. Those two girls have gotten as thick as mud."

"We're all happy you're going to stay, but I agree Hope might be just a little bit happier than everyone" Moses agreed. "She's never had a best friend until Gloria. I want that for her."

Alice stood back up. "I've got some work to do," she said briskly.

Thomas held up his hand. "Sit back down, Alice. You've had an extremely long day. There is nothing in the kitchen that can't wait until tomorrow."

Alice eyed him. "How do you know that?"

Thomas grinned. "Because I know you wouldn't have come out here until that was true."

"I reckon that would be true."

"Which is why you need to sit back down," Thomas repeated. "It's going to be a long night since you're determined to wait until the surgery is over. Breakfast will need to be served. One thing you have to learn around here is to rest when you can."

"Annie told me that, too." Alice settled back into the rocker.

Moses leaned back in his chair. Alice was going to fit in perfectly. He was free to do nothing but worry about his mama. He wished he was watching the surgery, hearing what Carrie and Janie were saying. He knew the operation was very risky – even *if* Carrie had experience.

Without experience, the appendectomy was terrifying.

Chapter Seventeen

Theodore Poulton pulled his horse to a stop and silently waved a group of ten armed men forward to the entrance of Blackwell Plantation. His sinister eyes glittered in the moonlight. His pudgy face seemed carved from stone.

A tall, lean man edged up beside him. "We ain't seen anyone, Theo."

Poulton wanted to tell Martin McNary that what he had seen, or not seen, meant nothing. In preparation for this night, he'd talked to men who had tried to attack Cromwell Plantation. They'd claimed even the trees had eyes. Every attack had been thwarted. Yes, they had killed Robert Borden, but that had been a mistake. The bullet had been meant for the little black girl Borden dove in front of. The shooter was rotting in prison.

Burning the barn down at Cromwell had been a success, but the man responsible for it had been found dead the next morning. Within a few weeks, a brand-new barn, bigger and nicer than the one destroyed, had been erected by an army of both white and black workers.

Poulton ground his teeth. That reality, more than anything, made him want to curse. If the Klan was going to take control of Virginia, they had to destroy white and black alliances, and also make certain blacks weren't treated equally. For their plan to be successful, all white Virginians needed to embrace the truth that blacks were inferior. Those who refused to accept the truth would pay.

It was time for Perry and Louisa Appleton to pay. Blackwell Plantation had fallen into disrepair when the older Blackwells, along with their son Nathan, had died during the war years. When Perry and Louisa returned to Blackwell plantation after the war, they should have run it the way her daddy would have. If they had, Poulton wouldn't be forced to teach them a lesson tonight.

Trying to calm his racing thoughts, his eyes scanned the woods around the pillared entrance. Were there Blackwell workers watching them right that instant? If they passed through the entrance, would they be mowed down by gunfire?

"You sure you want to do this?" McNary asked.

Poulton wanted to shout *no*, but he held his tongue. He realized that despite his wish to be home with his wife and children, he had been given the responsibility of teaching the Appletons how life worked in Virginia. He sensed the ten men with him were getting restless. If he didn't move forward with confidence, they would give into the fears of the unknown.

"Of course I want to do it." Poulton spun his horse and faced the group of men watching him with anticipation. None of them had been particularly eager to join this mission, but the Klan leader hadn't given them much of a choice. It was up to him to give them confidence.

"We've got this, men," Poulton proclaimed. "No one is out here at midnight. Blackwell Plantation doesn't have enough workers to provide a guard around the clock. Besides, our little conversation with Perry Appleton forced him to make some changes. He has workers, but they ain't gonna be as loyal." He hoped his lie was convincing. When he looked back at his men, he was relieved to see they were sitting straighter in their saddles.

He had already explained the plan to them, but he went over it again. When he finished the details, he smiled broadly. "No one will be expecting us. We're only going to hurt the Blackwells if they stand in our way. It's the house we're after. Not them." He didn't mention that jail time for murder would be much higher if they were caught.

Privately, Poulton hoped Perry Blackwell and that black who worked for him, Simon, would put up a fight. Nothing would make him happier than putting a bullet into both of them. He suddenly realized he was willing to risk jail time. That thought gave him the courage to pick up his reins and urge his horse forward through the entrance.

Every nerve was on alert as they trotted into the darkness.

Poulton took a deep breath of relief when the woods remained silent. No shouts. No gunfire. Just the sound of an occasional owl and the chattering of some nocturnal raccoons.

He stiffened at the sound of running footsteps. As the noise faded into the distance, Poulton relaxed. Whoever had seen them was running away in fear. Blackwell Plantation didn't have enough men to put up a fight.

Buoyed by the realization no one had attempted to stop them, he grinned and pushed his horse into a canter. He wanted the surprise attack to be as fast as possible. If all went well, they would achieve their purpose and be headed away within a few minutes.

He checked his saddlebag to make certain his supplies were ready, patted the pistol shoved in his waistband, and caressed the rifle hanging on his saddle. He was prepared.

Perry leapt up when pounding sounded at the front door.

"Perry!" Louisa pushed away her half-eaten dinner and stared toward the foyer with alarm.

June leapt up, lifted Nathan and Junior to their feet, scooped five-year-old Ella into her arms, and moved to stand in the dining room entry way.

Normally, they wouldn't have been up so late. With fewer workers, it had taken all of them to finish harvesting the tobacco. Even Ella had helped for the last few days. The crop should have been out of the field two weeks ago, drying in the barn by now, but there hadn't been enough help to make it happen. Nathan and Junior were practically asleep at the table, but he hadn't wanted them to go to bed hungry. Ella had fallen asleep the moment she sat down.

Perry silently pointed everyone toward the back room. Only when they had moved out of sight did he go to the window and peer out. He sagged with relief when he recognized Andrew, one of his workers, but his relief was short-lived. Why was he here past midnight? The men should be eating or asleep.

Perry opened the door and beckoned Andrew inside. "What's wrong?"

"There be eleven men coming," Andrew hissed as soon as he stepped into the foyer. "Me and another fella heard something bad might happen, so we been keeping watch. Just two of us couldn't stop them, but we came to warn you."

Perry would thank him adequately later. "We appreciate it," he said quietly. He opened the door and pushed him outside. "Go! You don't want to be here when they arrive."

Andrew hesitated, clearly torn between his desire to help and his desire to remain alive.

"Go!" Perry said urgently.

Andrew leapt from the porch and ran into the darkness.

Perry closed the door and beckoned to Simon. "It's happening," he snapped.

Their plan was well thought out.

Simon led the women and children to the back room. Perry knew he was opening the tunnel door and ushering them inside. He would close the door and pull a rug over it, making it invisible unless someone thought to move the rug.

They had planned for this moment.

They were ready.

Perry was waiting when Simon ran back through the door. Without speaking, they sprinted up the stairs to the second floor. They pulled down the wooden staircase leading to the rooftop and climbed up.

Perry was confident the attackers assumed they were catching them by surprise at this hour. He and Simon were counting on the attack coming down the driveway but were not taking any chances.

Perry opened the wooden box on the roof and pulled out an armful of loaded rifles that would provide fifty shots. When he looked over his shoulder, he saw Simon duplicating his movements. Simon's position on the roof overlooked the back of the house. Until they were certain no one was coming from the rear, they would cover both positions. If needed, Simon would join him at the front of the house.

They had talked through every possible scenario.

As he waited, Perry thought of the mistake the Klan had made in waiting so long for the attack. The three weeks since the tunnel had been dug had given them the time needed to create an elaborate plan and put everything in place to ensure its success. He grimaced, aware it wasn't actually *ensured* success. Andrew had said eleven men, but it could be more. The house was vulnerable from several positions, but they had given themselves the best odds possible.

Perry, Louisa, Simon, and June, had decided together that it was worth the risk to fight to save the house. They would do nothing to endanger the children – the reason Louisa and June were sheltered in the tunnel with them now – but Perry and Simon would fight.

Perry smiled tightly as he thought of the element of surprise they had been granted by Andrew's warning. He also acknowledged the fear tightening his throat. The beating he had received from the Klan had been brutal. He had healed from the bruises and cuts, but the memory refused to leave. He had yet to sleep through the night without waking up in drenching sweat. Louisa was used to pulling him close and singing softly until he could slip back into sleep. He hated the fear he lived with, but his years in the war had taught him it was possible to heal from trauma. It simply took time.

He welcomed the anger that swept up to swallow the fear. He had done nothing but treat his workers with integrity and fairness. He realized suddenly that if he survived this night, he would gather his workers and tell them they were going back to the working arrangement they'd had before the attack. He had allowed himself to be controlled by fear after the beating. He'd told himself it was to protect Louisa and Nathan, but it was mostly because of his own terror. Andrew had taken a risk to warn them. He would reward Andrew's courage by choosing to do the right thing, no matter the cost.

Perry took deep breaths as they waited. The cool air, after endless hours in the tobacco fields, was welcome. If he weren't waiting for an imminent attack, he would relish it. Leaves rustled softly, providing a chorus as the sliver of moon lifted above the treetops. The aroma of cut tobacco and churned earth filled his nostrils. How could such a beautiful night hold such danger?

An occasional whinny came from the barn. Perry berated himself. He should have told Andrew to let the horses out into the field so they could disappear into the woods. He cursed under his breath when he realized what could happen if the barn was set on fire. He looked around wildly. Was there time to dash across the yard to the barn, release the horses, and make it back?

The sound of hoofbeats in the distance silenced his thoughts. He had to focus on saving Blackwell Plantation, as well as ensuring the safety of his and Simon's family.

"It's time," Simon called softly.

"It's time," Perry repeated grimly. He lifted a rifle to his shoulder. He wasn't going to wait to ascertain the reason for a visit at midnight. He already knew the purpose. As soon as he had a target, he would shoot. Simon would do the same.

They would do everything they could to protect the house.

If they failed...

Perry fingered the rope next to his hand. It was tied to a bell secured inside the tunnel. If he rang it, Louisa and June knew to begin the escape. They had used the ensuing weeks to dig the tunnel wider and taller. They could maneuver through it easily now. There would be no delays.

Louisa and June had practiced running through the woods to where the boat was secured on the banks of the James River so many times, it was almost second nature. The children had run with them. They had cleared away the limbs and twigs that could make them stumble, or snap and alert the attackers to their location with the noise. The boys understood the terrible necessity of the exercise. Ella had seen it as nothing but a game.

Even if he and Simon weren't able to join them in the tunnel, Perry was reasonably certain they would make it to the James River before they could be caught. The attackers wouldn't have the advantage of knowing the woods like they did. From there, they would float down to Cromwell Plantation. June knew the location of the entrance to the Cromwell tunnel.

As he went through the details in his mind, Perry knew they had done everything conceivable to ensure the safety of the women and children.

The hoofbeats drew closer.

When Perry knew they were just around the last curve of the drive, the noise disappeared. They had slowed down to a walk, easing their way forward in the darkness. They had chosen the almost moonless night to give them an advantage. In truth, it had provided the advantage to him and Simon. They wouldn't be seen until they started to fire.

He forced himself to breathe slowly as he aimed the rifle down the road. The gun rested securely on the balustrade. No one would be expecting an attack from the rooftop. Neither would the invaders have a clear shot at them behind the solid balustrades. In the dark, they would be invisible. He and Simon planned to move around each time they fired, making it appear there were far more defenders than there actually were, as well as making it impossible to pinpoint their position. Any gunshot would simply go over the house.

Perry narrowed his eyes as the first man rounded the curve. As much as he wanted to fire, he forced himself to hold steady. The war had taught him control in combat. He wanted every invader to round the curve, assuring none of them would get away and attack from a different direction.

When he counted eleven men, he tossed a pebble toward Simon – the signal for him to join him. Andrew had told him eleven men were coming. They were clearly confident the attack was a surprise. They had not spread out to surround the house.

Another mistake.

When he felt Simon ease up beside him, Perry released his breath and pulled the trigger.

Boom!

Perry didn't wait to see if his bullet hit the mark. He simply kept firing at the eleven shapes – moving from left to right, and back again, shooting as fast as he could.

Simon's shots joined in the chaos.

Wild yelling filled the air as the men below panicked. They aimed toward the roof but had no way of knowing what they were shooting at. Were there two men? A dozen men?

Perry saw three men fall immediately. He smiled grimly as he imagined their shock and fear.

Another collapsed from Simon's well-aimed shot.

"Burn the house!" The hoarse order rang through the barrage of bullets.

Perry sucked in his breath and tightened his lips as he watched the remaining men reach into their saddlebags and yank out long sticks. He knew the wads of cloth at the end were soaked in kerosene.

Perry and Simon kept firing.

If the attackers got even one of those fire sticks close to the house, it could be impossible to extinguish it.

Three more men went down, tumbling from their horses onto the gravel drive. Their mounts bolted, disappearing into the darkness.

Only four men remained, trying to control their horses plunging with fear as they fired toward the roof.

Not a single shot had come close to them.

"Burn the house!" The hoarse order rang out again.

Somehow, the leader was still alive.

Perry recognized the voice this time. The man was one of his attackers from the road encounter. Rage roared through his veins, but his mind remained calm. He set his feet, aimed carefully at the portly man mounted on a towering bay, and pulled the trigger.

Poulton slumped forward but managed to retain his seat. "I'm hit! Retreat!" Holding on to the saddle horn, he kicked his horse into a gallop. "Retreat!"

Perry and Simon kept firing, but the remaining men had hunched forward on their horse's necks, making themselves less of a target.

Perry watched them retreat with a sense of satisfaction, but he was under no illusions the danger was over. When they disappeared, he shifted his attention to the men they had shot. None of them were moving but it didn't mean they were dead. They could be pretending, waiting for the moment they could fight back. Or run.

A movement in the woods across from the house brought Perry back to full alert. He pulled a rifle to his shoulder and took aim.

"Wait!" Simon hissed.

Perry moved his finger off the trigger. "Why?"

"They're Blackwell men," he said quietly.

Perry sucked in his breath as eight men moved from the woods, crept up to the fallen attackers, and leaned over them.

There was enough light to identify Andrew when he lifted his head. "Good shooting!" he called. "They're dead."

Suddenly, Perry felt fatigue rush through him. He felt sick to his stomach as he considered that seven men would never go home to their family; all because of senseless hatred. He had thought the end of the war would bring an end to the killing. "Will it ever stop?" he muttered. He had protected his and Simon's family, but other families had just been torn apart. Women had lost their husbands. Children had lost their fathers. "What a waste."

"I know what you mean," Simon said. He looked off into the distance. "What do you reckon we should do now?"

Perry was asking himself the same question. Would the four men leave, get reinforcements, return to retrieve their friends, and finish the job they had started? Or would they run for their lives like the cowards they were, with no concern for their fallen comrades?

Andrew asked the same question. "What you want us to do now?" He waved his hand toward the bodies.

Perry fought the impulse to yell with frustration. Blackwell Plantation was his responsibility. He was the only one who could make the decisions.

"We stay on the plantation," he told Simon, determined to protect his home. "You should go down and tell Louisa and June what is happening. They should remain in the tunnel for now. There are plenty of blankets and pillows down there, and enough food. They won't be comfortable, but they'll be safe."

Perry looked down from the roof. "Thank you for being here, Andrew."

Andrew nodded. "We was ready to join in the fight, but didn't look like you needed us none."

Perry recognized the wisdom of his decision. After tonight, the Klan's fight was still with Perry. If firing had come from the woods, the attackers would have known Blackwell workers had joined the battle. It would do nothing but make them more of a target.

"I appreciate your help, Perry said hoarsely. "Please pull the bodies back into the woods." He didn't want the children to see the dead men, but he wasn't certain what to do with them. Their families would want a proper burial. He supposed he could move them by wagon out to the entrance. It would provide a gruesome warning to anyone else who thought about attacking them, but also give the Klan a way to recover them. "We'll decide what to do with them in the morning." He would take no action without daylight.

As he headed toward the stairs, Simon suddenly jerked to a stop and pointed toward the tree line. "Look!"

Perry's head snapped in that direction. The instant he saw the glow, he knew. He stared in horror at the orange haze that lit the distant horizon.

The four remaining attackers, instead of leaving, had circled around the property and come up behind the tobacco barns. They had failed in their attempt to burn the plantation house, but they were destroying the entire tobacco crop drying after the harvest.

Perry was watching the destruction of Blackwell Plantation. The house may still be standing, but they needed that crop to carry them through.

Andrew, down on the ground, couldn't see over the trees. "I smell smoke!" he hollered. "You want us to go find out what it is?"

"No," Perry croaked, not certain his voice would carry down to Andrew. He knew it was too late. The barns would go up quickly, taking their hopes and dreams with them. Any satisfaction he had felt from saving the house vanished. He watched helplessly as the orange glow grew into leaping flames. He could hear the crackle of burning buildings and tobacco from where he stood.

"We need to go," Simon said.

Perry looked at him, dazed from watching the destruction. "What?"

"Burning the barns may give those men enough courage to come back here and attack the house again. We need to leave. There's no point in taking the risk."

Perry realized he and Simon had come to the same conclusion. Blackwell Plantation was finished. The only things they had left of value were their families. "You're right."

Perry looked back down toward the bodies. "Andrew, we're going to take our families to safety. We'll be back as soon as possible. Please take all the horses to the back fields where they won't be found. Go back to your cabins and don't make a sound. If you feel you're in danger, move everyone into the cover of the woods. In the morning, when you know it's safe, please put those men into the wagon and place their bodies beside the entrance. If they're not here, we'll know the men returned to retrieve them."

The words almost stuck in his throat. If the men returned to retrieve their friends and met no resistance, they would certainly burn the house. He forced himself not to think about it. Like Moses had reminded him, nothing was more important than his family.

Perry walked through the house slowly, as if he were seeing it for the last time. In truth, he most likely was. He ached at the thought of losing it, but he knew his pain would be nothing compared to Louisa's. This was her family home. All her memories were of this house.

Blackwell Plantation.

"You did everything you could." Simon's voice echoed up the winding stairway.

Perry heard him but didn't respond. Had he? Could he have done more to care for his family? To protect their home and livelihood? He suspected the questions would haunt him for the rest of his life.

"You're dead on your feet," Simon added.

Perry didn't resist when Simon took him by the arm and walked him through the house. He watched silently as Simon pulled back the rug and opened the door to the tunnel.

"Perry?" Louisa's frightened voice floated up to him. "We heard the gunfire. Are you and Simon alright?"

Perry reached down deep inside to answer her with confidence. "We're fine," he assured her. "We believe, though, that it will be best if we leave the plantation." He started down the stairs.

"Leave?" Louisa's face shone clearly in the lantern light. June, holding Ella, stared up at him. The boys remained silent, their eyes full of questions. "Through the woods? Down the river?"

"Yes," Perry answered.

Simon descended the steps and stood beside him.

Louisa, somehow sensing that this was not the time to ask any more questions, nodded.

Perry didn't want to tell her about the seven dead men and the destroyed tobacco crop while the children were listening.

"It's bad isn't it, Papa?"

Perry looked down at Nathan's grave expression.

"It's bad isn't it?" Nathan repeated. "Ella is asleep. Junior and I are old enough to know the truth, Papa."

Perry hesitated. They were mature for their age because they'd had to be, but the events of the night had been almost too much for him and Simon to handle. How could he explain it to children?

"Tell them," Louisa said quietly. "If we're running for our lives, we should at least know the truth."

Perry knew Louisa was right. He described what had happened in the last thirty minutes. The realization that it had taken only thirty minutes to lose what they had worked so hard for somehow made it even worse.

The expression on Louisa's face told him she realized the ramifications of what he had reported, but her voice was steady. "Let's go. It's safe for us to leave right now. We don't know how long that will be true."

"But mama..." Nathan said in a bewildered voice. "There are dead men outside the house."

"Dead men who aren't coming back to life," Louisa stated with no emotion. "Let's go." When Nathan started to say something else, she held up a warning finger. "Not another word, Nathan. Grab your bag of supplies and go down the tunnel. Not a word until we're down the river. Do it exactly like we practiced."

Nathan gulped and nodded. When his mama talked in that tone of voice, you didn't argue.

Simon leaned over and scooped Ella into his arms. She stirred and mumbled but didn't wake up. "Let's go," he said. He put an arm around Junior's shoulder. "We'll talk later. I promise."

"Yes, Daddy." Junior picked up his bag and fell in line.

June stood, kissed her husband on the cheek, and moved forward.

Perry walked quickly, leading the way with the lantern high over his head to illuminate the tunnel as much as possible. On the off chance someone had discovered the exit, he wanted to be the first to leave the tunnel. All he had left was his family. He would do whatever he had to in order to protect them. As he walked, he tried not to relive what had happened that night, but his efforts were futile. He could see the bodies of the seven dead men. He could see the orange flames licking toward the sky. The images would be forever seared into his mind and heart.

No one made a sound when they emerged from the tunnel. Silently, they made through the woods. Since they weren't being pursued, they walked carefully. There was no need to run. If anyone happened to be close by, they would not alert them to their presence.

Perry continued to lead the way.

Simon was grateful the path had been cleared of rocks and obstacles. Perry's prosthetic leg gave him impressive mobility, but he had to be constantly aware.

Simon brought up the rear. He never stopped scanning the woods for movement. He prayed Ella would sleep through the entire ordeal. She wasn't a baby who would cry, but she would be confused and want answers if she woke up. He tucked her closer to his shoulder and followed Junior closely.

The air was smoky and redolent with the smell of burning tobacco. In a different reality, he would have enjoyed it. He tried hard not to think about how much money had gone up in flames. He had no idea how he would care for his family now, but they had always found a way. This time would be no different.

It took only twenty minutes before they broke out onto the shores of the James River. The shifting wind had blown away the smoke and ashes. A canopy of stars blazed overhead, with the crescent moon floating over the water.

Simon took a deep breath. Even in a world of madness and hatred, there was always beauty to be found. The glory of the night sky restored a portion of his hope.

Ella stirred on his shoulder. She yawned and gazed upward. "It's pretty, Daddy."

"It is," Simon agreed in a whisper, watching as Perry and the boys pulled the large boat from its hiding place, climbed in, and positioned the oars. Louisa reached under the seats and pulled out thick blankets. As the temperatures plunged, they would need them.

Simon handed Ella to June once she was settled in the boat and took his place at the oars. The river current would carry them east toward Cromwell. His only job was keeping them in the center of the wide river, far from the banks. If someone was pursuing them, they couldn't be reached, even by gunfire.

"Mama, what are we doing?" Ella asked sleepily.

June's answer was barely audible. "We're going down to visit Grandma. And Uncle Moses and Aunt Rose."

"And Hope. And John. And Jed," Ella said sleepily.

"That's right," June said tenderly as she tucked the blanket around both of them. "You go back to sleep now. I'll let you know when we arrive."

Within moments, Ella was sleeping again, her breathing easy and steady.

Simon watched her, wishing life could be that easy. He wondered if his little girl would ever feel that safe in life again, and then scolded himself for thinking that. Whatever was coming next, they were going to Cromwell Plantation. They would all be safe, and they would be with family. The future would unfold as it was meant to.

A look at Perry's face revealed nothing. He knew Perry had locked his emotions away and was merely taking the next step. They'd learned to do that during the war. Simon ached for him. He and June had lost a lot, but Perry and Louisa had lost everything. He doubted the house would still be standing in the morning. Even if it was, the loss of the tobacco crop made it impossible for them to stay.

The boat glided through the water soundlessly. Frogs croaked and plopped into the water along the banks. Even this far out, the night was quiet enough for the sound to carry. A flock of snow geese, their white outlined against the dark sky, honked their way over as they headed south in anticipation of winter's arrival. Fish jumped as they snagged bugs from the surface of the river. Owls hooted their nighttime calls from leafy perches high in the trees.

Simon smiled when he realized both Junior and Nathan were sound asleep, curled up in the bottom of the boat beneath their blankets. He knew they were completely exhausted.

Despite the danger, he felt himself begin to relax. Both he and Perry could have died during the gunfight.

They had lived. June and Louisa were safe. So were the children. Everything truly precious to him was inside this boat.

Alive.

As the boat floated down the river, Perry could no longer push away his memories of the night. They came roaring back as he relived each moment. A feeling of failure threatened to swallow him. He leaned close to Louisa. "I'm sorry," he said softly.

"Hush," Louisa responded. Her voice was as soft as his, but it didn't hide the hint of steel in her words. "I'm glad it happened."

Perry gasped and sat back. "What are you...?"

"That plantation almost took away everything important to me," Louisa stated. "All I care about is you and Nathan. I was willing for you to fight to save the house, but when I was down in the tunnel listening to gunfire, I knew that if something happened to you, I would never forgive myself for letting it happen." Her voice faltered. "I didn't know if I would ever see you alive again, Perry. It felt like the war all over again. I almost lost you then. The idea of losing you because of a stupid plantation made me want to throw up."

"A stupid plantation?" Perry echoed. "How can you say that? It's your *home*. It's our *life*."

Louisa was shaking her head before he finished speaking. "It's a *house*, Perry. It was only my home because you and Nathan were there. Home is wherever you two are. I know what losing the tobacco crop means, Perry. I also know that if those men return for their dead friends, the house will probably be burnt." She looked over her shoulder to make certain the boys were still asleep. "I don't care."

Perry couldn't believe what he was hearing. "You don't *care*?"

Louisa was shaking her head again. "I don't care," she repeated. "I'm not naïve. I know we're going to have to start over. I know it will be hard." She took his hand. "Perry, we've been through hard times before. We had very little in Georgia, but we were happy. When the war ended, we claimed Blackwell Plantation as my inheritance, but we've lived with nothing except stress since we arrived. You think it's what I need and want, because it's where I grew up, but I'm not that person anymore." She smiled at him tenderly. "We can't keep the plantation running, but we have enough to start over somewhere else. We'll be fine."

Perry's reaction had changed from disbelief to awe. "You really mean that, don't you?"

"I do," Louisa said firmly. She looked toward the back of the boat. "We have enough for us to start over, and there's also enough for Simon and June to start fresh. We've only kept the plantation running for this long because of them. They're our friends. We'll all start over." She smiled again.

As Perry listened, it was as if he was watching a heavy weight lift from her and float up into the night sky.

"The workers can stay there as long as they want," Louisa continued. "At some point they'll have to find jobs, but there should be enough food stored away to carry them through the winter."

Perry chuckled. "You seem to have thought of everything."

"I have," Louisa agreed cheerfully. "I can hardly wait to have Annie's cinnamon rolls in the morning!"

———⚘———

Simon exchanged a look with June. Her eyes gleamed with tears, but there was deep peace on her face. The future was unknown, but they weren't starting from nothing. His mind began to spin with the possibilities.

Chapter Eighteen

Carrie straightened slowly, stretching out the painful knots in her back and shoulders. There was probably a time when she'd been this tired, but at the moment she couldn't remember it. A glance toward the window told her she and Janie had operated through the night. The sky glowed faintly over the line of trees in the distance.

"We did it." Janie's voice was laced with weariness.

"I hope so," Carrie replied. Using a medical book as their guide, they had painstakingly entered Annie's abdomen, found the ruptured appendix that extended from her colon on the lower right side of her belly, and removed it. Carrie had carefully examined other organs while she was in Annie's abdomen but hadn't found any other obvious problems. That didn't mean they weren't there. She just hadn't known how to identify them.

"Annie is still in danger," Carrie said soberly.

Janie nodded. "I know the infection could lead to inflammation in her abdominal lining."

Carrie was more concerned that the infection had already spread to her bloodstream. There was no way of knowing if Annie would develop sepsis, the same life-threatening condition that had taken Jed's father.

"There is no way Annie could have run that picnic today if her appendix had already ruptured, Carrie," Janie said. "Thanks to Rose, we caught it early. The infection had hardly any time to spread."

Carrie met her eyes but couldn't shake her uneasiness. "I know you're right," she said slowly.

"Stop thinking about Morris," Janie ordered sternly.

Carrie blinked at her. "How do you have enough energy to talk to me like that?"

"Habit. You need me to knock you out of your negative thinking."

Carrie managed to smile slightly, though the effort felt as if her lips were cracking. She allowed herself a groan as she rotated her head. "When I'm this tired, it's hard to think clearly."

"I know," Janie said sympathetically. "You did a beautiful job with the surgery."

"I couldn't have done it without you." Carrie walked to the window and gazed out at the approaching dawn. A smattering of stars, promising clear skies, rested above the treetops. They would soon be swallowed by the light of a new day.

"That's true," Janie acknowledged, "but you were the one who held Annie's life in your hands. That kind of responsibility saps the energy from your soul. You have every right to be exhausted."

Carrie turned away from the window and moved to the table set up near the bed. "Our job now is to make sure her body doesn't overreact to the infection." Carrie thought about the homeopathic remedies they had available. What would be most effective in stopping potential widespread inflammation and organ failure if sepsis was to develop? "I think we should begin treating her with Pyrogenium."

"Assume she has sepsis?" Janie asked.

"Yes," Carrie said, her tired mind coming back to life as she considered the options. "It's a wonderful remedy for sepsis, but it will support her body's ability to fight off other possible infection." She thought about the best ways to support Annie with the Pyrogenium. The remedy required fresh air to be most effective. She walked over and opened the window, breathing in deeply. The cool morning air, replete with the aroma of autumn leaves, revived her immediately. "There is no danger of contamination now. Annie will need fresh air and lots of rest."

"She'll also need cool cloth applications so that she doesn't get too warm, but I'm going to cover her with a blanket so she doesn't get chilled," Janie added. "When do you think she'll wake up?"

Carrie refused to admit or articulate her fear that Annie might *not* wake up. She'd done the best she could with the surgery, but having never done an appendectomy before, she had no idea what to expect with the recovery. In some ways, it was just like any other surgery, but she would have preferred not to experiment on Annie. "Within the hour," she replied.

"Should I go give everyone a report?"

Carrie hesitated. Other than the fact that they had successfully removed the appendix, they had no idea how Annie truly was. At the moment, all they could honestly say was that she was still unconscious.

"Stop thinking the worst!" Janie scolded.

"How can I not?" Carrie demanded. "I had no idea what I was doing, Janie!"

"Not true," Janie corrected her. "You had no idea what you were doing when you successfully performed an emergency C-section on me during Robert's birth. Since that day, you have performed hundreds of surgeries. You've learned so much. This surgery was different, but it wasn't anything you couldn't handle." She paused. "Actually, it wasn't anything you *didn't* handle. Dr. Wallington, the appendix is out. There was zero evidence of infection when you closed her up. No doctor can ever do more than that."

Janie's words pierced Carrie's uncertainty. "Thank you, Dr. Justin. You're right."

Janie returned to her earlier question. "So, do you want to give everyone the news or do you want to stay here?"

"Stay here," Carrie said promptly. "I don't want to take a chance on not being here when Annie wakes up. She will be disoriented and confused."

Janie pulled off the apron that covered her dress, patted her hair, and opened the door. "I'll be back in a few minutes with cool water. I'll also make some ginger and garlic tea for our patient."

Carrie pulled a chair next to the bed and sat down. "Thank you. Annie is going to get sick of that tea, but she's going to drink her weight in it. Garlic and ginger are the best herbal treatments for infection." She stifled a yawn and settled in to wait.

Moses jolted awake when Janie opened the screen door and stepped out onto the porch. He stood immediately, trying to calm the pounding of his heart. Was she bringing good news or bad news?

Janie looked around in astonishment. "Have y'all been out here all night?"

Anthony, Rose, Thomas, Alice, and Matthew yawned, opened their eyes, and stretched. They shoved aside blankets and pushed up from their rocking chairs.

"The entire night," Moses told her. "Not one of us was willing to go to bed until we had word on my Mama."

Instead of answering, Janie looked around the porch. "Where is Miles?"

"I'm right here," Miles said. His weary voice matched the speed with which he climbed the stairs. "I went to let the horses out." He walked over and took Janie's hands. "How is my Annie?"

Moses knew from the tone of his voice that Miles had prepared himself for the worst.

Despite the obvious fatigue, Janie smiled. "The surgery was successful, Miles. Carrie removed the appendix, made sure there was no infection, and then closed her up. She isn't awake from the anesthesia yet, but I don't think it will be much longer." Her voice was calm and reassuring.

Miles swallowed hard. "You tellin' me my Annie gonna be alright?"

Moses noticed Janie's slight hesitation, but her voice remained confident when she answered. "We believe she will be fine. There is a chance of internal infection, but we removed the appendix quickly." She turned to Rose "Your sharp eyes and quick action saved Annie, Rose. Thanks to you, we caught it early."

Rose breathed a sigh of relief.

Moses grinned. Now that he knew his mama would be alright, he could feel himself breathing again. He pulled Rose in close to his side. "It took extreme courage to tell Carrie something was wrong with Mama. I can imagine the death glare she gave you."

"She was not pleased," Rose agreed with a chuckle.

"We're going to treat her with a remedy for infection, but she may not even need it," Janie continued.

Moses allowed himself to absorb her hope. His mama hadn't died during the surgery. That alone was a reason for believing in miracles.

"My Carrie Girl did it," Miles said softly.

"She did," Janie answered. "Carrie is a top-notch surgeon. Just because she'd never done an appendectomy, she knew exactly how to find the appendix, and how to remove it."

Awe filled Mile's face. "I woulda never guessed my Carrie Girl would grow up and save my wife's life one day." He chuckled. "I woulda never guessed I would *have* a wife. Or be back here on the plantation workin' like a regular man." He looked up as the top of the sun peeked over the tree line. "I reckon this life done be filled with a lot of miracles."

"I'd say you're right," Moses agreed whole-heartedly.

Rose reached over, took his hand, and squeezed it tightly. "I'm going to tell the children. I promised I would let them know the instant we had news."

"Do you think we should wait until Mama wakes up?" Moses hated the fear still niggling at the base of his brain.

Janie shook her head. "There is no reason to think Annie won't wake up. She may be cranky for a while, but that's to be expected."

Miles laughed loudly. "My Annie is cranky when she's *not* had surgery. Why would this be any different?" He looked at Moses. "You go tell my grandchillun that their grandma is gonna be just fine."

Alice stood, raising her arms above her head to stretch further. "That's my signal to head to the kitchen. I'd say this news deserves some cinnamon rolls!"

"My Annie gonna be real glad you be here, Alice." Miles shook his head. "Don't know what we would do if you wasn't here."

Alice smiled. "I'm here. Annie can focus on getting well."

"Alice is going to work here from now on, Miles," Moses told him. "Even when Mama gets well, there's too much for her to do alone. Alice is going to be her assistant."

"That's a real good thing," Miles said fervently. "She weren't never gonna say nothin', but she was gettin' real tired. Help will be good."

Moses felt a stab of guilty regret. He should have recognized long before now that his mama was doing too much. Just because she would never admit it; he still should have seen it.

Miles laid a hand on his shoulder. "Get rid of them thoughts right now, Moses. Annie didn't want nobody to know that it be too much. You can't help somebody that don't tell you when they need it. Your mama be every bit as stubborn as you are."

Moses smiled. "At least I come by it honest."

"That you do, son," Miles answered. "That you do."

Moses moved toward the porch stairs. A walk would help him work off the stiffness after a night of restless sleep in the rocker. He would be back before his mama woke up.

"What was that?" Anthony asked sharply. He stood and walked to stand beside Moses. "I could swear I heard someone yell."

Moses didn't feel alarm. "Probably one of the men coming to tell me something. It's about time for work to start."

"Moses!"

Moses frowned and stared hard down the road. That had sounded like a woman.

"Moses!"

Suddenly, he recognized the voice. "That's June!"

In an instant, he was off the porch and running down the road, Anthony and Matthew right behind him.

———❧———

Moses didn't stop running until he reached the group.

Perry and Louisa, each with an arm around Nathan, were trudging up the road. Junior walked hand in hand with June. Ella was snuggled into Simon's arms.

"What are you doing here? What happened? Is everyone alright?" Moses asked.

Matthew and Anthony stepped up beside him. Their eyes swept the horizon, searching for signs of trouble.

"We will be," June replied wearily. "We're tired, but no one is hurt."

Moses looked at Simon with questioning eyes.

"The Klan came," Simon said, shifting Ella to his other shoulder. "They're not behind us." He paused. "At least, we don't think they are. Our escape was clean."

Moses reached out and took Ella from him. She made a small sound, curled into his shoulder, and continued to sleep.

Simon smiled. "I wish I could sleep like that."

Moses could tell from Simon's expression that sleep had not been an option that night. The dazed look on Perry's face revealed the same.

Moses turned to Perry. "Blackwell? The house?"

"My guess is that it's gone. We left before they came back to finish the job." Perry took a deep breath. "The tobacco crop is gone. They burned the barns."

Moses sucked in his breath. "The entire crop?" His mind whirled with questions.

"All of it," Perry replied.

"Seven men are dead," Nathan said. His voice was strangely void of emotion. "My daddy and Simon killed them."

"What did you say?" Moses knew Perry's son was practically dead on his feet. How could an eight-year-old boy process what had happened? How much had he seen?

"Eleven of the Klan came around midnight," Simon explained. "They would have surprised us, 'cept we'd been working in the fields the whole day to bring in the rest of the tobacco. One of the men warned us they were coming. Louisa and June took the children into the tunnel. Perry and me went up on the roof and waited for them. Turns out we surprised *them*. They'd come to burn the house..."

When his voice trailed off, Moses understood that he didn't want the children to hear what else they had come to do.

"We got seven of 'em, but the leader and the other three took off," Simon continued. "We hoped they were leaving, but it turns out they went around to the barns." His lips twisted. "They used their firesticks there. They only had four, but it was all they needed."

"No one was hurt," June said, as she stifled a yawn. "That's what's important."

"Yep," Simon agreed. "We figured the men would come back for the ones we killed. If they did, they would probably come with reinforcements. We surprised them by being on the roof when they showed up. They weren't gonna make the same mistake again, so we left. We decided all of us getting out of there alive was the best we could count on."

Moses gut clenched. The Klan might be filled with hatred, but they weren't going to leave seven of their men behind. The house was probably burned to the ground, or at least gutted. "You came down the river?"

"Yep. Decided to walk to the house." Simon looked at Anthony. "We didn't figure you and Carrie would appreciate us barging into your bedroom through the tunnel so early in the morning."

"We want some of Grandma's cinnamon rolls," Junior said sleepily. "I'm starving."

Moses frowned as he realized he had to give June more bad news. "You're going to have some cinnamon rolls, but Grandma isn't baking them."

June's eyes narrowed with fresh concern. "Why not?" she asked sharply.

"Because she got sick last night," Moses replied. He wondered how much to say with the children there, but thought about Janie's confidence that his mama would fully recover. "Carrie and Janie had to perform surgery."

"Surgery?" June clasped a hand to her mouth. Will she…?"

"She's going to be fine," Moses said firmly, praying Janie's confidence was justified. "She won't be cooking for a while, but I've hired Alice as her assistant. She'll take over for now, and help Mama when she's well enough to be back in the kitchen."

"She's really gonna be alright? Have you seen her?" June demanded. New fear was etched into her face.

"Not yet," Moses admitted. "She hasn't woken up from the anesthesia, but Janie assured us she'll be alright. It will just take time."

June took Junior's hand and started toward the house. "I'm going to see for myself."

Moses understood. He watched her move through the early morning sun glowing off the mist rising from the fields, before he shifted his attention to the rest of the group.

"We hate to impose like this," Louisa said softly. Her eyes were glazed with exhaustion.

"It's no imposition," Moses replied.

"We always have room for friends and family," Anthony assured them. "We've got two empty rooms in the guest house right now. It will be tight for you, but there will be plenty of food."

"Thank you," Perry said gratefully. "Tight is perfectly fine. We'll be safe. That's what matters."

Moses agreed. He was confident the Klan wouldn't consider an attack on Cromwell, even if they knew Perry and Simon were there. After losing seven of their men, they would be much more cautious.

Perry edged up next to Moses. "I know y'all have many questions. I promise we'll answer them later."

"Let's get back to the house," Moses said. "Mama should be waking up soon. There will be time for questions when y'all have eaten and rested."

―――❦―――

Carrie was struggling to stay awake when she heard Annie moan. The sound brought her instantly awake. She leaned over the bed so she would be the first thing Annie saw when she woke up.

Annie moaned again.

"Welcome back," Carrie said gently.

Annie's eyes fluttered open and closed for a few seconds.

Carrie was relieved beyond words to see no fever in her eyes. Infection could still come, but they were in the clear for now. That was an excellent sign.

Annie moaned again.

"You're alright, Annie," Carrie said soothingly. "You're here at home. You had to have surgery."

Annie's eyes opened again. "What?" she croaked.

"You had to have surgery," Carrie repeated. "You're going to be alright."

Annie swiveled her head, slowly scanning the room.

"I'll get Miles for you," Carrie said tenderly.

"Miles..." Annie whispered before she fell asleep again.

Janie opened the door and slipped inside. She looked toward the bed with a disappointed expression. "She's not awake yet?"

Carrie grinned. "She woke up! I told her where she was and that she'll be alright. She asked for Miles and went back to sleep."

"Yep," Janie said smugly. "I told you she would be fine."

Carrie chuckled. "I should know by now that my partner is always right."

"You should," Janie replied. "You've always been a slow learner, though. I'll give you more time."

Carrie stuck out her tongue. "Arrogance is not attractive."

Janie laughed. "My very brilliant partner once told me that confidence is not arrogance."

Carrie joined her in the laughter. "Your brilliant partner was absolutely right!"

A light tap sounded at the door.

Carrie opened the door and pulled Miles into a hug. "Annie is sleeping again, but she woke up a few minutes ago and asked for you. She doesn't have a fever. It's all good news!"

Miles wrapped his arms around her tightly. "You did it, Carrie Girl." His voice was husky with emotion. "Thank you for saving my Annie."

Carrie's heart swelled when she felt the tremor in his body. She'd never known Miles to cry. She breathed a silent prayer of gratitude. "You're welcome. We all love Annie."

"Not like I love her," Miles stated. He sat down on the edge of the bed and took Annie's hand. "I aim on bein' right here when she comes to again," he declared resolutely.

Carrie knew that look. She picked up the bucket of water and carried it to the bedside. "Annie needs to stay cool. I want you to bathe her face and arms with a damp cloth until she wakes again."

Miles nodded, dipped the cloth in the water, and wiped her face gently. His touch was so soft, it was more like a caress.

Carrie felt a lump in her throat as she gazed at the tender expression on Miles' face. She knew he loved Annie, but it wasn't until that moment that she fully understood the depth of his emotion. Miles had lived most of his life alone. He'd been a slave on the plantation for decades, refusing to take a wife because he knew she could be sold away from him at any time. When he escaped to Canada, he still chose to remain alone. It wasn't until he returned to the plantation looking for work, and met Annie, that he had fallen in love and married her.

"You go on and get something to eat," Miles ordered. "Both of you. Anything else I need to know when she wakes up again?"

Carrie pointed to the cup on the nightstand. "Give her that garlic and ginger tea. I've added honey, but the flavor is strong. She's going to hate the taste but tell her it's doctor's orders."

"She'll drink it," Miles vowed. "Don't you worry none about that."

Carrie's stomach growled loudly.

"Let's go eat," Janie said.

"Do you think there's any food?" Carrie asked.

Janie smiled. "Alice is taking over the kitchen until Annie is well again. Moses hired her to be her assistant. Annie will never have to do everything on her own again."

"That's wonderful!" Carrie exclaimed. She thought about adding someone else to the payroll but pushed worry from her mind. They would deal with everything one day at a time. Annie needed help. That's all that mattered. The details would work themselves out.

"We also have company," Janie told her.

"Company?" Carrie looked out the window. "Isn't it early for company? Who is it?"

"Blackwell was attacked last night," Janie replied.

Carrie closed her eyes for a moment to absorb the news. "Is everyone alright?"

"They are," Janie assured her. "The tobacco barns were burned, and the house is most likely gone.

Matthew told me he thought they would be here a while."

Carrie took a calming breath. They would do what they had always done. Make things work.

Chapter Nineteen

Abby lifted her face to the early morning sun as it climbed above the surrounding houses. She was finding it more difficult to find peace in New York City as the days unfolded. Visions of the plantation in fall called her, but she didn't feel she could go home.

It had been six weeks since the Stock Exchange had crashed. Almost five weeks since Wally had taken his life. Abby still couldn't detect a spark of life in Nancy's eyes. Her friend moved through each day in a numb fog, getting out of bed simply because Abby insisted. She scarcely ate anything, protesting she couldn't eat because she could barely breathe or swallow. She would answer if asked a direct question, but Abby couldn't make sense of the monosyllabic responses. She was a ghost of the vibrant, powerful woman Abby knew.

Wally had been Nancy's life. Her heart and life had been shattered by his death. The pain had been multiplied by the *way* Wally had died.

Abby had watched her friend die inside when Nancy saw Wally dead on the floor – his pistol lying next to his lifeless body.

At night, Abby heard the muffled screams of agony coming from Nancy's bedroom. She knew her friend was curled in a fetal position, doing her best to muffle the screams with a pillow, but desperate to find a release for the pain she was in. Most nights she crawled onto the bed to hold her friend while she cried, but there were some nights when Nancy couldn't stand even *her* presence. On those occasions, Abby would stand outside the door and pray for her friend to discover the will to live.

Nancy had never gone back into the bedroom she and Wally had shared. She had chosen a room as far away as possible, refusing to even look in the direction of the door when she walked by.

Abby thought often of what Carrie had gone through when Robert died. What other friends had gone through when their loved ones had died. What *she* experienced when her first husband, Charles, passed away. Five weeks was a blink in time; compared to decades of living and loving. She would stay as long as Nancy needed her.

Abby knew that the *way* Wally had died made it even more difficult for Nancy to process and survive. This day was going to be even more excruciating than the days that had preceded it since Wally's suicide.

The door creaked open as Nancy walked onto the porch. She stopped, staring out over the trees almost empty of leaves. The few still clinging to branches were brown and withered.

Abby was achingly aware the barren trees reflected Nancy's heart – empty, brown, and withered.

"This is the last time I will ever step out on this porch." Nancy's voice was both vacant and disbelieving. Her face revealed the bewilderment that her life had changed so drastically in such a short time.

Most of the time, the pain swallowing her made her completely unaware of Michael and Julie coming and going. She stared at him blankly when he asked her questions about the house. Somehow, though, it had registered that she was moving away from her home that afternoon.

Abby's heart swelled with sympathy and sorrow. Nancy had known this day was coming since the market crashed, but nothing could prepare her for losing the home she thought she would live in for the rest of her life, with the man she thought she would grow old with. Abby knew there were no words to make the stark reality easier.

The bank was repossessing her home.

Nancy was moving in with Michael and Julie.

"What am I going to do?" Nancy whispered.

Abby heard the same question from her friend every day. In truth, she had no answers, but she tried to come up with something comforting to say. She doubted the words were truly comforting, and she suspected Nancy didn't actually hear the words, but at least she knew she wasn't alone. "You know Michael and Julie want you to stay forever, Nancy. Your son and daughter-in-law love you very much."

Nancy shook her head. The morning sun emphasized the wrinkles that had multiplied in recent weeks. Her normally bright blue eyes were dull with pain and confusion. "How could I have not known?"

This was the other question Abby heard multiple times throughout every day of the last five weeks. She had failed to come up with an answer that relieved her friend's pain. She merely reached out and took her hand.

When Nancy turned to look at her, the dull pain had been replaced by a frantic wildness. Her voice came in shallow gasps. "Wally was my husband. I knew he felt terrible about losing our money, but I never dreamed he would ki..." She wrung her hands. "How could I not see how desperate he was? The Diamond Hoax. Investing in the Stock Market. It wasn't like him to be so risky. Wally was desperate. I should have known, Abby. If I'd known, I could have stopped it. My husband would still be alive." Her voice faltered away into a wounded whimper. "Wally would be alive."

Abby struggled for words but once again came up empty. She did the only thing she knew to do - she grasped Nancy's hands more tightly. She hated the feeling of helplessness that had become her constant companion since Wally's suicide.

They sat silently for several minutes. Nancy's breath eventually slowed.

"Why did he do this to me?" Nancy asked. Her words were barely audible.

Abby blinked away her tears. The longer she stayed with her friend, the more she realized suicide was not just a death to mourn. Suicide impacted every person left behind – leaving them with unimaginable pain and endless, unanswerable questions. She wondered if Wally had known how his suicide would impact Nancy, if he would have pulled the trigger. She couldn't imagine it. He had loved his wife deeply.

Michael had discovered a note on the bedside table. The words, scrawled almost eligibly, had been heartbreakingly brief.

I'm sorry. Everyone will be better off without me.

If Wally could see how everyone was suffering, he might have made a different decision.

Or not.

Every day was a guessing game of what she should say in the face of Nancy's grief, confusion, and guilt. She had dealt with the grief of loss many times, but with suicide as the cause of Nancy's loss, the right words seemed even more elusive.

"He didn't mean to do it to *you*, Nancy." Abby rubbed Nancy's hands, trying to force warmth and life into them.

"Well, he did," Nancy said flatly. She jerked away and walked to the edge of the porch. "I've heard it all in the last five weeks from my friends." She whirled around to stare at Abby. "I haven't told you about it. One friend told me Wally made a selfish choice. That my husband took the coward's way out. Another told me that he committed an unforgiveable sin. That killing himself was an act of weakness and went against God." She dashed away the tears streaming down her cheeks. "Someone told me his suicide was proof he wasn't strong and didn't love me."

Abby felt anger roar to life. Wally and Nancy were well known in New York City. They had scores of friends and colleagues, but few had come by since the poorly attended funeral service. When people realized Wally had killed himself, they had stayed away. She knew it was because they didn't know what to say, but their absence had devastated Nancy even more by heaping shame on her grief.

The few friends who had dropped by probably came with good intentions, but the words they had chosen were horribly destructive. "That is all complete nonsense, Nancy," Abby said fiercely. "Surely you don't believe any of that – especially the ludicrous suggestion that your husband didn't love you. Wally *adored* you."

Nancy's eyes had turned blank. "Did he, Abby? Or was I simply not worth living for?" Her voice broke. "I ask myself the same question over and over. *Why was I not worth living for? What did I do wrong?*"

Nancy's breath grew shallow and rapid. "I should never have talked to him about finances. I should never have asked questions. I made Wally feel like less of a man. When the market crashed and we lost everything, he couldn't handle it because of the things I had said."

Abby stepped through the invisible brick wall Nancy had erected around herself and pulled her tightly into an embrace. "It was not your fault," she said gently. "Asking questions did not cause Wally to kill himself." She held Nancy back so she could look at her closely and repeated her words more firmly. "*It was not your fault.*"

Abby knew she needed to say more. "You didn't know because Wally didn't want you to know. Your husband loved you with all his heart."

Tears filled Nancy's eyes. "Then why, Abby? Why did Wally leave me?" Her words ended on a wail. "I can't breathe most of the time. I don't *want* to breathe. I used to think I knew something about life. I know nothing." Her voice rose. "*I know nothing.*" She jerked away again. "How can I live life when I know nothing?" Her voice sharpened. "Actually, I do know one thing. I know *forever* doesn't exist. Wally promised to love me *forever*. I thought we would grow old together." Her voice crumbled into broken shards. "There is no *forever*, Abby."

Nancy collapsed onto the swing, sobs wracking her body that had become alarmingly thin in the past weeks. "Why do I have to breathe?" she cried. "How could he possibly think my life would be better without him?"

Michael had read Wally's suicide note to her. Her response had been to whimper and shake her head frantically, until she dissolved into tears.

Abby knew it was finally time.

"Wally loved you with all his heart," she repeated. "I'm certain he truly believed your life would be better without him. He simply had no hope left, Nancy. For that moment… when he pulled that trigger… he couldn't find hope."

"How do you *know*?" Nancy cried desperately.

Abby took a deep breath, releasing the secret she had sworn to take to the grave. "Because I tried to commit suicide."

Nancy's eyes bulged from her face. Shocked out of her crying, she stared at Abby with disbelieving eyes. "*You*? You tried to kill yourself?"

Now that the secret was finally out, Abby found the words she needed. "It was several months after Charles died. I felt so terribly alone and overwhelmed. Charles had left me the factories in his will, but I was a threat to the men in the industry. It's bad for women today, but it was terrible thirty years ago. They made it their mission in life to drive me out of business. They made fun of me. They lied in order to take business away from me. They mocked me in the streets. It seemed I couldn't go anywhere without one of them being there. I was afraid to leave the house." As Abby talked, all of it came roaring back to life. Even after three decades, it felt as if it were yesterday.

Abby fell silent for a long moment. She didn't want to talk about the next part but now that she had chosen to speak, she had to say everything. "One day, when I went out for groceries, one of the men appeared out of nowhere and shoved me into a dark alley." Her voice choked as she said the words.

Nancy held a hand to her throat. "Did he...?" she asked breathlessly.

"He ripped my clothing, but somehow I fought my way out of actually being raped." Abby's voice faltered as she remembered the bruises that had haunted her for weeks after the attack. She truly didn't know how she had escaped. She remembered fighting wildly... She could recall the moment she broke free. "When I got out of there, I ran home, closed myself in the house, and locked the doors. I had never felt so alone."

Abby turned away and sat down on the porch swing.

Nancy joined her, took her hand, and held it firmly.

The touch gave Abby the courage to continue. "I cried for hours. All I could think about was that it was never going to end. I was going to spend my entire life avoiding rapes and attacks unless I sold the factories and moved back to the country – back to the life I had fought to leave behind. I knew I was letting Charles down, but I couldn't continue fighting." She blinked back her tears. "I cried so long I could barely breathe. I realized I no longer cared if I *could* breathe. As I thought about unlocking my doors and stepping back outside, I realized I didn't *want* to breathe any longer."

Abby remembered the moment as if it was happening now. Reliving her experience gave her a deeper understanding of Wally's decision. She turned and looked Nancy directly in the eyes. "I lost hope, Nancy. I no longer hoped things would change. I no longer hoped life would get better. I was *done. Totally done.* I could live in total darkness, or I could choose death." She took a deep breath. "Death, as horrible as it might sound, was a more appealing option."

"What about your family?" Nancy whispered. "You had people who cared about you."

"I did," Abby agreed. "I also had friends trying to support me in the midst of all the pain and trouble." She paused again, choosing her words carefully. "I loved them. I knew they loved me. Quite honestly, it didn't matter. The truth was that they couldn't solve my problems. They couldn't make things better. They couldn't keep me from being raped in an alleyway."

Thoughts of Wally clarified her own experience. "I believed their lives would be better and easier if I died."

"No..." Nancy whispered.

Abby stood abruptly, her emotions churning so wildly she thought she might scream out from the awakened anguish. "I lost hope, Nancy. I didn't have anything left to push through and fight with." She paused again. She saw herself as she walked through the house with her torn dress and bruised face and arms. "I knew Charles had always kept a loaded pistol in his desk drawer. I hadn't touched his office since he died. It was as if I was in a trance when I went into his office and got the gun."

Nancy whimpered slightly.

Abby took a long, deep breath. "I wanted to be close to Charles when I died. My husband practically lived behind that desk, so I sat down in his desk chair, checked to make sure the gun was loaded, and held it to my temple."

As she talked, she saw Wally's lifeless eyes. She wondered if he regretted it the instant he pulled the trigger. She was certain he regretted it if he somehow knew the pain his loved ones were living with because of his choice.

"And then a very firm knock sounded at the door." Abby could hear the sound loudly in her mind. "I ignored it the first time... I put my finger on the trigger... A second later, the knock came again, louder that time." She shook her head. "Even now, I have no idea why I got up and answered the door. It was like an invisible force was pushing me to move."

"Was it more trouble?" Nancy asked breathlessly.

Abby finally smiled. "It was Matthew."

"Matthew? Matthew Justin?" Nancy asked.

"Yes. Matthew was a brand-new journalist, fresh out of college. He was searching for a story. He had heard tales on the street about how the men were attempting to force me out of business. That day, he had overheard the man who tried to rape me, boasting about how close he had come to having his way with me. The man was angry that I'd gotten away, and said I wouldn't escape the next time."

"Dear God..." Nancy's face turned white.

Abby's smile came naturally. Good memories flooded in to replace the bad ones. Matthew hadn't mentioned her torn dress or bruises. He already knew the reason. He just set about to fix things. "Matthew offered to help me. He told me he would be my bodyguard for as long as I needed him. He would run stories in the Philadelphia paper about the men who were doing such terrible things. He believed that when their behavior was exposed, they would stop."

"Did he do all that?" Nancy asked.

"Every bit of it," Abby replied. "He did so much more, however. Matthew restored my hope." She already knew what was rolling through Nancy's mind. Why hadn't someone come to save Wally? "I don't know why I was fortunate enough to have Matthew come to my house at the exact moment I was going to pull the trigger."

"Does Matthew know?" Nancy's eyes were latched on her.

"I've never told a soul that story. You're the only one who knows I almost killed myself."

"Why didn't you tell anyone?"

"Because I was ashamed," Abby answered. "I've carried the shame since that day. I had heard all the same nonsense you've heard. I believed suicide was an unforgiveable sin. I believed it was a sign of weakness. I believed I should be better able to handle my grief after Charles' death. I didn't believe there was anyone who could help me. It didn't matter that I didn't know how to ask for help. I couldn't see past the black hole of my grief, and my sense of failure." She thought about that fateful moment. "I longed for death, because I couldn't find a reason to hope. A *way* to hope."

"Like Wally couldn't," Nancy said with a heartfelt sigh.

"Like Wally couldn't," Abby agreed. She took Nancy's hands again, the words coming easily.. "You're going to hurt for a long time, my friend. You'll never be the same. Your pain will always be a part of you, though I believe you will find your way to a different kind of peace and joy." She knew Nancy couldn't believe that at the moment, but she wanted to plant the words in her friend's heart. "Understanding that Wally lost hope will not eliminate your pain. You will still fight to believe it's not your fault." Abby squeezed her hands tightly. "I'm going to keep telling you – for as long as you need to hear it – that his suicide is *not your fault.* It was a choice Wally made because he wasn't able to see beyond the black hole of hopelessness."

Nancy remained quiet for several minutes, but much of the tension had left her body.

Abby waited.

"I've thought about doing it," Nancy finally admitted in a broken voice.

"I'm certain you have," Abby said gently. "There's no shame in that. You've lost so much." She paused. "I'm awfully glad you haven't done it."

Nancy finally looked at her, tears pooling in her eyes. "I couldn't. I couldn't do that to Michael and Julie. They don't deserve the pain they are living with because of Wally. I won't multiply it," she said staunchly.

"I still don't know what I'm going to do about my life, Abby. After today, I will no longer have a home. Living with Michael and Julie will be fine for a time, but I can't imagine never being in control of my life again." She managed a dry chuckle. "It's funny. I was content for Wally to have control of my life for most of our marriage. When I finally started questioning things and learning things for myself, I learned I liked that feeling of control. To lose it again, after having it for such a short time, seems like an extra layer of cruelty."

"I understand," Abby replied. "Though every step of my life after Charles died was a battle, at least it was *my* battle. I had been taught that women were always to be taken care of by their husband. That was fine with me, until my husband was no longer there. Despite Charles having always taken care of me, I somehow knew I could make it on my own. Though he took care of things, he taught me everything I needed to know in our conversations. He was proud of my intelligence. Because of that, I believed I could run the factories successfully if the other business owners would simply leave me alone."

"Matthew helped you do that," Nancy replied.

Abby understood the tinge of jealousy she heard in her friend's voice. No one was coming to Nancy's rescue.

"He helped me," Abby acknowledged, "but that was *all* he could do. I was the one who had to make it happen. He wrote articles that exposed the men for what they were doing, but I had to work in the city where they ran businesses. They never quit hating me."

She smiled slightly. "Thankfully, most of them were old. They were all dead within ten years."

Nancy tilted her head. "Was Matthew really your bodyguard?"

Abby smiled fondly. "For five months. Matthew demanded that I not go anywhere unless he was with me. After the assault, I didn't argue with him. He took me to the factory each morning and picked me up each evening. Matthew and I had long conversations. He became the son I never had. Once the men understood I was never alone, they stopped bothering me. The articles were the icing on the cake. The day came when I was left alone to operate my factories. With the knowledge Charles had given me, I was able to make them a success."

"You certainly did," Nancy said admiringly.

Abby waited through another long silence. She could feel the wheels turning in her friend's head.

"I want to... do something with... my life," Nancy finally said. Her words were halting, but her voice was firm.

"You will," Abby assured her. She was thrilled to see hope and life simmering in Nancy's eyes.

"I don't know what it will be, though." Nancy's fearful look returned.

"You don't have to know that right now," Abby answered. "It's enough to know that you want to do *something*. Clarity will come in time." She glanced at her pocket watch and stood. "The movers will be here in a little while. Let's get some coffee and oatmeal."

"I miss not having a cook," Nancy said with a sigh.

Abby laughed. "I miss you not having a cook, *too*. You and I are both terrible cooks. I used to be able to make more than oatmeal, but after years of being spoiled by Annie on the plantation, it seems to be my entire menu."

"I know you've been waiting for me to be alright. After today, I finally feel I can breathe again. Are you going home when I move to Michael and Julie's?" Nancy asked.

Abby looked at the renewed spark in her friend's eyes. "I am. It's time." She kept her tone neutral, though inside she was jumping with joy. She didn't regret her decision to stay in New York, but she was eager to go home. She had missed most of the fall, but she adored every season on the plantation. She could hardly wait to sit in the library with Thomas in front of the roaring fireplace. She missed their conversations. She missed the children coming in and out in search of books. She missed watching Anthony and Moses battle over the chess board. She missed Carrie and Rose laughing through an intense game of backgammon. She missed the aroma of food wafting from the kitchen, and the love that surrounded the table during long meals. When the days grew shorter, the meals grew longer.

"How is Annie?" Nancy asked. "I don't think I even responded when you told me Carrie performed an appendectomy on her, but I heard you."

Abby understood that Nancy hadn't been able to reach beyond her pain the day the telegram had arrived. "Annie is fine," she said gladly. "She's had to take it easy, but there was no infection. Carrie will remove the stitches soon. She won't let Annie cook, but she's in the kitchen ordering everyone around as much as she can." She laughed as she envisioned it.

Nancy smiled. "I understand why you want to go home. Cromwell Plantation is a special place," she said wistfully.

Abby felt a catch in her heart. "Will you be alright, my friend? I told you I would stay as long as you needed me. I meant it."

Nancy leaned forward and wrapped her arms around Abby. "I will be fine," she assured her. "Michael and Julie will take good care of me. I know I'm welcome to stay with them for as long as I need to. I know I'll still grieve, but..." her voice trailed off and then strengthened. "But I won't lose hope," she finished. "I'm going to figure things out. I'm on my own, but if you can build a factory empire alone, surely I can find a way to take care of myself and create a life."

"I know you can," Abby said. "I completely believe in you."

Nancy smiled her gratitude. "Thank you. When will you leave for Richmond?"

Abby opened her mouth to answer, changing her mind before the words could escape. "Actually," she said slowly, "I believe I'm going to Boston first." The idea had formed in her mind as she spoke.

"Boston?" Nancy asked with surprise.

"Boston," Abby repeated, the surprise thought crystallizing into certainty. "I want to visit Frances and Felicia before I go home. They'll be on the plantation for Christmas in a month, but I want to experience their new life in Boston. Frances has been writing letters, but it's not the same as seeing it for myself." She realized she didn't know when any of them would feel free to make the trip again. The economic crash was spreading financial woes across the country.

They would know within a week, when the crop was taken into Richmond, how much it was going to impact the tobacco market. There was already a slowdown in their garment factories, though they continued to remain in a better position financially than other factories because they had been cautious. The added cost of going to Boston before she returned home would be minimal from New York City.

"I'll leave in two days," Abby said.

"Michael and Julie will be thrilled to have you for those two days," Nancy replied. "I'll be glad to not say goodbye quite yet."

Abby was looking forward to long conversations with Michael. She read the papers daily, but most of her time had been spent trying to be a support to Nancy. There was what seemed like an endless number of questions she wanted answers to.

Chapter Twenty

Rose found Carrie sitting on the porch, huddled under a blanket and holding a steaming mug of tea. "It's time," she announced as she sat down and pulled a blanket around her shoulders.

Carrie blinked at her. "It's time?"

"Minnie is unhappy," Rose said bluntly. "She agreed to come back to school, but Phoebe tells me she's not the same girl. She's quiet and she refuses to go outside at recess time. She insists she wants extra study time. We both know that's not Minnie."

Carrie sat up straight. "Actually, it's far beyond time. I promised Minnie we would solve her problem when we got home from Boston, but Annie got sick, and..." Her voice was remorseful. "It's my fault she's so unhappy. When she agreed to go back to school again, I assumed things were better. I should have known she was simply trying to make life easier for me by hiding it."

Rose frowned, her confusion deepening. "Her problem? Hiding it? What are you talking about?"

"Minnie told me before we went to Boston." Carrie paused. "It's about Missy Highland."

Rose's frown deepened. "Missy? The little girl Graham and Melissa Highland adopted? One of the Bridge Children?"

"Yes. Evidently, she's quite jealous of Minnie. She tells Minnie that she's ugly and stupid. She makes fun of what she wears and tells her she isn't good enough to live on Cromwell Plantation." Carrie felt her anger returning. "She tripped her one day and made her fall. Then she stood and laughed."

Rose was horrified. It was easy to imagine how hard that was for tender-hearted Minnie. "I had no idea! How could that happen without Phoebe being aware of it?"

Carrie shrugged. "It's one more reason I hate that the Board of Education made you separate the white and black students. I love Phoebe Waterston. She's a wonderful teacher, but I still wish every day that you were teaching my children. I don't believe this would have happened."

Rose knew that fact probably wouldn't have protected Minnie in this situation. "I wouldn't be so certain of that. No teacher can see everything," she said. "Especially at recess. We try and watch every child, but it's not possible. There are too many of them." She thought about all the big trees that could hide interactions.

"That's the reason Minnie won't go out for recess anymore. She doesn't feel safe," Carrie said sadly. "I'm not blaming Phoebe," she said earnestly. "I just don't know what to do."

"We're going to figure it out," Rose promised. "We're not leaving this porch until we have a plan of action."

"How well do you know Missy?" Carrie asked.

"Enough to know she struggles," Rose replied. She made it a point to know all of her students, even the ones who didn't attend class with her during the day. Combining recess for both schools gave her the chance to mingle with every child, for at least a few minutes. "I've never had Phoebe tell me Missy is a problem. She evidently conceals it well."

"Minnie told me that Russell said Missy didn't used to be mean," Carrie offered.

"None of us knew Missy before she came out here. Russell would know better than anyone else since they shared the experience," Rose replied. "None of us truly knows what it was like for any of the children who lived under the bridge, but it's easy to imagine it was horrific."

"Russell has told us enough stories to understand why he sometimes still has nightmares." Carrie took a deep breath. "I remember how skinny Missy was, but I mostly remember her haunted eyes when she crept out from under the bridge the day we found them. I knew something awful must have happened to her." Carrie's voice grew quieter. "Do you know what her life is like with Graham and Melissa Highland?"

Rose thought about the question. "I know she is well-fed. I know she comes to school dressed in clean clothes. They aren't fancy, but it's obvious she is cared for. I believe she's smart, but Phoebe tells me she is progressing more slowly than some of her other students. I'm certain her two years under the bridge set her back in her development."

"Do the Highlands love her?" Carrie asked.

"That is a difficult question to answer. I'm certain they're caring for her," Rose said slowly. "Do they love her like we love our children? Do they show her the kind of affection we lavish on ours? I doubt it." Rose picked her words carefully. "The Highlands never had children. They strike me as being rather stern and unyielding. Not abusive," she said hastily. "Just not overtly affectionate." As she spoke, she thought about how desperate Missy must be for warmth and love after what she had experienced.

Carrie looked conflicted. "I understand life might be harder for Missy, but I hate what she's doing to Minnie. My daughter used to love school. She could hardly wait to go. It breaks my heart that she no longer feels that way."

"We're going to change that," Rose considered possible solutions. "You said Missy told Minnie she doesn't deserve to live on Cromwell Plantation."

"That's true," Carrie answered.

Rose smiled. "There's not a child at school that doesn't wish they lived on the plantation. Most of our students come from good families, but their lives are quite different. Our children regale the other students with stories about swimming in the river, the picnics Annie makes for them, and the hours they spend riding horses." As Rose talked, she wondered how many other students secretly resented their children.

Carrie looked thoughtful. "I can imagine that would make anyone jealous."

"I know exactly how she feels," Rose replied. "When I was your slave, I spent every moment dreaming of what my life would be like if I was you. There were times when I hated you – even though you were my best friend." She smiled. "Mama did everything she could to make me feel special, but I knew my life would be much better if I were actually a Cromwell."

"Which you actually were... the entire time..." Carrie shook her head. "We can't go back in time to rewrite history."

"We have to focus on the present," Rose agreed. Her thoughts slowed enough to reach at least one conclusion. "I don't believe punishing Missy is the answer."

"I agree," Carrie replied. "Punitive action will only make her more vindictive. Not to mention the fact she needs love – not punishment." Her troubled look cleared. "Rather than punish her, why don't we involve her more in our world?"

Rose cocked her head. "Meaning?"

"Missy is jealous of the life Minnie has here. If I believed Missy is nothing more than a bully, I would tell Minnie to stand up to her and not let it happen." Carrie stared off into the night for a long moment. "I don't believe Missy is simply a bully. Russell said she was nice. I believe she is a child in pain because of her past. Instead of Minnie responding like she would to a bully, I think she should become friends with her."

"How do you propose that happen?" Rose asked. She was intrigued but knew her job at the moment was to ask questions. Carrie was finding her way to a solution.

"Swimming season is over, but Anthony and Russell built new swings for the children. The tobacco barn will be empty in a couple days. Moses is going to help them hang the swings from the rafters, so the children have a place to play all winter. They're bringing in huge wagons of hay that they can jump into." Carrie looked into the darkness for a few moments. "What if...?"

"What if Minnie invited Missy to come play?" Rose finished. She was thrilled with the idea. "Alice can fix a huge picnic for them."

Carrie nodded enthusiastically. "Russell knows Missy better than anyone. He's angry at her because of how she's treating Minnie, but he's old enough to bring in on the plan. He and Minnie could invite her together. I don't believe Missy will say anything hateful if Russell is there." She hesitated. "Do you think Missy will come?"

"I think the first question is whether Minnie will want her here?" Rose answered. "I believe it would be a mistake to force her. If it goes badly, it will only make things worse."

"I believe I can convince her to give it a try," Carrie responded. "I'm sure she'll be skeptical..."

"As you or I would be," Rose added.

"I most certainly would be skeptical," Carrie agreed. "I think I would have been willing to give it a try with Louisa, though, if I had thought it would make my life easier."

"It will be wonderful for Missy if it happens," Rose said softly. "Perhaps she and Minnie could actually become friends. She's had a very tough life, Carrie. While we've been talking, I've been remembering more details about Missy." She frowned, the memories making her feel nauseous. "Missy's father died quite early in the war. She and her mama didn't have any family, so they came to Richmond to start fresh. I've been told Missy's mother is quite beautiful. There was an older man who took an interest in her, but he didn't want children. Her mother knew about children living under the bridge on their own, so she stuffed Missy's belongings in a bag and took her out to the bridge." Rose felt the bile rise in her throat as she imagined how terrified the little girl had to have been. "Missy was eight."

Carrie held a hand to her mouth. "No..." she whispered.

Rose nodded. "Her mother left Missy there and told her she was on her own. Missy has never seen her again."

Carrie shook her head with disbelief. "I don't understand people. How could a mother do that? What would possess her to simply abandon her child?"

Rose scowled. "One thing I've learned from years of teaching is that many adults should never be parents. They don't know how to love and give. They don't know how to put their children first. Just because a woman is biologically able to give birth, it doesn't mean she should."

Carrie sat in silence, horrified by what she'd heard. She hated what Missy was doing to Minnie, but she was better able to understand the child's actions. Could her plan possibly make a difference?

"Mama..."

Carrie was surprised when Minnie materialized from the darkness. "What are you doing outside this late?" Had she overheard their conversation?

Minnie climbed the stairs to the porch. "I couldn't sleep. I kept thinking about going to school tomorrow. You've always told me being outside helps you feel better, so I came outside. I've just been walking around." She looked down at the floor. "I don't feel any better."

Carrie held out her arms. When Minnie came to her, she gathered her close and pulled her onto her lap. "Honey, I'm sorry I let you down, especially after promising you before we left for Boston that it would get better. I didn't understand school was still difficult for you. I should have asked you. We should have talked about it." Her remorse felt like it would swallow her.

"I didn't want you to know, Mama," Minnie said in a small voice. "You were taking care of Annie, and Grandma is still gone. I didn't want to make life harder."

Carrie was glad the darkness hid the tears in her eyes. "You could *never* make my life harder," she said fiercely. "You are nothing but a joy to me. I love you, Minnie." She hugged her tighter, feeling her heart melt when Minnie rested her head on her shoulder.

"I heard what you and Rose said about Missy," Minnie said quietly.

Carrie knew she should probably admonish her for eavesdropping, but she would have done the exact same thing at her age. "I see... What do you think about what you heard?"

Minnie remained silent for several minutes.

Carrie was content to wait her out. It was enough to hold her daughter in her arms and let her feel how treasured she was.

When Minnie spoke, her voice was low and hesitant. "I was lucky. When my family died, I could have ended up in a bad place, too. Instead, I got to come here..." Her voice trailed off. "I guess I could have ended up being mean too if I'd been left under a bridge."

Carrie doubted it. She didn't think there was a mean bone in her daughter's body, but she needed to let Minnie work through her feelings without saying anything.

Another long silence ensued.

Flocks of geese migrating south for the winter passed overhead, their honking loud in the stillness of the night. Owls hooted as they searched for prey. The remaining leaves, many of them still colorful, rustled in the slight breeze, barely loud enough to be heard.

Carrie reached for the blanket on a nearby rocker and pulled it snuggly around Minnie's body. As the night deepened, the temperature was steadily dropping. Winter was not far away.

"I'd like to invite Missy to play in the barn with us," Minnie finally said. "Well, I can't really say I would *like* to, but I think it's the right thing to do." She snuggled deeper into Carrie's embrace. "Perhaps it will turn out better than I think it will."

"I admire your honesty," Carrie said tenderly. "If I were you, I would feel the same way."

"Really?" Minnie breathed.

"Really," Carrie assured her. "I'm proud of you. If someone had made the same suggestion to me about

Louisa, I'm not certain I would have been as willing as you are."

Minnie peered up at her. "Louisa said you were very kind and nice to her. She told me so at dinner that night."

"When I was *much* older," Carrie replied. "When Louisa no longer had the power to hurt me. I don't know what I would have done when I was the age you are now. You are choosing to be very compassionate and giving *right now*. I'm proud of you."

Minnie considered that for several moments. "Isn't that what a Bregdan Woman would do?"

Carrie caught her breath. Her heart swelled with admiration for her brave daughter.

Rose laughed lightly. "You're absolutely right, Minnie. I'm as proud of you as your mama is. Giving Missy a chance to act differently is a huge act of compassion."

Minnie turned to look at Rose. "What if it doesn't work? What if she's still mean?"

Carrie had wondered the exact same thing. She waited for Rose's answer.

"We'll go back to the drawing board and come up with a new plan," Rose said confidently.

"What if Missy is just a *mean* girl?" Minnie demanded. "What if she doesn't know how to be nice?" Her voice trembled with emotion.

"Do you believe that?" Carrie asked, preparing herself for whatever answer Minnie gave her.

Minnie took the question seriously. "Can I think about that for a minute?"

"You may," Carrie answered.

Once again, the porch lapsed into silence. There were no honking geese to fill the quiet. Instead, they were treated to the sounds of the horses in the field as they whinnied and snorted into the cold night. Sleek summer coats had been replaced with thick fur to protect them from the rapidly approaching change in season.

Carrie took deep breaths of the chilly air, relishing the absence of summer heat and humidity. She never tired of the changes in the seasons. She loved every one of them.

"I don't think Missy is truly mean," Minnie finally said. "I think she's hurt, so she *pretends* to be mean."

Carrie sucked in her breath and met Rose's eyes over her daughter's head. She had not expected such an insightful response. "I believe you're right, honey. I'm proud of you for knowing that."

"When will Daddy and Moses have the swings put up?" Minnie asked.

"I believe if you invite Missy to come spend the day next Saturday, everything will be in place," Carrie answered.

"Alice will be able to put together a picnic? I'll help, of course," Minnie added.

Carrie knew her daughter was spending extra time in the kitchen, helping out while Annie recovered. "We'll make certain of it."

Minnie peered up at her. "You aren't going to cook anything, are you?"

Rose laughed loudly. "That's a very smart question."

Carrie pretended to be hurt. "What an awful thing to say. Are you telling me you don't like my cooking?"

Minnie smiled coyly. "You tell me to always be honest, Mama."

Carrie joined in the laughter that rang through the night, and then pulled Minnie close to her body again. Her daughter rested her head on her shoulder. "I love you, Mama," she said sleepily.

"I love you too," Carrie whispered. She was content to rock quietly.

"So, I have a whole week of school before Missy comes out?" Minnie eventually asked.

Carrie knew the wait would seem interminable. "Yes, but if you ask Missy on Monday, the odds are that she'll be nice for the rest of the week."

"Why will she be nice?" Minnie demanded.

"Because Missy won't want you to rescind the invitation," Rose said promptly.

Minnie looked puzzled. "Rescind?"

"Rescind means to cancel or take away," Rose explained. "Missy won't want you to take away the invitation. She's going to want to come play in the barn on the new swings."

Minnie didn't look convinced. "I suppose that could be true."

Rose came to the rescue again. "I'll talk to Miss Waterston and let her know what is going on. She will keep an eye on Missy and make sure there is no more trouble."

Minnie looked doubtful that it would work, but she nodded her acceptance. "I guess a week isn't so terribly long," she said quietly.

Carrie hugged her tightly. "I feel good about this, Minnie. I'm proud of you for being willing to give it a try. It's a very brave and mature thing to do."

Minnie brightened slightly, yawned and stood. "Thank you for making me feel better, Mama. You too, Rose. I think I'll go to bed."

"Good night, sweetheart." Carrie watched her walk into the house.

"She is really something," Rose said softly. "I've seldom seen such a compassionate heart in a child that young."

"She's survived a lot of pain," Carrie replied. "We both know pain either toughens you or softens you. Unfortunately, far too many people choose to let it toughen them. They turn bitter and resentful, unable to see beyond their pain." She paused. "My amazing daughter has chosen to let it soften her."

"As you have," Rose told her. "Minnie has a good role model."

Carrie thought about that statement. "I suppose that's true. We both have every right to be bitter and resentful, Rose. What kind of life would that have given us, though? I don't know anyone who doesn't experience pain. It's what we choose to do with it that matters."

Thomas materialized from the darkness. "My daughter has become quite the philosopher." He sat down in the rocking chair next to her.

"Where did you come from?" Carrie peered into the night. First Minnie; now her father. "Is there anyone else out there waiting to come startle me?"

Thomas chuckled. "Not that I know. I was coming home from the guest house. After the day we had, I went to check on Perry and Louisa."

"How are they?" Carrie asked. She'd arrived home late from her day at the clinic. "What did they discover at Blackwell?"

Today was their first return to the plantation since the attack. Her father, Matthew, and Harold had joined Perry, Louisa, and June on the trip. No one knew what they would find. They had insisted the children attend school.

Anthony had gone into Richmond on business. Moses and Simon were on their way into the city with the wagons of tobacco.

The group hadn't arrived home until after dinner had been put away, though Alice had left food for them in the kitchen. Carrie had been upstairs putting the children to bed. She knew Rose had been doing the same.

"They're putting on a brave front," Thomas replied as he relaxed into his chair. "I believe Louisa means it when she says she's ready to start over somewhere new, but I also saw the expression on her face when she caught sight of her family home burnt almost to the ground."

Carrie felt ill. "The Klan destroyed Blackwell?" She had vivid memories of horse tournaments, fancy balls, and family picnics throughout her childhood. She had danced with Robert for the first time at Blackwell Plantation. He had crowned her the Queen of the Ball, after winning the tournament on Granite. Memories engulfed her. She could hardly believe it was all gone.

They had talked about the possibility of the Klan destroying it, but possibility and reality were two different things entirely.

"It's really gone?" Rose whispered.

Rose had spent almost as much time as Carrie at Blackwell. Her experience as a slave had been vastly different, but she knew it well.

"The house, the tobacco barns, and the horse stables," Thomas said somberly. "That could have been us when the barn was burned. We were lucky."

Carrie knew he was right but her mind was fixed on something else. "The horses?" she asked sharply, not certain she wanted to hear the answer.

"They're fine," Thomas assured her. "The workers released them from the barn and took them to pastures on the other side of the plantation before the Klan returned. The Klan didn't find them. That's where they are now."

Carrie knew without asking what Perry and Louisa needed. "When are the horses coming to Cromwell?"

Thomas eyed her. "You don't mind?"

Carrie shook her head. "It's the only way to keep them safe, especially with winter coming. We'll make it work." She pushed away the thought of all the River City Carriages horses coming to the plantation if it were necessary. They would cross that bridge if they came to it.

"Perry and Louisa are going to ask you tomorrow. The workers will bring them next week." Thomas paused. "They'll figure out the next step in the future."

Carrie knew her friends had massive decisions to make.

"The workers?" Rose asked. "Did the Klan go after them?"

Thomas' tight smile was humorless. "They tried. Everyone moved into the woods and hid in the darkness. The Klan fired shots into the trees, but no one was harmed."

Rose grimaced. "The worker quarters?"

"They're gone," Thomas said grimly.

Carrie thought of the thirty-five men, many of them with wives and children. "Winter is coming. What are they going to do?"

"They're building new homes," Thomas told her. "They know they can only stay through the winter because there are no jobs, but the Klan didn't find their food stores in the root cellars they dug. They won't starve, at least. They're cutting down trees and building homes. Most of the Cromwell men, now that the tobacco crop is gone, are going there for the next few days to help."

Carrie was happy to hear that, but she couldn't ignore the spark of fear she felt. What if the Klan decided to attack Cromwell while the men were gone?

Her father read her mind.

"Twenty men are staying behind to act as guards," Thomas said. "I doubt the Klan will do anything so soon after losing seven of their members, but they may have been emboldened by burning Blackwell. We're not taking any chances," he stated.

Carrie nodded with relief, hating that the conversation was necessary. "What are Perry and Louisa going to do? Are they truly not going back to the plantation?"

"They say they're done," Thomas answered. "They don't, however, know what their next step is going to be. Until the attack, they'd not considered anything else. I've told them they can stay here at Cromwell through the winter. They might decide to leave before spring, but there won't be any pressure."

Carrie looked at Rose. "What about Simon and June? Have they made any decisions?"

"I don't know," Rose answered. "Simon is with Moses. Moses is going to talk to him and see if he can get any clarity on what they're thinking. I've tried to talk with June, but she's not ready to communicate. All she wants to do is spend time with Annie."

"That makes sense," Carrie responded. "She could have lost her when Annie's appendix burst. Now, she and Simon are planning to leave the area. She doesn't know when she'll see her again. Of course she wants to be with her."

"That's true," Rose conceded. "Nothing is quite as we hoped."

Carrie narrowed her eyes. Even though it was too dark to see Rose's expression, she could feel her friend's angst reverberating in her words. "What is it?"

A long silence stretched out on the porch. Carrie grew increasingly anxious. "Rose?"

Rose sighed heavily. "The country is changing, Carrie. I remember believing, after the war, that Reconstruction was going to alter things for the freed slaves – for *all* blacks. Alter them for the better." She took a deep breath. "For a while, it was happening. Now? It's scary to watch and hear what is going on. The horrors in Louisiana. The tens of thousands of black men, probably more, enslaved in the prison system throughout the South. The KKK attacking so many of my people."

Rose stood abruptly and walked to the edge of the porch. Her tense shoulders, illuminated by the lantern in the parlor window, formed an outline against the night sky. "Things in Virginia are scarcely better. The Democrats are in power again. The Virginia Republicans have gone back on almost every promise they made to my people. Life in Richmond is getting progressively worse. The Klan is growing in power because they know President Grant doesn't have the support here to uphold his policies. No one has gone after the men who attacked Blackwell." Her voice grew bitter. "If the white supremacists can get away with what they did at Colfax, what's to stop all the white bigots from believing they can do whatever they want?" Her voice sharpened. "I'm frightened."

Rose whirled around. "Black people are scared. They should be," she said flatly. "On top of everything, the economy has crashed. You don't have to be a genius to know unemployment is going to skyrocket. Whites will resent blacks even more, because they'll see them as stealing the white man's job. The Depression is going to hurt everyone, but it will hurt blacks more." Her voice trailed away. "Simon and June haven't said so, but I know they're planning to leave the South. They don't want Junior and Ella to grow up in constant fear. They don't want to live in fear themselves."

"Prejudice is everywhere," Thomas reminded her. "Even in the North."

"Yes," Rose agreed. She looked at her brother. "Do you honestly believe the South is safer than the North, however?"

"No," Thomas admitted as he leaned forward. "Are you saying that you and Moses are thinking about leaving?"

"No," Rose said quickly. "This is our home. Moses loves farming, and I can't imagine leaving my school, but..."

Carrie's heart quickened. She understood the fear Rose felt, but she couldn't begin to fathom what life would be like if her best friend was to move away. "But...?"

Rose shook her head. "I can imagine a time when we'll feel we have no choice." Her voice caught in her throat. "Felicia is safe in Boston, but what about John? Jed? Hope? What kind of world will they grow up in? Will I always be afraid of what can happen to them if they leave the plantation? Will they have to be afraid? Will they have the opportunities Moses and I dream of for them?"

Carrie had no answers.

Thomas was quiet, as well.

Anything they said would be nothing but empty words.

"Annie is about to lose her daughter," Rose said. "She hasn't seen her often, but she knew June was close. She knew she could see her grandchildren. And Simon. We may all have the winter, but when spring comes, everything is going to change." Her voice thickened. "I'm going to miss them. Moses will miss Simon terribly." Her voice trailed away again. "More than anything, we're losing faith that things will actually be better for blacks in the South."

Carrie walked to Rose and slipped an arm around her waist. Despite the fact they were best friends, this was one of the times when she couldn't say she truly understood. How could she? She was white. She had all the privileges that came with being white; with having been born a wealthy plantation's daughter. All she could do was let her know she was standing with her.

Carrie heard nothing but the soft rustle of leaves. The horses had settled down for the night. Even the owls were silent. She simply couldn't imagine the plantation without Moses and Rose. She *refused* to imagine it.

"We're going to keep fighting," Rose said. "We're not giving up. We're not leaving."

Carrie heard the unspoken *yet* in her friend's words.

She knew sleep would be elusive that night.

Chapter Twenty-One

Abby sat down in a wingback chair close to the roaring fire. Mid-November in New York City could be cold. This was one of those nights. She rested her head back against the velvety material and closed her eyes, reveling in the warmth spreading through the room.

The parlor, though small, was tastefully decorated. Abby recognized Julie's touch with the colors and the textures of the fabrics. Glowing lanterns sent flickering shadows through the room that still carried the aromas of the evening's delicious dinner. A cold wind slapped limbs against the windows, creating a rhythmic drumming sound that somehow added to the sense of peace.

"Still want to talk?"

Abby's eyes snapped open.

Michael smiled. "I understand if you're too tired."

Abby shook her head forcefully. "I'm not too tired. I was merely resting my eyes and enjoying the fire. I was afraid we wouldn't have the opportunity to have a conversation. I have so many questions." She was leaving the next day for Boston.

Michael settled into the opposing wingback, dwarfing it with his tall frame.

Abby smiled. "You should get bigger chairs."

Michael returned her smile, but his eyes remained serious. "I doubt I'll be spending money on new furniture any time soon."

Abby looked at him closely. She had known Michael far too long to not see the strain in his eyes. Though she had seen him almost daily for the last six weeks when he came to visit Nancy, they'd had no opportunity to talk alone. With Nancy in her room and Julie in the kitchen, now was their chance. "How are you?"

Michael looked away. "I'm fine."

Abby leaned forward and put a hand on his knee. "It's me, Michael. How *are you*?"

Michael took a deep breath and met her eyes. "How do you think I'm doing, Abby? My father killed himself. Mother lost her home and is here with us. We're thrilled to have her, but I hate the reason. Business is struggling. Every day, something else bad happens."

Abby could feel the pain radiating from him in waves. She reached out and took his hands. "Your father committing suicide was not your fault, Michael."

Michael jerked, looked away, and then back at her. "Yes. It is," he said harshly. "I might as well have killed him myself."

"How can you say that?" Abby saw in a single blinding instant that she should have made more of an effort to talk to him. She was horrified that he had been carrying this belief since finding his father. Being there for Nancy hadn't been enough; he needed her to be there for him, too.

"Because it's true." Michael looked both defiant and devastated. "Father wanted me to join him in those investments. Actually, he begged me to. I told him no, but I didn't try to talk him out of them." His voice faltered. "If I had, he would still be alive."

"You couldn't have talked him out of them," Abby told him. "Your father was desperate."

"Why?" Michael demanded. "He had everything he could ever want. A successful business. A beautiful home. A wife who adored him... *Me.*" His eyes filled with tears as his voice broke. "Why was he desperate?"

"He believed the lies," Abby said gently. "America seems to have gone crazy with greed. Your father had everything he could ever want, but the lies told him he didn't have enough. The men who talked him into those investments only cared about themselves – the money *they* could make. They knew the risk he was taking. They lied. They told him wealth was a sure thing. Your father wanted what those men have."

Michael shook his head. "My father taught me that risky investments were never a good idea! He drummed that into me my whole life, but especially when we went into business together."

"And he meant it," Abby assured him. "Your father was human. He lost his way." She searched for the right words to make sense of what was impossible to understand. "We can't know what motivates people sometimes."

"Fear," Michael said flatly. He pulled his hands away and clenched them in his lap.

Abby was alarmed by what she was seeing in his eyes. They seemed to be boiling with both sadness and anger. "What do you mean?" she asked carefully.

"Julie and I have talked at length about this." Michael hesitated but then forged ahead. "Her father committed suicide too. Because of fear."

Abby gasped. "What? I had no idea!" How could she not know? She and Julie had talked many times, but his wife had never mentioned why she came to the city.

"Julie left the farm where she grew up because her father killed himself. Her mother died from grief just a few weeks later."

Abby tried to absorb this new information. "You said he committed suicide because of fear?"

Michael nodded. "The railroad took his farm." His eyes flashed with anger. "They came and just *took it* because it was in the way of their tracks. The government let them. It's happening across the country. Julie would have had to leave anyway, but she didn't have to lose her family."

Abby listened closely. "Her father was afraid?"

"Yes," Michael said sharply. "He knew he couldn't support his family without the farm. It had been in his family for generations. It's all he had ever done. All he had ever known. He believed he was too old to start over." He flushed with anger. "The railroad told him to move into the city and get a factory job. He couldn't imagine it. Julie told me she had never seen him so afraid." His words broke off as he looked into the flames. After several moments, he continued. "He went outside and walked around the farm for hours. Every memory he had was there. He had a good life."

Abby felt bile rising in her throat. "He was saying good-bye to it."

Michael nodded. "He killed himself the next day."

Michael's anger bloomed inside of Abby. "Because they wanted what he had." She gritted her teeth. Corporate greed was destroying so much of the country she loved.

Michael leaned back in the chair. Just as quickly as his anger had erupted, it disappeared. A haunted look took its place. "I miss my father, Abby. I think about all the good times we had. How much he meant to me. I want to talk to him every day." He paused, his voice cracking. "Every night, when I close my eyes..."

Michael didn't have to finish the words.

"The same nightmares are haunting me," Abby said quietly. She would never forget the blood splatter behind Wally's slumped body, nor the vacant stare of his eyes. "But he wasn't my father, Michael. It's immeasurably harder for you."

Michael blinked away tears. "Will I ever get over seeing him dead like that?"

Abby had never been anything but honest with Michael. "You'll never be the same, honey. You don't just forget something like that." She rested her hand gently on his knee again. "But that doesn't mean you can't move beyond it. In time." She was determined to be real with him. "It could take years, Michael, but you'll find joy again. You'll create a life for yourself, Julie, and your mother. You will be able to think about your father and feel more than ragged pain."

Michael looked doubtful.

Abby stared into his eyes, willing him to believe her words. "The most important thing is to know *it was not your fault.*" She let the words sink it, hoping one day he would believe them. "Your mother believes it was *her* fault."

Michael looked startled. "What? How could it possibly be *her* fault? My father was her whole life. She adored him. She gave him everything!"

"It's *not* her fault," Abby assured him. "No more than it is *your*s. Your father made a terrible decision at the moment he lost hope. Unfortunately, the people he left behind are trying to find a way to keep living. You're trying to make sense of something that is completely senseless."

"Did he truly believe our lives would be better without him?"

"He did at the moment he pulled that trigger," Abby told him. "We all know he was completely wrong, but he was consumed with regret and fear. He couldn't find hope to keep going." The crackle of the flames offered their peace. "Your father loved you so much, Michael. He was prouder of you than you may ever know."

Michael's face crumpled as a sob gripped his body. "He shouldn't have left us, Abby. He shouldn't have left us."

"You're right," Abby said tenderly. She stood and enveloped Matthew in a hug. Once again, he was a small boy who needed to believe his life would be alright again. "I have to believe your father regrets his decision. Unfortunately, you can't go back and undo a decision like the one he made."

Michael took deep gulps of air in order to bring his emotions under control. He looked at her after several minutes. "You've helped me more than you can imagine, but would it be alright if we talked about something else?"

Abby smiled. "Of course. Would it make you feel better to talk about the crisis of our economy?"

Michael barked out a small laugh. "It would be nice to focus on a different pain for a while."

"How bad is it, Michael? I've been reading the papers, but I know they're not giving the whole story. I'm hoping you can help me understand the full scope of what has happened. I know you have your finger on the business pulse of the city."

Michael met her eyes and spoke evenly. "It's bad, Abby. Really bad."

Abby tensed. "How bad is *really bad?*"

"You know the Stock Exchange was closed for 10 days. When it opened back up, they wanted to believe the worst of the crisis was behind us. The truth is being experienced every day. The number of bank and brokerage house failures continues to climb. You were right that a crash would throw us into a lengthy depression. It's only been six weeks, but things are steadily getting worse."

"Across the country?" Abby asked. "Or mostly here in New York City?"

"It's worse here because it started here," Michael told her. "It's spreading, though. As this goes on, more banks will fail. There has already been a run on banks all over the country. The collapse has destroyed American's faith in the banking system. They want their money in their hands, where they can touch and feel it. It's just a matter of time before more banks go under."

Abby could understand people feeling that way, but she knew it would exacerbate the crisis. "America's first great crisis of industrial capitalism," she said. "It's come." Abby thought about what she had feared for the last several years. "This is going to alter the entire economy, Michael. Despite people's blind faith in the inevitability of constant economic progress since the war ended, they're going to have to face the truth. We're going to have to deal with things as a country that we haven't been forced to deal with before."

"Yes," Michael agreed. "The long-term repercussions will be painful, but it's what is happening right now that has people panicked. They're losing their money, but the impact is much broader. There are many millions of bushels of grain stuck in the Midwest, because the money can't be found to export them to Europe."

Abby frowned, realizing she hadn't considered agriculture. While millions had come to the cities to work in the factories, there were still millions of Americans working on the farms and ranches that provided food to the entire country. "It's that bad?"

Michael's grim expression spoke volumes.

Abby's thoughts flew to Cromwell. "What will this do to tobacco?" She knew Moses was on his way to Richmond to sell their crop.

"Everyone will suffer," Michael told her. "Prices are plummeting, because there's no way to move the crops. There have been pleas to the government to step in with enough money to relieve the pressure, but what they have done to help isn't enough. Nothing is moving."

Abby's frown deepened. She, Thomas, and Moses had prepared for this time, but she wasn't sure they had prepared well enough. "It's beyond frustrating. Large corporations and greed crash the economy, but the government, paid for by American's taxes, is supposed to bail everything out." She shook her head. "I've known for years this was coming."

"I know you have," Michael told her. "I'm grateful Julie listened to you. She is the reason I turned down all the investments my father wanted me to join him in. She kept repeating the things you told her."

"The economy has always been volatile," Abby stated. "I'm afraid, however, that this crash is going to last longer than any other. There's more money at play and at stake. The Industrial Revolution has changed everything. Corporations control more than they ever have." Her thoughts flew back to the plantation. "Are you telling me tobacco isn't being shipped to Europe?"

"*Nothing* is being shipped to Europe right now," Michael said bluntly. "Or at least very little. The shipping companies have zero confidence that the credit is there to pay for their services." He scowled. "Unfortunately, they're right. There are millions of bushels of crops still in the Midwest, but there are more than a million bushels right here in New York City – languishing in warehouses, but with nowhere to go. Oh, it will sell eventually, but it will sell for such low prices..."

"No money will be made," Abby finished for him. "The farmers have already been paid for this year, but the companies they sold to are likely to go under."

"Meaning next year will do nothing but make this depression worse." Michael stood up and stared out the window. "The farmers won't have companies to buy their crops. Farmers will suffer, but so will the families who can't get the food they need."

"More family farms will be lost." Abby felt nauseous. She thought about Julie's father committing suicide because the railroads had claimed his land through the government. More farms were going to be lost because of the crash. The ripple effects of corporate greed would be felt throughout the entire country.

Michael swung around. "What about Cromwell?"

"The plantation will be alright for a while," Abby replied. "We prepared for an economic downturn. We saved most of our profits from the last few years – both with the plantation and with the factories." She thought about the Richmond tobacco factories and the thousands of men who counted on them for their livelihood. It wasn't just New York workers who were facing a daunting winter. "America can never go back to business the way it's being done," she stated firmly. "Things have to change."

"Like labor practices." Michael voice was intense.

"Exactly," Abby agreed. "What is happening in New York?"

Michael frowned. "Unemployment is growing. Factories have laid off workers in anticipation of what is coming. There are tens of thousands looking for jobs." He sat down again but his body was rigid, his face agitated.

Abby considered the ramifications of vast unemployment at the beginning of winter. Corporations had lured people to the city, away from the farms and small towns, with the promise of stable employment. Immigrants were pouring in from all over the world, pulled by the assurance of American wealth to provide jobs.

"People are going to starve," Michael said grimly. "Or freeze. Poverty is rampant in New York City already, but the layoffs are going to take it to a level we haven't yet experienced. When I was a policeman, I got to know many of the factory workers. We became friends. They are men I respect..." His voice trailed away before he continued. "Most of them traveled across the world to make a better life for their families. Few have found what they were looking for, but it will soon be much worse. They won't be able to eat. They won't be able to heat their homes. There are already rumblings of protests. Workers have begun to demand the city create jobs through work projects."

"Will New York do that?"

Michael's eyes blazed. "Not at this point. No one knows exactly how bad this depression is going to be, or how long it will last. I don't think anyone has a clue what to do." His voice sharpened. "Except let people starve in the name of corporate profits. Many of the companies will continue on, because they've laid off so many. The robber barons will sleep well at night, not caring about the people who made their wealth possible."

"What are you going to do?" Abby asked quietly. She had seen him before when anger smoldered inside him in regard to injustice. She had never known him to not take action. While she admired his commitment to justice, she was afraid for him. And for Nancy. She had just lost her husband. She couldn't take the double blow of losing her son. She knew the country was simmering with barely constrained violence.

"I don't know yet. I do know that I can't just sit by and watch while more and more men become as desperate as my father. Suicides are already rising around the city." Michael scowled and clenched his fists. "I don't know what I will do yet, but I will do *something*."

Abby was certain of that. She also knew when Michael wore that expression, there was no talking him out of what he decided to do. She had more questions. "Is the newspaper correct about the number of railroads that are failing?"

Michael shook his head. "As you suspected, they're not telling the full story. They're afraid it will cause even more panic. The truth is, at the rate things are going, more than half the country's railroads will fail. Speculative investment has been rampant. The time has come for these companies to pay the piper. It's just a matter of time. I don't believe it will take long."

"*Half?*" Abby's head spun with the information. "That will have a massive ripple effect on *everything*. The railroads have made themselves integral in almost every aspect of American life."

"The ripple effect is already happening," Michael replied. "Iron furnaces all over the country are suspending operation and laying off every worker. There are no new tracks being laid. Every single industry that supported the railroads has been impacted." He scowled. "It's simply the beginning. It will get worse. As people have less money to spend, more businesses will close. Homes will be lost. Men will roam the country, looking for jobs that can't be found."

Abby sat silently, absorbing the ramifications of what she was hearing. She had suspected it was coming, but it was immeasurably worse than she had envisioned. Millions of Americans would suffer.

"This is our first truly *international* crisis," Michael continued. "It's being called The Great Depression. It's not limited to America."

"Europe is suffering as well," Abby agreed. She had known it would. "They were already struggling, but the collapse of the American economy has hit them hard, because there was so much European capital invested here."

"That's true. European banking institutions are failing almost as quickly as ours," Michael acknowledged.

"What is President Grant going to do?" Abby asked. Though she didn't believe it was the responsibility of the government to bail out corporations who made abysmal business decisions, there were millions of innocent hard-working Americans who were going to pay the price if relief wasn't provided.

"As far as I can tell," Michael answered, "our president doesn't have a clue *what* to do. New York City bankers and business owners have begged him to take action. While I applaud much of what President Grant has done, especially in relation to civil rights and women's rights, he's unfortunately quite naïve about finances. I also believe he is totally overwhelmed by the scope of what has happened. His approach to economics has relied mainly on listening to the advice of successful businessmen. They're telling him the crisis isn't as bad as the media is reporting, and that the economy will stabilize itself if left alone."

Abby found it difficult to breathe. Grant was listening to the very men who had sent America's economy into a spiral. "Surely, you're not telling me President Grant will do nothing."

"Oh, he and Secretary of the Treasury Richardson, have released some funds, but it's a mere pittance of what is needed to right the boat," Michael told her. "Some of the smaller banks have been bailed out, and more people have been able to claim their deposits, but much of it is being hoarded. The men who created this debacle are being bailed out, but it's not stretching to the rest of the country. It's done little to change the downward trajectory of the economy. It hasn't done anything to pay for the export of crops. Confidence has been shattered. Men and women will continue to be laid off. Banks will continue to close."

Abby listened closely. Historically, depressions would create lower prices for products, because people had less money to spend. Lower prices would mean lower wages for people who managed to stay employed. Wages had been growing since the end of the war.

Michael seemed to read her mind.

"Wages have gone up nearly twenty-five percent in the last eight years," Michael added. "That is about to change," he said darkly.

He pivoted to a new subject. "Cotton is going to be a real problem, too."

Abby was puzzled by the sudden change in topic. "Cotton?"

Michael nodded. "I was focused on tobacco because of Cromwell, but prices for cotton are falling drastically. I've heard cotton will be impacted even more than tobacco because so much more of it is grown. Some people are projecting cotton prices will fall as much as fifty percent."

Abby was overwhelmed by what she was hearing. There were many states who didn't harvest cotton until October through December. The crops in the fields would be practically worthless. "That will devastate the South. The war ravaged their economy. The majority of southern states are completely dependent on their income from cotton."

Abby's mind continued to spin as she considered where the consequences would lead. "People will blame the government, Michael. They always do, even when they aren't the ones responsible." She felt a renewed flash of anger toward the greedy men and corporations who had brought this on the country.

"I know what you're thinking, Abby. The Democrats could take over at the next election. The Republican administration will take the blame. They'll pay the price at the ballot box." He paused. "If Grant can't find a solution to the suffering of millions of Americans, they won't care about anything except not voting for the party that was in power when the crash happened."

Abby knew he was right. Both Republicans and Democrats in Congress had allowed corporations to take over the country. They had opened the door to give them a foothold and then accepted bribes to give them unfettered power. Both parties carried a portion of the blame. The Republicans weren't blameless, but she knew what would happen if the Democrats took control. Reconstruction was already fighting an uphill battle. Though Northerners didn't believe blacks should be slaves, they weren't terribly concerned with their civil rights, especially when it impacted their lives. With the economy in tatters, fewer people would care about black rights. They would be solely focused on their own survival, seeing the black man as the competitor for the few jobs still available.

She shuddered when she thought about what life would be like for blacks in the South if the Democrats took control.

"I know what you're thinking, Abby, but you can't cross bridges until you come to them."

Abby knew he was wrong. "I would normally agree with you, Michael. Not this time. I don't like to borrow trouble, but I do believe in being prepared for possibilities. Such as the economy crashing," she said bluntly. "If Reconstruction fails and the Democrats take power, the South is going to become a terrifying place for millions of Americans."

Michael eyed her. "What are you saying?"

Abby sighed. "The KKK and other white supremacy groups are already ignoring the laws put in place to protect the freed slaves. If the Democrats take control, they'll simply abolish those laws." She gritted her teeth. "Close friends recently had their plantation completely destroyed by the KKK. We've been able to protect Cromwell so far, but it wasn't that long ago that Robert was murdered by the KKK... that the barn was burnt by the KKK." Her voice caught. "I've not wanted to believe this was possible. We must continue to fight for equal rights for everyone... and then deal with what happens." Her words did nothing to resolve the burning feeling churning in her stomach.

She needed to leave New York City. After tonight, her heart yearned to go home to the plantation more than before, but the girls were expecting her. At least Boston would remove her from the epicenter of the crash.

While she didn't regret her decision to stay, the last weeks had taken a toll on her.

Chapter Twenty-Two

Anthony was waiting on the porch of Thomas' Richmond home when Moses and Simon trudged up the steps.

Moses had seldom felt so exhausted. "Hello, Anthony."

Anthony peered at him. "Do you feel as bad as you look?"

Moses managed a slight smile. "Probably."

"It's that bad?"

Moses walked toward the door. "Can we go inside?"

Anthony stepped back quickly and held the door open for them. "Of course. May has dinner waiting for you."

Moses was starving but so utterly exhausted he wasn't sure he could eat. He simply nodded and walked inside.

Micah, hanging up coats in the foyer, eyed him. "That bad?"

Moses heaved a heavy sigh. He would have to answer questions whether he wanted to or not. He might as well eat. He jabbed Simon. "Ready for dinner?"

"I was ready a few hours ago," Simon replied.

"Wash up," May said crisply as she pushed through the swinging kitchen door with a platter. "It will be waiting for you when you return."

Moses eyed the roast beef, green beans, corn and fluffy biscuits with appreciation. As far as he was concerned, no one could beat his mama's cooking, but May came in a close second. She had been cooking for Thomas since the war had started. She and Micah had first been his slaves, purchased at the beginning of the war as his house servants. They were now his trusted employees and close family friends. When May had married Thomas' driver, Spencer, he had moved in.

"May I eat before I deliver the bad news?"

Spencer nodded. "Bad news makes a man hungry. 'Course, I already knew it was gonna be bad. Every man I know who worked for the tobacco factories has been laid off."

Moses' appetite disappeared. He pushed away his plate.

"I told you to let him eat first," May scolded. "I'm real sorry, Moses. My husband doesn't know when to stop talking." She glared across the table at him.

Spencer looked remorseful. "She's right. I talk too much. Carrie used to tell me the same thing when I drove for her during the war. I'm sorry."

Moses shrugged. "I might as well get it over with." He thought about the long day he and Simon had endured. They'd left the plantation before dawn at the head of twenty Cromwell wagons with towering loads of tobacco, arriving at the warehouse before lunch. There were already wagons lined up in front of the docks, but nothing was moving. There was none of the usual yelling, laughter, and jostling. A somber silence had laid over the entire scene. The sick feeling in his gut had started then.

"Mind if I eat?" Simon asked. "I don't have to talk, so I might as well."

Moses chuckled. "Some things don't change. I've never known you to miss a meal."

"I spent plenty of days hungry when I was a slave. More when I was fightin' during the war," Simon retorted in a wounded voice. "I see no reason to not take advantage of May's hard work. It would be pure disrespect to not eat this meal."

May laughed heartily. "Such a noble man you are, Simon!"

Simon's eyes twinkled. "June tells me that all the time."

Moses was grateful for the brief moment of levity before he had to face reality. "They at least took our crop," he started. "There were moments I thought they wouldn't."

"They took *all* the crops," Simon added around a mouthful of green beans. "At least from all the wagons that got there before lunch. Cromwell wagons were the last ones, before they put up a barrier at the entrance. Of course, their willingness to buy the crops ended up not being such a good thing."

Moses eyed him. "You eat. I'm telling this story."

Simon shoved a forkful of roast beef into his mouth obligingly.

"They bought everything," Moses continued, "but prices are down almost thirty percent."

"*Thirty percent?*" Anthony looked shocked. "Why?"

"Because all they're doing is filling up their warehouses, hoping the day will come when they can sell it," Moses explained. "They have nowhere to send it."

Anthony shook his head. "I don't understand."

"Some of our tobacco goes up north, but the majority of it is exported to Europe. When the economy crashed, shipping companies lost confidence in getting paid. Nothing is leaving the country."

"Nothing is being exported?" Anthony asked. "How is that possible?"

Moses shrugged. "It's not just tobacco. It's happening with crops all over the country. Grain. Corn. Cotton." He scowled. "Cotton prices are down almost 40%. They're predicting they will go lower."

"Will there be any profit at all from the Cromwell crop?" Anthony demanded.

Moses heaved another heavy sigh. "No. We barely covered our costs for the year. There is no profit." His mind ran through the ramifications. "There won't be enough money from the sale of the crops to pay for next year's planting. We've prepared for this time, but it's still going to hurt. We can plant next season but if the economy doesn't improve, there may still be no profit." *And no way to recoup the losses*, he thought silently. Depressions could go on for years.

"What about your workers through the winter?" Spencer asked.

"I believe everyone will be alright. No one will make a percentage of the profits this year, but they still have the wages we paid them. The gardens produced copious amounts of food this year and the smokehouses are full. The greenhouses will be in full swing through the winter. No one will go hungry, at least." Moses was deeply grateful for that knowledge.

Spencer looked at Simon. "What about the families on Blackwell Plantation?"

Simon swallowed a bite of his biscuit before he spoke. "They've built homes for the winter. Nothing fancy, but they'll stay warm. They have enough food." His voice sobered. "Next spring, they'll have to figure out what they're gonna do."

"Can they stay there until the economy turns around?" Spencer asked keenly.

"I don't know," Simon replied. "They can stay as long as the plantation belongs to Perry and Louisa, but when they sell it..."

Moses listened intently. He had intended to talk with Simon while they were here. Perhaps he would find out what he wanted to know during dinner.

Spencer's eyes widened. "They're selling Blackwell?"

Simon nodded. "They're done. I don't know if they finalized their plans, but I know Louisa wants to head north. This ain't a great time to sell, but they ain't in a hurry. They have enough money to start over. The plantation will sell in time."

Spencer absorbed that information. "What about you and June?"

Simon shot a look toward Moses before he answered. "We don't know yet. But..." his voice faltered.

A silence stretched through the room. The only sounds were the crackling of the fire in the parlor and the wind battering the windows.

Moses remained quiet.

"But...?" Spencer finally prompted.

Simon looked trapped. "I don't see us staying down here," he admitted.

"In the South?" Spencer pressed.

Simon hesitated and looked directly at Moses. "I wanted to talk to you privately."

Moses accepted that as true, but since the conversation was happening, he needed to know more. "You and the family are leaving?" He tried to keep his voice even, but was certain he had failed.

Simon wiped his mouth with a napkin and settled back in his chair. "The South ain't what we hoped it would become after the war ended and we all got our freedom, Moses. You know that. It's getting worse."

Moses wouldn't argue what was obviously true.

"We're real tired of living in fear," Simon said. "Tired of waiting for the KKK to come after us. Even if they hadn't destroyed Blackwell, we were talkin' about leavin'. We don't reckon any black person is safe down here."

"Mama is going to miss June and the grandchildren. So will the rest of us." Simon was his best friend. He was also family.

"It's gonna be gut-wrenching to leave," Simon replied. He shook his head. "But it's more gut-wrenching to think of staying. We don't have what you have at Cromwell. Andrew saved us when he came to warn us, but Perry and me know how lucky we were that night. There weren't enough men, and not enough money to put guards around the property. Most of the time, me and June felt like sittin' ducks."

Moses hated that he understood. "You could stay at Cromwell," he offered. "Y'all would be safe there."

Simon smiled. "That's a real fine offer, but June and me need to create our own life."

Moses shook his head. "I could use you on the plantation, Simon. I've missed you since you left."

"In the middle of a depression? We both know you have enough men to do everything you need. Besides, at some point..." Simon's voice broke off abruptly.

"At some point *what*?" Moses demanded.

Simon shook his head but didn't answer.

Moses was aware of everyone else in the room listening to their conversation. He gritted his teeth with frustration.

"What Simon don't want to say is that at some point, you and Rose might gonna have to decide the same thing," Spencer said quietly.

"We're not leaving the plantation," Moses retorted. He refused to acknowledge that he had wondered in private if that time might eventually come.

"Not now," Spencer agreed, "but Simon is right. The South ain't what we hoped it would be when the war ended, and we all got our freedom. Every one of us has got a decision to make."

Moses had come to Richmond to deliver the tobacco, but also to find out the true state of events. He hadn't been off the plantation since arriving home from San

Francisco the last week of July. "Tell me what is going on, Spencer."

"When things fell apart up in New York City in September, all the Richmond business leaders told us we ain't got nothing to worry 'bout," Simon began. "By October 1st, the bottom had completely dropped out of the city's economy. Most of the fellas I know have been laid off. Factories are closing faster than we can keep track of. That place you found to take your tobacco be one of the last few still open. I 'spect your wagons were the last ones to pass through to any of them. They only took that tobacco 'cause it came from Cromwell. They know it be real high quality. They figure they might get a little more money for it."

Moses glanced at Anthony for confirmation.

"Spencer is absolutely right. For workers that weren't laid off, their hours have been cut back and their wages have been lowered," Anthony told him.

"What about River City Carriage drivers?" Moses asked. He had noticed how much quieter the city was. Factory whistles had been silent. There was no drumming of heavy machinery. The air had been almost clear of industrial chimney smoke. The quiet had been a nice change, but it also foretold the unannounced suffering.

"I haven't let anybody go, but the majority of their income comes from their fares. There aren't many businesspeople coming to Richmond. The trains are practically empty. People in town mostly choose to walk so they can save money. My drivers are hurting. Unfortunately, it's going to get worse. I can help a little with wages, but I can't cover what they've lost."

Anthony's eyes darkened. "I have money saved, but if this stretches out, I'll be forced to lay off workers too."

Moses knew that was true. From what Thomas told him on a daily basis, the depression was likely to stretch out for a lengthy period of time.

"At some point, I'll have to take most of the horses out to the plantation," Anthony continued. "It makes no sense to continue feeding them here if they aren't able to bring in income."

Moses understood the necessity of the decision but knew it would make life even harder for the farmers counting on the income from feeding Anthony's stable of horses. Any action taken would create an impact on others.

"How bad is it for the tobacco workers, Spencer?" Moses wanted to understand the full picture.

Spencer scowled. "Real bad. By October 1st, half of the workers had been laid off. We thought that was bad, but it's only gotten worse. There ain't many still got a job. Now that the warehouses are full, the rest gonna lose their jobs." He shook his head. "I got friends who were trying to save some money, but they been fighting to make up what they lost in the spring when the factories tried to pressure the government about the tobacco tax. They agreed back then to go without some pay. The factory owners convinced them it would pay off, but now they lost everything."

"Have they at least been paid for their work before the layoffs?" Moses demanded.

Spencer's scowl deepened. "Nah. The factory owners telling them they ain't got enough money on hand, 'cause the banks ain't giving the factories anything. Everything is drying up."

Moses was certain that was true. While he had been busy with the harvest, Thomas had been reading newspapers voraciously and reporting on what was happening. Banks that hadn't failed yet were barely hanging on and had no money to loan.

"It ain't just the tobacco workers," Micah said. "It's happening to ever'body. Iron workers. Flour factory workers. Barrel manufacturing. Everything, really." His voice was grim. "People losing their jobs all over the place. I never imagined things could get so bad this quick."

May broke into the conversation. "Mr. Cromwell going to keep this house?"

"As far as I know," Moses answered honestly. He understood why she would ask. It was something he and Thomas had discussed. Selling the house would be a decision made out of dire necessity. It made no sense to sell during a depression. "If Thomas and Abby had feared having to sell the house because of a crash they anticipated, they would have already sold it. I don't think you have anything to worry about."

"At least not today," May said crisply. "Miss Abby taught me that you gotta be prepared for anything."

Moses remained silent. None of them could truly know what was coming. He could feel the pressure building inside. "How are the secret societies doing, Spencer?"

"We gonna keep caring for our own, Moses. Long as the Freedman's Bank don't go under, we'll be alright. Nobody gonna have much, but nobody gonna starve.

There be enough to pull us through for a while. There ain't many of our people had to ask for help from the city since the end of the war. We intend to keep it that way."

Moses tensed. "Is all the secret society money in the bank?"

"Of course," Spencer replied. "Where else we gonna keep it? We don't figure we have anything to worry about."

"Why?" Moses asked, surprised by his casual approach. Banks were failing all over the country.

"You know who John Mercer Langston is?" Spencer asked.

"Of course. He's the president of Howard University's law school." Moses knew Langston had worked tirelessly for abolition, had escorted many slaves to freedom through the Underground Railroad, and had been fighting for equal rights for his people since the end of the war.

"That's him," Spencer agreed. "Him and Frederick Douglass came to Richmond not too long ago. They done assured us our money is safe in the bank. I ain't got much of my own money in the bank, but the societies got almost all their money there. Mr. Douglass told us that if they was to take all that money out, that they gonna cause the bank to fail."

Moses hated how his gut was churning. What the two black leaders had told everyone about the Freedman Bank needing their money was true, but what if the bank still failed? There would be no money left to care for the people suffering from the depression.

Rather than save the bank, wouldn't it be wiser to save the people?

"I'm thinking the same thing you are, Moses," Micah ventured.

Moses eyed him with surprise.

"You be thinking that saving that bank ain't what is most important," Micah said earnestly. "What if that bank fails like all the others? I read the paper to May every morning while she be cooking. Miss Rose told me that was the best way to improve my reading, so I been doing it. I know what's going on! If that bank still fails, even though we did what they said and left our money there, there ain't gonna be money to help our people. We're gonna have to depend on the local government for help."

"A *Democratic* government," May snapped. "They are already treating us black folks like we don't matter. I don't think they'll care much if a bunch of black people starve or freeze to death during a depression. They'll just figure there be less of us to compete with the white folks looking for work. Everybody is counting on the Secret Societies to help if things get worse. I don't know what we're gonna do if the bank closes."

Moses looked at Spencer with a raised brow.

"I ain't gonna argue with my wife. She be a right smart woman. I'm just telling you the Societies ain't gonna take the money out," Spencer said flatly. "At least not right now. Can't say what they gonna do in the future."

Moses decided to change the subject. "How is your new governor?"

Spencer shrugged his massive shoulders and rolled his eyes. "Won't know till he takes office on January 1. What I do know is that Kemper is a *Democrat*. I reckon that says it all. He shook his head. "Not many of us cared too much for the Republican running for governor again either, though. Walker let us down. Seems like Republicans ain't doing much for us anymore. As far as most of us can tell, they just want us to work hard for their benefit. When we do it, we don't get much more than empty words and contempt." His eyes flashed. "Still, maybe he would have been better than who we getting'. We fought a war to keep Democrats from doing terrible things, but they be back in power again. How is that even possible?"

Moses wondered the same thing every day. "What are you and May going to do, Spencer?"

May answered his question. "We ain't going anywhere as long as we have this home to live in, Moses. Things might be hard here for most people, but we be some of the lucky ones. Mr. Cromwell pays me and Micah regular. We have a beautiful roof over our heads, a big garden out back, and a cellar full of food. If that ever changes, we'll have some decisions to make, but that time ain't now."

"May is right," Spencer agreed. "We're staying put. Leavin' a good thing during a depression don't seem very smart."

Moses shot a pointed look at Simon, but his friend's focus was on the last bites on his plate.

Simon looked up briefly. "You gonna eat that dinner, or not?"

Moses pushed the plate of food to his friend. The churning in his stomach had done nothing but get worse during the conversation. He pushed back from the table. "Please excuse me. I need some air." He was quite certain he would explode if he didn't escape the confines of the house. He longed for the plantation, but Thomas' back yard would have to do.

He had one final thing to do the next day before he went home.

Simon found Moses out back, staring up into a moonlit sky. "I'm sorry about that. I didn't want to have that conversation with other people."

Moses sighed. "It wouldn't have mattered. Even though I suspected what you were going to do, I didn't want to admit it." He shoved his hands into his pockets. "I'm going to miss you, Simon. We haven't seen each other enough since you moved to Blackwell, but I knew you were there. We saw each other. June and the kids could visit Cromwell."

"We're not excited about leaving," Simon said gruffly. "We need to get out of the South."

Moses saw an opening. "In the midst of a depression? What are you going to do?"

Simon looked uncomfortable. "I don't know," he admitted. "Perry and Louisa are giving us some money to get established as payment for what we've done for 'em. It ain't a lot, but it's more than I ever dreamed we would have at one time."

Moses listened carefully. "Are you going to look for work? Start a business?"

Simon shrugged. "I'm still trying to figure that out."

"Simon, you're my best friend. You're also my brother-in-law. I have my sister to think about too; not to mention my nephew and niece. I don't believe this is the time to make a move like you're considering. Finding a job is going to be next to impossible in this economy. You've been a slave, a soldier, and a farmer. What kind of job does that prepare you for?" He answered his own question. "The kind of job that millions of laid off workers are going to be looking for."

"I could start a business," Simon said weakly.

"What kind?" Moses asked. "Every business in America is hurting right now. Starting a business in the middle of a depression doesn't make sense."

Simon eyed him. "Then why is Felicia still in Boston?"

Moses wasn't offended. "That's a very good question. Now that I know how bad things are getting, we're going to have to re-evaluate everything. This conversation, however, isn't about Felicia. It's about you and June."

Simon shifted his feet.

There was just enough light from the street lantern filtering into the back yard, for Moses to see Simon's expression. His friend resembled a trapped animal. "Stay on the plantation until the economy gets better. If you still want to leave after that, I'll do everything I can to help you and June."

"The house is already stuffed with people," Simon objected. "The room in the guest house is fine for a little while, but I can't see my whole family living in a single room through the winter."

"We'll build you a house." Moses hadn't considered it before, but Simon was right. Once he had said the words, he knew it was the perfect solution.

"Are you crazy?" Simon blurted. "It's the middle of November. Winter is around the corner."

"Which is why we'll build it quickly," Moses replied, the plans coming together in his head as he spoke. "There won't be time for anything fancy, but we'll build a house that will keep you warm and give Junior and Ella a bedroom. You can work on fixing up the inside through the winter. The men helped build a dozen houses at Blackwell. One more won't be anything." He could tell from the expression on Simon's face that he was making headway.

"My boy eats a lot of food," Simon warned.

Moses chuckled. "Not as much as his daddy does, but it doesn't matter. There's plenty of food to get everyone through the winter. Next year, if the economy is still bad, we'll plant more of the land in food and we'll raise more animals. It's not anything that didn't happen all over the South during the war. We'll be fine."

Simon was silent, obviously deep in thought. "June could help Annie in the kitchen."

"Which would make both of them happy," Moses replied. "Junior and Ella will go to school. June and Louisa have done a fine job of teaching them, but Rose will love having them as her students."

"They would love to go to school," Simon allowed. He stood quietly for several moments but his body was still tense. "What about the KKK?" he demanded.

"They're out there," Moses allowed. "I believe, though, that they'll steer clear of Cromwell after you and Perry killed seven of their men. They know we have armed guards watching the perimeter of the property all the time. They've tried before and failed – taking the bodies of their men with them. They counted on the element of surprise to attack Blackwell. They know that won't happen at Cromwell. I don't believe any of them are brave enough to take the risk – not after burying their friends so recently."

Simon's breathing evened out and his shoulders relaxed.

Moses waited for what seemed like an eternity, but was probably less than a minute, before he blurted, "You'll stay?"

Simon nodded slowly. "As long as June agrees. She wants to get out of the South real bad, Moses."

Moses allowed a broad smile to spread over his face. "My sister is a smart woman. She'll know this is for the best. And remember, when the time comes, I'll help y'all leave."

Simon finally smiled back. "It will be good to work together again, Moses."

Moses, free from the dread he had been feeling, reached out and slapped Simon on the shoulder. "Nothing could make me happier."

"We headed home tomorrow?" Simon asked.

"Yes," Moses said firmly. "I have one stop to make."

The Freedman's Bank was empty of customers when Moses walked in. He had questioned his intentions throughout the night, but in the end, he was confident he was taking the wisest action. Abby's telegram, waiting for him when he arrived at the house, had confirmed his belief. He'd had to ponder what Spencer had told him, but it hadn't changed his mind.

He strode across the floor of the simple clapboard building, stepped up to the counter, and slid a piece of paper across to the bank teller. He had no interest in broadcasting how much money he was withdrawing from his account. He had done business with the teller many times over the years, but they weren't friends.

The teller's eyes widened when he saw the amount he had written. He looked around for the bank manager, who had evidently stepped away from his office.

"The amount is correct, Gerald," Moses said quietly. "Please check."

The teller gulped and nodded. "I'll be right back, Mr. Samuels."

"Thank you. I would appreciate you putting it in a single bag," he said authoritatively.

The teller gazed up at his towering height, hesitated, and then nodded again. Moses had no desire to intimidate him, but if his size increased the teller's willingness to do as he asked, he was fine with it.

Simon was waiting for him in the wagon when he returned. Moses had already sent the rest of the wagons and drivers on their way to Cromwell as soon as dawn had arrived.

"You got it?"

"Yes." Moses pulled the large bag from under his coat and secured it beneath the wagon seat carefully, but quickly. If they were stopped for any reason, it was unlikely anyone would look there. He had parked around the corner in the alley in order to avoid prying eyes. Carrying so much money was a bit overwhelming, but he wouldn't leave it in the bank. His revolver was tucked into his waistband. He prayed he wouldn't need it, but he was ready.

"They give you a hard time?"

"They weren't happy about it, but it's my money," Moses replied. Not even Simon knew how much he had withdrawn. "The Secret Societies may be alright with risking their hard-earned funds, but I'm not. I'll feel awful if my withdrawal causes the bank to fail, but I have to believe it won't. Obviously, most of the depositors have opted to leave their money in the bank. Langston and Douglas did a good job of convincing them. That should protect the bank for a *while*." He was fairly certain the Freedman's Bank would follow the pattern of other bank failures. Abby's telegram had been cryptic, but quite clear that bad investment decisions by white trustees had put the Freedman Bank in jeopardy.

"Where you gonna put all that?" Simon asked.

"In the tunnel," Moses replied. "It's the safest place I can think of."

"Seems safer than the bank," Simon agreed.

Simon and others knew about the tunnel's existence, but very few knew of the nooks and crannies he and Anthony had built into the brick walls to hide valuables. The money would be secure.

Moses settled onto the wagon seat and raised the reins. When the horses stepped out in unison, he felt a surge of relief. He was ready to be out of the city and back on the plantation. He wouldn't fully relax until he was home and the money was secured, but he already felt better.

No one in Richmond knew what he had done. He doubted the bank, fearing his action would encourage others to do the same, would broadcast his withdrawal.

"You did the right thing," Simon said as they moved through the relatively quiet streets toward the outskirts of town.

"I believe I did," Moses said gravely.

Richmond had been a bustling, rapidly growing city since the end of the war, but the deepening depression seemed to have dropped a blanket of gloom over the entire town. Broad Street, usually thronged with wagons carrying supplies and goods of every sort, was eerily empty. There were people out and about, but there was no energy in the air.

Moses wished his withdrawal wasn't necessary, but he'd taken the only action he'd felt good about. He had been proud to be a major depositor in the Freedman Bank. He believed he was helping secure prosperity for more blacks by supporting the only black bank in America.

The economic crisis, caused by greedy white men had changed everything. His family depended on the money they had earned. The plantation would need extra funds to survive if the depression lasted for years. Felicia was counting on him to help her in Boston. He doubted the wisdom of investing in anything during the current economic crisis, but he and Rose would carefully examine any plans she sent them, and then consult with Abby. Felicia was an astute businesswoman. If anyone could find a way to launch a successful business venture during a depression, it would be her. He would not diminish her ability to do it.

Moses took a deep breath when they reached the open countryside outside the city. He'd been carefully watching every movement around him, wondering if they would be accosted before they left town. Having so much money with him was making him paranoid. Being on the open road in the country would eliminate the element of surprise available in Richmond. He believed they were in the clear. "Let's go home."

Chapter Twenty-Three

Minnie shouted with joy when she saw the new swings her daddy and Moses had installed in the tobacco barn. Now that the crop was gone, it had become the perfect playground for them through the winter. It was easy to envision hours of fun waiting for them.

She and Russell watched the pile of hay grow as the plantation workers pitchforked it from the two wagons they had brought into the barn. Pitchfork after pitchfork soon resulted in a pile of hay that towered over their heads. When they got tired of swinging, they could launch from the swing into the fluffy hay.

Without warning, a wave of sadness swept through her.

"Hey," Russell said. "Why are you looking sad?"

Minnie sighed. "I miss Frances. She would love the swings."

"She'll be home in just twenty-three days to enjoy them!" Russell exclaimed.

"But she'll only be home for Christmas," Minnie said sadly. "After New Year's Day, she goes back to Boston."

"That's true," Russell conceded. "Would you rather her not come home at all?"

Minnie was shocked. "How could you ask that? Of course I want her to come home."

"Then you have to accept she'll go back to Boston," Russell replied. "We don't have her all the time like we want, but at least we have her part of the time."

Minnie hated when her brother became all logical. Her daddy told her it was because he had an engineer's mind. He might see things *clearly and analytically*, but she found it merely annoying most of the time. This time, however, she supposed he had a valid point. "That's true."

Russell changed the subject. "Missy will be here soon."

Minnie frowned. She had been trying not to think about it. Missy had accepted her invitation with surprise, and had left her alone through the week, just as Mama said she would. She was glad for the reprieve from the bullying but had no confidence it wouldn't start up again after Missy's day on the plantation.

"Missy isn't a mean person," Russell reminded her, as he had many times.

Minnie eyed him. "That's what you keep telling me, but she does very *mean* things."

"I know," Russell said sympathetically. "I talked to her about it."

"What? When? I didn't know. What did you say?"

"I told her to stop being mean to my sister," Russell answered. "I told her she had never been that way when she was forced to live under the bridge, and that I didn't understand why she was being mean now."

"Thank you," Minnie whispered. Her first brother, the one who had died in the fire, had never stood up for her. It felt good. "What did Missy say?"

"She told me to mind my own business," Russell said ruefully.

Minnie's nervousness increased. "Why do you think she's coming today?"

Russell's expression revealed he wondered the same thing. "I guess she's curious. Other than the day she arrived from Richmond, she's never been on the plantation. Her new parents haven't brought her to the picnics, so she doesn't know what it's like."

Until that moment, Minnie hadn't realized that Missy's family hadn't brought her to the picnics they'd had for the Bridge Children. "Why haven't they brought her?"

"I don't know. I asked Missy, but she wouldn't tell me. She told me it was none of my business again." He frowned. "I don't think they're mean to her, but..." He looked at the new swings swaying beneath the sturdy beams. "I don't think they do things like this, either."

"Mama says she's probably jealous of me," Minnie confided. "That makes me sad."

"She probably is," Russell replied after a lengthy silence. He looked uncomfortable. "I was jealous of you in the beginning."

"Why?" Minnie cried. "You're my brother."

"Yes, but you were adopted two years before me. You belonged in the family more than I did. Besides," he added, "you didn't end up a part of the family because you were stealing from Daddy."

That made Minnie smile. She loved the stories about how he stole small things from River City Carriages, so he could sell them to buy groceries for the children under the bridge. It may have been wrong, but it had also been extremely brave. She admired him for it, but hoped she would never need to do it. "You don't still feel that way, do you?" she asked.

Russell shook his head. "Of course not, but I can understand why Missy might. She's glad she doesn't still live under the bridge, but she probably wishes every day that she lived on the plantation."

"What should I do when she gets here?" she asked nervously.

"Don't hog the swing."

Minnie punched his arm. "I don't hog things!"

Russell eyed her. "Really?"

Minnie started to deny the accusation again, but paused, thinking about the night before. "I might have played with the bubble machine longer than I should have last night," she admitted.

"While Bridget begged you to give her a turn," Russell reminded her.

Remorse swept through Minnie as she thought of her little sister staring up at her with beseeching green eyes while she begged her for a turn. She had ignored Bridget and kept blowing bubbles. "I was awful, wasn't I?"

"Pretty awful," Russell agreed. "It's a good thing Mama and Daddy weren't out there to see how you treated her."

Minnie's regret grew. "I'll make it up to her," she vowed. "We'll play with the bubble machine tonight. I won't take a turn at all. I'll give my turn to Bridget."

Suddenly, she wished her two-year old sister was older, so she could play on the swings with them.

The doors swung open as John and Jed ran into the barn, followed seconds later by Hope.

"Look at the swings!" Hope squealed.

Minnie could see the raw desire in Hope's dark eyes.

Hope ran for the swings, but John and Jed were faster than she was.

Minnie, using the impressive speed she had discovered, beat all of them to the first swing. "Give Hope a turn first."

John shook his head. "No. Jed and I got here first."

"Actually," Minnie said smugly, "I did. Because I'm faster than you. I say Hope gets to swing first. The two of you can take turns on the other swing."

John scowled but turned away.

Jed dashed over to the other swing. "I'm first!"

"Get on fast, Hope. You'll be the first to use the new swings!"

Hope grinned and clambered onto the shellacked wooden swing. "Push me!"

Minnie grinned, stepped behind her, and gave her a big push. Hope soared into the air before Jed settled onto his swing. "Now, pump your legs," she ordered. "You'll be able to go as high as you want!"

Hope laughed with delight and pumped her short legs as hard as she could.

When Hope was swinging higher than Minnie could reach to push, she stepped away and joined Russell.

"That was nice," Russell observed.

Minnie noticed he hadn't moved. "Why aren't you fighting over one of the swings?"

Russell hesitated before he answered. "Swings make me sad."

"Why?"

Russell remained silent for a long moment. "When I was six," he finally said, "my mama made me a swing. Not as big and high as this one, but I loved it. It hung from the limb on a big tree where we lived. You know my daddy was killed in the war, so I never met him, but I was real happy with my mama. She was seeing a man for a while. I liked him alright. I figured he was going to be my new father, but when he found out my mama was pregnant, he left us. Mama promised me everything would be alright, anyway. She was excited to have another child. I guess I was, too."

Minnie listened carefully. She and Russell had both been through hard things. It's one reason they were so close.

Russell looked wistful. "I used to swing every single day. Nothing made me happier than to climb on that swing." He watched Jed for a few moments. "I never had to share with anyone, but I thought it would be fun to teach my little brother or little sister. One day, I had been swinging for hours when I heard my mama scream real loud. I ran inside and she told me to go get the doctor. She said something was wrong." His eyes filled with tears. "I ran as fast as I could, but it wasn't fast enough. She was dead before I got back with the doctor." He took a trembling breath. "The doctor told me he couldn't have saved her even if I'd found him sooner, but I don't know if I believed him." He sighed. "The baby died with her."

He glared at the swing. "I never got on that swing again. I cut it down. Not too long after, I had to move under the bridge."

Minnie had no words for the pain she saw in his eyes. She grabbed his hand and held on tightly. Sometimes, the only thing you could do was hurt with someone.

Together, they watched Jed and Hope laugh as they pumped their way high toward the rafters.

"They're here!" Russell said thirty minutes later.

Minnie walked to the barn door, trailing behind her brother. Each of them had invited a friend. Her father had taken a wagon and picked everyone up.

Missy, Cassandra, Luke, Paul, and Grant jumped from the wagon. All of them, except for Missy had been to the plantation many times to play.

Minnie noticed Missy hanging back, obviously unsure of her welcome. She had invited her; it was up to her to treat her as a guest. Her mama would expect nothing less. "Hello, Missy!" she called cheerfully.

Missy's blond hair hung down her back in long braids. Her blue eyes were dark with suspicion and nervousness. "Hello, Minnie."

Minnie relaxed slightly. At least Missy wasn't going to start out being mean. "I'm glad you're here." She supposed it was alright to lie if it was for a good cause.

Missy didn't look like she believed her, but she didn't challenge it.

"Do you like to swing?"

Missy shrugged. "Ain't done it before."

Minnie thought about what she had overheard her mama and Rose saying. Missy's mother had abandoned her beneath the bridge three years earlier, leaving her there when the man she was interested in told her he didn't like children. Obviously, her mother had not had much interest in Missy either. "It's great fun," she said enthusiastically. "Come on. It's my turn. You can take it."

"Why would you do that?" Missy demanded.

Minnie sensed that any sympathy would make Missy angry. She had thought a lot about how she would feel if her mama had done to her what Missy's mama had. She didn't know if she would be mean or not, but she was sure she wouldn't trust people. "Because I like to be nice," she replied. She walked over to the swing; aware Missy was following her.

Hope ran up to them, Cassandra by her side. "Do you know how to swing, Missy?" she asked. "It's the most fun thing in the world! Minnie taught me! I can swing very high!"

"I don't," Missy admitted with a smile. "It sounds like you're a good swinger. Will you show me how, Hope?"

Minnie couldn't believe what she was hearing. Missy was being *sweet* to Hope. Was it only because Rose was her mama? Or because Missy wasn't quite as terrible as she thought she was? If that was true, why was she so mean to her?

"Of course!" Hope said brightly. "First, you sit on the swing." She waited until Missy was on the board. "Someone needs to push you the first time until you learn how to pump your legs." She frowned. "I would push you, but I don't think I could get you very high."

Russell appeared. "I'll push you," he offered.

Minnie shook her head at him and stepped behind the swing. "*I'll* push you," she stated.

Russell smiled. "Have fun, girls." Moments later, he was back with John and Jed.

"Hold on to the ropes tightly," Minnie instructed. "When you start going higher, you can pump your legs to keep going."

"Like this!" Hope yelled. She straddled a nearby sawhorse and pumped her legs, her face beaming with excitement..

"Got it!" Missy hollered back, her eyes beginning to sparkle.

Their voices echoed through the cavernous barn.

Minnie pushed as hard as she could. She moved away from the swing when Missy was going higher than she could reach. She walked over to join Hope and Cassandra, glancing up at Missy. What she saw made her freeze in place.

"This is fun!" Missy called, pumping her legs as hard as she could.

What had frozen Minnie in place was the exuberant smile on Missy's face. As she watched, Missy burst into happy laughter.

"Now that's something I've never seen before. I don't believe I've ever seen Missy laugh."

Minnie wasn't aware of Russell's presence until he spoke into her ear. "I've never seen her laugh, either. She's having so much fun!"

Russell looked serious and far older than his years when he answered. "Missy hasn't had much fun in her life. Not before the bridge. Not during the bridge. And probably not with her new family."

Minnie suddenly understood what her mama had been talking about the night before when she came to tell her goodnight. She had suggested to her daughter that while she might not like Missy, she could perhaps look at things from her point of view and imagine herself in Missy's place.

"She looks different when she's laughing," Minnie observed. The hard lines had disappeared from Missy's face. Her blue eyes, usually dull with suspicion, were bright with joy.

When Anthony arrived back at the barn with two huge baskets of food, the children swarmed around him.

"I'm starving!" Russell exclaimed.

John reached for one of the baskets. "I never knew swinging could make you so hungry!"

Minnie laughed. "You did as much leaping into the hay as you did swinging."

"That's as much fun as the swinging!" Jed added.

Anthony eyed the pile of scattered hay. He reached for the basket John was holding, and then held both of them high above their heads. "No lunch until you've piled that hay back into the heap it was. It will only protect you when you're jumping if it's very high." He nodded toward the corner of the barn. "There are three pitchforks over there. When you're done, you can eat."

"But we're hungry now," Hope said plaintively. "And, I'm too little for the pitchfork."

Anthony squatted down in front of her. "You'll need to think of a different way you can help, Hope."

Hope looked defiant but finally gave in. "Fine," she muttered.

Minnie had grabbed a pitchfork. She was shocked when Missy appeared beside her with another one. John claimed the third one.

"Let's see how fast we can do this," Minnie said as her stomach growled loudly.

Hope reached down and grabbed Cassandra's hand. "We can't pitchfork, but we can cheer them on!"

Cassandra grinned and started jumping up and down. "Go! Go! Go!"

Hope started leaping with her. "Go! Go! Go!"

The rest of the group scattered around the pile and threw handfuls from the wooden floor for them to fork onto the pile.

Minnie and Missy looked at each other, laughed, and forked hay as fast as they could.

———⚜———

Anthony had all the food out of the basket and laid on the blankets he had brought with him. The children descended on it like a pack of wild animals.

Minnie noticed Missy hanging back, so she grabbed extra food. When her plate was heaped so high it couldn't hold more, she motioned to Missy. "Come on! I have food for both of us."

Missy's eyes widened, but she followed her willingly.

Minnie pulled out the second tin plate she had grabbed and divided the food carefully. Fried chicken. Deviled eggs. Fluffy biscuits still warm from being wrapped in cloths. Oatmeal cookies.

"Let's eat!" Minnie said eagerly.

Missy took her plate, but just held it. "Do y'all eat like this all the time?"

Minnie remembered what it meant to look at things from Missy's point of view. She also remembered what Russell had said about Missy not having the same life with her new family. "We do," she admitted. "I know we're very lucky. Annie, who cooks for us, is John, Jed, and Hope's grandma."

Missy thought for a moment. "So, she's Miss Rose's mama?"

"No. Have you ever seen Rose's husband?"

Missy nodded. "He's the biggest man I've ever seen!"

"Me too, Minnie agreed with a laugh. "Anyway, Annie is his mama. They got separated before the war at a slave auction. Moses came here to be a slave. His mama went somewhere up in the mountains. When the war ended, he went and found her and brought her back here. She's been here ever since. She got real sick, but she's doing better now." She suddenly frowned and looked over at Hope. "Hope, where is Gloria? Why isn't she playing with us?"

Hope shrugged. "I tried to get her to come, but she said she had to help her mama in the kitchen."

Missy looked surprised. "Gloria lives here too?"

"She does," Minnie told her. "She and her mama were attacked in Richmond. Her mama was almost killed." She decided not to tell the story of how Gloria had ended up at the black orphanage. She was already talking far more than she thought she would. "They came out here to live. Alice helps in the kitchen now, because it's too much for Annie to do all on her own anymore."

"How many people live out here?" Missy asked.

Minnie shrugged. "I don't know. I've never counted. I'll think about it and let you know on Monday at school."

The mention of school made Missy look uncomfortable. "Why are you being so nice to me?"

Minnie thought about the question. "I guess because it's easier than being mean," she replied. "And because you have a great laugh."

Missy looked startled. "What?"

"It's true," Minnie replied. "Until today, I never heard you laugh. You have a really great laugh." She decided to take a huge risk. "And because I would like us to be friends." As soon as the words came out of her mouth, she wondered if she should regret saying them.

Missy looked even more startled, but after a long moment a soft smile formed on her face. "I'm sorry for being so nasty and mean to you."

Minnie was too honest to deny the truth, and she wasn't going to say it was alright. Nothing about it was alright. She thought about how she had treated Bridget the night before. "We all do stupid things," she replied. "I know I do. I guess all we can do is try not to do them again."

"I'll never be mean to you again," Missy said fervently. She dropped her eyes. "I'd like to be friends."

Minnie stared at her. Missy's voice had become so quiet that she wasn't positive she had heard her correctly. "You want to be friends?"

Missy nodded, finally looking up. "Yes."

Minnie grinned. "Then we're friends!" She handed Missy another cookie to seal the deal.

Missy returned the grin and took a big bite of the cookie. "These are the best cookies I've ever eaten."

"I made those last night."

Missy stopped chewing. "*You* made them?"

Minnie hesitated, wondering if Missy was about to say something mean, but nodded. "I did. I love to cook!"

Missy held the cookie up and stared at it. When she looked up there was a mist in her eyes. "Mrs. Highland says I'm too stupid to cook. She told me that any little girl whose mother left her under a bridge must not be very smart. Her and Mr. Highland are trying to make me smart."

Minnie gasped. "That's horrible!" Her mind raced. When she overheard her mama and Rose talking about Missy, they'd said the Highlands took good care of her. They must not know what terrible things were being said. Instantly, it was easier to understand why Missy had been so mean. Missy's lips trembled, but Minnie could tell she was trying to stay in control.

Minnie reached over and grabbed Missy's hands. "Sounds to me like *they're* the dumb ones," she said indignantly.

She pulled Missy to her feet and raced over to her father. "Daddy, can Missy stay the night with us? We're going to cook together."

Missy's mouth dropped open. "Stay here? We're going to cook together?"

Minnie was certain she was doing the right thing. She watched her father cover his look of surprise before Missy could see it. "Is it alright, Daddy?"

"It is with me," Anthony assured her. "As long as the Highlands say it's alright. I'll swing by their place when I take the rest home."

"They won't care," Missy muttered.

"She can wear one of my nightgowns," Minnie said, the plan coming together quickly in her mind. "We're close to the same size, so she can wear some of my clothes, too." She grabbed Missy's hand. "I'll teach you how to make oatmeal cookies tonight!"

Missy looked stunned but returned her smile.

Minnie was satisfied for the moment, but she knew much more needed to be done.

Chapter Twenty-Four

Abby looked up when Alice pushed through the front door, allowing in a blast of frigid air. A cold front had blown in the night before. Snowflakes swirled through the air, but no one believed there would be much accumulation. She had enjoyed watching the white flakes dance through the air in celebration of a new season. The day had been spent reading *The Scarlet Letter* by Nathaniel Hawthorne. She had enjoyed it immensely.

Abby had been in Boston for a week. After the intensity of New York City, her visit had been a welcome reprieve. In another seven days she would head south again. She had no plans to leave the plantation again for a long time.

"Hello Abby!"

"Hello Alice," Abby replied. She pulled her sweater tighter around her body. The fireplace, combined with the oil furnace, kept the house pleasantly warm, but the air gushing in was cold enough to penetrate her clothing. "It's getting colder."

"It is," Alice said cheerfully, "but this is a day to celebrate justice."

Abby raised a brow. "Regarding?"

Alice shrugged out of her thick coat, unwound the navy-blue scarf from her neck, placed her hat on the coat tree, along with her coat, and then came to sit beside her. "Who would you love to see behind bars more than anyone else?"

Abby suddenly remembered what was happening in New York City shortly after she left. With everything going on with Nancy and with the economy, she had forgotten. "The Boss Tweed trial." She was almost afraid to ask. "Boss Tweed was convicted?"

Alice grinned. "Of 102 felony crimes!" she said triumphantly. "The prosecutor is pushing for one hundred and two years in prison, since each crime carries a sentence of one year. He is trying to have Tweed fined $25,000, as well."

Abby clapped her hands, thrilled to discover there were still enough citizens in New York with the integrity to hold Tweed accountable. There were many times she had doubted it. "That's wonderful!" she exclaimed. "He deserves to languish in prison for the rest of his life for what he has done." Then she frowned. "A fine of $25,000 is ludicrous, however. Tweed has stolen close to $45,000,000 dollars from New York City taxpayers."

"What he has stolen may well end up being much higher than that. New fraudulent schemes are being discovered every day," Alice said grimly. "Our country has never experienced such a corrupt politician."

"Which is saying a lot," Abby said wearily, thinking of all the damage that had just been wrought by the corrupt politicians and businessmen that crashed the economy. Tweed's corruption had been limited to New York, though she was certain the effects would ripple much further out. The depression was reaching into every corner of the country. His theft would increase the impact.

"Tweed got away with everything for so long," Alice said. "How was that possible?"

"How is so much of what happens in this country possible?" Abby replied. "People turn a blind eye, or they're simply too afraid to stand up against bullies like him. Tweed started defrauding New York and taxpayers back in 1852. Matthew kept me apprised of his activities for years. Tweed extorted everyone he could, climbing the political ladder at a staggering speed."

"Was what they called the *Tweed Ring* real?" Alice asked.

Abby scowled. "Unfortunately, yes. Tweed was quite adept at having his friends elected to office. He granted businessmen city contracts at ridiculous profit margins, in return for the money he extorted from them. He bought off an untold number of lawyers and judges. The combination of their powers for corrupt behavior was staggering. It made Tweed staggeringly wealthy, but the men in his ring profited greatly, as well. That's why they were willing to do whatever he told them." Abby paused, the extent of the fraud sweeping over her. "It will take decades for New York to recover from the damage they've done. The people of New York will suffer greatly."

"In the middle of a depression," Alice remarked ruefully. "Recovery will be that much more difficult here in New York."

"Exactly," Abby muttered. "I'll grant that Tweed was brilliant in knowing how to consolidate power and buy off, or intimidate, anyone who stood in his way, but the damage he has done is unimaginable. Four years ago, on top of everything he'd already done, he took control of the New York City government. When he accomplished that, it took his fraudulent schemes to a new level. Not only had he bought the judicial system – I believe they were actually afraid of him. There was practically no stopping him."

"But they have." Alice sat down in the chair across from her with a steaming cup of tea. "How did they finally stop him?"

"He started to fall two years ago," Abby answered. "It began with a cartoon campaign by Thomas Nast in *Harper's Weekly*. He was under attack from *The New York Times*, as well. It's not that people didn't know what he was doing. Tweed truly thought he was untouchable and above the law. He threatened Thomas Nash, but the cartoonist didn't care. He was determined Tweed would be brought to justice."

"Were Nash's cartoons that powerful?" Alice asked.

"They were powerful," Abby confirmed, "but it was more than that. Tweed had little respect for his constituents but was savvy enough to realize he needed them to hold on to power. He didn't care so much what the *New York Times* said, because most of his supporters can't read. He built his power from a base of constituents who didn't have the education and knowledge to question him. They were swayed by his powerful personality; not aware he was lying to them about everything. Tweed knew, however, that the cartoons could be his undoing. Pictures say far more than words can, and anyone can understand them."

"So, it was just the cartoons?" Alice asked.

"No. They got people's attention, but the cartoons wouldn't have been enough on their own," Abby replied. "The cartoons forced an examination of the city's books, but the men who examined them were part of the Tweed Ring," she said contemptuously. "They reported the books had been *faithfully kept*," she said sarcastically.

Alice rolled her eyes.

"Tweed's fall continued when members of the Tweed Ring began to turn on him. Most turned on him as revenge for Tweed not giving them what they wanted, but a few turned on him because of a late discovered integrity. They realized he was on the verge of bringing down the entire city. They couldn't stomach being a part of that, no matter how much they were making. They finally decided to do the right thing."

Alice looked thoughtful. "I suppose $45,000,000 is a lot for any city to lose."

"It's a lot for a *country* to lose," Abby retorted. "Tweed embezzled so much money that it provoked an international crisis of confidence in New York City's finances. There was a very deep concern from other countries about the city's ability to repay its debts. There were enough clear-thinking men left to realize that if the city's credit were to collapse, it could potentially bring down every bank in the city with it. It took them time to dig through all the deception and coverups, but Tweed's crimes were finally discovered. His first arrest was two years ago."

Abby shook her head in disgust. "Until this trial, he's been able to avoid justice. He practically owns every judge in the city, but he was immensely popular with the masses, despite his having defrauded every person in the city who pays taxes. They didn't know about what he had done. His powerful personality made them think he was a far better man than he actually is. Not only did they fail to convict him two years ago; he was actually elected to the state senate again."

Alice stopped in the middle of a sip of tea. "That's not possible."

"Oh, it's possible," Abby told her. "When a reporter confronted him and asked him about the charges, Tweed arrogantly asked him, *'Well, what are you going to do about it?'*"

"He knows now," Alice said indignantly.

"Yes," Abby agreed. "They failed to convict him in January of this year during another trial, because the jury couldn't deliver a verdict. There were still too many people in awe of his power and personality."

"Well, they got him this time!" Alice said.

Abby grinned. "They did. It renews my faith in the justice system." A frown replaced the grin. "It remains to be seen, however, what the sentence actually is. The prosecution asked for one hundred and two years, but there is little chance that will happen. If the sentencing judge is one of his cronies, the sentence could be far lighter."

"Perhaps," Alice agreed. "But surely his power has been stripped away. I would imagine there are far fewer men who will want to be connected with a convicted felon."

"Indeed." Abby found comfort in that knowledge. "Tweed is a man who lives off power and intimidation. I've never been able to understand it. I've heard him speak. He is a blowhard who lies constantly. He thrives off lying – the bigger the better. He has been able to convince men to do just about everything for him for decades."

"But not anymore," Alice said. "The tides have turned against him."

That statement made Abby much happier. "The tides have indeed turned."

The door opened again, allowing a bigger gust of cold air as Frances and Felicia entered.

"It's snowing again!" Frances called. "It's beautiful!"

Felicia shook her head. "You won't think it's beautiful after six months of it. I thought snow was *beautiful* until the winters I spent at Oberlin College in Ohio. I understand Boston is worse."

"Or better," Frances said cheerfully. She hung her coat up and moved to the fireplace to hold her hands out to the flames. "I refuse to let your poor attitude diminish my joy!" She stuck out her tongue impudently.

Abby laughed. She loved the banter between the girls. The last week had been a delight. She had thought she would stay with the Gilberts, but the girls had begged her to stay with them. After Alice had assured her there was room, it had not been hard to persuade her. She adored being with the girls in the cozy cottage tucked near Boston Common. She and Alice had grown close during the time she'd been there.

The cold, blustery wind and snow had kept her inside that day, but she had spent hours during the other days roaming the city and watching the new construction in the financial district. In some areas, it was practically impossible to see the effects of the fire the year before. In others, the devastation was still terrible. It was easy to imagine the terror that had consumed the city when the fires were blazing.

"How was your day, Frances?" Abby asked.

"I'm smarter than when I left this morning," Frances said, her tone still cheerful.

Abby, however, saw the angst in her eyes. She reached out to snag her hand, holding it closely between her own. "Hard day?" she asked gently.

Frances sank down on the sofa. "Yes," she admitted. "Mama warned me this could happen, but I didn't want to believe her."

"What has happened?" Abby hated the sadness lurking in her granddaughter's brown eyes that usually bubbled with happiness.

"My age," Frances said bluntly. "No one will take me seriously, because I'm so young." She shook her head. "I asked Mama if I should wait until I'm older, but she insisted I'm ready."

"Then you're ready," Abby said calmly.

"Other students don't believe I belong there!" Frances exclaimed. "I can hear them talking about me and laughing at me."

Abby felt a flash of anger but kept her voice calm. "People did the same thing to me when my husband died, and I took over the factories. They made my life miserable."

Frances frowned. "That's terrible, Grandma. I've never heard this story. What did you do?"

Abby smiled. "I proved to them that I belonged. My factories became more successful than those owned by the men who mocked and ridiculed me. It took time, but I proved they were wrong about me."

Frances was silent for a moment. "How long did it take?"

"As long as it took," Abby replied.

Frances looked confused. "I don't understand."

"I don't have a definitive answer for your question," Abby replied. "You will prove to people that you belong at medical school by doing the best you can. In time, they will realize how incredible you are."

"You're a little biased," Frances said dubiously.

Abby laughed. "I'm supposed to be. I'm your grandmother. If I can't be biased, who can be?" She turned serious. "I'm also right, but that doesn't truly matter. The most important question is whether *you* believe you're going to be an incredible doctor." She let the statement hang in the air for a few moments. "Do you?"

"Grandma..." Frances squirmed and looked away.

Abby held up a hand. "I want an answer, but I'm not interested in a *fake* answer, Frances. No false humility. *Do you believe you're going to be an incredible doctor?*"

Frances took a deep breath and met her eyes. "Yes," she said confidently. "I've learned from my mother, the best doctor I know. I've learned from Janie." Her eyes went to her landlord. "And from Alice. She helps me each day when I come home with questions. I've even spent time with Dr. Gilbert and Elizabeth at the clinic. They let me work with them."

Abby was delighted. "Do you realize how lucky you are, my dear? How many other students do you know who have learned from such amazing physicians? How many other students do you know who have the opportunities you have right now?"

Understanding dawned in Frances' eyes. "No one."

Abby smiled broadly. "You've been in medical school a little more than a month. That may seem like an eternity, but it's merely a second in your life." She remembered something. "You had an exam today. How did you do?"

"I believe I did alright," Frances replied.

Felicia cut in. "You said it was so easy that it didn't feel like a test at all. You're confident you got every question right."

"Don't you suppose that will show people what you're capable of?" Abby asked.

Frances looked uncomfortable. "I suppose..."

Abby waited for her to finish her thought.

Frances became quite interested in something on the floor. "I don't want to make other students feel bad, Grandma. They might not have done as well."

Alice started laughing. "Darling Frances, I can assure you that your mother never hesitated for a moment to show all of us how much better a student she was than us."

Frances looked startled. "She didn't?"

"Your mother studied more than all of the rest of us put together," Alice's voice was intensely serious now. "She had waited so long to come to medical school. After the war, she was fiercely determined to be the best doctor she could be. None of the rest of us had spent years working with wounded and dying Confederate soldiers. It gave your mother a passion the rest of us couldn't share. Janie came the closest but even she hadn't experienced all your mother had..

We would try to talk your mother into doing fun things with us, but she refused. She said she had to study. Nothing would deter her from that. She spent her entire time at the top of the class. She earned it."

"I didn't know that," Frances murmured.

Alice wasn't finished. "She did something much more important than studying, though."

"What?" Frances asked.

"She treated people every chance she got. She wasn't going to wait until she got out of school. School gave us some opportunities to practice medicine, but it wasn't enough for your mother. She constantly looked for people she could help. When we were all in school, we lived in your grandma's house. It was wonderful for us because we were together, and we felt safe. Until the cholera epidemic swept through the country."

"Mama told me about that," Frances replied. "That's when she discovered Homeopathy."

"Yes," Alice agreed. "When cholera killed so many people seven years ago, your mother discovered the power of homeopathy." She paused. "The rest of us, however, were not impressed."

"Why not?" Frances demanded. "Mama told me about what happened. Traditional medicine couldn't help all the thousands dying in Philadelphia. Mama found out about homeopathy and started treating people. They lived and got well. How could you not be impressed by that?"

"Because we were idiots," Alice replied "We didn't want to rock the boat. We'd been told by the Women's

Medical College of Pennsylvania, where we were students, that if we were to start using homeopathic remedies, we would be told to leave."

Frances was shocked. "Why?"

"Because traditional medicine has always been threatened by homeopathy," Alice explained.

"Threatened by treatments that work?" Frances looked disgusted. "Doctors treated cholera patients with things they knew wouldn't work. They closed them away in hospitals that were more like warehouses and waited for them to die. Doctors are supposed to make people better!"

Alice smiled. "You are definitely your mother's daughter, Frances. That was exactly how she felt. That's the reason she left medical school and went to the Homeopathic Medical College of Pennsylvania. When Janie saw how many people she was saving from cholera, she joined her." Shame filled her face. "The rest of us, me, Elizabeth, and Florence moved out and ended our friendship."

Frances stared at her for a long moment. The only sound in the room was the crackle of the flames in the fireplace. "You're teasing me."

"I'm not," Alice assured her. "We were awful and ignorant, but we finally saw the light. All of us apologized to her and Janie for being so blinded. We all use homeopathy in our medical practices now. We incorporate traditional medicine practices when we know they will be effective, but we're simply committed to making our patients better. That's what matters most."

Frances sat in silence while the fire crackled and the wind roaring down the chimney got louder. "Why didn't Mama ever tell me about this?"

"Because your mother knows how to extend grace and compassion. By the time you became her daughter, we had all seen the error of our ways. I'm sure she saw no purpose in giving you reason to view us poorly," Alice replied. "That's who your mother is."

Frances finally looked at Abby. "I understand what you mean about being lucky to have Mama and Janie teach me about being a doctor." She took a deep breath. "I want to make her proud."

"Then do what your mother did," Alice said firmly. "*Be the best.* Study harder than anyone else in your school. Do the best you can on every test. Look for every opportunity to help people. Learn from everyone who will teach you."

Abby chose her words carefully. "Frances, there will always be people who try to bring you down. People who are jealous or insecure think they will feel better about themselves if they can bring you down by destroying how you see yourself. Honey, never be less than your best in order to make others feel better. That won't help anyone – you *or* them. When you commit to doing your best, you will inspire others to do the same."

"Abby is right," Alice continued. "When the other students see what an excellent doctor you *already* are, it will make them want to be better. You'll end up helping patients all over the country that you will never see, because you will make the other students become better doctors."

Felicia joined the conversation. "Listen to them. I've been told many times that I'm too young to do the things I've done. I go ahead and do them anyway."

Abby turned to her with a smile. Frances had plenty to think about after their conversation. "Which brings us to you, Felicia. How was your day?"

Felicia shrugged. "The highlight was getting two letters. The first was from Mama. She wrote to tell me Grandma is doing much better. She's still healing from the surgery, but she's back in the kitchen driving Alice crazy." Her eyes sparkled. "Grandma keeps telling everyone that she doesn't need help all the time, but Daddy told Mama that she came to him privately and thanked him for hiring Alice. Besides the fact that she needs the help, she likes having Alice around, and has fallen in love with Gloria."

Abby felt the tug to go home become stronger. "That's wonderful news! Who was the second letter from?"

"Mrs. Pleasant wrote to tell me not to let the economic downturn dissuade me from making investments. Most people won't be able to, so I'll be able to purchase property at a lower price." Felicia's voice was full of doubt.

"Still not finding the right properties?" Abby knew Felicia had been roaming the Boston streets for weeks, searching for opportunities.

Frustration filled Felicia's face. "No."

"You knew it wouldn't happen quickly," Abby reminded her. Once again, she was glad she had decided to visit the girls in Boston before returning home. Normally brimming with confidence, Felicia was struggling to remain positive. Studies had come easily to her. Putting her knowledge into practical business investments was proving a daunting challenge.

"That's true," Felicia acknowledged, "but Boston is booming, even with the economic downturn. I've found wonderful properties, but they cost too much. I don't believe they'll be profitable in the long run. I refuse to put my parent's money, nor Mrs. Pleasant's money, at risk by making a poor investment."

"That's the perfect attitude," Abby assured her. "I've seen far too many people make risky investments because of impatience and lose everything." She raised her brow. "The country is rather full of those people right now." She couldn't help thinking about Wally – which led her to wonder how Nancy had been doing without her for the last week.

"Do you believe I can find the right property?" Felicia demanded. "Perhaps this is simply not the right time to attempt what I want to do." She hesitated. "Or perhaps I chose the wrong city."

Frances looked alarmed. "You're not thinking of leaving, are you?"

Felicia continued to watch Abby. "I need to know what you think, Abby."

Abby considered the question carefully.

Alice stood to add more logs to the fire. "I'm glad you're here, Abby. I can answer medical questions, but I'm useless when it comes to business."

Abby smiled as she continued to ponder the question. What did she truly believe? Felicia deserved a thoughtful response. "What are you finding in the city?" she finally asked.

"The majority of the boarding houses I've found are nice places. I've talked to a few of the tenants. They love Boston, the rents are reasonable, and they plan on staying where they are for a long time. That would be positive if the purchase price wasn't so high. Rents would cover expenses, but they wouldn't make much profit. I could raise rents, but my goal is to create *affordable* housing. It would be different if I were well established and could invest solely for future profits, but I need investments to create income now in order to expand."

"That sounds wise," Abby responded, listening carefully. "What else have you found?"

"I've found boarding houses that are quite rundown and in a bad part of the city. They were nice when they were built, but they haven't been cared for. I'm not interested in those, because Mrs. Pleasant told me those types of tenants are more likely to not pay, and they are less likely to take care of their rooms." Felicia frowned. "I never thought it would be so difficult to provide affordable housing for women. I don't want to have boarding homes that only a few people can afford."

Abby appreciated that Felicia's values were dictating her business decisions. She wasn't done asking questions, however. "What have you learned about the history of Boston? How have the areas in the city changed over the years?"

"Those are good questions," Felicia answered. "Give me a minute."

Abby waited patiently. She knew Felicia was thinking.

"Every area has gone through a transformation," Felicia finally said. "Boston has been expanding in size as they claim more of the land around the city. They've spent a lot of time and money to fill in the bays and wet areas. As they create stable land, they build on it. When they do that, the existing areas improve." She fell silent, continuing to think.

Abby was content to look outside. Snowflakes still swirled through the lantern light. She knew it was brutally cold, but Alice's home was warm and cozy. It was easy to relax in the chair and enjoy the flames in the fireplace while Felicia thought.

Alice and Frances remained quiet, as well.

Peace pervaded the room.

"Boston is doing well, even with the current economic crisis. More and more people are moving here, but it doesn't have the same problems New York City has. The people coming seem to have more money. They are looking for opportunities," Felicia said.

"And a safe place to live?" Abby asked.

"Yes," Felicia replied.

"And areas that have struggled in the past are doing better now?"

"Yes."

"Is there a reason to believe this pattern will continue?" Abby asked. As she asked questions, a plan was forming in her mind.

"Yes," Felicia said again. Her eyes began to shine. "You're telling me to invest in the rundown boarding houses, because those areas are going to improve. I can be a part of making that happen!"

"Is that what you believe?" Abby asked carefully.

Alice began to laugh so hard she had to lean over to catch her breath. "Oh girls..." She fought to speak clearly. "You told me Abby did this. I didn't believe you."

Frances joined her in laughing. "She taught Mama to do it, as well. Trying to get a straight answer from either of them is nearly impossible. They do nothing but ask questions."

"You did it to me again, Abby!" Felicia exclaimed. "I didn't even realize it, this time."

Abby took a sip of her tea. "You don't need me to give you answers, my dear. You need to answer questions and find the solution for yourself."

"Have I found the solution?" Felicia demanded.

Abby smiled as she put her cup down. "Do you believe you have?" She held up her hand when Felicia opened her mouth to protest. "I can't answer this for you, Felicia. It's far too important. Whatever you decide to do, it needs to be something you believe in. You're going to face challenges and obstacles along the way. It will take time for any area of the city to transform. It won't happen quickly."

"That's true." Felicia's eyes were sparkling again. "But I can see it. I'll be getting in on the ground floor of those areas. I can help with the transformation by carefully selecting tenants and encouraging new businesses to open. I can't be the only one having a hard time affording things in the city. Other people are too. I can lead the way and open their eyes to the opportunity waiting for them."

Abby clapped her approval. "It's a brilliant plan." The very one that had been formulating in her mind.

Felicia walked over to the table beside the fireplace to get a pencil and a pad of paper. "I need to make a list." She scrunched her forehead in thought. "I will need workers to help me improve the buildings."

"Which should be easy to find right now," Abby replied. "There is a lot of building going on in Boston to recover from the fire, but the economy *will* slow things down. Men will be looking for jobs. When men discover there is work to be found, they will come in from other areas of the country suffering from the depression."

Felicia grew serious. "Do you think they will listen to me?"

Abby acknowledged it was a valid question. Men weren't used to taking orders from a teenage girl. "You will have to be strong and positive. You may be female, and you may be young, but you are also the one hiring them. You have what they need..."

Felicia grinned. "Money!"

"Exactly. You may have to fire a few men along the way, until your workers realize you truly are in control. It won't be fun. However, once you have a group of workers you can trust, I believe you'll get things done quickly."

Felicia eyed her. "You had to do this with your factories, didn't you?"

"I did," Abby replied. "There were men who thought they could walk all over me because I was a woman. They were rather shocked when I told them they were fired, but it taught my other workers to treat me with respect. As time went on, they appreciated the respect I showed them, as well. I believe it's what made my factories so profitable. I treated my workers well. They treated me well. It's how Thomas and I operate our factories today. A work environment should be positive for everyone."

Felicia was listening intently. "How many buildings should I buy?"

"What has Mrs. Pleasant taught you?" Abby was curious to see how Felicia would approach this issue.

Felicia's lips twitched. "You're right. I know the answer to this one. I have to add the cost of the building to what I believe it will take to renovate them. Once I have the cost, I need to figure out what I will charge tenants, and the number of tenants it will take to break even. There will be maintenance costs, but anything after that is my profit. It will take me a while to pay off the investment, along with the interest I've negotiated with Daddy and Mrs. Pleasant, but the boarding houses will continue to make money for as long as I own them."

"Once you have those figures, you'll be able to develop a solid business plan to share with your parents and Mrs. Pleasant," Abby told her proudly.

"Will you tell them you believe I have a sound plan?"

Abby raised a brow. "If you put together a solid plan, with numbers that work, you won't need my endorsement. The numbers will speak for themselves. Assuming you do that, however, I will gladly tell them I think you're onto something."

"Thank you! I have a lot of work to do before we go home!"

Abby was thrilled to see the light shining in her eyes again.

Alice stood. "Now that we have all the problems of the world solved, can we eat?" She sniffed the air. "I believe I smell chicken soup. Abby, did you actually cook for us?"

"I'm not certain chicken and vegetable soup is *cooking*, but since I didn't go out today, I decided to putter. I've practically forgotten how to do anything in a kitchen, but at least I've moved beyond the oatmeal I cooked in New York. When I have Annie cooking for me, there is no need to get anywhere near a kitchen."

"With the exception of Minnie, any woman who comes from Cromwell Plantation is doomed to starvation," Felicia observed.

"That's true," Abby said. "I'm afraid we've done a poor job of preparing the group of you for your life."

"Not true," Frances protested. "Alice is already a doctor. I will be one in the future. Felicia is going to be a wealthy businesswoman. We'll just hire someone to cook for us, treat them with respect, and help make the world better for women!"

Once again, the room dissolved into laughter.

Snow continued to swirl through the air, bringing the promise of a winter full of new beginnings.

Chapter Twenty-Five

"What happened to your family, Minnie? Why did you get adopted?"

Minnie leaned back against the trunk of the sprawling oak they were sitting beneath. Instead of dreading school, it had been a joy to walk through the doors hand in hand with Missy. They were sharing the lunch Alice had fixed for them. The Highlands had been more than happy to have Missy spend the weekend at the plantation. They'd had great fun baking cookies, playing on the swings, blowing bubbles, and talking for hours.

"My daddy died in a factory accident when I was eight. My first mama never told me exactly how it happened. When he died, I had to go work in the same factory he died in. I almost died there too," Minnie said matter-of-factly.

Missy looked properly horrified. "How?"

"My hair got caught in one of the machines. I thought it was going to rip my head off." Minnie could almost feel the pain again. "I'm still not sure how I got away from it. I guess it finally pulled enough of my hair out. I was bleeding real bad, but no one offered to help me. I was walking home when there was a fire engine accident. Mama came to treat the men who got hurt. That's when she found me. I didn't want to tell her how I got hurt, but I finally did. She took me back to her clinic, fixed me up, and took me home."

"Why didn't you want to tell her how you got hurt?" Missy asked.

"I didn't know her. My first mama said we needed me to work at the factory if we were going to eat. When I first met Mama, she told me she was Dr. Wallington. What if she had gone to the factory and saw the conditions I was working in?" Minnie still had occasional nightmares of the horrendous factory full of clanking, grinding machinery that ran around the clock. She had worked twelve-hour days. In the winter, she never saw the sun. She had only worked there a year, but it had seemed like an eternity. "I couldn't risk losing that job."

Missy's eyes were wide. "What happened when you told her the truth?"

Minnie smiled. "She hired my first mama to be her and Daddy's cook." Her voice dropped. "Mama is a *real* bad cook. She is a wonderful doctor, but you don't want her to feed you."

Missy giggled.

Minnie giggled back; certain she'd never get tired of hearing Missy giggle. "Anyway, Mama told my first mama that the only way she could cook for her was if I never had to go back to the factory. She said I needed to go to school."

Missy's eyes grew wider. "What did she say?"

"She agreed, because they were paying her a lot of money. None of us would have to work anymore. We wouldn't be rich, but we could all eat and stay warm, so we *thought* we were rich." Minnie smiled wistfully.

"Mama loved being a cook. She was real good at it, too. She taught me the first things I knew about cooking." Her mind traveled back in time. "I loved being at that house. Mama was doing a surgical internship with Dr. Wild. That's why she and Daddy were living in Philadelphia, instead of on the plantation. That's when I met Frances."

"She moved to Boston didn't she?"

"Yes. We loved each other right away. She's five years older than me, but it didn't matter. We did everything together. When I was at the house, if I wasn't helping my first mama, I was with Frances." Minnie smiled. "I pretended we were sisters, but I knew it wasn't real..." Her voice trailed off.

"Until?" Missy prompted.

Minnie hesitated. She hated to talk about that night.

"You don't have to tell me, if you don't want to," Missy said softly.

Minnie was comforted by the fact that Missy saw her pain. "No, it's alright. One night, Frances asked me to stay late, because we were playing. My first mama said it was alright, as long as Mr. Anthony brought me home. I don't remember what Frances and I did, but I do remember smelling smoke when me and Daddy got close to where I lived." Suddenly, she couldn't bear to relive it in detail. It was enough that the flames were practically searing her brain. "It was my family's boarding house," she said quickly. "My whole family died that night in the fire."

Missy clapped a hand to her mouth. "*All* of them?"

Tears pooled in Minnie's eyes as she fought to push away the memory. "My mama. My brother. My two sisters."

Missy stared at her, aghast. "That's awful. I'm so sorry." She reached out and took Minnie's hand.

"Thank you," Minnie whispered. It had been a long time since she'd told that story. She guessed it would always be hard.

"How did you end up with the Wallingtons?"

"Mr. Anthony brought me home with him. He didn't know what else to do. That night, they decided I would become their little girl." Minnie smiled as she remembered. "They brought me to the plantation. Frances became my real sister. They became my new Mama and Daddy."

"And then Russell and Bridget got adopted too," Missy observed.. "All of you are real lucky."

"I know," Minnie agreed. "Russell and I talk about how lucky we are."

"So, Frances is their only real child."

"No, Frances is adopted too. Mama can't have children of her own. She had a little girl, but the birth almost killed her. It killed the baby. They told her that if she tries to have another one, it will mostly likely kill her."

Missy's eyes were wide again. "How did they find Frances?"

Minnie told the story of how Mama had met Frances on a wagon train to the New Mexico Territory to help the Navajo people. "Frances' first family was killed by the flu when they were living back in Illinois. She was in an orphanage, until Mama found her and brought her home."

Missy's blue eyes brightened with unshed tears. "I wish I had been lucky like all of you," she said softly.

Minnie frowned. "Me too. I don't want you to back to the Highlands."

Missy shrugged. "Maybe they won't treat me as bad since I spent the weekend at the plantation. I reckon they won't want your folks to know the truth." Her voice grew sad. "Mrs. Highland told me once that they wished they had never adopted me. She said I wasn't so bad, but that they didn't really want a child around the house." A single tear spilled over, but she wiped it away impatiently. "If I was a little older, I would run away and live on my own." Her voice grew frightened. "I lived like that under the bridge. I don't want to do it anymore."

Minnie silently reached over and took her friend's hand.

They sat that way until the bell called them back to school.

Carrie was relaxing on the porch after a long day at the clinic. It was too cold to be outside, but she needed the quiet after an endless stream of patients. She pulled her hat down and wrapped the thick blanket more closely around her. She felt like a caterpillar encased in a warm cocoon. It wasn't quite dark, but the dusk would finish swallowing the daylight soon.

When it did, the full moon she could see peeking above the horizon would rise in all its glory. She leaned her head back and drew in deep lungfuls of the frigid air. Miles had told her to expect snow tonight. Since he was never wrong, she knew the skies would cloud over soon and obscure the moon.

"Mama?"

Carrie smiled when Minnie appeared, clad in coat, gloves and a thick hat. "Hello, darling daughter."

Minnie's expression was serious. "Mama, we need to talk."

Carrie nodded toward the rocking chair next to her. "Alright. What are we talking about?"

"You and Daddy adopting Missy."

Carrie hadn't know what to expect, but it wasn't this. "Why don't you tell me where this is coming from."

Minnie sat down, her freckled face set in intense lines. "The Highlands are not nice to Missy."

"Are they hurting her?" Carrie asked sharply.

"Not on the outside," Minnie replied. "They're hurting her on the *inside*. They tell her she's stupid and can't learn. They told her if she was smarter, that her mama wouldn't have left her under the bridge."

"No!" Carrie cried.

Minnie nodded, her voice growing more distressed. "They even told her they wished they hadn't adopted her, and that they don't want a child around their house."

Tears filled Carrie's eyes. After what Missy had endured and survived, to live with a family who didn't want her had to be heartbreaking. It was easy to understand why Missy had been mean. It was also easy to understand why she loved being on the plantation. Anthony had told her the expression on Missy's face when he dropped her off at the Highland's after the weekend with Minnie had made him want to snatch her up and take her away.

"So, we need to adopt her," Minnie said matter-of-factly. "Missy is my best friend. She shouldn't have to live that way. Now that Frances is all grown up and lives in Boston, there is room in our family for another little girl."

It was hard to debate the logic, and it warmed Carrie's heart to see how much Minnie cared. "This will have to be a family decision, honey." She was already imagining how wonderful it would be to grow their family again. Once again, they had not gone looking for a child – one who needed them had been brought to them.

"Russell agrees with me," Minnie told her. "We talked about it before I came to find you. Bridget is too little to understand, but she loves Missy. Missy told me she has always wanted a little sister. She's very kind to her."

Carrie had seen how drawn Bridget was to Missy. She'd witnessed how Missy came to life on the plantation. She was a little girl when she was with them. "I'm not opposed to the idea," she said quietly.

The moon chose that moment to burst above the horizon, its full glory casting a silver glow over the plantation.

Minnie grinned when she saw it. "I believe Rose would call that a sign, Mama!"

Carrie laughed. "It might be," she agreed. "I still have to talk to your father, honey. I'll see him tomorrow when I go into Richmond with Hobbs."

"I know," Minnie replied. "Russell and I figured it made sense to get you on our side before you talked to Daddy."

Carrie laughed again, harder this time. Her daughter was definitely honing her skills of persuasion. "We should also talk to Frances."

Minnie frowned. "Why? She doesn't live here anymore."

"This is still her home, Minnie. I would never want her to feel that there isn't room for her here." She saw hope flash across her daughter's face.

"Do you know something I don't know?" Minnie demanded. "Is Frances coming home for good? Is she staying here after Christmas?"

"No, honey," Carrie said gently. "Frances will go back to Boston, but she'll come home every chance she can." She paused. "Are you sure you want to share your alone time with Frances, with Missy? It will change things if there are three of you in your room."

"Four," Minnie reminded her. "Felicia will be home sometimes, too. We're all in the same room." She sighed. "How can such a big house be so crowded?"

Carrie asked herself the same question on a regular basis. "It's full of people we love."

"That's true," Minnie agreed.

They sat in silence for a while, watching the moon rise higher in the sky. The barn roofs gleamed silver. Even the horses still in the field reminded her of silver statues. She knew the clouds massed on the far horizon held snow. She expected flakes to start falling before midnight. She pulled the blanket more closely around her, wishing for the hot tea brewing in the warm kitchen.

Carrie was content to let Minnie think.

"Mama?"

"Hmm?"

"I want us to adopt Missy," Minnie said firmly. "I know it will change things with Frances, but things have already changed. She'll always be my sister, and I will always love her, but Missy is *here*. I miss having a sister to share things with. Bridget isn't old enough yet. And besides, Missy needs a family that loves her. I can't stand the thought of her living with the Highlands."

Carrie had reached the same conclusion while they were sitting there. "I'll talk to your father when I'm in Richmond. We'll both be home in three or four days. We can discuss it then."

"What about Frances?" Minnie said. "She won't be home for two weeks. I realize she needs to be part of the decision, but would it be alright if we invited Missy to stay with us through Christmas? Tomorrow is the last day of school before Christmas break. The Highlands will be glad she's gone, and it will give Frances a chance to get to know her."

Carrie smiled. "I believe that's a wonderful solution! It will give Missy an opportunity to see what it's like around here all the time. If she doesn't want us to adopt her, we'll find another family she'll be happy with."

"Oh, she'll want to be adopted," Minnie assured her. "She tells me all the time how lucky Russell and I are. And Bridget. She loves it here."

It would be good for her and Anthony to have time with Missy. Adding another child to their family was a heavy consideration. When they had talked about it in the past, they'd agreed they wouldn't go looking. Just as they had with their other children, they would wait for God to bring them. It seemed as if this was one of those times, but she was grateful for time to make a firm decision.

Chapter Twenty-Six

Carrie was delighted when she woke to a thin layer of snow covering the world. It wasn't enough to change her travel plans, but it made everything more beautiful. She looked at her breeches longingly. No matter how comfortable they were, she wasn't willing to appear in public in breeches. She slipped into a navy-blue woolen dress, pulled on woolen stockings, and carefully plaited her hair into braids before she coiled them into a bun.

Hobbs smiled when Carrie walked into the barn. "Good morning!"

Carrie started laughing as soon as she saw her friend. "I wouldn't recognize you if I didn't know it was you!" She walked around him, looking carefully. "It's perfect!" she exclaimed.

"You told me the black walnut hulls would do the trick," Hobbs said. "I followed your instructions exactly. I ground up a bunch of the hulls and added them to the hot water just like you said and let it steep overnight. Last night, I applied it to my hair and beard and let it sit for an hour. I even put it on my eyebrows. I wanted it really dark, so I did it four times."

Carrie grinned. "How does it feel to not be a redhead?"

"Strange," Hobbs admitted. "But if it keeps me alive when we go into Richmond, I will happily be a brunette."

Carrie sobered. Hobbs had wanted a Hanger prosthetic since the moment he laid eyes on Perry's several months earlier. With Perry on the plantation, his desire had grown. She understood his desire for a leg that would give him increased mobility, especially on the horses, but both she and Anthony were hesitant about taking him into Richmond. There was a very good chance a Klan member would recognize him and remember his betrayal at the KKK convention in Nashville.

"It's going to be fine, Carrie," Hobbs said. "It's been seven years! And besides, you just said you wouldn't have recognized me the way I look now."

Carrie chose not to remind him of the Klan's increased activity in the last several months. They were becoming bolder all over the South. They seemed to know that since the economic crash, the government had more important things to focus on than how the blacks in the South were being treated. Not to mention the revenge the Klan was determined to exact on whites that didn't share their beliefs in black inferiority. It made her furious, but all they could do was be more aware and more cautious.

"Do I pass inspection?" Hobbs asked.

Carrie shook her head. "Not yet. I want you to come back to the house with me for the final step."

Hobbs frowned. "Final step? It's not enough that I've ruined perfectly good red hair?"

Carrie smiled. "You haven't ruined it. It will wash out when you get back to the plantation."

"So, what are we doing?"

"You'll see," Carrie said teasingly.

"I'll get the carriage ready." Miles walked up carrying a steaming mug of coffee.

"Thank you." She eyed the mug. "Is that for me?"

"Nope." Miles took an easy sip. "You got coffee in the house. You ain't got no need to take mine."

"It smells good!"

"I reckon it does. Don't mean I got to give it to you."

Carrie smiled at her old friend. "How is Annie this morning?"

"Complainin' that she oughta be back in the kitchen full-time. Keepin' her still is harder than trying to quiet the wind durin' a blizzard!"

Carrie laughed. "One more week," she told him. "I will not take any risk of her developing an infection."

Annie's voice sounded from the stairs leading to their apartment above the barn. She had descended halfway. "Ain't no chance of me gettin' an infection. I reckon I could go swimmin' in mud and still be right as rain. You done poured enough garlic tea in me to fill the James River."

Carrie smiled. "There is more waiting for you in the kitchen," she said calmly.

Annie scowled. "That burst appendix might not have killed me, but I be pretty sure that garlic tea will."

Carrie had learned to ignore Annie's complaining. "Stop fussing and go drink your tea," she retorted. "I did not save your life just so you could throw it away again."

Annie snapped her mouth closed.

Carrie hid her smile. Being reminded of dying had a calming effect on Annie. She was used to demanding her own way, but Carrie knew her bluster was for show. Her voice grew gentler. "You're too important to us, Annie. I won't take even one chance that something could go wrong."

Annie acknowledged defeat, but she wasn't going down gracefully. "I'm going to the house to get garlic tea. When I get that poison down, will *Dr. Wallington.* let this old woman eat one of them cinnamon rolls me and Alice started last night?"

Carrie was aware that no matter what she said, the first thing Annie was going to do was eat a cinnamon roll, but she would play the game. "Only if you make sure there are enough for Hobbs and me to take with us to Richmond."

Annie smiled coyly. "I reckon maybe we can do that."

Carrie turned back to Hobbs. "Let's go."

Once they were inside the house, she led him into a small room off the kitchen. She pointed toward a chair next to a small table. "Sit."

Hobbs raised his brows. "Bossy."

Carrie smirked. "Some things never change." She reached for the bowl she had prepared that morning.

Hobbs peered into it. "What's that?"

"Cornstarch, cocoa and turmeric," Carrie answered. "It's makeup that I made this morning.

Close your eyes and lift your face."

Hobbs stared at her. "Are you crazy? What are you going to do?"

"Cover your freckles with this makeup," Carrie replied. "I don't know any brunettes with bright blue eyes and freckles. I can't do anything about your eyes, but I can cover the freckles. If someone is paying attention enough to note your freckles, they'll recognize you're trying to disguise your identity. Once that happens, they'll start looking more closely to attempt to discover who you are."

Hobbs sobered as her words sunk in. "You've thought of everything," he muttered. "I'm sorry to be this much trouble."

"You are most definitely a lot of trouble. I suppose it's a good thing you saved Robert's life, got Matthew through the door of the Klan convention, and are so wonderful with the horses." Carrie smiled tenderly. "We love you, Hobbs. Keeping you safe is not a lot of trouble. It's what we do for people we care about."

Hobbs closed his eyes and lifted his face. "Do your magic. I need to go to Richmond so I can get a new leg!"

———

Thirty minutes later, cinnamon rolls in hand, Carrie and Hobbs rolled down the drive. The sun was above the trees, but it was still early. She hoped Richmond would be busy when they arrived in town. Empty roads would make them stand out.

It was the four hours of travel to get there that were making her uneasy. She hated feeling this way, but she couldn't stop thinking about how Anthony and the rest had been stopped by Klan members on the way home from Blackwell Plantation. If they had stopped a wagon of men to intimidate them, they wouldn't hesitate to stop a carriage with a woman and a man. Once they realized who she was, they would not be pleased. If they recognized Hobbs, things would turn ugly.

Hobbs spoke the words she was thinking. "You reckon the Klan will stop us?"

"They might." It would do no good to pretend differently. They might as well be prepared. "They'll most likely recognize me, but they'll think twice before they do anything that will bring the wrath of the plantation down on them."

Hobbs looked nervous. "What if they recognize me?"

"Then we'll be in trouble," Carrie said honestly. She wanted to assure him it wouldn't happen, but the possibility was why she had been hesitant to let this trip happen in the first place. "Let's not cross that bridge until we come to it."

Hobbs stiffened. "Trouble," he muttered.

Carrie stared at the two figures on horseback she could see next to the gate. Surely the Klan wasn't bold enough to come right up to the plantation entrance. Surely, they knew there were Cromwell guards watching them from the woods right that second. It comforted her to know they were there, but she could still be moving toward trouble. She considered turning the carriage around and going home, but anger kept her driving forward. She refused to let fear keep her from doing what she wanted to do. Both she and Hobbs were armed. She hoped they wouldn't need their guns, but they were prepared. She hated the thought of more violence. She was sick of all of it.

As they drove closer, she smiled and relaxed. "It's Matthew and Harold!"

Carrie pulled the carriage to a stop when they reached the pair. "Good morning! What are you doing here?"

Matthew, bundled against the cold, lowered his bandana enough to smile at her. "We're going to Richmond with you."

"What?" Carrie asked in astonishment. "Why?"

"For a lot of reasons," Matthew replied. "The first is that my wife told me she would refuse to feed me for a week if I didn't." His eyes gleamed with amusement.

Justin chuckled. "Susan made the same threat."

Matthew's voice turned serious. "Things are volatile, Carrie. Hobbs is at risk of being recognized, but you are equally at risk. Being a Cromwell is a wonderful thing, unless you're living in Virginia at this moment in time."

Carrie found it suddenly difficult to swallow. "Is it ever going to change?" she asked wearily.

Matthew lifted one shoulder. "Only time will tell. What I do know is that it's not going to change today. My wife wants her partner in the medical clinic to return. Seems she doesn't want to have to handle it all on her own."

"Susan said the same thing about her partner in Cromwell Stables," Harold said. "Then she gave me a list of things I could buy for her in Richmond."

Carrie laughed. "So, she used her concern for me as a ploy to get you to shop for her."

"Basically," Harold agreed.

Carrie appreciated their lighthearted approach, but she knew the true reason they were there was to protect her and Hobbs from the Klan. She wished she didn't feel the relief pouring through her, but she wouldn't pretend otherwise. "Thank you."

"My pleasure." Matthew shifted his focus to Hobbs. "How does your hair look?"

Hobbs smiled and pulled off his hat.

Matthew stared at him with disbelief. "It worked? You actually covered all that red with something made from black walnut hulls?"

"Just think what it could do for your and Harold's red locks," Carrie teased.

"No, thank you," Matthew retorted. "I was born a redhead. I intend to stay that way." He leaned closer to stare at Hobbs. "Where are your freckles?"

Hobbs rolled his eyes. "Carrie covered them with makeup."

Matthew threw back his head and laughed. "You have *makeup* on?"

Hobbs scowled. "Keep laughing and you'll be sorry. If it weren't for you and that Klan convention you were so fired up about getting into, I wouldn't be sitting here with brown hair and no freckles. I would have left the Klan, but I wouldn't have had to run away to Oregon."

Matthew quit laughing as remorse swept over his face. "You're right, Hobbs. I'm sorry."

Carrie felt like the wind had been knocked out of her. Until that moment, she hadn't fully comprehended the price Hobbs had paid for his decision to help Matthew infiltrate the Klan convention. His move to Oregon had been an absolute necessity – not a choice. His sacrifice had turned his whole world upside down. He'd been brave enough to return, but he wasn't safe. He would pay for his actions for a long time. She suddenly understood how much they owed him.

"I'm sorry, too," Hobbs muttered. "I shouldn't have said that. No one made me help you get into the convention, Matthew. I made that decision on my own." He looked west. "Let's go. Klan or no Klan, we've got to get to Richmond."

Matthew reached into his pocket. "Put these on. It won't hide your blue eyes if someone is really looking, but they'll do a good job of obscuring them."

"Glasses?" Hobbs asked.

"The lenses are fake, but they look like the real thing. They'll help conceal your identity."

Carrie grinned when Hobbs slipped them on his face. "You're actually quite handsome as a brown-headed, bespeckled man."

Hobbs looked doubtful but nodded west again. "If brown hair, glasses, and makeup will keep me alive long enough to get a new prosthetic leg, I'm fine with them. Richmond is waiting."

Relief flooded Carrie when they reached the city limits without incident. The hours had passed pleasantly, filled with talk and laughter. The sunshine had quickly melted the light layer of snow and dried out the road. The basket Alice had stuffed full of food was empty.

Hobbs' appointment wasn't until the next day, so they were headed to her father's house on Church Hill.

Carrie was alarmed as they rolled down Broad Street. She'd not seen it this deserted since the war years. "This is what the depression has done?"

"Yes," Matthew answered. "Most of the factories are completely shut down or operating with very few employees. There aren't many goods coming in or out of the city."

"What are people going to do?" Carrie demanded. "How will they eat? Or pay for heat?"

"It's going to be a long winter," Harold said grimly.

"Is it happening everywhere?" Carrie was dismayed by the hopeless expressions on pedestrians' faces. The streets were clear from the snow the night before, but the wind blowing in from the north was frigid. Miles had warned her it was going to be a cold winter. There were many months of suffering ahead.

"New York City is the worst," Matthew continued. "It's spreading, though. The railroads had a long reach. Every business connected with them has either gone out of business or is barely operating. The number of workers who have been laid off has reached the hundreds of thousands."

Carrie's memories of Richmond during the war were crystal clear. Hunger and cold would replace eating and celebration. "Christmas is coming," she said sadly.

Hobbs' expression revealed he remembered the war years, too. "It won't be a happy one this year for most of Richmond."

Carrie was eager to be off the desolate streets, and in the warmth of her father's house. She had thought about going to River City Carriages first, but if Anthony wasn't already at her father's house, he wouldn't be far behind them. Seeing the empty streets made her understand why business had slowed down so drastically. She began calculating what needed to be done in order to care for his horses on the plantation. It would be a waste of valuable resources for them to stay in the city.

So far, Cromwell Stables hadn't been affected by the economic crash. All their foals had been sold and paid for that spring, even before they were born. The six-month-old colts and fillies had been taken to their new homes several weeks earlier. A few buyers had ordered for the following year, but not as many as usual. The ones that hadn't had explained they needed to hold on to their money because of the crash. Cromwell Stables would begin to feel the impact of the depression in the spring. There was little chance the economy would recover before then. It remained to be seen how many of the normally coveted foals would be purchased. Thankfully, because of Abby, they had prepared for a crash. They would be alright for two years, if necessary. Things would be tight, but they would be able to care for the horses.

Anthony was waiting on the porch when Carrie pulled up to the house. "I'll be in once I care for the horse," she called.

"I should think not," Hobbs protested. He waved his hand. "Get out of the carriage. I'll take the carriage around back and make sure Eagle has everything he needs for the night."

"Harold and I will be in as soon as our horses are settled," Matthew said. "Tell May we would appreciate some hot tea to thaw our bones."

Carrie stepped down from the carriage. In truth, she was frozen to the core. She was warmly dressed, and had been covered with lap blankets, but the frigid air had still seeped in. The bright morning sunshine had faded as more clouds rolled in. She didn't know if it was going to snow, but the temperatures had dropped.

Anthony swept her into a hug when she reached the porch. "I'm glad you're here," he said. "I've been missing my wife."

Carrie raised her face for his kiss. "I missed you, too," she said softly.

When she shivered, Anthony released her and opened the door. "You're freezing. Let's go inside."

Carrie was more than happy to oblige. Fires burned in every fireplace. The crackling sound, the warmth, and the smell of a delicious meal almost made her swoon. She closed her eyes and breathed it in.

"Why are Matthew and Harold here?" Anthony asked. "Was their trouble?"

"No," Carrie assured him. "They came with us to make certain there *wouldn't* be trouble."

May swept into the room carrying a tray. "Welcome back to Richmond, Miss Carrie. Have some hot tea."

Carrie reached for the steaming cup, inhaled the rich aroma, and then took a sip. The warmth spread through her body. "Ahhh..." She closed her eyes and took another sip. "Thank you, May. This is delicious."

May smiled. "Dinner will be ready in one hour. Spencer is taking hot water up to your room for a bath. It will be ready in about fifteen minutes."

Carrie gasped with delight, already imagining the feel of the hot water wrapping around her. "Really?"

May sniffed. "You think I don't know how to take care of guests, Miss Carrie?"

Carrie laughed at her look of pretend offense. "I'm just not used to being spoiled. I'm absolutely thrilled to have a hot bath. Thank you."

"Sittin' on that carriage seat for four hours will stiffen up every part of your body," May replied. "You sit there and relax."

Ten minutes later the back door pushed open. Cold air came rushing in, but Matthew closed it firmly as soon as the three men entered.

May stepped out of the kitchen. "Hot tea and cookies are in the parlor, Mr. Matthew and Mr. Harold." She stopped when Hobbs appeared behind them. "Who are you?" she demanded.

Hobbs grinned. "You don't recognize me, May?"

May stepped closer to get a better look. Her eyes widened. "That you, Hobbs?" Her eyes narrowed. "What happened to you?"

Carrie laughed. "He's in disguise, May. Evidently, it's quite an effective one."

May continued to stare at him. "Who you hiding from, Hobbs?"

Hobbs stopped grinning. "The Klan."

May slapped her hand to her mouth. "The Klan be after you? Why?"

Matthew answered. "Hobbs got me into the KKK Convention in Nashville seven years ago. Because of him I was able to publish information about their inner structure. I couldn't have gotten that information any other way. They were going to eventually figure out how I infiltrated their inner sanctum, so we got Hobbs out of town."

"That's why you went all the way out to Oregon?"

"That's why," Hobbs confirmed.

"And now you're back," May observed. "How do you figure that's a good idea?"

"I'm not sure I figure it is," Hobbs admitted. "I missed home. I'm working at Cromwell Stables for Carrie. Being home and being on the plantation is what I needed, so I decided it was worth the risk. Especially after Portland, Oregon almost burned to the ground a few months ago. I was ready for something different."

"What were you doing out west?" May asked.

"Working for the railroad," Hobbs answered.

"Then your leaving Oregon was the best thing for you to do. You woulda lost your job anyway. Better to do it on your own terms," May said wisely. "Ain't nobody with the railroads working much anymore." She caught Carrie's look of surprise and raised a brow. "What? All you have to do is read the newspapers to know what's going on, Miss Carrie. Mr. Thomas and Miss Abby buy about every newspaper there is. Mr. Thomas told me I could read them before I send them on out to the plantation. That's what I do."

"With Miles' help," Anthony interjected with a smile. "She has him well trained."

"That's true," May agreed. "He reads to me every morning while I'm cooking. I explained to him that if he wanted to eat, he needed to read." Her eyes twinkled. "I read the rest of them at night. I've done learned a lot about this country."

"You probably know more than I do," Carrie told her. "I try to read them, but when I come in after a long day at the clinic, and spend time with my children, I don't have much energy left to read."

"When you get as old as me, you'll have more time to read. I'm going back in the kitchen to finish up dinner. You go on up for your bath."

"Bath?" Matthew said hopefully.

May chuckled. "You want a bath, you can carry up the water yourself, Mr. Matthew. I'm not having my Simon haul water up for you strong men."

Matthew looked wounded. "I can assure you Carrie is every bit as strong as we are, May."

May raised a brow. "That may be, but she has something else you don't."

"What?" Matthew demanded.

Carrie was as curious as he was to hear the answer.

"She has a daddy that pays my salary every month!"

The room erupted in laughter.

"On that note, I'm going up to take advantage of hot water," Carrie said. In truth, she felt a little guilty that she was the only one to enjoy the luxury of a hot bath, but not guilty enough to miss her opportunity. "I'll let all of you know just how wonderful it was."

Matthew eyed her. "You're going to pay for that last comment, Carrie Wallington."

Carrie shrugged. "I doubt it," she said serenely. "I have a big strong husband to protect me."

Anthony stepped away from her. "Your big strong husband will not protect someone taunting cold men who accompanied you from the plantation to keep you safe. You're on your own, wife."

Matthew grinned and started forward.

Carrie bolted from the room and raced up the stairs. She slammed her bedroom door and locked it just as she heard boots pounding down the hallway. "Sorry," she called sweetly. "I'm busy taking a *bath*."

Matthew's amused voice sounded outside her door. "Just remember, you're going to pay. You may not know what, and you may not know when, but you will certainly know *why*."

Carrie laughed, pulled off her clothing, and stepped into the steaming water. She closed her eyes and allowed the water to soak away the chills and tired muscles. Her bath would be worth whatever retribution Matthew designed.

Later that night, Carrie curled into Anthony. "How many of your horses are we taking back with us when we leave?'

Anthony sighed. "Most of them. It makes no sense to keep the horses here. Since Matthew and Harold came with you, we'll be able to take five wagons back to the plantation. We'll tie ten horses to each wagon. Marcus and Willard will make sure the remaining twelve are cared for. If there isn't enough business to keep them here, we'll bring them out in January."

"You're going to shut down River City Carriages completely?" Carrie asked with surprise. "What about Marcus and Willard?"

"I couldn't run River City Carriages without them. Bringing the horses out to the plantation will allow me to continue paying them."

"For how long? I know you've been saving money, but this depression could stretch out for a long time. It seems like no one has any idea how far reaching it will be."

"The last year has been extremely profitable. If all of us take half pay, I can stretch it out for three years."

"Three years? That's wonderful!" Carrie exclaimed.

"Thanks to Thomas and Abby," Anthony said ruefully. "I thought Abby was creating a worst case scenario in regard to the economy. One that wouldn't actually happen. I wanted to expand the stables last year. Your father convinced me otherwise. I'm grateful he did."

Carrie listened carefully. "I should have known all this. Why didn't I know this?"

"We're busy when I'm home. Between the children, your clinic, and Cromwell Stables, you barely have an opportunity to breathe at times."

"Which is no excuse." She was exhausted from her long, cold day, but had an important question that needed asking before she could sleep. "Do you resent it?"

"Resent what?"

"How busy I am."

"If you weren't busy all the time, you wouldn't be the woman I married. I knew who I was marrying, Carrie. I love our children. I love what you do at the clinic, and I love the stables. There's nothing to resent." He chuckled as he nuzzled her neck. "Besides, when we're together, there is nothing to interrupt us. Even Bridget is old enough to sleep through the night."

Sleepiness forgotten, Carrie wanted to dissolve into his arms, but this seemed like the opening she had been waiting for. "How would you feel about one more child?"

Anthony went still for several moments before he spoke. "You want to adopt Missy."

It wasn't a question.

Carrie sat up, pulling the blankets off both of them. Cold air rushing in revived her. "How could you know that?"

"It's freezing out there!" Anthony pushed her down and pulled the blankets around them again. "Missy is an unhappy child. Minnie adores her new best friend. I see how happy Missy is when she's with us. I also see how eager the Highlands are for her to leave when I go to pick her up." Anthony smiled. "So, I'm right?"

Carrie told him what Minnie had revealed about Missy's life with the Highlands.

Anthony's eyes darkened with anger. "That poor little girl! The Highlands don't deserve to have a child, especially not one that has endured what Missy has."

Carrie couldn't have agreed more. "Minnie asked me last night if we would adopt her. She said that with Frances in Boston, we have room for another little girl."

"That's my girl," Anthony said softly. "What did you tell her?"

"That I would talk to you, and that we would talk to Frances when she comes home. Russell is already completely on board, and Bridget loves Missy. Minnie is inviting her to spend the school break with us. She'll be with us for Christmas and New Year. If we all agree as a family to adopt her, she'll never go back to the Highland's house." Carrie felt happiness pulse through her. "We both know how quickly life can shift. This year has been full of new beginnings, but this was not one I anticipated."

Anthony smiled. "Me either. I can't wait to see Missy's face on Christmas morning."

"On Christmas Eve, when she sees the tree with all the candles glowing!"

"When she sees all the food. Her first Christmas with us will be one to remember."

Carrie snuggled closer to him. "You're quite an amazing man," she said tenderly.

"Because I love children?"

"No, because you're willing to continually have your life turned upside down to make life better for children," Carrie replied.

"Every time we make room for another child, our own lives improve immeasurably. If it were possible, I would have dozens."

Carrie laughed. "I believe five is a good number for this year." She kissed him gently. "You truly are amazing, Anthony Wallington."

Anthony pulled her closer. "I'm happy to let you show me how amazing I am."

Chapter Twenty-Seven

The J.E. Hanger Artificial Limbs waiting room had four men sitting in upright chairs. Crutches leaned against the wall. Three of the men had a pant leg hanging loose, indicating an amputation. One had a wooden peg leg, like Hobbs', stuck out in front of him. Their facial expressions were a combination of nervousness and hopeful anticipation. Carrie knew they had come looking for a new way of living after injuries she suspected they had obtained during the war. They had lived with their challenges for at least eight years.

While Hobbs and Anthony, who had insisted on joining them for protection, sat down, Carrie walked around the room and looked at the glass-fronted cases displaying prosthetics. She had known for years that Perry had a prosthetic leg quite different from a peg leg, but it had seemed rude to ask him to see it. She eagerly examined the prosthetics constructed of whittled barrel staves and metal. There were separate prosthetics for above the knee amputations, and below the knee amputations. The design used rubber bumpers, and featured hinges at both the knees and ankles. She could imagine how much easier it would be to walk in this prosthetic, compared to the peg leg.

She had done research since learning of James Hanger. Hobbs had told her about Hanger losing his leg in the first battle of the war when he was eighteen. Further research revealed Hanger had left George Washington University, where he was an engineering student, to fight. He had only been in Philippi for two days before the battle began, so new he hadn't even officially enlisted. He wasn't a soldier at Philippi when the Union Army attacked. He had been given orders to care for the horses in a nearby barn, and to keep them calm when the battle began.

A cannoneer with extremely poor aim had shot a tree. The cannon ball had boomeranged off the tree into the barn, shattering boards on its way toward Hanger. The impact had been enough to destroy his leg. A Union doctor committed to the Hippocratic Oath had treated him. His leg had been amputated and he'd been provided care. He had been given a peg leg and told to learn how to use it.

After time in a Union prison camp, he had been exchanged for a Yankee prisoner and sent home to Virginia. He hated the peg leg and was determined to create something that would work far better than anything currently invented. He spent weeks in his bedroom, refusing to come out, while he perfected his design for the new leg. His family heard him hammering and sawing, but it wasn't until he walked downstairs with his new leg that they discovered what he had been doing.

Hanger patented his most recent model of the prosthetic just two years earlier, in 1871. Virginia had commissioned Hanger to manufacture the above-knee prosthesis for wounded soldiers.

Carrie leaned closer to the display case. She was fascinated by the knee hinges, but the ankle hinges were especially intriguing. She read that Hanger dissected a squirrel in order to discover details about how the joints worked. Besides supporting the foot and being able to withstand someone's body weight, the ankle had to twist and rotate laterally – not to mention working in conjunction with a wooden foot. Attaching the prosthetic to the stump was equally challenging. It had to be secure and as comfortable as possible.

Hanger had made countless versions of his leg; learning something new every time he tested his newest creation. She was certain he was still working to perfect it.

"I lost mine because of a wound at Antietam. At first, I was able to keep my leg. An infection after the war caused the doctors to take it off."

Hobbs' voice brought her attention back to the room. The men had started talking to each other.

"Gettysburg," an older man said. "I've been wearing this peg leg for ten years now. I hate it." he said vehemently.

"I hate mine, too," a slender man with blond hair and blue eyes said. "I lost my leg at Fredericksburg. I figured my life was over. I was right," he said bitterly. "My wife left me not long after I got home from the war. She couldn't get used to seeing my stump. She said it scared her."

Carrie's heart ached for the veteran who had paid such a heavy price for his part in the war. She thought of the veterans she had helped through the years. She hadn't been able to replace their peg legs, but now she could tell them about a better option and would help them travel to the clinic. What she had done was to alleviate their pain with the homeopathic remedy, *Hypericum*. She wondered if James Hanger knew about its effectiveness in reducing phantom pain.

"Mine got cut off at the Battle of the Wilderness," a man with stringy black hair and haunted brown eyes said. "I heard they never decided who won that battle, but I can tell you I lost my leg there." He scowled. "I was twenty. I'd been fighting for three years, but never been hurt. I figured I was one of the lucky ones. I'd go home from the war and go back to blacksmithing. Ended up not being so lucky." He stared down at the empty pant leg hanging loosely from his body. "I tried one of them peg legs, but I hated it more than I hated not having a leg. It hurt all the time. I decided I was better off just using crutches since I was a cripple who couldn't work. People gonna stare at me all the time, anyway."

The fourth man stared at the floor, refusing to look up and engage in the conversation. Carrie was curious what his story was, but he was clearly not interested in telling it.

"I know a fella with one of these legs," Hobbs said. "I would never have guessed he had a fake leg. He even rides a horse like he has a real leg."

Every expression in the room brightened with hope.

"He rides a horse with a fake leg?" the older man asked. "I ain't been on a horse since I lost my leg. Having a peg leg stick out is more than I can stand.

Besides, how are you supposed to grip when your leg can't hold the saddle?"

Carrie knew that's how Hobbs felt, too. He'd only been on a horse a couple times since returning to Virginia. He said not riding at all was easier than having to ride with a peg leg. He had tried riding without having his leg attached. It had been a little better, but he still hated it. She prayed Hanger could help Hobbs as he had so many others.

The door to the back offices opened. The room grew quiet as a man walked out. He had a broad grin on his face. He stopped when he saw the men in the waiting room. "Hello fellas," he said cheerfully. He lifted his pants leg to show them his prosthetic.

Even though the men had seen the ones in the display case, they all leaned forward to look more closely at the leg that was actually being worn.

"What's it feel like?" Hobbs asked.

"Like I have a leg again," the man replied. "I've had it for three months now. It took some getting used to and I'm still learning how to use it, but for the first time since the war, no one even knows I don't have a real leg," he said proudly. "When the war ended, people called me *the man with the peg leg*. It's like losing my leg completely stole who I was before the war. Having this leg has changed my life! Unless I choose to tell people, they don't even know I have a fake leg!"

It was mid-afternoon before Hobbs made it into the back office.

Carrie hadn't minded the lengthy wait. Watching each of the men go in with nervous anxiety, only to see them emerge later with eyes full of hope and belief had been wonderful to watch. Each man would have to wait until their legs could be manufactured, but they had been measured and had received the promise of a new leg. Carrie knew they were actually receiving the promise of a new life. She was thrilled for them, but Hobbs was the focus of her attention today.

When Hobbs walked back through the door, his face positively beamed with excitement. "I qualify for a new leg!"

Carrie grinned and clapped.

"I knew you would," Anthony said enthusiastically. "How long before you have it?"

"I'm to come back the first week of January," Hobbs answered. "They'll have it for me then."

"That's hardly any time to wait," Carrie said encouragingly.

Hobbs stared at her without speaking.

Carrie laughed. She knew that expression well. "Alright, so it's forever to wait. But, it's better than being told you can't have a leg at all."

"That's true," Hobbs conceded before he changed the subject. "Hanger wants information on the Hypericum."

Carrie grinned again. "You told him about it?"

"Of course. He asked me how bad my phantom pain is. When I told him I didn't have any, he was shocked. I told him about the homeopathic remedy you give me and your other veteran patients. He wants to know more."

"I'm happy to provide him with everything he needs."

"That's what I told him. You're to come back to meet with him tomorrow morning."

"What?" Carrie exclaimed. "We're going home in the morning."

"I told him that, too. I also told him you're as passionate about helping veterans as he is. I assured him you would meet with him." Hobbs smiled. "I did make him agree to meet with you at seven o'clock in the morning. I figure we'll still have plenty of time to make it home before dark."

Carrie couldn't argue with his plan. She glanced at Anthony.

"It's fine," he assured her. "It's going to take time to get the horses ready to be led out of the city. I didn't figure we would leave before eight o'clock, anyway. If it's a little later, it won't matter. I'll have Spencer drive you here and then back to the stables."

Before Carrie could answer, the door to the office opened again. A tall, slender man with vibrant eyes above a mustache and goatee appeared. He looked around the room, his eyes settling on Carrie.

"Hello Mr. Hanger," Carrie said.

"You're Dr. Carrie Wallington?" Hanger's voice was both smooth and direct. He was clearly a man focused on his mission of helping veterans.

"I am."

"You can help my veterans who are in pain?"

"I've helped dozens. Almost all of them have responded favorably."

"Wonderful!" Hanger said. "Will you be able to meet tomorrow morning? I understand it could be an inconvenience."

"It will work," Carrie assured him. "We'll head home after our meeting. I'm looking forward to talking with you."

Hanger regarded her more closely. "I understand Cromwell Plantation is a unique place."

Carrie hesitated. She knew James Hanger was a miracle worker with prosthetics, but she knew nothing about his racial or political attitudes. "It's home."

Hobbs grinned. "He's not a KKK member, Carrie."

"Certainly not! I've made legs for many black veterans. I don't care if someone is white or black, Confederate or Yankee. If I can help them with a prosthetic, I will help them."

Carrie smiled brightly. "I'm very happy to hear that!"

Hanger eyed her. "I suspect we're close to the same age."

"Close," Carrie agreed. "My husband and I are thirty-one; three years younger than you." She smiled at his surprised expression. "I like to do my research on people. My father has an extensive library of magazines and newspapers. It wasn't difficult to find information on you."

Hanger smiled. "I suspect my wife would love to meet you. She doesn't know many people in the city yet. Nora and I were married just this year. She is fourteen years younger than I am, and a graduate from Hollins Institute."

Carrie smiled graciously. "I would be pleased to meet your wife." She did not, however, believe Nora would be as pleased to meet her. Hollins Institute was known for academic excellence, but the Institute was based upon the southern sensibility that a lady was to be trained to submit to the order of men. She and Nora would find themselves on very different sides of that issue. "There won't be time on this trip, but I look forward to it in the future."

She wanted to give Dr. Hanger the information he desired and return home.

A cold wind was blowing when they arrived back at the Church Hill house. She was happy to see smoke curling from the chimneys. The day had been exhilarating and fulfilling, but she was ready to eat dinner and settle in for a relaxing evening. She stepped from the carriage, grateful for Hobbs taking care of the horse, and looked at Anthony. "I've been thinking about something. Should we wait two more days and take Abby back to the plantation when she arrives from Boston? It seems silly for one of your men to drive her out when we are right here."

"I thought you were anxious to get Hobbs out of Richmond." Anthony looked surprised.

"I was, but we haven't had any trouble at all," Carrie replied. "I don't anticipate any, especially if Hobbs stays in the house until we leave. I would love to surprise Abby and be here to take her home."

"She may not be the one who will be surprised."

"What are you talking about?" Carrie stopped walking and looked up at him appraisingly. "I know that expression. You're hiding something."

"Not for much longer." Anthony turned her to face the porch.

Abby was standing on the top step with her arms spread wide.

Carrie laughed and ran up the steps to embrace her mother. "What are you doing here? You're not due home for two more days!" She hugged her tightly. "I've missed you so much!"

"And I've missed you," Abby assured her.

"I want to hear everything," Carrie said. "But first, how are the girls? I'm counting the days until they come home. I'm not sure I'll survive ten more days."

"Good thing you won't have to."

Carrie spun around when Frances' voice sounded behind her. She started laughing the instant she saw her daughter appear from the doorway. "Frances!" she cried. She grabbed her daughter and pulled her close. "What? How?"

Frances hugged her tightly. "I couldn't survive ten more days either. Since I'm the top student in my class and I'm ahead in my studies, the dean agreed to allow me to come home early – as long as I agreed to talk to my classmates about my amazing physician mother when I return."

Carrie laughed and hugged her tighter. "I'll write a thank you letter to the dean when you return. You have no idea how happy I am to see you. I've missed you so incredibly much!"

Anthony's voice broke in. "Would it be alright if I hugged my daughter, too?"

Frances pulled away and leapt into her father's arms. "Daddy! I missed you too!"

Carrie watched them, still laughing. When they pulled apart, she grabbed Anthony's arm. "You knew about this?"

"I only found out last night. Abby sent a telegram. Thankfully, you were upstairs preparing for dinner when it came. She asked me to keep it a surprise."

"You're terrible at keeping surprises," Carrie reminded him.

Anthony pretended to be offended. "Even I can keep a secret for *one day*," he protested. "May is evidently quite good at it, however."

May pushed open the door. "Yep. Which is why I'm the only one who has known for five days."

"Five days?" Carrie cried.

Abby grinned. "May is the only one I could trust to not talk. It was important to the girls that we surprise you. When Thomas wrote about your coming to town to get Hobbs a new leg, we concocted our plan."

Carrie shook her head. "I don't believe my father has known about this. He's worse about keeping a surprise than Anthony is."

"They're both hopeless," Abby agreed. "He doesn't know, either. Your father is going to be equally surprised when we arrive tomorrow."

"Where are Felicia and Alice?"

"Inside," May answered. "Where anyone with any sense would be on a day like today. They are sitting by the fire." She waved toward the house. "Get out of this cold," she ordered. "There are hot tea and cookies waiting for everyone."

The evening passed with endless stories and laughter.

Carrie and Frances arrived at the Hanger clinic, sharply at seven o'clock the next morning. Frances, once she had discovered the purpose for the visit, had insisted on joining her. Carrie had been delighted.

Spencer pulled back on the reins and grinned at them. "Seems like old times, Miss Carrie." He eyed Frances. "Me and your mama got in some awful fixes back during the war, when your grandpa hired me to drive her."

Carrie smiled mischievously. "We did an awful lot of good, Spencer. I could never have done what I did without you."

"Have I heard all those stories, Mama?" Frances asked eagerly.

"She tell you the one where a group of white men came after us? Your mama lit into them with a whip and saved my life."

"A whip?" Frances' mouth gaped open. "Mama, did you really do that?"

Carrie's mind flooded with memories. She and Spencer had been on their way home from the black hospital. They had left after dark, something she knew not to do, because the streets of Richmond during the war had grown increasingly dangerous. "It was my fault we were out so late. I had some patients I refused to leave. We should have just stayed there for the night, but I knew your grandpa would have worried terribly. I suspected there would be trouble but decided it was worth the risk." She grimaced. "I was wrong. We'd only gone a few blocks when a group of men appeared on the road in front of us and forced us to stop."

She could see it clearly in her mind. "They demanded I get out of the carriage, but I knew what would happen if I did. Spencer would have tried to protect me, but it would most likely have cost him his life. I wasn't going to let that happen. I got their attention by snapping the whip at their feet a few times in quick succession. They hated me for helping Richmond's black residents, but they weren't interested in feeling the whip." They hadn't known that she also had a pistol inside her coat. She would have used it, if necessary, but the whip had done the job. Cursing, they had turned and disappeared into the dark shadows. "They decided they had better things to do that night."

"Weren't you afraid to keep going back to the Black Hospital?" Frances asked.

"I reckon we both were," Spencer answered. "Them folks needed her real bad, though. She wasn't gonna let nothing stop her from taking care of them."

Carrie reached over and squeezed her old friend's hand. "I made sure we left well before dark, or spent the night, for the remainder of the war."

Frances' eyes were full of admiration. "I'm going to tell that story when I go back to school in January."

Just then, the door to the clinic opened. James Hanger stepped out onto the porch. "Come inside, Dr.

Wallington," he called. "I have hot coffee and biscuits waiting. Bring whomever you have with you. It's much warmer in here."

Carrie introduced Spencer when they stepped inside.

Spencer settled down in a chair with a steaming cup of coffee, leaned his head back against the wall, and closed his eyes.

Carrie knew he had been out late the night before, helping distribute food to the poorest of the freed slaves suffering from the depression.

"This is my daughter, Frances, Mr. Hanger. She insisted on coming when she discovered we were meeting. She's a student at Boston University School of Medicine."

Hanger smiled. "You're going to be a doctor like your mother?"

"I can only hope I'll someday be as good a doctor as my mother, Mr. Hanger. I've seen firsthand the veterans she has helped with their phantom pain."

Hanger stepped back. "Please come into my office. I know our time is limited, so I don't want to waste a moment of it." He sat down behind his massive desk after they had settled into large, comfortable chairs. "Dr. Wallington, please tell me how you have helped your patients."

"I understand you're not a doctor," Carrie began.

Hanger shook his head. "Far from it. I was a student at George Washington University, on my way to being an engineer, before the war broke out. When I lost my leg, I dedicated my life to creating prosthetics that are the best in the world. I believe I have done that, but I still can't help my veterans with their endless pain."

"Or with your own, I imagine," Carrie said sympathetically.

"That's true," Hanger conceded. "I've learned to live with it, however."

"Admirable, but unnecessary." Carrie reached into her bag and pulled out a vial. "Through my years of practice, I have discovered that Homeopathy offers hope where other paradigms fail. This remedy is called *Hypericum*. When I first started treating my veterans, I used it exclusively. It's highly effective, but further research has expanded my treatment options."

Hanger leaned forward; disappointment evident on his face. "That's how you help your patients? What do you do with it?"

Carrie smiled. "I take it you're not familiar with Homeopathy?"

"I'm not," Hanger acknowledged. "I've heard the word at some point in the past, but I can't tell you anything about it."

Carrie could talk for hours about homeopathy, but since their time was limited, she chose to be brief. "In it's purest form, Homeopathy is the treatment of disease by minute doses of natural substances that in a healthy person would produce symptoms of disease." She held up her hand when she saw Hanger's confused look, reached into her bag, and pulled out a book. "You're going to have far more questions than I can answer in the time we have. This book will provide answers to most of them."

Hanger reached for it gratefully. "I appreciate the fact that your patients get better, but my engineer's mind has to understand the reasons. I will read this carefully."

Frances chuckled. "My brother is like you. He has to know the reason for everything."

"I'm sure I would like your brother."

"You would," Frances assured him. "His name is Russell. He's only eleven, but he already has his own shop at the plantation. He makes all kinds of things."

Hanger raised his eyebrows. "That right? The next time you come to Richmond, bring Russell with you, Dr. Wallington. I would love to meet him."

"Thank you. I'll certainly do that." Carrie could easily envision Russell's excitement at meeting James Hanger. She reached into her bag and pulled out another vial. "This is *Calendula officinalis 200*."

Hanger repeated his earlier question. "What do you do with it?"

"With both of the remedies, you add five drops to water and drink it twice a day," Carrie instructed. "Within a week, your pain will lessen. Continue the use and it will disappear completely. I would start with *Hypericum*. If you aren't experiencing the results you want, switch to the *Calendula*. There are some cases in which it is far more effective. I've had a few patients who didn't respond well to the *Hypericum*. When I switched them to *Calendula*, their pain went away."

Hanger reached for the vial and peered at it. "That's it? A few drops in water?" He looked dubious. "It actually works?"

"It works," Carrie assured him confidently. "I'm here today, because Hobbs told you he has no pain. You're not the first person to believe the process is far too easy to be effective. In time, they become believers." She smiled brightly. "You will too."

Hanger's expression changed from dubious to astonished. "Why am I just learning about this, Dr. Wallington? Why doesn't every amputee in the country know about Homeopathy?"

"Because the American Medical Society doesn't care about people getting well!" Frances said vehemently. "They don't want patients to know about Homeopathy."

Hanger's eyes widened.

Carrie appreciated her passion, but knew she was overstating the issue. There were allopathic physicians who cared deeply but were mired in ignorance. She and Janie had fit in that category at one point. "I'm afraid Frances is largely correct. It's accurate to say there are forces at work within America that are more concerned with profits than they are with a patient getting better. There are physicians who don't use homeopathy but do their best to help their patients." She paused. "I don't believe they can help their patients effectively, however. I believe it takes both traditional and homeopathic approaches to help patients achieve ultimate health."

Hanger shook his head. "We have veterans who have been in agony for more than a decade," he said angrily. "You're telling me they have suffered without reason?"

Carrie knew some of his frustration was for the pain he had suffered himself. It was completely justified. "You're right to be angry. That's why I was happy to meet with you this morning. You will connect with far more of these men than I ever will. You can help them. The remedies are very inexpensive and can be bought right here in Richmond. You don't have to be a doctor to be able to share them with your clients. The wonderful thing about homeopathy is that while there are some people it doesn't seem to help, there are *none* that it hurts."

"Not like the so-called elixirs on the market now." Hanger's words dripped with disgust.

Carrie scowled. She saw ads for the elixirs in every one of her father's newspapers and magazines. They were being peddled and distributed across the country, but especially in rural areas that didn't have easy access to medical care. "They are nothing but alcohol and opioids. Those elixirs are the reason our veterans are suffering from addiction. Their lives were destroyed by the war. Now, they're being destroyed by charlatans focused on making profit from their pain." Anger flashed through her. "It's criminal."

Hanger lifted the vials and the book. "I will read everything, Dr. Wallington. Once I have, I will test the remedies on myself. If they have the effect you tell me they will, I promise my clients will be told about this."

"I'll look forward to hearing from you about your results," Carrie said. "The book will tell you how to administer the remedies to your clients. I wrote the name and address of the homeopathic pharmacy here in Richmond at the front of the book." The chiming of a clock in the waiting room made her stand. Their time had passed quickly. "I have a wagon of horses to lead out to Cromwell Plantation, Mr. Hanger."

Hanger stood quickly and opened the door. "Please know how much I appreciate your time, Dr. Wallington."

"It was my pleasure," Carrie said graciously. "I truly hope the men you supply with prosthetics will be helped with their pain."

Hanger turned to Frances. "It was very nice to meet you, Miss Wallington."

"The pleasure was mine, Mr. Hanger."

Carrie remembered something she had recently learned. She turned away from the open door. "Mr. Hanger, I heard about the new plan Congress passed last year for the veterans. It's my understanding that dismembered veterans have been given the choice of receiving either a prosthetic or cash to move on with their lives. How is that working?"

Hanger shrugged. "If I had been asked, I would have told them a much better alternative would have been to provide the veterans with both, but no one asked. No one should be forced to make a choice like that. My records show that my company has provided prosthetics for one hundred and forty-two Virginians in the last twelve months. Unfortunately, there were four hundred and thirty-two veterans who chose the cash." He frowned. "On the one hand, I understand their choice. They returned from the war unable to provide for their families. They believed choosing the cash was a better option."

"But the money will run out," Frances protested. "They'll be back where they started; without money and with no way to earn more."

"You know that, and I know that, Frances. It's a shame you aren't in Congress. I learned long ago that desperate people find it difficult to see past the immediate moment. It's hard to envision the future when the present is completely overwhelming."

"They don't have hope," Frances said softly.

Hanger looked at her more closely. "How old are you, Frances?"

Frances flushed. "I'll be seventeen next year, sir."

Hanger looked astonished. "And you're already in medical school?"

"Frances has been working closely with me for close to five years. She passed her entrance exams easily and is at the top of her class," Carrie added proudly. Frances had told her the night before about her struggles to be taken seriously because of her age.

"Oh, I'm not questioning her ability to be in medical school," Hanger answered.

Hanger looked back at Frances. "Age should never mandate our ability to do what we want to do. What surprises me is that someone your age understands that too many veterans have lost hope for the future."

"We lost a close family friend to suicide after the Stock Market crashed, Mr. Hanger. He lost everything and couldn't find a way to hold on to hope. I've thought about his decision all fall. Hope can be quite elusive."

Carrie listened to her daughter with astonishment. She wasn't certain she had ever felt prouder. Frances was exhibiting a maturity and sensitivity that many adults never achieved.

"I can understand how someone who has lost a limb, and can't support their family, would find it difficult to have hope for the future." Frances smiled "You're giving them hope, Mr. Hanger. My mother is giving them hope by alleviating pain. I want to do the same thing when I become a doctor."

"I'm quite certain you will," Hanger said sincerely. "One thing I tell every client is that the prosthetic is much more than just a new leg. A prosthetic will give them what mine gave me – a new beginning."

Carrie smiled brightly. "I love that! And, on that note, we must be going."

A few minutes later, Spencer was driving them at a rapid clip toward River City Carriages.

Carrie's thoughts had already moved beyond Richmond. She and Hobbs had made it into town without any trouble, but they still had a long trip before she could relax at home.

Chapter Twenty-Eight

Carrie was surprised when she arrived at River City Carriages and saw Abby sitting on the driver's seat of one of the wagons. Hobbs was busily tying horses into place. Marcus, Willard, and Anthony were helping him.

Carrie hopped down from the carriage and walked to Abby. "Why are you driving the wagon?"

"You don't believe I'm capable?" Abby asked with amusement.

Carrie laughed. "Oh, I know far better than to suggest you're not capable of doing whatever you want." She felt Frances come up behind her. "Darling daughter, never make the mistake of doubting your grandmother's abilities."

"I wouldn't dream of it," Frances replied. "I've heard rumors of what happens to people who do that. The stories are disturbing."

Abby joined in the laughter, but her eyes were serious as they scanned the area around the stables.

"Abby, what's wrong?" Carrie demanded. "Why are you driving?"

"Miles arrived home from an errand this morning with some possibly bad news," Abby replied. "Seems he overheard some men talking about catching sight of a Klan traitor in town."

Carrie stiffened. "Hobbs?"

"He doesn't know," Abby answered. "The men quit talking when someone else came in the store."

"We have to assume they were talking about Hobbs," Carrie muttered.

Abby nodded. "The consensus is that having Hobbs drive a wagon is not a wise idea. Leading the horses home means there will be a large gap between each wagon. It would be difficult to give him protection if the Klan suspects who he is and comes after us."

Hobbs appeared beside her. "Wipe that worried look off your face, Carrie. I'm going to be the most comfortable person on this little wagon train. May fixed us a big basket of food. I'm going to sit in the back of Anthony's wagon with blankets to cover up with if anyone tries to cause trouble. I'll be eating the whole way!"

His blue eyes twinkled with fun behind his fake glasses, but Carrie knew him well enough to recognize his nervousness. "We'll get you home," she promised. "I warn you, though. If you eat all the food in that basket before we stop for lunch, I will hurt you when we get there." Her stomach was already growling. "In fact, take me to that basket now. I haven't had breakfast."

"I'm coming with you," Frances said. "I'm starving."

Carrie had finally stopped scanning every movement on the horizon when they were about halfway to the plantation. She and Frances, who had chosen to ride with her, talked nonstop, but she remained vigilant.

Years of dodging and confronting danger had taught her to expect the unexpected.

Felicia was sitting on the wagon seat with Anthony, talking and laughing. Carrie could see Hobbs' head resting against the back of the wagon seat, but the rest of him was invisible. She wondered how much of May's food he had devoured.

Alice had chosen to ride with Matthew. She knew he was peppering her with questions about her time in the asylum and her years on the road with Elizabeth Packard.

The River City Carriage horses were all behaving remarkably well. They didn't seem at all alarmed by their unexpected adventure. It was easy to imagine how delighted they were going to be when they were released in a massive field, after years of confinement in the stables.

"Are we stopping to eat soon?" Frances asked.

Carrie smiled. "Are you hungry again?"

"Of course. One thing living with Alice has taught me is that it's wise to make the most of good meals when they're available."

Carrie laughed. "The three of you are hopeless."

"Says the woman who is the worst cook of all," Frances retorted.

"What kind of a way is that to speak to your mother?" Carrie demanded with outrage.

Frances smirked. "I learned a long time ago that your eyes speak far more than your words. You're not angry, because you know what I'm saying is true."

"Just because it's true doesn't mean it needs to be spoken," Carrie protested, fighting to control her amusement.

"Says the woman who taught me to tell the truth from the moment you adopted me," Frances responded calmly.

Carrie couldn't stop the amusement bubbling from her. "I love you, Frances Wallington," she said between bursts of laughter. "I'm happy you're my daughter."

Frances stopped laughing abruptly, her eyes glued on the road ahead. "Mama…"

Carrie caught the appearance of five men on horseback at the same moment Frances did. Even from this distance, their body language revealed it would not be a friendly encounter.

A hand motion from Anthony made Hobbs disappear. She could only imagine what Hobbs was thinking as he hid beneath the blankets. He was concerned for his own safety, but more concerned for the increased risk he had put all of them in. She hoped the day would come when he fully understood that his value as their friend, and as a valuable employee of Cromwell Stables, made him worth the risk.

Carrie clucked to her team of horses, moving them up as close to Anthony's wagon as she could. They had talked through what they would do if they were threatened. While the road wasn't wide enough for all of them to be side by side, they would draw in closer together. Abby pulled her wagon next to Harold's, making sure the horses they were leading didn't feel crowded. If the horses panicked, they would have a mess on their hands.

Matthew pulled his wagon forward as close as he could at the back.

Carrie waited as the men approached, watching every movement carefully. Each one had their hands close to their firearms. "Frances, get in the back of the wagon, please. You too, Felicia."

"Mama, I…"

"Now," Carrie said sternly. She was not going to worry about the girls being cut down by gunfire if the men started shooting. "Please don't argue."

Frances gulped, swung her legs over the wagon seat and slipped down behind her.

Felicia followed suit.

Carrie could see the girls staring at each other. She had known there was a risk when they decided to take Hobbs into Richmond, but the girl's surprise appearance had added an increased level of risk that she hadn't anticipated. She never would have combined the two events by choice, but there was nothing she could do to change it.

Alice was the only one who remained in her seat. Carrie was certain it was because she had simply refused to move when Matthew told her to. Alice wasn't armed, and had no idea how to use a firearm, but she would refuse to back down to danger; however foolish her decision was.

No one spoke as the men approached.

"Expecting trouble?" The man at the front of the line spoke in a pompous, oily voice.

Anthony eyed the portly man astride a large bay gelding. "I've heard that trouble seems to follow you, Mr. Poulton."

Carrie controlled her reaction. Theodore Poulton was the man who had attacked and burned Blackwell Plantation. His presence meant trouble.

Poulton scowled, but then looked pleased. "You know who I am?"

"Certainly," Anthony answered. "You're rather infamous in this part of Virginia."

Carrie fought to keep a neutral expression on her face as Poulton puffed with pride. His face, even in the cold, shimmered with sweat. His attitude was an attempt to hide his anxiety. She was aware her brilliant husband was setting Poulton up for something, but she had no idea what.

"I suppose I am," Poulton agreed. His prideful voice shifted into a dangerous anger. "I hear Cromwell Plantation is harboring a fugitive. We're after Warren Hobbs."

Carrie stiffened. She didn't know how Hobbs had been discovered, but it was obvious they knew, or at least suspected, that he was on the plantation.

Anthony raised a brow. "A fugitive? I hardly think so. We don't hire criminals."

"I hear you took on a traitor to the Klan," Poulton said harshly. "In our world, that's worse than being a criminal."

Anthony paused for a long moment, letting the silence grow.

Carrie was careful not to look in the direction of Anthony's wagon. She wouldn't do anything to reveal Hobbs' presence. She examined the four men with Poulton. They seemed young and nervous.

Anthony finally spoke. "In *our* world, it is *worse* than criminal when you allow seven of your own men to be shot down in a fight they weren't prepared for." His voice shifted from calm to cutting. "Poulton, what was it like when the Klan had to notify those seven families that their husbands and fathers were killed in a midnight raid on Blackwell Plantation?"

Carrie watched the four men's expressions change to fear.

"Those men were heroes," Poulton snapped.

Anthony snorted. "Those men were led down a dark road and cut down like sitting ducks by men on the roof of Blackwell Plantation. They never had a chance to be heroes, even if activity in the Klan *had* any valor – which it doesn't." He eyed the four men. "Those men killed that night were led by *you*, Poulton."

Carrie knew Anthony was planting doubt and fear in the men's minds.

Poulton's eyes narrowed with anger, but his expression resembled a trapped animal. "That ain't got nothing to do with today," he whined. "We're looking for a Klan traitor."

"That you won't find here," Anthony answered coldly. He reached into his waistband and pulled out his pistol smoothly.

Carrie reached for her own weapon and pulled it out, knowing each of the five of them had done the same thing. Five against five. She prayed with all her might that gunfire wouldn't break out, but if it did, it would be a fair fight. Actually, since they had drawn first, they would have the advantage.

"What you will find," Anthony declared, "are five people who are sick of how you and the Klan keep believing you have the right to terrorize innocent Virginians." He paused. "It probably wouldn't look good for the Klan if you and your *friends* here didn't make it back from this *supposed* little raid." Sarcasm dripped from his words.

Anthony looked away from Poulton. His gaze swept the four men staring back at him with startled expressions. "Your leader here doesn't have such a good reputation when it comes to bringing his men home. Are you ready to give your life for him today?".

One man was brave enough to speak up. "Theodore Poulton was responsible for setting fire to Blackwell Plantation. He burned up the house and the barns," he said proudly.

"That's true," Anthony agreed. "Do you believe those men rode into Blackwelll Plantation planning on giving their lives? Do you think it was worth it to the families of those seven men who will never see their husband or father again?" He didn't wait for an answer. "The way I see it, you men are already at a disadvantage. We already have our guns pulled." He held his up a little higher but didn't aim it away from Theodore Poulton. "If you look carefully, you'll see that each of my friends are aiming at one of you. They all happen to be very good shots. By the time you finish reaching for your weapons, all of you will be dead on the ground."

Carrie felt sick at the possibility of what Anthony was describing, but she knew she would shoot to protect any of them. She understood his strategy. She prayed he was instilling enough fear in the Klansmen that they would refuse to follow Poulton's lead.

"Now, it's cold today." Anthony spoke in a conversational tone. "We would like to continue down the road so that we can get home. So, here's what we're going to do. I'm going to count to five. If any of you are still blocking our way by the time I finish counting, we'll start shooting. It shouldn't take more than one shot each to take care of this situation," he said calmly. "It would be best if you continue riding toward Richmond. I'm not interested in any of you being stupid enough to lie in wait for us in the direction we're going." He let his words hang in the air. "If you make the mistake of going back the way you came, I'm afraid we'll have to shoot you in the back."

Carrie kept her pistol aimed on the man farthest to the right. She watched his brown eyes dart around in fear. His hat covered blond curls. He couldn't be older than his early twenties.

"*One.*"

Anthony's voice rang out in the frigid air.

Carrie thought about Abby. Her mother had never shot anyone before. She hadn't either, but was certain she would have no trouble protecting her family. Could Abby do it? She hoped she wouldn't have to find out.

"*Two.*"

The men in front of them exchanged increasingly nervous looks. Their horses, reacting to their anxiety, shifted restlessly and tossed their heads.

"They ain't going to shoot us," Theordore Poulton snarled.

Anthony smiled. "That's probably what he told the seven men who died at Blackwell Plantation."

"*Three.*"

Anthony's voice grew louder and more authoritative. He glanced over his shoulder. "Remember what I said about aiming for the middle of their chests," he called. "Oh, and if any of them reach for their guns, go ahead and shoot them now. I'm cold and I want to go home."

"*Four.*"

The man Carrie was watching suddenly went from nervous to decisive.

He spun his horse around quickly. "I ain't dying here today!" He leaned close to his horse's neck and galloped away in the direction of Richmond.

In less than a moment, the other three Klansmen were racing after him, leaning low on the horse's necks to avoid gunfire.

Anthony opened his mouth to call five, his finger on the trigger of his gun as he set his gaze on Poulton.

Poulton looked both terrified and infuriated. Before Anthony could speak, he was flying down the road after his men. "This isn't the end!" he hollered over his shoulder.

Carrie sagged with relief and put her pistol back in her waistband.

"Anthony, you were magnificent!" Abby called. "You had *me* actually believing we were going to shoot those men."

Anthony caught Carrie's eyes. In that one look, she saw how stressful the encounter had been for him. She recognized he would have shot Poulton in order to protect the people he loved. She was grateful it hadn't come to that. She could tell by the expression on Matthew's and Harold's faces that they had been prepared to kill the Klansmen.

Fatigue seeped into every pore of her body. "Let's go home."

Frances stood in the back of the wagon and crawled onto the bench with her. "Might I suggest we forget lunch?? I don't really have much of an appetite left," she said shakily.

"I think that's a splendid idea," Abby called.

Moments later, they were in formation and moving steadily east.

Chapter Twenty-Nine

Russell walked into the parlor, his arms loaded with boxes from the attic.

Missy turned around when she heard him. "What's all that?"

Russell placed the boxes on the floor around the tree. "Christmas tree ornaments," he announced.

Missy eyed the boxes. "Is that all of them?"

"No. There are more upstairs. John is bringing them down. We're all going outside later to get pinecones and any dried flowers we can still find. There are a lot of flowers down in the basement. We dried them this summer, so we would be ready for Christmas, but it's fun to go out and see what new ones we can find. You can never have too many!"

"Why? What are you going to do with them?" Missy asked.

Russell suddenly realized Missy had never had a Christmas tree. She was staring at the massive tree Moses and his men had carried in earlier as if wondering why it was taking up so much space in the parlor. He had been completely overwhelmed by his first Christmas the year before, but at least he had experienced small and simple Christmas' when he was growing up. Clearly, Missy had had nothing. Suddenly, he knew why the thought was bothering him so much. "Didn't you have Christmas with the Highlands last year?"

"They said Christmas is a waste of money. They told me it was one reason they'd never had children. They didn't want to have to buy Christmas presents for 'em. They figured since I weren't their real child, they didn't need to do anything for me." Missy's voice was soft and trembly.

Russell tightened with anger. Before he could say anything, Minnie's voice broke in.

"The Highlands are terrible people." Minnie had walked into the room while they were talking.

Missy didn't turn around. "I don't want to talk about the Highlands. It makes me sad. I don't want to think about going back there after the school break."

"Then we won't talk about them," Minnie said brightly. She exchanged a knowing look with Russell. "We're going to start decorating the tree after lunch. It will be the most beautiful thing you've ever seen."

"Why today?" Missy asked.

"Because tomorrow is Christmas Eve!" Russell exclaimed. "Minnie is right. When Daddy, Grandpa, and Moses light the tree tomorrow night, it will be the most beautiful thing you've ever seen!"

When Missy turned away from the tree, Russell knew she couldn't comprehend what was coming.

Missy walked around the room, leaning over to sniff the greenery that had been brought in to decorate the mantels, windowsills, and tables. Red candles stood tall in silver candlesticks; ready to cast their light. "Everything smells good."

Missy moved to the fireplace and stared down at what Moses and Simon had carried in that morning. "What is that? Other than the biggest log I've ever seen in my life!"

"It's a Yule Log," Russell told her. "It's another Cromwell Plantation tradition."

"*Another* Christmas tradition?" Missy asked. "There sure seem to be a lot of them."

Felicia walked into the parlor in time to hear the last part of the conversation. "Every single one of us have had to get used to Cromwell Christmases."

"Did you not like Christmas here at first?"

"I loved them from the very beginning," Felicia said enthusiastically. "I'd just never experienced anything like it. I wasn't sure it was alright for me to love it as much as I did, because my first parents were too poor to do anything like what is done here."

"How old were you when you came here?" Missy asked.

"I was ten, Missy. The same age you are now. My parents were murdered in Memphis, Tennessee during a riot. Moses brought me here to the plantation. Not too long after that, they adopted me."

Missy absorbed her story with a sad expression. "I'm real sorry that happened to your folks." She paused. "Is everyone in the house adopted?"

"Most of us," Russell replied. "John and Hope are the only ones born into their family. Jed was adopted, too."

Missy thought about that for a moment. "Are John and Hope more important than the rest of you?"

"No," Russell said confidently. "We're all family." It had taken him time to realize that, but he was comfortable with being adopted now. "Mama and Daddy say we're extra special, because they got to *choose* us."

Russell saw the longing in Missy's eyes. He wanted to blurt out the news but Mama had sworn him to secrecy. He was glad it was almost Christmas Eve. He was certain he was going to explode with the importance of the secret soon.

Missy turned back to the fireplace. "What is a yule log?"

Moses walked into the parlor as she was speaking. "It's only the most important part of Christmas," he said jovially. He was carrying a smaller piece of wood that he laid carefully on the huge log.

"What's that?" Missy leaned over to look more closely at the massive log filling the fireplace.

"That, Miss Missy, is a piece from last year's Yule log. It's how I will light this one."

"Miss Missy?" Missy giggled. "That's a funny name."

"Miss Missy," Moses repeated. "That's what I'm going to call you from now on."

Missy giggled again as she looked back at the log. "What if it doesn't light?"

Moses grew serious. "Well, Miss Missy, that would be very bad luck," he replied. "Bad things could happen." His deep voice rumbled through the parlor.

Missy looked nervous. "Has that ever happened before?"

Thomas joined them. "Never. The Yule log always lights from the one the year before. There has been a yule log burning in this fireplace for as long as I can remember."

Missy regarded him with appraising eyes. "I bet you can remember a long time."

Thomas chuckled. "Are you calling me old?"

Missy looked horrified. "Oh, no sir. You're not old at all!"

Thomas laughed harder. "That's alright, Missy. I'm a lot older than you. I grew up here, you know. We had a yule log for every Christmas. It's one of my favorite traditions."

Amazement filled Missy's eyes. "You grew up here? In this house?"

Thomas nodded. "I did. So did my daddy. The Cromwell family built this plantation and the house."

Missy looked suitably impressed. Russell remembered being equally impressed, even though he hadn't really understood what that meant when he first heard it. He understood more about generations now. He would talk with Missy about it later.

Thomas waved his hand toward the massive oak log. "When this log is finished burning, we'll take the ashes and sprinkle them on the soil in the tobacco fields. Doing that guarantees we will have a good harvest."

"Really?" Missy looked skeptical.

"Cross my heart. I've never understood *why*, but it works."

Missy still looked skeptical.

"Most importantly," Felicia said, "the Yule log is a symbol of light prevailing over darkness. We burn it as a beacon of hope for the new year."

Book # 21 of The Bregdan Chronicles 501

Missy stared at the log with a new expression. "I wish we'd had a Yule log under the bridge. It got real dark under there at night."

Russell walked up beside her and stood close. More than anyone there, he understood what she meant. The long nights under the bridge, in darkness so intense he couldn't see his hand in front of his face, had seemed endless. Though they didn't happen as often, he still had nightmares about those nights.

Carrie stopped in the doorway before she walked into the parlor. The tree, resplendent with its decorations, was ready to be illuminated by the candles. The Yule log crackled merrily in the fireplace. It had been burning all day, but it had hardly diminished in size. Anthony and Thomas were seated in front of the fire, engaged in a game of backgammon. Perry was waiting for his turn to take on the victor.

The children were on the floor, working hard at a new jigsaw puzzle of Central Park that Abby had brought home from New York City. Puzzles had quickly become a favorite pastime.

Abby and Alice were deep in conversation in chairs next to the window. They had become close during Abby's weeks in Boston. Alice was enchanted by every single thing about the plantation and had questions about all of it.

Rose, June, and Louisa watched the children work on the puzzle, offering hints when they saw something they thought might be helpful. Cheers rang out every time a new piece fit into place.

Moses and Simon focused intently on the chess board, their brows knit with concentration.

Carrie watched the scene with delight. It was everything she dreamed Christmas should be. The parlor pulsed with family, love and laughter. Her stomach was stuffed from a delicious dinner. She counted the moments until the Christmas Eve secret would be revealed. She had thought about little else since the decision had been made.

Carrie's eyes settled on Missy. Missy, instead of working on the puzzle, was standing next to a window, obviously trying to take it all in. Carrie had grown used to the expression of confused wonder on the children's faces when they experienced their first Christmas at Cromwell. Like her father, a Cromwell Christmas was all she had ever known. Not so for the children. She walked over and laid her arm across Missy's shoulder. "It's a lot, isn't it?"

"It is, but Russell and Minnie told me they felt the same way when they were here for their first Christmas," Missy replied. "It's real beautiful!"

Carrie held back her chuckle when she thought about Minnie's statement to Russell the year before. *It's just the way things are when you're adopted by a rich family. You have to get used to things.*

"Besides, I'm not your child," Missy added sadly. "I'm just here for now. I'm going back to the other place when school starts." Her expression was a mixture of sadness and determined bravery.

Carrie's amusement evaporated. Missy never called the Highland's house her home. She simply referred to where she lived as *the other place*. There had been no need for persuasion when Anthony had approached them with their request. They had eagerly relinquished rights to Missy. She tightened her arm around Missy's shoulder, her heart melting when the child pressed as close as she could to her side.

"Mama!" Bridget ran into the room and stared up at the tree. She spun around until she caught sight of Carrie. "Mama!"

Carrie was still surprised by her youngest running around the house. Her time living under the bridge had delayed her development, but once she had started walking a few months earlier, she had become unstoppable. When she had discovered running, walking seemed to no longer be an option. She ran everywhere she went.

Carrie walked over with Missy, took her arm from her shoulder, and scooped her youngest into her arms. "Yes, Bridget?"

Bridget waved her arms toward the tree. "Pretty tree!"

"It is," Carrie agreed. "Missy helped decorate it."

Bridget grinned at Missy. "Pretty tree!"

Missy grinned back at her. "It was fun, Bridget! You'll be old enough to help next year."

Carrie loved how gentle Missy was with Bridget. The day before, Russell had reminded her that Missy was one of the two girls who had cared for the infant when they found her abandoned in a trash can. Carrie had no idea how she had forgotten that important information. The girls had kept Bridget from freezing to death. They hadn't known how to care for a baby, but they'd done the best they could.

They had kept her alive.

Carrie placed Bridget on the floor. "Missy, will you show her the ornaments?"

Missy brightened. "Yes, ma'am."

Carrie watched as Missy knelt beside Bridget and pointed out the bows and ribbons, the pieces of glass, the dried flowers and pinecones, and the small tin ornaments Russell had hammered out in his workshop. Bridget touched each one gently, a look of awe on her face. Carrie wondered if she remembered her first Christmas the year before but didn't think it likely.

"Why is Christmas Eve so important?" Missy had appeared by her side again, holding Bridget by the hand. Her youngest seemed content to stand quietly at Missy's side.

"That's a good question," Carrie responded. "It's special for many reasons. The most important thing is that Christmas is a celebration of the birth of Christ, but it's more than that. When I think of Christmas, I think of family and love. I think of light because of all the candles and the yule log. I think of music because we do so much singing."

"You have to think about food, too," Missy said. She looked through the door at the dining room buffet laden with food. "I've never seen so much food in my whole life! We ate a massive dinner, but there's more food waiting for us. I've never eaten so much food at one time. I'm so full I might pop!"

Carrie laughed. "Yes, I definitely think about food. Annie believes food is an expression of love. That's why she feeds us so well."

Annie had been thrilled when Carrie had finally agreed she could spend however much time she wanted in the kitchen. She and Alice were having a marvelous time together.

"She must have a lot of love inside her," Missy commented. "Cause there sure is a lot of food."

Carrie laughed again. "That's true, Missy. Annie has a lot of love inside her." She thought about what Annie had told her. "I understand you've been helping in the kitchen."

Missy's head bobbed up and down. "I have! It's really fun. I never knew nothing about cooking, but I like it a lot. Minnie has been teaching me. So have Miss Annie and Miss Alice. *Both* the Alices. It can be real confusing to have two Alice's in the house. We finally solved it, though. We call one Miss Alice. The other we call Doctor Alice."

Carrie thought that was a brilliant solution, but she was surprised by the information. "I didn't realize Dr. Alice was spending time in the kitchen."

"Yep," Missy replied. "She said she's real tired of not knowing how to cook. She told me that she gets tired of eating the same old thing for almost every meal. She wants to go back up there to Boston and know how to cook more."

"Are Felicia and Frances learning too?" Carrie asked. She was quickly learning that Missy seemed to never miss what was going on. The little girl paid attention to everything.

"No," Missy said earnestly. "Miss Alice asked them if they wanted to learn. They told her they were going into the library, because one day they would just hire someone to cook for them."

Carrie laughed heartily. "That sounds like my daughter."

Frances looked up from the section of the puzzle she was working on. "I'm simply following in my mother's footsteps," she called.

Since Carrie couldn't dispute what she said, she chose to remain silent.

Missy smiled shyly. "I helped make the oatmeal cookies last night. And Annie let me help her with the apple pies. I got to go down into the cellar where she kept the apples from the fall harvest." Her eyes got wide. "That cellar is bigger than anything I ever lived in."

Carrie smiled. "I used to be afraid to go down there when I was a little girl. I was certain I would get lost and never find my way out."

Missy gazed up at her with an earnest expression. "What's it like to live in one place your whole life, Dr. Wallington?"

Carrie sat down on a chair and pulled Missy onto her lap. Missy looked startled, but then smiled and relaxed. Carrie stroked the gleaming blond braids that Minnie had plaited into Missy's hair that morning. She had already fallen deeply in love with this child. She could hardly believe this was the same girl who had tormented Minnie at school. She had mellowed and softened with each day on the plantation.

"It's wonderful, Missy," Carrie admitted. "I didn't understand how lucky I was when I was a child growing up here. It was simply all I'd ever known. As I've gotten older, I recognize how many children aren't as lucky as I was."

Missy's eyes filled with sadness. "You were *real* lucky. Course, I don't reckon I even know what I'm missing, because I ain't never had it." Her eyes shifted from sadness to resolution. "I reckon it's better that I don't know, because I ain't ever going to have it. This Christmas has been real nice, but I'm going back to that other place."

Missy crawled out of her lap to stand on the floor. "If you don't mind too much, I'm gonna go out on the porch for a little bit."

Not waiting for permission, Missy walked away.

Carrie heard her pull her coat and hat on, and then heard the door close behind her. She knew Missy had gone outside to cry alone.

Carrie felt tears stinging her eyes as her heart lodged in her throat. When she looked across the room, Rose met her eyes.. *It's time,* she mouthed.

Carrie knew her best friend was right. She stood and motioned for Anthony and the children to join her. When they were standing in front of her with quizzical expressions, she said, "Put on your hats and coats. It's time."

Minnie grinned and clapped her hands. "It's time!" Then she looked confused. "Why do we need our hats and coats?"

"Because Missy went outside to cry," Russell said. "She's real sad."

Carrie wasn't surprised that her observant and sensitive son had understood why Missy left the room. He had made it his mission to look out for her.

Bridget frowned. "Missy sad? Why?" Her green eyes were distraught.

Anthony swung his youngest into his arms. "She won't be for much longer, honey."

"Let's go tell her," Frances said eagerly. "We all know exactly how she's going to feel. She should know before we light the tree!" She looked at Carrie. "I know you wanted to wait until after, but..."

Carrie's heart surged with tenderness when she looked at her oldest child's excited expression. Frances had been eager to adopt Missy from the moment they had first talked to her about it. Her entire focus was on how much better another child's life would become. "Now is the perfect time," Carrie agreed.

It took only a few minutes for everyone to bundle up against the cold.

Missy looked up and swiped at her face when they all trooped out onto the porch. She looked both embarrassed and defiant as she turned to face them.

Carrie knew the little girl was ashamed of her emotions. Life had taught Missy to never show weakness. Weakness had been a luxury she couldn't afford.

"Am I in trouble?" Missy asked. "Should I not be out here?"

Carrie walked over and took Missy's hand. "You are most certainly *not* in trouble, dear. We just want to talk to you."

"*All* of you?" Missy asked. "Why?"

"Because we want to talk to you about a decision we made as a family," she said gently. She sat down in a rocking chair, waiting until Anthony and the children each found their own and pulled them together into a circle.

Missy stared around her with confused eyes. She clearly expected trouble, despite what Carrie had said.

Carrie reached out and took the little girl's hands. They felt like icicles. "Honey, you don't have gloves on!"

Missy shrugged. "I forgot to put them on, but I'm fine. When I lived under the bridge, there were lots of times I didn't have gloves. It ain't so bad. You get used to it."

Carrie took a deep breath. There would be plenty of time for the little girl to get used to wearing gloves. There were more important things to talk about. "Missy, we would like to ask you something."

"Alright..." Missy's voice was uncertain, but she met Carrie's eyes bravely.

Carrie smiled. "The Wallington family would like to ask you to join our family."

Missy gasped. "What?" She took several quick breaths as she stared around. Her eyes returned to Carrie. "You mean...?"

"Anthony and I would like very much if you would be our little girl, Missy," Carrie said tenderly.

"And all of us want you to be our new sister," Minnie shouted, unable to remain quiet a moment longer.

Missy gasped again and stared around the circle. "You want to adopt me?" she whispered.

"Yes," Carrie and Anthony said in unison.

"Yes!" the children shouted.

"Please say yes," Minnie cried. "You're already my best friend here in Virginia. Now you can be my sister, too!"

Carrie bit back her smile. She knew the addition about Missy being her best friend in *Virginia* was meant to let Frances know they would always be best friends, too.

Missy continued to stare around the circle. Finally, she turned to Russell. He had clearly become her lifeline. "Is this real? Is this really happening?" Tears pooled in her eyes. "All that time under the bridge. The last year at the other place..." Her voice faltered as tears swallowed her words.

"It's real," Russell assured her. "We want you to be our sister."

She swung back to Carrie. "Really? You really want *me*?" She began to shake with sobs. "*Me*?"

Carrie knew Missy would be haunted for a long time by the mother who had cruelly dropped her off under the bridge because she didn't want her any longer. Her year with the Highlands had done nothing but intensify those feelings. Instead of answering with words, she pulled Missy into her arms and held her tightly.

As she rubbed her back, she whispered. "I love you, Missy Wallington. You will always be our little girl. *Always.*"

Several minutes passed before Missy could control her sobs. When she had finally regained composure, she stepped back and looked around the circle.

"Yes."

Everyone looked up expectantly when Carrie and the rest stepped back into the parlor after shedding their winter clothing. Everyone had been told what was going to happen. The original plan was that they would ask Missy after the Christmas tree lighting and singing, but the time on the porch had actually been the perfect time.

Minnie grinned. "She said yes!"

The room erupted in clapping and cheers as everyone rushed forward to welcome Missy to the family.

Carrie was quite sure she had never seen an expression on anyone's face quite like what she saw on Missy's. It was a combination of joy, wonder, disbelief, and perhaps the purest expression of love she'd ever seen.

When the commotion died down, Abby sat down at the piano and began to play softly. The Yule log, burning brightly, cast off a delicious warmth that reached every corner of the room.

A moment later, a match flared. Thomas lit the candle he held, and then touched his flame to Anthony and Moses' candles. Abby continued to play as the men carefully lit the candles on the Christmas tree.

When the towering cedar tree stood glowing in all its beauty, there were several minutes of silence. The ornaments the children had spent the day decorating the tree with, caught the light and came to life.

Bridget, snuggled onto Carrie's lap, sighed happily. "Pretty tree. Pretty, pretty tree."

Anthony had claimed a chair once the tree was lit. Minnie rested on one knee. Missy, her face beaming, sat on the other.

Missy's face was illuminated by the candlelight. "That is the most beautiful thing I've ever seen," she breathed. She turned to grin at Russell. "You were right."

Abby paused in her playing and then began again, singing as she played. Thomas' baritone joined her, followed by Rose's sweet soprano, Moses' deep bass, and Miles' rich tenor. Everyone joined in, filling the house with song.

Silent night, holy night!
All is calm, all is bright.
Round yon Virgin, Mother and Child.
Holy infant so tender and mild,
Sleep in heavenly peace,
Sleep in heavenly peace.

Silent night, holy night!
Shepherds quake at the sight.
Glories stream from heaven afar
Heavenly hosts sing Alleluia,
Christ the Savior is born!
Christ the Savior is born

Silent night, holy night!
Son of God love's pure light.
Radiant beams from Thy holy face

Book # 21 of The Bregdan Chronicles

*With dawn of redeeming grace,
Jesus Lord, at Thy birth
Jesus Lord, at Thy birth.*

When the song came to an end, Carrie sat silently, allowing the pureness of the moment to fill her.
Christmas had once again come to Cromwell.

Chapter Thirty

Rose leaned back against the log and gazed up into the sky. What must certainly be a million stars glittered across the black canopy. A narrow sliver of the moon rested on the horizon, as if waiting for the sun to appear and grant permission for it to slip out of sight.

As she watched, the stars faded on what was rapidly turning into a cobalt blue canvas.

She looked over and saw Carrie watching her. Rose knew she was thinking about their early years of celebrating New Year's Day. Just the two of them, perched on a rock in the James River, they had waited for the sun to rise. They had been just children when they began the tradition that had grown and changed with time.

Her eyes swept the circle as the sky lightened. Abby. Felicia. Frances. Hope. Minnie. Missy. June. Louisa.

Rose was thrilled that Annie had joined them. Usually, she insisted on staying behind in the kitchen. This year, she had been eager to join them.

Miss Alice was there with Gloria tucked beneath her arm, her face turned to the horizon as she eagerly watched for the sun to rise.

Dr. Alice was seated next to Abby, her face revealing how special the moment was for her.

Rose knew they still had at least thirty minutes before the sun crested the line of trees in the distance.

"I got me something to say," Annie said brusquely.

Rose was surprised, but thrilled.

"We'd love to hear it," Carrie said.

Annie turned to look at Carrie. "I reckon you saved my life, Miss Carrie." She paused. "I reckon I should say *Dr. Wallington*."

Carrie chuckled. "I would prefer Carrie, please."

The serious look on Annie's face intensified. "I been real sick before. I know you and Miles was afraid I was going to die when I had that flu, but I kept on livin'. This last time, I reckon I could feel that ole life force draining right out of me. I kinda knew when you put me under to cut me open, but I didn't figure I was gonna wake up again. I made my peace with it, cause these last years with y'all on the plantation been better years than I thought I would ever have. My whole life been a lot of misery up till then."

Tears pricked Rose's eyes. She was certain she had never heard Annie utter so many words at one time. She watched her mother-in-law struggle for control.

"When I done woke up and I weren't in heaven, I knew right then that God done give me another chance at life," Annie said quietly. "I'm still figurin' out just what that means, but I reckon I'm gonna help find homes for more of those orphans at the Black Asylum. If I ain't dead, I'm supposed to be doin' somethin'. It be mighty special that I'm here to watch the sun rise on a new year." She set her eyes on the horizon. "1874. It's a year I didn't reckon I was gonna see." She cleared her throat. "I owe that to you, Miss Carrie. Thank you." She quit talking as her eyes swept the circle. "I reckon that's all I got to say."

"Thank you, Annie," Carrie said softly. "That means more than you can know. I'm excited to see what this new year is going to bring for you."

"Mama?"

Rose turned to Felicia. "Yes."

"I would like to share something."

Everyone turned to Felicia eagerly. Rose knew they all hoped she had another poem to share, but she hadn't heard anything about a new one. "We'd love for you to, honey."

Felicia's eyes swept the circle. "I can hardly believe only one year has gone by since we were here last year. So much has happened." She reached up and placed her hand close to her neck. "You can't see it, but beneath all these clothes is the diamond star necklace I've worn every day since I did my Kinaalda. I was thirteen when I did my Navajo rite of passage to womanhood. I've held on to all the lessons I learned during those four days. They have guided my life from that point forward. Whenever I have big decisions to make, I hold my necklace and remember that time. It is my foundation.'

Rose thought about the special time she had designed for Felicia. Five years later, she had grown into a truly extraordinary woman.

"Moving to Boston has been a big change for me," Felicia continued. "I've spent days wandering the city as I have searched for the right investment opportunity. During those days, I made time to walk through the parks. I listened to the wind in the trees. I sat in silence as I thought about the last year." She stopped speaking.

Rose knew that everyone was doing what she was doing in the silence – thinking about all that had happened during the last twelve months.

Hardships that could have destroyed them. The Angola Massacre still haunted them all. Financial ruin had struck the country, bringing uncertainty and suffering to many. Wally had succumbed to despair. Nancy was fighting to emerge from the depths of grief and guilt. She would fight for years to come. Sickness and medical emergencies had been dealt with.

"I imagine we're each thinking about the hard things," Felicia continued.

Rose was startled by how right she was.

"I'm learning, however, how to focus on the good things that happen in the midst of the hard." Felicia smiled. "I think about Grandma Annie swimming in the James River."

"Yes, child!" Annie said happily. "I can't wait till this ole river be warm again."

Everyone laughed. Rose thought about the look of pure joy on Annie's face when she had finally gone into the water after years of refusal.

"I think about June going swimming," Felicia said.

June smiled and nodded her head happily.

Rose knew how hard it had been for her sister-in-law to overcome her fear of the James River, after watching her best friend drown. It had taken tremendous courage. A courageous act that had resulted in triumphant joy.

"I think about Missy joining our Cromwell Family. What joy that has brought to us!"

Rose watched Carrie pull Missy closer to her side and lean down to kiss her hair. Missy was beaming with complete happiness.

"I think about all the laughter. The love. The courage that we all have," Felicia continued. "There has been so much change as we have each moved toward different things in our lives. This was a year of new beginnings. Old things ended. I've learned old things *have* to end, in order for new beginnings to happen. 1873 has ended, but I know all of life is nothing but new beginnings, so they will continue to happen for each of us."

Felicia took a deep breath. "As I move into this new part of my life, I've thought so much about the women who have come before. The women who have created who I am today. There are so many of them – starting with the woman who gave birth to me when she was a slave. She and my daddy fought to get us to Memphis so we could have a new life. I loved them deeply. "I miss them every day. I was certain my life was over when they were murdered, but their presence sooths me even today. I know they hoped for a different life for me. A better life. A freer life than what they lived."

Felicia looked at Rose. "Their murder turned out to be a new beginning for me. I didn't die that horrible day. I lived. I woke up a different person. Very different. But I didn't die. I lived. Most of us can say that exact same thing. *I didn't die. I woke up. I lived."*

Rose was stunned by the power of her daughter's words. The raw truth of what she was saying. Her eyes swept the circle. Felicia was right. Most of them could say the same thing.

Felicia said the words again, her voice louder in the frosty morning air. *"I didn't die. I woke up. I lived."*

Felicia stopped talking. Silence followed her words. The fading twinkling of stars in the crisp winter night gave the only response.

The love around the circle was as tangible as the numbing air tickling her nose. Rose knew that no matter where destiny beckoned, where life might lead, what challenging decisions lay ahead or how far apart they might live, the bonds between these women would never fade.

Never.

Felicia wasn't done. "I was brought here to Cromwell for that better, freer life that my parents dreamed. Their dreams for me became my reality. Because of my past and my present, I have a destiny to fulfill. Thanks to my parents, I lived. Thanks to each of you, I live.

Felicia turned and smiled at Rose. "I love you, Mama. I know that who you are was created largely by your mama – the lady I know as Old Sarah. I've learned so much through you because of what your mama taught you. Grandma Sarah will forever be a part of me, as well."

Rose returned her smile, once again amazed at the maturity Felicia had.

Felicia addressed her grandma next. "Grandma Annie, you have taught me about bravery. Bravery to continue living when your husband was murdered, and when your children died or were taken from you. Bravery to start a brand-new life when daddy saved you from slavery. Bravery to fight back this year when you almost died. Bravery to find homes for so many children who need one." Her eyes softened. "You also taught me how to bake love into my actions."

Annie, though her eyes were gleaming with tears, snorted. "Felicia, you never baked a thing in your life, girl."

Felicia grinned as everyone laughed. "That's true. But if I ever do, I know to add lots of love.

Felicia turned back to Rose. "You have made me who I am more than anyone, Mama. You are my example of love and integrity every single day. You taught me that I could love and trust again. Daddy saved me, but you've taught me what it means to be a woman. I will be forever grateful."

Rose wasn't ashamed of the tears streaming down her face. She was grateful this year wasn't as cold as others. If it had been, the tears would be frozen streams on her cheeks.

Felicia glanced at the horizon.

The glow was getting brighter as the sun kissed puffy clouds with pink and orange.

"I'm almost done," she promised. "I owe something to every woman who is in this circle." She looked at each of the children. "The rest of us are growing up. Because of these women, we have a future that is wide open with possibility. We have a future because of the generations that have come before us, even though we might not be able to understand how it all fits together. Each person is important in our own life's journey. We need to hear their stories. We need to listen deeply."

Her eyes swept the circle. "Every life that has gone before is part of our destiny. Our future."

Felicia smiled. "So, after all that thinking, I sat down and wrote a poem last night. I knew I couldn't end this year, or start a new one, without writing what I was thinking and feeling." She opened the black notebook she pulled from her coat and began to read.

<u>Lifted on the Wings of Destiny</u>

"i am the voice of old. the generations past. the legacy of ancient.

'i teach you the secrets of mother earth. i whisper secret wisdoms in the wind.

i am hawk: guardian of secret wisdoms' - Old Sarah is my hawk

'i am strength. i am experience. i am determination to live. i am welcoming. i am action into love.

i am eagle: strongest of the brave' - Grandma Annie is my eagle

'i transform. i wait. i hope. i bless. i beautify. i dignify. i believe.

i am butterfly: magnificent metamorphous of harmony - My Mama Rose is my butterfly

speak hawk, for we listen. act eagle, for we watch. believe butterfly for we doubt.

Gateway To A New Beginning

together we go forward, forward to the future.

look hawk, look eagle, look butterfly, look: we create each other. we belong to each other.

i am because you are. you are because i am. we are ubuntu.

we look to the past and listen: we are Dynasties of power

we look to legacy and trust: we are Lineages of potential

we look to the future and live: we are Vessels of change

Vessels calling possibilities - Vessels answering yes - Vessels yearning serenity

Mama Rose, my butterfly: as we transform: We Believe

Grandma Annie, my eagle: as we express truth: We act in Love

Old Sarah, my hawk: as we yield to the air: We Ascend
We ascend unto tomorrow: Lifted.

we who are enfolded in – embraced by– protected with wings of love, we ascend

We ascend unto tomorrow: Lifted.

Lifted to breathe – heal – live

Lifted by the Wings of Destiny

When Felicia finished reading, Rose jumped up and rushed to embrace her. "Oh, honey," she whispered. "Thank you. That is so powerful and beautiful."

The next minutes passed in a blur as everyone in the circle stood to embrace each other.

"Here it comes!" Missy yelled. "Here comes the sun!"

Carrie reached down and lifted Missy into the air and then pulled her close in a fierce embrace. "Happy 1874!"

"Happy 1874!"

"Happy 1874!"

The wild cries lifted into the air and collided with the clouds dancing above their heads.

1874 beckoned them all forward into their destiny.

To Be Continued...

Coming Spring 2025!

Lifted By The Wings Of Destiny

January 1874 - July 1874

Ginny Dye

Would you be so kind as to leave a Review on Amazon?

Go to www.Amazon.com

Put Gateway To A New Beginning, Ginny Dye into the Search Box.

Leave a Review.

I love hearing from my readers!

Thank you!

Book # 21 of The Bregdan Chronicles

The Bregdan Principle

Every life that has been lived until today is a part of the woven braid of life.

It takes every person's story to create history.

Your life will help determine the course of history.

You may think you don't have much of an impact.

You do.

Every action you take will reflect in someone else's life.

Someone else's decisions.

Someone else's future.

Both good and bad.

The Bregdan Chronicles

- # 1 - Storm Clouds Rolling In
- # 2 - On To Richmond
- # 3 - Spring Will Come
- # 4 - Dark Chaos
- # 5 - The Last, Long Night
- # 6 - Carried Forward By Hope
- # 7 - Glimmers of Change
- # 8 - Shifted By The Winds
- # 9 - Always Forward
- # 10 - Walking Into The Unknown
- # 11 – Looking To The Future
- # 12 - Horizons Unfolding
- # 13 – The Twisted Road Of One Writer
- # 14 - Misty Shadows of Hope
- # 15 - Shining Through Dark Clouds
- # 16 - Courage Rising
- # 17 - Renewed By Dawn
- # 18 - Journey To Joy
- # 19 - Courage To Stand
- # 20 - Walking Toward Freedom
- # 21 - Gateway To A New Beginning

Every book ends with To Be Continued…
There are MANY more coming!

Book # 21 of The Bregdan Chronicles

Other Books by Ginny Dye

Pepper Crest High Series - Teen Fiction
Time For A Second Change
It's Really A Matter of Trust
A Lost & Found Friend
Time For A Change of Heart

Fly To Your Dreams Series – Allegorical Fantasy
Dream Dragon
Born To Fly
Little Heart
The Miracle of Chinese Bamboo

All titles by Ginny Dye
www.BregdanPublishing.com

Author Biography

Who am I? Just a person who loves to write. If I could do it all anonymously, I would. In fact, I did the first go 'round. I wrote under a pen name. On the off chance I would ever become famous - I didn't want to be! I don't like the limelight. I don't like living in a fishbowl. I especially don't like thinking I have to look good everywhere I go, just in case someone recognizes me! I finally decided none of that matters. If you don't like me in overalls and a baseball cap, too bad. If you don't like my haircut or think I should do something different than what I'm doing, too bad. I'll write books that you will hopefully like, and we'll both let that be enough! :) Fair?

But let's see what you might want to know. I spent many years as a Wanderer. My dream when I graduated from college was to experience the United States. I grew up in the South. There are many things I love about it, but I wanted to live in other places. So I did. I moved 57 times, traveled extensively in 49 of the 50 states, and had more experiences than I will ever be able to recount. The only state I haven't been in is Alaska, simply because I refuse to visit such a vast, fabulous place until I have at least a month.

Along the way I had glorious adventures. I've canoed through the Everglade Swamps, snorkeled in the Florida Keys and windsurfed in the Gulf of Mexico. I've whitewater rafted down the New River and Bungee jumped in

Book # 21 of The Bregdan Chronicles

the Wisconsin Dells. I've visited every National Park (in the off-season when there is more freedom!) and many of the State Parks. I've hiked thousands of miles of mountain trails and biked through Arizona deserts. I've canoed and biked through Upstate New York and Vermont, and polished off as much lobster as possible on the Maine Coast.

I've lived on a island in the British Columbia province of Canada, and now live on a magical cliffside in Mexico.

Have you figured out I'm kind of an outdoors gal? If it can be done outdoors, I love it! Hiking, biking, windsurfing, rock-climbing, roller-blading, snowshoeing, skiing, rowing, canoeing, softball, tennis... the list could go on and on. I love to have fun and I love to stretch my body. This should give you a pretty good idea of what I do in my free time.

When I'm not writing or playing, I'm building Millions For Positive Change - a fabulous organization I founded in 2001 - along with 60 amazing people who poured their lives into creating resources to empower people to make a difference with their lives.

What else? I love to read, cook, sit for hours in solitude on my mountain, and also hang out with friends. I love barbeques and block parties. Basically - I just love LIFE!

I'm so glad you're part of my world! ~**Ginny**

Join my Email List so you can:

- Receive notice of all new books
- Be a part of my Launch Celebrations. I give away lots of Free gifts!
- Read my weekly BLOG while you're waiting for a new book.
- Be part of The Bregdan Chronicles Family!
- Learn about all the other books I write.

Just go to www.BregdanChronicles.net and fill out the form.

Made in the USA
Las Vegas, NV
13 October 2024

cc5a3fdd-af79-4f3b-b68b-b95a6f9938a2R01